SALTED
WITH
FIRE

GRIF STOCKLEY

ROSE
Publishing Company, Inc.

ROSE
Publishing Company, Inc.
2723 Foxcroft Road
Little Rock, Arkansas 72207

DESIGNED BY GARY WAYNE GOLDEN
MANUFACTURED IN THE UNITED STATES OF AMERICA

10 9 8 7 6 5 4 3 2 1

LIBRARY OF CONGRESS CATALOGING IN PUBLICATION DATA
STOCKLEY, GRIF
SALTED WITH FIRE / GRIF STOCKLEY
P. CM.

1. ARKANSAS—FICTION   I. TITLE
PS3569.T612S25
813'.54
00-136249

ISBN 1-930728-00-X

To Teresa and Andy

PREFACE

From 1936-1938 in the former Confederate states, interviews were conducted with ex-slaves by men and women employed by the Federal Writers' Project, which was a negligible part of the Roosevelt administration's effort to jumpstart the economy during the Depression. These interviews have become known as the Slave Narratives. Yet the only booklength treatment of the slave period in Arkansas, *Negro Slavery in Arkansas*, published by Duke University Press in 1958, by the highly respected historian Orville Taylor, makes no mention of these interviews. Though the University of Arkansas Press has recently reissued Taylor's Book in a handsome paperback format, Arkansas historians agree that a new history of slavery in the state is long overdue. References and excerpts from the Slave Narratives and Professor Taylor's book in my work of fiction are taken often verbatim from these materials. The books *Coming to Terms with Slavery: Torture and Rape in Arkansas* and *Salted With Fire* are of course fictional, as are the characters of this novel.

And if thine eye offend thee, pluck it out; it is better for thee to enter into the kingdom of God with one eye than, having two eyes, to be cast into hell fire.

Where their worm dieth not, and the fire is not quenched.

For every one shall be salted with fire, and every sacrifice shall be salted with salt.

Salt is good; but if the salt have lost its saltness, with what will ye season it? Have salt in yourselves, and have peace one with another.

Mark 9:47-50

1

"Call me, Miller. I'm in trouble."

As I work my way through our messages (most are for Laurel), I become progressively disturbed by the tension I hear in my oldest friend's voice. By the third call, not more than an hour ago, he has figured out when we were due back—the 5th of May—but he has left no clue what is bothering him.

"Have you ever heard Cormorant's voice sound like that?" I ask my wife. We are both fuzzy with exhaustion after a trans-Atlantic trip. Laurel led me on a forced march all over France and in particular Paris for three weeks. I was lost in Paris much of the time, but armed with a compass and enough maps to have allowed us to explore the sewer systems of the entire country, my wife of twenty-five years was in her element, taking enough pictures of the gargoyles on the North Tower of Notre Dame to open her own museum. Their purpose, Fodor's told us, was to keep bad spirits from the cathedral. Insurance, Laurel, a life-long Episcopalian, without a trace of irony, called the gargoyles' placement when I laughed.

"He sounds like she caught him in bed with another woman," Laurel guesses, already beginning to unpack. "As much as he talks, I can't imagine he was doing anything but putting a woman to sleep. Go call him. I want to get this stuff in the wash before it gets up and walks off."

"Thanks." I get the phone from the kitchen and move out to the deck. Laurel, I know, likes Cormorant, a tenured history professor at the University of Arkansas at Little Rock, as much as I do, but can't resist making fun of him for his propensity to put his foot in his mouth. Yet, like me, she admires his stainless-steel honesty and integrity. We know of no one like him, which is a relief in a way to his friends, for invariably he reduces the South to its proper size, having nothing but scorn for the inevitable exaggeration, the embellishment of reality, the preference for the story over the facts, everything dear to the Southern mentality that I've reveled in for my fifty-five years on this planet.

As I punch in the number for his home in the upper Heights in Little Rock, I realize that what Laurel objects to about Cormorant is that he is an impostor, not Southern at all. His insistence on saying exactly what he thinks at any time, publicly and privately, she likens to someone with a severe case of Tourette's Syndrome. The difference is that Laurel thinks Cormorant can act otherwise. After all these years, I'm not sure he could. I know he doesn't want to. Like his efforts to quit cigarettes, his willingness to speak the truth when it is not convenient or politic has come to be an immutable habit, one not easily shed. Character takes practice, I have often reminded my daughter.

Over the years, I have become cautious and circumspect, learning the lessons of adulthood—sometimes all too well, according to Laurel. A lawyer for almost thirty years in the Arkansas Delta, I know I am trusted and respected by my colleagues and clients. Cormorant is often regarded, unfairly, I think, as a royal pain in the ass because of his penchant for noticing and calling to attention the nakedness of not just emperors but subjects alike. I've often thought that if the two of us were on a sinking boat and one of us had to jump into the water, my region of the country would be better off if I would do the honors. In the states of the Confederacy, the society pages positively teem with respectable, well-heeled lawyers; courageous, intelligent, honorable men who are willing to take a stand on principle are as rare as bald eagles in our relentlessly materialistic world of the so-called "New South."

"Hello!" Cormorant shouts. At Rhodes College in Memphis in the sixties (it was still called Southwestern then), he was the sound man and manager of a rock and roll band and had paid the price of losing a bit of his hearing. Proud of this youthful rebellion, every couple of years or so he teaches a course he designed called "History and American Pop" and plays for his surely bemused students Jimi Hendrix's version of the "Star Spangled Banner." If he still wears a bow tie in class, he must look a little silly, especially if he starts to dance.

"Cormorant!" I shout back. "We just got in. What's wrong?"

"I'm scared, Miller," he says, his voice dropping to a confidential whisper. "I think I'm about to be charged with murder."

I look across the deck and see the high water still flooding my soy bean fields to the east. It is so beautiful here in the spring. A storm is moving in from the west. The clouds overhead are purple black. A huge fist seems to be protruding from them. I wonder if I am so tired that I've begun to hallucinate. "Murder?" I finally rasp into the phone. "You're not serious."

"Oh, yes," Cormorant answers grimly. "I sent you that book by Damascus Merriweather. I'm convinced the cops think I killed him because of it."

I haven't talked to Cormorant since Easter, but he had sent me a book by a colleague of his just as we were leaving. "I haven't gotten to it yet," I explain.

"It's trash, Miller," Cormorant says, his voice hoarse with emotion. "There's nothing to it. I said that to his face, but I wouldn't kill a man over a book."

I look at my watch. It is five on a Wednesday afternoon. It seems preposterous that he is worried. I'd like nothing more than to get in bed. "You want to drive over now?" I offer, hoping he will say it will be tomorrow. Laurel would have a fit, but she'd get over it.

Naturally, he says he is on his way. He has to pass out final exams tomorrow, so he will have to get up early. I hang up, telling myself I couldn't possibly represent him because we are too close. There are plenty of good lawyers in Little Rock if it actually comes to a murder charge, which I can't imagine. Before I break the news to Laurel, I go to the den and find the book in its manila envelope where I left it and take it to the deck. Then I drag the deck furniture out from the storage shed behind the house. I sit down in one of the wrought-iron chairs and open the book, propping my feet on the west railing toward the building storm and study Damascus Merriweather's picture on the back. He is a black bear of a man with a beard straight out of the Old Testament. He looks our age. The flap says merely he is a professor of history at UALR and is a native of Forrest City in the Arkansas Delta. The title, *Coming to Terms with Slavery: Torture and Rape in Arkansas,* sends a strange chill through me.

Squinting against the glare as the sun momentarily peeks through the clouds, I turn to the beginning and read the first sentence. *Nestled deep in the psyche of white Arkansans is the quaint belief that their ancestors were largely innocent of cruelty and abuse of African-Americans during the long period of slavery in this country. The silent screams of their victims, suppressed and then ignored for more than a century, despite the evidence, demand a hearing. The white Arkansan's bedtime fable, repeated from generation to generation, is at odds with history. The white population has not yet come to terms with the sins of their fathers and mothers.*

I skim the preface, which explains that only one book has ever been published about Arkansas slavery, and that account in 1958 by a white history professor named Orville Taylor is devoid of any reference to the "slave narratives," a collection of interviews by the Federal Writers' Project during the 1930s. *If Arkansas whites want to make the attempt to understand what they have done to African-Americans, they must begin with the work of a black man from Little Rock named Samuel S. Taylor who took his notes in shorthand as he conducted his interviews of the former Arkansas slaves. It is in those 129 interviews conducted by Samuel Taylor, rated to be the best of the twenty WPA workers, that one begins to develop a sense of the truth of what it was like to be owned by white Arkansans.*

"We et out of a trough with a wooden spoon. Mush and milk. Cedar trough and long-handled cedar spoons. Didn't know what meat was. Never got a taste of egg. Oo-ee!! Weren't allowed to look at a biscuit."

I rub my eyes. Somewhere I must have read that some slaves were sometimes fed like livestock, but I don't think I ever really believed it. I had assumed they ate in their own cabins and had imagined a homely scene of a family gathered around a fire before heading off to the fields singing Ole Black Joe, I guess.

The preface continues:

"We hardly knowed our names. We was cussed for so many bitches and sons of bitches and bloody bitches, and blood of bitches. We never heard our names scarcely at all. First young man I went with wanted to know my initials! What did I know 'bout initials? You ask 'em ten years old now, and they'll tell you...Initials!!!"

I have a sick feeling in my stomach. Despite what Cormorant

said, I have the feeling I am reading a real person's words. It doesn't sound made-up.

"My mars used to throw me in a buck and whip me. He would put my hands together and tie them. Then he would strip me naked. Then he would make me squat down. Then he would run a stick through behind my knees and in front of my elbows. My knees was up against my chest. My hands was tied together in front of my shins. The stick between my arms and legs held me in a squat. That's what they called a buck...you couldn't git your feet out. You couldn't do nothin' but just squat there and take what he put on you. You couldn't move no way at all. Just try to. He would whip me on one side till that was sore and full of blood and then he would whip me on the other side till that was all tore up.

Still in the preface, in a section on the fate of runaways, the author includes another quote from Sally Crane, the former slave who talked about eating from a trough and wasn't called by her name:

"I have worn a buck and gag in my mouth for three days for trying to run away. I couldn't eat or drink—couldn't even catch the slobber that fell from my mouth and run down my chest till the flies settled on it and blowed it..."

I have to put the book down when the author says Samuel Taylor reported that the old lady had shown him the scars on her body where maggots had eaten in. I stand up and study the water in the fields, wondering if I would feel better if I had a drink but knowing that as tired as I am, alcohol would knock me out. I look down at the book again. It was published in Little Rock by something called Freedom Press, and I wonder if it was self-published. I have never heard of the slave narratives. If Cormorant called the book trash, these interviews must be apocryphal. Cormorant, who received his Ph. D. from Ole Miss, is a historian who has made a reputation by debunking other historians' work instead of constructing some grand historical design that doesn't hold water. If he says something is garbage, it probably is.

"Would you roll the windows up?" Laurel calls from the kitchen door. "In case you hadn't noticed, it's going to storm."

I look up and see the trees beginning to sway. Tornado weather. Twenty years ago Laurel planted just off the deck a wild flower garden that includes Solomon Seal, columbine, maidenhair fern, clematis, and crepe myrtle, which grows well here but is not native to Crowley's Ridge. The Ridge was formed in the Arkansas Delta (if you believe geologists) only ten thousand years ago. These gentle hills in the Delta extend north and south a good bit of the state.

My family has farmed in Jeffersonville since my great-great-grandparents crossed from Tennessee into Arkansas in 1830 in a flatboat and floated down the L'Anguille River to the point where it joins the St. Francis River, just a few miles from the Mississippi. At one time in its history, the site was inhabited by the Akansa, Quapaw, and Chickasaw Indians, and the town of Jeffersonville, thought to be the oldest town in what is now Lee County (which was carved out of four adjacent counties in 1873, courtesy of Reconstruction politics), was in the 1800s a thriving community with hotels, saloons, churches, blacksmiths, commercial fishermen, slaves, and steamboats. Today, Jeffersonville, a victim of progress, is just a few farms, and my law office is fifteen minutes away in Marianna, the county seat. All around the house there are tulip poplars, oaks, elms, sycamores, sweet gums, black gums. Laurel will never get over it if these trees are damaged by a storm. "I've got some terrible news," I call over the wind. "Cormorant thinks he's going to be charged with murder."

Her arms full of laundry, Laurel glares at me as if I am a small child who won't pick up his room. Clearly, she thinks Cormorant is exaggerating. "You still need to roll up the windows. Then come tell me. I'll be in the laundry room."

I trot across the deck and down the steps and circle around the house to the Olds in the yard, feeling momentarily exhilarated by another clap of thunder and a flash of lightning over my shoulder. When we were younger, Laurel and I would strip off our clothes and make love on the deck in the storms. We have no neighbors for miles. But we haven't done that for years. As tired as I am, all I could do today would be to lie on top of her, but that would be okay. I dread telling her about Cormorant. She is bone weary of the problems of race. Long after I quit, she stayed involved in community projects in Marianna, trying futilely to help blacks and whites not completely turn away from each other. If she had her way, we'd sell Sunnyside and move to Mars. Like all of the Delta, Lee County can't escape the past. I get the windows up and run toward the house as the first drops splatter on my face. My heart is racing, and I don't know why.

Over the noise of the washer, I tell Laurel about my conversation with Cormorant and about the book.

"We don't have any food in the house," my wife responds. Her voice is clipped with fatigue, and her drawn face is etched with lines that only time and weariness can give you. If she had been born in the middle ages, she jokes that she would have been a lady and I would have been a peasant sent off to die in the Crusades.

So much for my oldest friend's guilt or innocence. "Make me a list. I'll go," I say, hoping we don't fight. "He sounded serious. You heard his voice."

Laurel picks up a white tee shirt of mine and makes a face. The underarms are almost brown from sweat stains. Her expression suggests we can afford some new underwear for me. "He always sounds serious," she says. "It doesn't matter whether he is talking about the World Bank or bad breath. It's his way of getting attention. Is Beth coming?"

She hasn't even asked a single question, but I can't take my conversation with Cormorant seriously either. I've never seen him even draw back his fist, and I've known him all my life. "No," I say, making a reasonable assumption but not wanting to send my wife into a cleaning frenzy. Beth, who regularly appears in the *Arkansas Democrat-Gazette*'s society section at one charity function after another, irritates Laurel with her incessant talk about Little Rock. I think there is some envy. Beth has escaped the Delta, and she hasn't. "Do you want me to call back and ask?"

As I think about it, I realize there has always been an undercurrent of competition between them. Laurel, despite our trips, is still a small town girl; Little Rock, though hardly Memphis with its Old South social pretensions, has its own pecking order, and Beth has developed a pretty sharp beak. If Cormorant could keep his mouth shut, no telling where she could be. Family money and connections they both have in abundance, but if you want in the Little Rock Country Club, you still need a husband who will not write letters to the editor of the *Arkansas Democrat-Gazette* agreeing with out-of-state pundits that Little Rock is a back-slapping, good-ole-boy bastion of white male privilege and that one of the main nerve centers for these activities is the LRCC.

Laurel produces a pencil and begins writing on the back of a paper sack as she says, "No, she might come, and I look and feel like hell. Besides, this house is as dirty as an Algerian commode."

I let that go, and twenty minutes later I am cruising the aisles of Food Giant in Marianna buying the ingredients for dinner as well as milk, paper towels, coffee, and razor blades. It has become the only store in town that really sells food, and thus blacks and whites are forced to interact. It even has a few black employees. As I contemplate chicken breasts (do I want them without ribs?), for some reason I am reminded of Laurel's comments to her sister, Eve, who flew over from her home in England and met us in the south of France for a week. Maybe we should just sell out and leave. Together, we've made Lee County a third-world country. I decide to get the breasts with ribs attached, realizing that my theory of race relations is a lot like my theory of chicken buying. It doesn't really matter what I think. Hollys have lived in this area for a long time. I like living in the Delta on my own land. Granted, I no longer tilt at windmills. It is true that, as Laurel says, I have made an accommodation to the present, but I've had no choice. Behind me, a black woman warns her child, "Don't you be puttin' that in your mouth!" As long as it is not my chicken, I'm not going to even look.

At the checkout counter I say "thank you," and "yes, ma'am," to the young woman who gives me my change. I walk toward the door, and somehow my dime-store glasses fall out of my left front pocket. The sacker, an African-American young man who looks about twenty-five, reaches down and scoops them up for me. I thank him and make a little joke about how my eyes are getting so bad that I couldn't even see them on the floor. He laughs obligingly. Manners. It's too bad the South couldn't have taken a patent on them and plowed under the cotton fields.

Superstitious (I would have received a call), I decide to swing through town on my way back to Jeffersonville just to make sure my law office hasn't burned or been hit by a tornado. As I drive around the square, I am struck as I haven't been for years by the bleak shabbiness of the downtown area. Leaving for three weeks must have given me a slightly different perspective, because I feel the town's deadness like a weight on the back of my neck. It is as if one of those neutron bombs had been exploded years ago leaving the buildings standing but killing the people. When I was a child, on Saturdays especially, the square was alive with humanity as farmers of both races came into town to buy supplies and let their families have some time away from their chores.

I look up at the soaring statue of Robert E. Lee, from whom the county took its name, and though I have seen it almost every day of my working life, it occurs to me that I have never once considered the irony of having the county named during Reconstruction after the north's greatest military antagonist. A history buff, I know the first sheriff of Lee County was a black Republican named Furbush who was a state representative from adjacent Phillips County. Since the other county officials were all white Democrats, obviously some deals were made. I decide I don't have time to go into my office and head down Poplar, realizing how inured I have become to the lack of economic activity in downtown Marianna. At the corner of Main and Chestnut, the city has pulled down a row of condemned buildings that at one time housed, among other businesses, a black movie theater. Supposedly, low-rent apartments for the elderly will be erected through some federal grant. Why bother? Lee County has lost approximately a third of its population since 1970. As I travel up and down the Delta, it is much the same in every county. Last month I tried a case in Helena and had to drive three miles to find a place to eat. There was nothing open on Cherry Street, which is looking these days as desolate as Poplar. Every problem we have seems connected to race.

It is hard to not think of Merriweather's preface. Could it have been as bad as those excerpts suggest? My ancestors owned slaves in what was then Phillips County, and so did Cormorant's. I know nothing about the conditions except for having a vague recollection that my grandfather used to say they had been treated like family and had the audacity to run away when the

Yankee soldiers came.

By my side in the kitchen, Laurel, who reminds her friends of the Energizer Bunny with her ceaseless activity, gestures at me with the knife she is using to cut up carrots and cucumbers. "If Cormorant is charged, are you going to represent him?"

My hands smell of chicken fat. I wash them in the sink. "He can afford to get a hot shot in Little Rock. I'm too close to him. Besides, I've never done a murder case."

Almost five-eight and lithe as the day we were married, Laurel arches her back. "How are you going to turn him down? It might be good for you to get your hands dirty."

I dry my hands on the blue and white cloth dish towel on the counter. I'm not sure what she means, but she sounds angry. My law practice, which consists mainly of insurance defense work and white-collar crime, takes me all over the Delta. True, the rent from our farms and income from investments over the years have made it possible for me to slow down, but I've chosen not to. "What is this about?" I say, smiling to take the sting from my tone. "We've only been back a couple of hours."

When Laurel gets emotional, her neck muscles tighten, and now they look like the sinewy cords on those women kick-boxers I've started to see on television. "All you do is work," she says, her voice as bleak as the expression on her face, "and then come home and sit on the deck. You've got all this respect from everybody, but you don't risk any of it. Granted, people around here think you're some kind of god—the last of the great Holly family—but what good does it do anybody? This last year it's as if you've died. I was hoping the trip would make you interested in things again."

Stung, I keep my mouth shut and return to the stove to inspect my handiwork. The last time we had guests I undercooked the chicken. It was embarrassing to watch them pretend they liked their poultry half-raw. Southerners are good at that sort of thing, though. "I thought I was interested," I say finally. Laurel isn't usually so direct. She must be more tired than I thought. "We made love a bunch of times over there."

"As long as you had a nap," she says, her voice affectionate, but suddenly she begins to cry. "I don't want to stay here and watch you start to drink yourself to death."

I bend down to get a frying pan from the bottom cabinet. I should have told Cormorant I was driving over to see him. "This is our home," I say quietly. "Running away isn't going to make things better. We're just very tired."

In a single motion that is a blur, Laurel turns and hurls the knife against the window, but it does not break. I have never seen her throw anything before. Her face is terrible.

"Miller!"

I look up and see coming through the living room my oldest friend. I put a smile on my face and go to him.

2

"Why is it trash?" I ask, wanting to understand how the book he sent me fits in before he gives me the details of the murder of his colleague. He has told me that he had been called to Merriweather's house and may have been one of the last persons to see him alive in the last hour of his life. "I've only read a few pages of the preface, but it sounded real to me." Cormorant is seated at the kitchen table nursing a bourbon and Coke while Laurel and I finish cooking dinner. We could have eaten at the club in town tonight, but it is too public a venue for all of us. If he has noticed the tension between me and Laurel, I can't tell it, but Cormorant is not a man who spends time consulting the emotional temperature of the group he is in before he starts talking.

"A historian's only loyalty is to the truth," Cormorant says, waving the copy he has sent me. "On every page of this damn thing, he violates that precept. He has to say what he doesn't know, and Damascus seldom does. It's a polemic, not history."

"What about the slave narratives?" I ask. "Why didn't the one historian who has written a book about slavery in Arkansas use them?" Cormorant is stirring his drink with a carrot. When he begins to talk, he forgets what he is doing. It is talk he loves, according to my wife. She says he is in love with his brain and masturbates it instead of his penis. When it comes to Cormorant,

Laurel has a pretty sharp beak, too.

Ignoring the avocado dip Laurel has set out for him, Cormorant sucks on the carrot as if it were a sugar stick and begins to talk in his low gravelly voice, made hoarse by a lifetime of Camels. "Because they're not trustworthy as sources. Think how old those ex-slaves were when they were interviewed. When the interviews were done, it was more than sixty-five years since slavery. How can a person remember those kinds of details? Besides, a number of the slaves interviewed in the Arkansas narratives only came to Arkansas after the Civil War. Orville Taylor, the man who wrote that book in 1958, was a first-class historian who will be remembered as having written a classic study. His book is so well-respected, it has preempted the field in this state. Sure, it's dated now, and but even today it still holds up. The University of Arkansas Press has just reissued it in paperback. Duke University Press was his original publisher. Damascus couldn't find a publisher for his, so his brother shelled out for a vanity press operation, according to the papers."

I sprinkle some Cavender's on the chicken. If somebody put me in a "buck," and fed me out of a trough, I think I'd remember it if I lived to be a hundred and twenty. "What motive would they have to make something up?" I ask, trying not to think of the maggots entering that woman's body.

Cormorant knocks back a healthy slug. "Come on, Miller. You sound like one of my graduate students. Blacks were going to say whatever they thought the interviewer wanted to hear. A number of the interviewees said they haven't been treated badly at all. Of course, they were being interviewed by mostly whites. They didn't trust the whites, so you can't swallow whole those interviews either. It's not that the narratives don't hold interest for historians; they do. But as historical sources they are suspect: If Orville Taylor had relied on them for his conclusions about slavery, his book would have been suspect among professional historians. He didn't whitewash the slave era in the state and cites plenty of instances where brutality was documented through court cases and letters from the period, but it's a balanced treatment. A historian can't judge another era by the present. Whipping was common as punishment back then in a number of situations. Hell, school boys in England expected to be caned. You're not a historian if you ignore that."

Not as interested as I am in the book he is holding, Laurel interrupts to ask how how he could be a murder suspect. "Was there an accident?" she asks, reaching for the glass of Chablis on the counter she has poured herself. "Did you run over him or what?"

Cormorant, who is making one of his annual efforts to quit smoking, slams the book on the table and shakes his head. Only about five-six, he is a little tubby now, and his jowls are full. "He was shot in the chest. I had just been to see him. The damn cops have been swarming the department, trying to get something on me. It's ridiculous."

"Have you talked to them?" I ask, turning over the breasts with a spatula that had belonged to my mother. When we were boys, Cormorant and I used to shoot turtles and gar with a .22 rifle off the St. Francis bridge at Cody. He was a terrible shot because of his eyesight. If he hit anything, it was by accident. Both of us would laugh out loud when he tried to shoot something with a little .22 pistol. Dust would fly up all around the tin can as if he were deliberately trying to miss it.

"Once," he says, his voice bitter. "Then I realized they actually thought I might have done it."

"What did you tell them?" I ask, knowing how many of my clients have hung themselves over the years by their tongues. The urge to explain is irresistible. Yet, if you are not guilty, why wouldn't you talk? After being a lawyer for more than a quarter of a century I know the answer to that question. My white-collar clients are almost always better off taking the 5th Amendment. They rarely feel guilty and explain vaguely that their business practices are the essence of American capitalism. That is why Cormorant has always seemed remarkable to me. He may not spare others, but he doesn't exempt himself either.

"Like a fool, I told them we had bantered like we always did," Cormorant says gloomily. "See, unlike his goddamn brother, Ezekiel, Damascus was alright. On a personal level, I liked him, and I think he tolerated me. And this was despite the fact that I voted against him being hired and voted against him being tenured. I told him to his face once that he would be better off in the journalism department."

Laurel laughs out loud at this impertinence. I think she is probably delighted to see Cormorant sweating a little. I know he's just being honest, but he can be destructive. He hurts people, she said once. Herself, she means. He had told our daughter Cynthia that he wouldn't write a recommendation for her to get in graduate school because she wasn't smart enough. There are too many mediocre graduate students already. She had cried for a week, but today is a sales rep in Atlanta for pet pharmaceuticals and makes twice Cormorant's professor salary at UALR. On her last visit, she took him and Beth to dinner at Alouette's and picked up the check to thank him.

"What did he say to that?"

Cormorant examines his glass as if there were a hair on it. "That I would have made a great lieutenant in the Confederacy, meaning that I would have fallen on my sword to make a point."

Laurel frowns, being one of those Southerners who actually think the South would have been better off if we had won the Civil War. Slavery, she says, would have died a natural death, and we would have ended up like South Africa. Laurel is not a person who shrinks from the judgments of history.

"So why did you go to see him?" I ask, smelling the meat. Maybe I just need some food to feel better.

"He wanted me to take his place on a panel at the law school to discuss the impact of the 1954 Brown decision," Cormorant explains. "You need to know he was dying of cancer. Actually, he was alone in his brother's house in a wheelchair. This is one of the things that make it absurd that I would be considered a suspect. We all knew he was dying. I had heard that months ago. You don't shoot a man who is dying anyway."

I've had to bite my tongue to keep from interrupting. "The school integration decision?" I ask, incredulous. "I can't imagine you weren't on opposite sides philosophically on that case."

Laurel begins to set the table for dinner, and Cormorant lifts up his drink. "Of course we were," he replies. "Brown was based on little but bad sociology and liberal guilt, and its implementation for years was disastrous for the black community, which lost their schools and their jobs. And talk about reinforcing the notion of black inferiority! The idea that a black child would learn better if he was sitting side by side with a white child had to be one of the most insulting notions a race of people has ever had forced down their throats." He wags his head sadly as if I had argued the case myself. "Miller, there has been nothing more tortured in our society than the meaning of the 14th Amendment."

Laurel smiles at his earnestness. Though he can infuriate her, Cormorant makes her laugh, too, especially when they have both had something to drink. I think at one time in the past she might have been attracted to him, and he must have hurt her feelings. She wouldn't talk about him so badly otherwise. In high school I had a major crush on Beth, who was homecoming queen our senior year and the most popular girl in our class. Pecking her on the mouth on the football field Thanksiving Day before the

Helena game is a cherished memory. Co-captain of the Marianna Porcupines. Quill 'em, team, quill 'em! I add a little black pepper. Lust. If you've known someone for fifty years, it's not unexpected somewhere along the way.

Brushing by him, my wife says, "Why did he ask you?"

Before he answers, Cormorant makes a show of sniffing Laurel's perfume. I can't begrudge him that. After all, she has just been to Paris. "See, that's what nobody understands but me. For all his ineptness as a historian, Damascus was amazingly tolerant of other viewpoints. He used to say, the truth will emerge. Hell, that's about the only thing I really agreed with him about."

Laurel picks up the book and studies the jacket. "So the cops say you were the last person to see him, huh?"

Cormorant pushes back his chair and stands up. "Have I got time for another one of these?" he asks, abruptly.

"Sure," I reply. Alcohol might loosen him up. From the way he is holding his shoulders, he has been tense for weeks. Even if he gets shit-faced, I don't anticipate a confession. Cormorant never could stand the sight of blood if my memory of a rabbit-cleaning episode is correct. He knows where the booze is kept and goes to the cabinet to pour himself a couple of fingers and a splash of Coke on the remaining ice cubes. It is during the summer and Christmas holidays when we usually see Cormorant and Beth. He drags her back to the Delta every chance he gets. It is in his blood, too. Beth would prefer to socialize in Little Rock, but she has a mother who is in a nursing home in Helena and can't avoid coming back either.

"Is all they have the fact that you saw him the afternoon he was killed?" I ask, wondering if Cormorant is getting paranoid in his old age. Investigations have become a way of life in Arkansas since Whitewater and Kenneth Starr decided to pick on us.

"That's something I can't tell," Cormorant says, looking out the window wistfully. It has stopped raining, and everything is clean in the long twilight. "I'm beginning to think the cops might have my pistol."

I laugh out loud. "A cap pistol?" I ask. "You couldn't hit this house at twenty paces. What are you doing carrying a weapon?" The thought is ludicrous. Cormorant tells the story on himself that in basic training during the Vietnam War he couldn't even see the 200-meter targets on the firing range, and because every one of the instructors cheated to make themselves look good, he fired "Expert" to the consternation and ridicule of his buddies. He said he spent his year in Vietnam in Saigon as an order-of-battle analyst, hoping he didn't catch VD.

"We own some rent houses in some bad areas in Little Rock," Cormorant explains, his tone almost sheepish. "I guess, to prove I can do it, I collect the rent myself."

Laurel, back beside me at the counter, hoots loudly. The thought of Cormorant, usually so priggish about money, squeezing deadbeat tenants, makes me smile, too. "So, you pull a gun on them?" I ask.

"No!" Cormorant exclaims, seeming horrified at the thought. "But Little Rock has so many damn gangs and crack addicts that you never know who's going to cause you trouble. I keep the damn thing in the car, or I did until it got stolen."

I turn the chicken breasts over again and turn the heat down. They are done, but I don't want to rush Cormorant. I'm learning things about him that I never knew. "Did you report it?" I ask, realizing now that he is deadly serious about being a suspect.

"I didn't know it was stolen," he complains. "I hadn't checked the glove compartment in a month."

Laurel, too, seems to sense for the first time that Cormorant is truly worried and not just concerned about some awkward publicity for being in the wrong place at the wrong time. "Do you think someone stole it and is somehow trying to frame you?" she asks, leaping ahead to a conclusion I hadn't reached. Laurel is a conspiracy buff. The Kennedys, Martin Luther King, Amelia Earhart. Every time a plane goes down, she thinks Iraq, Iran, and Libya are celebrating another victory over the Great Satan.

"Maybe," Cormorant says softly, gulping his liquor. "I just know this black cop loves coming to the department and snooping around. He talks to everybody. Hell, I don't know what's going on. I didn't kill Damascus Merriweather. I swear to God."

"Of course you didn't," I say automatically. It is a bad moment, summoning a favorite saying of Cormorant's from childhood: it's a bit dog that barks. "What makes you think they even have your gun?"

Cormorant drinks down the rest of his bourbon and says that it was just the look on the detective's face when he reported that he had lost the pistol. This conversation took place two days ago. "This black cop seemed to already know."

I haven't seen him chug alcohol like this since we were teenagers. Actually, I am remembering myself more than Cormorant, who, come to think of it, seldom drank in high school and college and only started smoking (as well as drinking) in Vietnam. I acquired a taste for marijuana and Vietnamese women myself, activities which weren't particularly Southern. I decide maybe we better eat after all. I suggest that we sit down, and Laurel agrees it is a good idea. Now that Cormorant is worried, she is protective of him and helps his plate.

"If they really thought you were a suspect," I say, pouring myself a glass of iced tea, "you'd have gotten your Miranda warnings."

"Actually, he wanted me to come down to the police station yesterday, but I put him off," Cormorant says, buttering a roll but not eating it. "I think that's coming. See, you haven't been here or you would realize the cops are getting a lot of pressure to make an arrest. His brother is just going nuts. He's been on the news at least three times, saying I was one of the last persons alive to see Damascus. He's gotten the damn blacks stirred up, and to make it worse, the Associated Press has played up the story, and his damn book has begun to get national attention. Last Sunday the *Democrat-Gazette* mentioned on its book pages that it has already gotten a good review in the *Boston Globe.* Of course, anybody outside the South is going to love it." Cormorant jerks up out of his seat and says, "I've got a tape out in the car of his brother. I want y'all to see it." Though Laurel volunteers to get it, Cormorant, already made unsteady by the bourbon, lurches through the house toward the front door and outside to get it.

"What do you think?" I ask Laurel, who is chewing thoughtfully. "Why would he shoot him?"

"He's been set up," she says, her mind on automatic pilot. "A black cop over there is out of control, and his boss is letting him get away with it. It was probably a robbery that turned into a murder, and this is the easiest way to solve it. You don't think it couldn't happen here?"

The mayor of Marianna is now black, and he has appointed a black police chief. I bite into the chicken. Little Rock now has its first black chief of police, too, so I guess what she is suggesting is plausible. I mull over this possibility. Now that the blacks are taking over, we blame everything that goes wrong on them. It is a hard habit to break. "Sure," I say.

Back inside the house, Cormorant yells from the den, "Come see this! It won't take but a minute."

I follow her into the den to find Cormorant inserting a tape into the VCR. "Raven got this for me. She knows somebody at Channel 7."

I sit down in the recliner, thinking that I should call Cormorant's sister to find out how much of this story is real and how much is his imagination. Raven has more common sense in her little finger than Cormorant (only a woman as eccentric as his mother would name her children after birds) has in his entire body. The owner of her own ad agency in Little Rock, she adores her brother though they are as opposite as night and day.

When the tape begins, the person speaking is Janie Stoner, a second-string newscaster for Channel 7, who is reporting from outside the Little Rock police station. In the background a group of blacks are carrying signs reading, "Arrest the murderer of Damascus Merriweather," and "Chief Casewell, why are you protecting a professor at UALR?"

Stoner, whom I've seen on television for years, holds up Merriweather's book and says, "Every bookstore we've called has sold out its supply of this book since the murder of Damascus Merriweather two weeks ago. No one has been arrested." As the picture pans to the group of blacks, her voice continues, "As our viewers can see, a number of individuals in the African-American community are clearly upset. Overnight, Damascus Merriweather, once an obscure African-American history professor at UALR, has become as famous as Nolan Richardson, the coach of the Razorback basketball team, because of his book about slavery in Arkansas. With me is the murdered man's brother, Ezekiel Merriweather, a pharmacist and entrepreneur in Little Rock. Mr. Merriweather, what is this group protesting and why?"

Ezekiel Merriweather, who looks like an older version of his brother, replies, "For the first time in our history, someone has told the truth about what slavery was like for black Arkansans. That person was my brother. For the first time, the pain and horror of what happened to our ancestors has been set down in a book. We always kill the messenger in this society, and that messenger was my brother. I say to you that we won't rest until his killer is brought to justice."

Stoner asks, "And do you think the Little Rock police department is not attempting to do just that?"

"Absolutely not!" Ezekiel Merriweather responds emphatically. "Our sources in the department tell us that the person believed to have shot my brother is a fellow faculty member but that he is being protected for some reason. And don't ask me why or his name. I don't know."

"Bullshit, he knows! And, protected, hell!" hisses Cormorant. "It's been like a dragnet at the school."

Stoner continues, "As tragic as his death is, would you agree that his murder has had the effect of getting people to read his book? Everywhere I go, people, black and white, are talking about it."

The brother has an immense air of dignity about him. His black pinstriped suit makes him look like an undertaker. His broad face, mournful and grave, hidden somewhat by whiskers, reminds me of James Earl Jones. His voice measured, he says, "My brother's book would have been recognized at some point in time as the truth of what happened to us here as a slave people. If that notoriety comes sooner than later, so be it. I certainly can't be expected to agree that it was worth shortening his life, but if he becomes a martyr in the name of truth, that will happen whatever I think. The least I can do in his memory is to insist that the person who took his life be held accountable, and that is the only reason we are here today."

From the couch, Cormorant snorts, "They say he put up the money to publish the book. He'll probably get rich off of it. The best thing that ever happened to the book is Damascus's murder."

I don't know. Unless the man is a great actor, his grief seems genuine. What else can he do? The tape continues with Stoner asking, "Mr. Merriweather, is it true that your brother was dying of cancer? That is a report we've heard but can't confirm since the authorities have not released the autopsy report."

Mr. Merriweather studies the floor, and for a moment appears as if he is going to cry. Finally, he says, "He was quite ill. I would hope the media would respect the family's privacy."

As the tape ends, I ask, "Was Damascus as classy as this guy?" I find I am moved by this man's dignified persona. I wonder if Laurel agrees, but her face in profile is impassive.

Cormorant clicks off the VCR and locks his hands behind his head. "Don't be fooled by this fake humility. You haven't read but a few pages. Damascus really gets into the crap. He traces slave owners' families to the present. Names names of mulattoes at the time of slavery and claims to identify their fathers. Tosses the word rape around a lot. And he had the nerve to call this book history when it is basically propaganda and gossip. Of course no real publishing house would touch it."

My skin goes clammy. Now I think I know why Cormorant sent me the book. There are all kinds of stories in the Delta about liaisons between Negroes and whites, most not going back to the days of slavery. "Are our families in there?" I ask weakly.

"No," Cormorant responds. "I would have called you, Miller."

Laurel insists that Cormorant eat something, and leads us back into the kitchen where we again sit down at the table.

I ask, "Are there people in the book we know?"

"Of course," he says, finally beginning to eat, and names off half a dozen families in Lee County alone.

I sit in stunned silence, trying to assimilate what I am hearing. What possible good can come from a recitation of this hoary gossip? Between mouthfuls, Cormorant reads from the book: *The white Southerner's secret shame has always been the rape committed by his forebears. And make no mistake about it, each time a white man entered the slave quarters, there was no question about consent. Evidence? The evidence is all about us. Every light-skinned Negro in Arkansas has a story to tell you. It may not date from slavery, but many do.* In his 1958 book, Negro Slavery in Arkansas, *Orville Taylor, using the 1850 and 1860 census data which shows the percentage of mulattoes in each state, asserts correctly that no definitive statistical conclusions about white-fathered births can be gleaned from such data. And though Taylor does not ignore this subject, what is absent from his treatment is a discussion of how the Arkansas slave, both male and female, reacted to the master or his sons or the overseer entering the slave quarters. The 1850 census records that 15.6 percent of the slave population was mulatto in Arkansas, so indirectly we know what was occurring. The trouble with Taylor's book is that it is accepted as the official history of slavery in Arkansas, but there is not one word in it from the mouth of a person of color about how he or she felt about the torture and rape that was a daily part of slave life in Arkansas. Why?*

The answer is obvious to black Arkansans and part of the unending racism that permeates our lives. Orville Taylor's book was acceptable to the white establishment and considered credible precisely because he ignored those who could have told him the most about his subject. Everybody knows blacks are untrustworthy as sources. To rely on the slave narratives and the oral history of the black experience would have been too risky, would have compromised his reputation as a scholar and made his book less authoritative, less the truth. Is it any wonder there is such a gulf between white and black in this state? He slams the book down on the table. "This is just outrageous!"

"But isn't he right?" I ask, wondering how well Cormorant knew this man. "Isn't history always written by the winners?"

Cormorant picks up the book and studies Merriweather's

picture as if he has never seen it. "If you truly give history its due, you have to admit how little you can ever know anything about the past. When my beginning students get the urge to talk about the causes of the Civil War, I tell them to go take a walk and come back when it passes. The most they can do is tell what the soldiers ate, what their weapons were, perhaps what they were thinking before the battle if they wrote a letter home." He pushes food around on his plate and adds, "I'm not worried about the book. What bothers me is the ability of this man's brother to force the police to make an arrest."

I think how frustrating Cormorant must be as a professor. What was the point of grinding out the semester if you couldn't fill up five or six blue books pontificating on the causes of the Civil War?

"Let's assume the worst," I say. "Let's say the police have your gun, and the ballistics come back showing it was your pistol that murdered Merriweather. Apparently, they have found somebody else's fingerprints on it, and are trying to find them. That's why you haven't been arrested."

Cormorant takes a deep breath. "Do you really think that's what's going on?" he asks, visibly relaxing for the first time tonight.

I reach over and touch Cormorant on the shoulder, thinking how human it is that even the smartest people I know are victims of wishful thinking. "Yeah, probably," I say.

"Miller!" Laurel yelps, her voice thick with fear.

Through the kitchen window we can see a line of red lights blinking. Two minutes later, Cormorant is arrested for the murder of Damascus Merriweather.

3

"You can tell him later that you're not going to be his attorney if that's the way you feel," Laurel says as I dial Cormorant's number in Little Rock to tell Beth.

I look down at the warrant, which seems more real than the arrest. "They must have somehow thought he was about to run and followed him all the way over here."

The look on Cormorant's face is one I will never forget, and made me tell the arresting officer I was representing him and show them my Arkansas Bar Association card. Terrified, resigned, but with an air of dignity as they were handcuffing him, he confirmed that, yes, I was his lawyer. To me, he said he knew he would have to spend the night in jail but that he hoped I could get him out tomorrow. I said I would try.

Beth sounds in shock but clearly has been expecting this arrest. She listens quietly as I instruct her to get in the car and drive to her sister-in-law's house and wait for me. Except as support to Cormorant, I doubt if Beth, who usually does not cope with stress well, will be much help, but Raven will be invaluable for a number of reasons. I tell Beth not to call anyone until she speaks to Raven, whom I call next. Close to Cormorant, maybe even closer than Beth, she immediately and correctly assumes that I'll need a place to spend the night. The first task I give her is to begin rounding up as much as perhaps a hundred thousand dollars for ten percent of a bond. I admit I have no idea at this point how much it will be. Cool under fire, Raven says glibly we can be sure that the NAACP will be watching.

We discuss whom she and Beth should call besides Cormorant's grown children, Miller Ray and Catherine. "What about your father? Will he understand?" I ask, watching Laurel repacking a bag for me. She does not care for Raven, who is such an overachiever that she intimidates most women. Laurel complains rightly that she is bossy and compulsive, admitting that she can tolerate those behaviors better in a man.

"I've got to call him," Raven replies. "If it's on the news, he might have another stroke. He just can't talk, thank God."

Despite myself, I laugh, thinking of the many times Mr. John terrified me as a boy. When he was angry at Cormorant, who couldn't even change a flat tire on a truck without help, he would throw a hatchet against the side of his tractor shed until he calmed down. Despite the old man's temper, Cormorant has worshiped his father, and even now he is a force to be reckoned with. Raven tells me she and Cormorant will drive to Phillips County tomorrow after I get him out of jail.

"How did Cormorant take it?" she asks.

"He was pretty shaken," I say. "Listen, don't you think you need a Little Rock lawyer on this? They've got an excellent defense bar, and they've been getting a lot of practice these days."

"Are you crazy?" Raven cuts me off. "You're the only one Cormorant is capable of trusting. I know him, Miller. He won't listen to anybody but you. If you refuse to take it, he might as well not have a lawyer, and you and I both know that would be disastrous. He's never been able to keep his mouth shut and that's why he's in trouble."

More than one hundred miles away, I nod in agreement. Not

only does Cormorant write letters to the editor of the *Arkansas Democrat-Gazette*, he tells off college presidents, mayors, Baptist preachers. "Why have a First Amendment if you're afraid to use it?" he routinely asks me when he has pissed someone off and needs a lawyer to do his heavy lifting. After one particularly candid speech eight years ago to a North Little Rock Kiwanis Club meeting, in which he attacked everything from the belief in the divinity of Christ to the morality of hunting and fishing (fishing, for God's sake!) as well as questioning the sanity and integrity of a member who belonged to the National Rifle Association, he was hit with a slander suit by the guy, who took it personally. We have laughed about that one for years. It wasn't funny until the guy settled for an apology that I wrote and forged Cormorant's signature to. The plain truth is that I marvel at my friend's willingness to stand up for what he believes. That kind of conflict isn't worth it to me, but Raven knows I treasure him for it. There is no point in arguing that I am too close. She knows what I have done for him in the past. "Okay," I say, suppressing a sigh.

"Thanks, Miller," Raven says, meaning it. "We can get him out of this."

"Somebody better," I warn her, though she knows as well I do that Miller would have his teeth knocked down his throat if he had to spend even a week in jail. The First Amendment isn't a high priority in prison.

"Miller, he isn't capable of killing a person in cold blood," she says. "Maybe talking someone to death, but I can't imagine him shooting someone."

I wonder if she knows he had begun carrying a pistol in his car. A workaholic, she may not see him all that often these days. Raven has been married and divorced three times. Each time I have handled her divorce, and each time she has thanked me and sworn she will stay away from bad men. Still attractive at fifty-three, with frosted blonde hair, blue eyes and a sensational smile all packaged in a size-five figure, she is irresistible to men over the age of forty and bowls most over like twigs. If I hadn't known her all my life, I surely would have been interested in that side of her myself. She claims the only men she can't boss are her father, Cormorant, and me, and probably for this reason has been devoted to each of us. Her friendship with me irritates and confounds Laurel, who is suspicious of the motives of most other women. She is certain that one day I will leave her, even if I am seventy-five when I do it. I tell her that I don't think there would be many takers at that age, but she says women would climb out of the grave to get their hands on a man like me, whatever that means.

"After the bond," I tell her, "the most important thing is what tack we should take with the media tomorrow. It's going to be a circus and the sooner we figure out how to deal with it, the better off we'll be."

Though perhaps not as smart as her brother, she is more savvy and practical. She will be worth three lawyers in this case. "I'll start thinking about a statement now," she responds, "and we can talk about it when you get here."

I hang up a few moments later, my mind whirling with the events of the last four hours. Laurel pleads with me to spend the night and get up early and drive over, but now I am so keyed up that I know I won't sleep for hours. "Don't you let her come into your room in the middle of the night," Laurel says, only half joking as I start up the Olds.

Sex between me and Raven is something that I can't really imagine. She is so aggressive she makes me wilt just thinking about it. "I'll nail it shut," I tease her.

"Call me to let me know what time you're coming home,"

she says, reaching in and pecking me on the mouth. "If you get too sleepy, pull over. Remember you have a deposition down in Hamburg Friday. I'll check on everything at the office in the morning."

"Thanks," I say, grateful I have nothing scheduled for tomorrow, which was supposed to be set aside for recovering from jet lag. Though I have a secretary, Laurel has managed my office for me for the last decade and has done all the accounting. Great with numbers and details, she has been an invaluable part of my defense preparation in several white-collar cases over the years. Once the CPAs have finished thoroughly confusing me, it is Laurel who has a knack for going through the books, breaking down the figures, and showing me how much my clients have actually stolen. She is steady as a rock. I don't know what I would have done without her. "Are you okay?" I ask, thinking about the knife.

"I'm fine," she says quietly. "I'm sorry I lost it. I'm worn out from the trip. Be careful, please."

I tell her I love her, and roar off, leaving her in the yard with her hands on her hips. To get to Little Rock, I have to drive back through Marianna, and on my way to I-40, as I pass the cemetery on Highway 79 where my parents are buried, I begin to wonder how much longer Laurel will tolerate living in Lee County. Many of our friends have already moved away, and once the blacks take over complete political control of the county, I can't imagine who of the rest will remain except people like us who have land here. What is incomprehensible to me is that their transition to power has taken so long. With seventy percent of the population, how can they not control county government? Even Cormorant, who has an answer for everything, professes to be mystified and pretends to believe that whites won't let them, which is not true. My theory is that ninety percent of our best people, black and white, have already left Lee County.

As my mind replays the events of the evening, the only thing I am certain of is that Laurel is about to crack, if she already hasn't, and I am going to have to deal with her feelings or I will come home some day and find a note that she has gone to Alaska. I think of Laurel's face as she let go of the knife, and I realize that I blame Cynthia for not leaving this subject alone. Hardly a month goes by that she does not write or call asking when we are going to move. When I remind her that eight generations of Hollys have lived in this area, she laughs and says that was seven more than necessary. She will be shocked when Laurel calls her tonight about Cormorant. Now that she has found herself, she calls him the last honest man from Marianna. She no longer appreciates the fact that if everyone in Marianna said aloud what they thought, the entire town would be burned by nightfall.

By the time I reach the county line, the crick in my neck which had begun about halfway over the Atlantic reinforces how bad an idea this was, but I know Cormorant is feeling a lot worse than I am, and I drive on, trying to force myself to concentrate on the little he has told me. My mind keeps tuning out. I know that if Laurel, normally the gentlest of souls, is capable of sudden violence, Cormorant, being a man, could easily have shot someone in anger, however improbable it seems. On the interstate the lights of the truckers coming from the west seem distant to my sleep-deprived brain, like messengers from another planet.

How could we have come to this? I realize I am glad Mother and Daddy both died young and missed the last thirty years. They would not have understood how we can simply capitulate as if there had been another Appomattox . As I pass the Brinkley exit, with only another hour to go, I think of how Daddy said that one of the greatest thrills of his life was the day Strom Thurmond visited Marianna in 1948 when he temporarily bolted the Democrat Party and ran on the Dixiecrat ticket for President. He would have stroked out today upon seeing their godson taken into custody for killing a black man. And he would have refused to read a single word of the victim's book. How can I be so different from him? I wonder if I really am. If there is anything I understand, it is that he had to die for me to be different. I wouldn't have been strong enough to oppose him.

As I think of my father, my mind flits back to Cormorant's situation. Surely, this man Damascus Merriweather had a number of enemies who could have killed him. There is too much anger in what I read to believe he didn't incite people in person as well as on paper. His brother certainly has that capacity. Before Cormorant's trial, I must find a way to rub the jury's nose in his enemies' hatred so that it will believe a number of people could have murdered him.

Finally getting into Little Rock at ten thirty, I pull off at the Center Street exit and turn left onto Louisiana. Raven and her most recent husband, a trader at Stephens, bought one of those old houses in the Quawpaw Quarter that take half the gold in Ft. Knox to fix up. Admittedly, it is lovely inside, but at night it is said you are a virtual prisoner because of the crack dealers and gangs downtown. She swears she loves it, but as far as I am concerned, she is in major denial. If I were going to seriously consider living in the Little Rock area, we'd buy in Conway or Cabot and drive in. Those palaces I read about on Chenal Parkway out west don't interest me at all.

Standing in the door in shorts in full view of the probable crack dealer across the street, Raven hugs me, making me wish I'd taken the time for a shower. After a twenty-two hour day, I'm not exactly fresh. "I'm so glad you've come."

I have gotten sleepy again, but as soon as I see the mask cracking on her face, I feel my exhaustion retracting like a gonad on a cold winter's day. Raven usually hides her feelings behind a bluff, take-charge exterior, but there is none of that tonight as she leads me to a phone in her kitchen. I call the Pulaski County Sheriff's Office to find out if Cormorant will be held all night or transferred to the Pulaski County detention facility, and am put on hold. While I am waiting, I get a good look at Raven, who looks her age for the first time I have known her. Her blonde hair, usually down to her shoulders, is drawn tight behind her head in a bun. If she lives long enough, she will look like her mother, who died last year at eighty with a patch of goat hairs on her chin that she refused to let anyone get close enough to clip. *Nature's way of reminding women we were made from Adam's rib*, she said in a firm rasp the last time I saw her alive. Despite this unique interpretation of the aging process, Cormorant said that she hadn't been dead a minute before Raven had found her scissors and said their mother had been one of the most ignorant women she had ever known.

Told Cormorant will be taken to the Pulaski County jail within the hour after he finishes in-processing, I hang up and Raven takes me upstairs to my bedroom. "Did Beth get hold of Miller Ray and Catherine?"

"They were hysterical just like their mother," Raven answers without an ounce of pity in her voice as she pulls out my underwear. Childless and glad of it, Raven pokes through my bags as if she were a child promised a gift from my trip. We have always been like a brother and sister though I see her only occasionally now. "I gave Beth a pill, and she went to sleep thirty minutes ago in the bedroom next to mine. Miller Ray cried like a five-year-old."

My namesake is gay, a development his family hides from the world, especially east Arkansas, which, as Cormorant says, still isn't ready for prime time. More liberal than my wife, I found myself growing used to the idea after we met his companion in Miami Beach last year. I was hoping they would show affection toward each other, so I could test my reaction, but understandably, they acted quite circumspectly. Laurel is appalled and insists for some reason on associating homosexuality with pedophilia. Cormorant, ever the truth teller, told my wife her homophobia is consistent with her refusal to accept any social behavior not openly practiced in small southern towns in the 1950s.

"What about his sister?" I ask, embarrassed by the grayness of my underwear.

"Catherine kept saying over and over that her father never even spanked her," she says dryly. "I told them not to come until they are all through with their exams. Cormorant doesn't need their hand-wringing at the moment. Would you like to borrow some of my ex-husband's tee shirts?"

Downstairs in her den, which is more of a library, Raven hands me a cup of coffee and picks up a copy of *Coming to Terms*. "What do you think of the book? If Cormorant hadn't been so hard on it, he might not be charged with murder. This guy's brother is riding it for all he is worth."

I explain that I have only read the preface. "Why would people care now if they haven't for two hundred years?" I muse. "We're not responsible for what our ancestors did."

Raven begins flipping through the pages. "See, what I believe got this Merriweather character started on his high horse was Bill Clinton. When he came to Little Rock for the fortieth anniversary of the Central High crisis, he came within an inch of apologizing to blacks for slavery. Merriweather's book in the first chapter picks up where that visit ended, with the president of the United States, the governor of Arkansas, and the mayor of Little Rock symbolically holding the door open at Central for the Little Rock Nine. Listen to this: *In every generation there is a window of opportunity for a people to understand and to come to terms with their past. For a brief period of time, they may be ready to receive the truth, psychologically prepared perhaps by a tangible reminder and symbol of their victims' oppression and humiliation. By the symbol of a door held open in September 1997 (so Southern a gesture), these nine now middle-aged and weathered African-Americans were invited to recall for all the world their memories of the embarrassing and shameful era of legal segregation and their personal struggles to overcome it. For an instant, it seemed as if the President of the United States, a Southerner, so flawed and yet so human a man, might go further and invite the country to reflect on its earlier history of slavery and issue an acknowledgment and apology to the millions of African-Americans whose ancestors were made chattel by their fellow countrymen. Had he been able to summon the courage and exercise the moral leadership of the great man he so desperately wanted to be, perhaps white Arkansans (and the rest of the country, by implication) could have been persuaded to explore an even darker era of their history. Perhaps one of them could have been moved to write a history of that time which credits the words and memories of the victims themselves. Even the Jews, so persecuted for much of recorded history, have been allowed the dignity of telling their stories of the Holocaust and of being believed. Not so in the state of Arkansas, where the Slave Narratives lie gathering dust. In these documents there is evidence of what slavery was really like for the slave and not just for the master...*

Raven lays the book face down on the table, cracking its spine. "If this book touches a nerve like some of these out-of-state reviews are implying that it does, then there's going to be some major pressure to offer up Cormorant as a victim."

I sip the coffee and realize I haven't had a full cup since France. I could never make myself understood that I wanted something more than a thimbleful. "I've begun to worry about that, too," I confess. "This is the chance for Little Rock's redemption and who better to put on the fire than a Delta planter's son, especially somebody like Cormorant."

Raven, reminding me of my own mother, bends and picks up from the deep Persian rug a paperclip I couldn't even see. "But it may be the kind of finger-pointing we can exploit. I want us to think about it."

Now that I'm sitting down without having to concentrate on the road, the pressure on my spine begins to ease. "What do you mean?" I ask, thinking of Cormorant, who is probably being fingerprinted at this moment. Don't talk, I had mouthed to him as he was led away. That's like asking a river not to run, he told me once when a Chi Omega pledge at the University complained how he wouldn't shut up after I had fixed them up on a blind date.

Raven, seated across from me at an antique glass table that was in her mother's house, hands me a sheet of paper. "I'll tell you tomorrow. This is my idea what you say when you get Cormorant released. There are going to be a dozen cameras outside the jail. It's short, but it will set the stage for maybe where we ought to go."

I pick up the paper and squint, having left my reading glasses on the dash. *Though I have not seen the prosecutor's file in this case, I can only tell you that my client is merely guilty of having been in the wrong place at the wrong time. Because of the highly controversial book he had written, Damascus Merriweather unfortunately had many enemies. Dr. Ashley was not one of them and had no motive to shoot his colleague of ten years. He may have, indeed, been one of the last persons to see Dr. Merriweather alive that afternoon, but as you may know, Dr. Merriweather was dying of stomach cancer. Dr. Ashley, at Dr. Merriweather's request, had driven to his brother's home that afternoon to discuss filling in for him on a panel at the law school. Anyone who knew of Dr. Merriweather's condition and wished him ill had only to wait and watch him suffer. I am not in a position to take your questions at this time. Suffice it to say now that my client expects nothing less than a prompt acquittal.*

"You don't think I should say that Cormorant was less than overwhelmed by his book but that was hardly a reason for murder?" I ask when I have finished reading the statement. I wonder what else she knows. Cormorant has always confided in her.

"I don't think we want to do that yet," Raven muses. "There will be plenty of time to pick it apart. It's more than enough right now to get the media to begin to speculate about who could have been his enemies. Surely, the police have been looking at other suspects."

I reread the statement and marvel at how much her mind works like a lawyer's. Maybe there isn't much difference between her profession and my own. Her statement says just enough. Raven has wisely kept it short. Right now, I should get out to the jail to check on Cormorant, but before I can ask Raven for directions, she looks down at her Rolex and clicks on her television and we watch a brief news break at eleven p.m. on Channel 4 that a professor at UALR, Cormorant Ashley, has been taken into custody. The local tv news stations pretty much are put to bed after the ten o'clock news programs, so there is not much more.

I find Roosevelt Road and head toward the Pulaski County Detention Center, bemused by the fact that when this morning began my only concern was to spend the French coins in my pocket at Charles DeGaulle Airport. Driving west on Roosevelt, I realize that this area of Little Rock is all black and wonder how much the issue of race influences this city. Preoccupied with the Delta, I have only marginally kept up with Little Rock but know vaguely that like all urban areas it is deeply divided by white flight and that much of the political rhetoric is conducted in code so as not to scare off any more industry than necessary. As I stop at a light at what used to be High Street and is now M.L. King, I glance warily at the neighborhood around me for signs of gang activity. Though I haven't read more than a few pages of Merriweather's book, I realize that what is extraordinary about it is its lack of restraint. The language is deliberately inflammatory. He surely knew what he was unleashing if he were able to get any attention for it. The white heat of the man's prose is infuriating, and I remind myself again that I have seen Cormorant lose his temper when his patience runs out. But murder? I still can't imagine it.

It is shocking to see Cormorant in an orange jump suit as if he were already convicted and serving time. If this had happened in Lee County in the old days, I could have bonded him out in an hour. "Miller, where have you been?" he almost sobs after the guard shuts the door on us.

His attempt at bravery at the moment of arrest has given way to panic. Over the years I have seen scores of criminal defendants and none of them except maybe some kids have cried. "They don't let the lawyers hold their clients' hands while you're being processed," I say, feeling testy rather than sympathetic as I should. "I've been at Raven's, working on a statement for tomorrow." I should have known better than to think he would remain calm and stoical.

The relatively spacious room provided for defendants and their attorneys, with its table and chairs, is better than the jail cells I've often been provided. Built in the last seven years or so, the Pulaski County Detention Center, I've read, is already busting at the seams.

"When can I get out?" Cormorant asks pathetically, his small white hands clutching his thighs through the orange material. He must be humiliated by what he is wearing. I've never thought of Cormorant as a sartorial dandy, but now I think of the bow tie he affects in his classroom and suspect I haven't paid attention to that aspect of him. Dapper is how I would have described him and let it go at that. His physical appearance is much more important to him than I would have thought. Yet, I know I shouldn't be too hard on him. Cormorant rarely displays the usual defense mechanisms that drive most men. The psychological filtering which allows us to wall ourselves off from a catastrophic event is often absent in him. When a favorite student of his died last year in an accident, Beth said he broke down in tears at the service during the eulogy he was delivering. Despite my knowledge of how his psyche works, I want him to act like a man.

Perversely, I am tempted to tell him that it will be a couple of weeks. I think of all the defendants, usually black, who have no chance of making bond and yet are no threat to escape. "No later than five tomorrow, I expect," I say gruffly. "If you want me to get a Little Rock lawyer, you probably could get out by noon. I don't know the judges and the system here. I can get somebody to work with me. It wouldn't be a bad idea at all. Every judge has his favorite. Once we find out who it is, I can ask around."

"No!" Cormorant barks, now running his hands through his sandy hair, which unlike mine, is still thick without much gray. "I don't trust anybody in this town. The blacks have got them all scared to death just like at home."

Cormorant is talking nonsense. Little Rock's racial composition is pretty much the reverse of places like Lee and Phillips County. More like 70-30 white, instead of 30-70. But after watching the tape of Ezekiel Merriweather's interview, I realize I might be feeling the same way and cut him some slack. "Everything's going to be okay," I say soothingly. "Raven's taking care of the bond."

"How's Beth?" he asks, his voice more normal. "Has she called the kids? I should have prepared them, but I just didn't know what the hell to tell them."

"They're going to be fine," I lie. What else can I tell him? Whatever happens, they will be scarred for years, maybe the rest of their lives. The odd thing is, so will I. When I saw those lights outside the house, I had the strange feeling they were coming for me. "Beth is spending the night at Raven's, too. She's asleep. Raven gave her a pill."

Cormorant laughs sourly. "You should have brought me about ten. You can't imagine what it feels like. I've been claustrophobic since the second they put handcuffs on me. Does Daddy know?"

"When I get you out tomorrow," I explain to him, "you and Raven are going to drive to Helena. We'll have plenty of time later to talk about the details. Raven had to call his night attendant. She was afraid he'd see it on tv tomorrow."

"Doris is there tonight," Cormorant says softly. "She'll watch him."

It is Cormorant, not Raven, who looks after his father, traveling back and forth to Helena and handpicking the women who stay with him on a twenty-four basis now. Cormorant would prefer to have him in an apartment in Little Rock, but Mr. John couldn't be pried out of the Delta with a crowbar. His father has never forgiven him for not wanting to farm, nor has Cormorant ever forgiven himself for not being the man his father wanted. Teaching isn't a man's job, Mr. John told him the day Cormorant called him to say that his thesis on the Battle of Helena had been accepted. Cormorant, I think, began to formulate his theory of history the day his father said that. History wasn't worth much after his daddy got through with it. *All we can hope to know is what the soldiers wore, what they ate...* Actually, Mr. John wouldn't have minded if Cormorant had taught a couple of courses at the community college in Helena just as long as he was farming at the same time. *He could never believe that thinking and writing about the past was a full-time job*, Cormorant has said more than once.

"Your father is the last person who would ever believe that you shot another man."

A rueful expression steals over my friend's face. "He wouldn't think I had the guts is what you mean. Now, if it had been Raven..."

Despite myself, I smile, knowing exactly what he means. Raven was driving a combine twelve hours a day when she was fourteen; a year earlier, from a standing position, she shot a cottonmouth in the head with a .22 rifle just as it was about to bite Franklin Roosevelt, the family mutt. She should have been the farmer, stayed in the Delta, but she didn't do either. And Mr. John never held it against her, the way he did with his son. "You didn't talk to anybody, did you?" I ask, worrying that Cormorant can't resist the need to vindicate himself. I have to make him focus on the present. "From this second forward, we have to think of ourselves as being at no-holds-barred total war with the prosecutor, the police, the press, the judge, the jury, every black person, every white person in the state of Arkansas. It's all of them against you. Forget the notions of reasonable doubt and presumption of innocence. Now that you've been charged, the presumption is that you shot this wonderful, truth-telling, black man at close range in the chest because you were jealous of him or because he made you mad. I don't know what the prosecutor is saying your motive was, but we have to go to war with all of them, and every moment of the day I want you to be thinking about how we can convince twelve people you didn't shoot that man. Do you understand?"

Cormorant nods. "I think I voted for the prosecutor, a guy named Latting. He's not supposed to be such a bad guy."

That's not what you will be thinking when he's cross-examining you, I think, but don't tell him. I'll have plenty of time to disabuse him of the notion that the prosecutor is his friend. "We both know you've made people mad over here from time to time," I say, remembering not for the first time tonight how surprised he always was when the victims of his remarks took his comments personally, "and I want you to draw me up a list of your worst enemies, especially on campus."

Cormorant rubs his hands on his orange pants. "Nobody I know would do this to me," he says automatically.

To shock him out of his lethargy, I am tempted to say something sarcastic to him, but he doesn't have a clue, possibly because his mind works so abstractly. He can't conceive that a person would hate him over an idea. What he forgets is that he strikes at a person's core beliefs. To Cormorant, there are no absolutes, so why should he get his feelings hurt? "You offend the hell out of people. They aren't like you. They may not say anything back, but inwardly, they are seething. Remember that guy who sued you."

Cormorant's eyes glitter with scorn. "What an idiot he was!" he says, derisively. "We should have gone to court with him. It would have been like our creation science case."

My eyes feel like I have sand in them. Blinking, I look around the room, hoping they don't start to water. I don't have a handkerchief with me, and my hands feel grimy. Like most people, Cormorant is a mass of contradictions. He thinks words are sacred, but he uses them as weapons. "Everybody has people that hate them. For God's sake, you know that."

"You're a lawyer, Miller," he points out. "People hate you, but I'm a college professor, and this isn't the Wild West."

I don't think of myself as being hated, but I suppose he is right. The public reaches for its wallets whenever a lawyer comes around. However, within the profession I am known as someone who recognizes that disputes have to be settled and who can preserve everyone's dignity in the process. If you have to try the case, even a criminal case, essentially, it's because you've missed an opportunity to deal it down. Every case has its weakness and can be settled or plea-bargained successfully. "You are the one who carried a pistol with you," I remind him. "You flunk students, piss off your colleagues, evict tenants. Don't act like you're so damn innocent. You're the opposite of a murderer; you make people want to murder you."

As if to answer me, Cormorant farts, sending a ripping, ridiculous sound through the bare, empty room, but I resist even smiling at him. Normally, he would giggle, but tonight he is under such pressure that it may not have even registered. He says, "So you think I've been framed, and it wasn't just a coincidence that somebody came after me?"

Instead of his bowels, Cormorant's stomach now rumbles from beneath the table. I can't imagine he has been able to eat much lately. The last forty-eight hours must have been hard. I suspect that if he had been interviewed again, he would have been asked to take a polygraph. "The last thing we want to do is exclude any possibility. This is a war about creating reasonable doubt."

"You sound like you think I'm guilty," he accuses me.

Until I get Cormorant out of jail, there is no point in talking to him. Perhaps, because of her job, Raven already understands what it is we have to do. Cormorant, despite thinking the truth can't be known, still believes in it. "You're the one thing standing between this prosecutor and sainthood. A judgeship, maybe the office of Attorney General. If he puts you away, a lot of people in this city are going to feel good about themselves. Between now and the trial, we have to change that culture of thinking."

Cormorant rubs his hands together, an old sign that I am making him nervous. "You get so damn intense, you know it? You always have. When you get this way, you actually give off a stench. I swear to God. I'm glad I'm not Laurel."

I stand up, ready to go back to his sister's house. "I'm glad you're not either. When I get you out of there, I want you to sit down and write down everything you know about the brothers Merriweather, you understand? I want a book as thick as the Bible from you."

Cormorant nods but stares down at his knees. "It's good my mother isn't here to go through this. She wouldn't know who to be for."

"Probably not," I grunt, shoving my hands in my pockets. At the age of sixty, Miss Ella woke up one day and threw off her lukewarm commitment to mainline Christianity and became an unforgivable embarrassment to the family by embracing the views of every New Age evangelist she could find on cable. Even after it was discovered that she was suffering from Alzheimer's, it was hard to overlook her obsessions. She began visiting black churches in the 1980s and asking for their forgiveness for her Methodist great-grandfather, who, she had discovered during a genealogical exercise, had preached during the 1850s that God had ordained slavery. Cormorant had innocently explained to her that this was a normal theological position for a Southern clergyman of his day and time, an observation that had incensed his mother, who unilaterally decided great-granddaddy had been the anti-Christ and that it was her duty to apologize for him one hundred years later. Shades of Bill Clinton. Almost.

As I open the door, Cormorant says quietly behind me, "Thank you, Miller. I know what I'm asking. I won't forget it."

For an instant I am tempted to say that we won't be friends until this case is over, and if he is convicted, never again, because blame is inescapable. Instead, I reach back and he clutches my hand. "I know," I say.

4

"Just keep smiling," I whisper to Cormorant, who is back in street clothes after his arraignment and bond hearing, as reporters yell questions while we make our way to Raven's waiting Lexus in the parking lot at the Pulaski County Detention Center. Though I have represented many high-profile criminal defendants (mainly white-collar east Arkansas businessmen in federal court), nothing has prepared me for the Whitewaterlike atmosphere that is attending Cormorant's release. With Cormorant at my side, my brief statement must have drawn thirty reporters, including television cameras from Shreveport and Memphis. On the other side of him, holding tightly to Cormorant's right hand, Beth, despite my entreaties, is wiping her face. Maybe on television it will look like sweat. Two in the afternoon, it is ninety degrees and the humidity must be worse.

Beth ought to be smiling. We have drawn the best judge we could have. Minor Latting, the prosecutor for the 6th District, has taken the unusual route of filing charges directly in circuit court, bypassing municipal court, which is the typical procedure, but it may have backfired on him. Though he has lived in Little Rock since his graduation from Vanderbilt Law School twenty years ago, Judge Harry Cato's family is from West Memphis. Cormorant whispered to me during the arraignment that the judge's parents knew his mother from the time when she was a girl and used to travel to Crittenden County to visit a cousin. Whatever his motive, Cato had set a paltry $100,000 bond and then had lectured the prosecutor when he dared to complain. *I can't believe this defendant is much of a threat to flee the court's jurisdiction, and I can't imagine you actually think he is either.*

Implicit in his tone was a not so subtle warning to Latting that he will not be stampeded by the publicity this case is apparently going to generate. Cato is used to being in the limelight in Little Rock, primarily because of his political background: Once a partner in the Rose law firm who surely must have left because of the problems and conflicts generated by Webb Hubbell, Cato served briefly as an advisor to Jim Guy Tucker after Bill Clinton resigned as governor to become President. Nimble as the quarterback he used to be for Tulane, he left after a year before Tucker's troubles began with Kenneth Starr, and ran for a circuit judge seat that came open. With his contacts and smarts, Cato could make a lot more money practicing law, but I suspect he doesn't want to or have to.

As we struggle toward the car, we can't escape the sounds of a noisy rally being staged to our right. It is my first time to see Ezekiel Merriweather in the flesh. I was too busy in the courtroom to pick him out, but there is no mistaking him as he gestures emphatically to a group of primarily African-Americans. "Don't look," I whisper to Cormorant as he turns his head. "I don't think we want a photo op with the brother just yet." Ezekiel in person, I notice, has a head as big as a lion and the wounded air of a disappointed politician as he jabs the air with his fist. The low bond obviously didn't set well with him, and I suspect we will read about his complaints in the *Democrat-Gazette* tomorrow morning. Besides the media, the courtroom had been packed with Merriweather sympathizers, many carrying copies of the victim's book, apparently as a gesture of solidarity. Already I have seen television cameras pointed to it as if it were a sacred text. "A publicist's dream," Raven called this trial last night before I went to bed. Damascus Merriweather must be smiling.

With cameras and microphones still shoved in our faces, Cormorant and Beth follow me through the crowd. Despite my announcement a few moments ago that we would take no questions, they're still coming. A reporter yells in Cormorant's face, "Is it true that you thought Damascus Merriweather was unqualified to teach?"

Cormorant's jaw tightens, and I know he would like nothing better than to deliver a lecture on the evils of affirmative action. He does not know that Raven and I already are hatching a plan that may allow him to become more than a human punching bag between now and September 9. "Raven!" I yell, seeing her Lexus come into view.

I open the back door and Beth and Cormorant scramble into the backseat, and like a bodyguard I climb into the front beside Raven, who, judging from her grim expression, wouldn't mind running over some of the media despite the fact that she is doubtless on a first-name basis with most of them from Little Rock. "I can't stand this!" Beth wails as we inch our way forward. "We've never done anything to blacks! Did you see their faces? They're so full of rage! How could they get this stirred up over a book?"

"Have you read it?" I ask, irritated with Beth, though it is hardly the time for a book discussion. Beth, based on her performance today, is going to be even less help than I thought, but maybe I am being too hard on her. While I was waiting for her to get out of the bathroom this morning (naturally Raven was in the other bathroom), I read more of *Coming to Terms*, which Laurel had remembered to pack for me. A line from the first chapter that

Cormorant could have written comes back to me now: *Morally bankrupt like the rest of the South, this generation of Arkansans has escaped history's microscope until outsiders investigating Whitewater re-exposed the venality and cupidity of the white elite who defend themselves by insisting that their incestuous self-dealing is inevitable because Arkansas is "such a small place."* It occurs to me that Cormorant probably had more in common intellectually with Damacus Merriweather than with his own wife. What they differed over was the fact that Cormorant would never have written that sentence unless he had a hundred footnotes to back him up.

"Why should I?" Beth sniffs. "Cormorant says it's trash."

I turn and say to Cormorant, "You meant that as history the book is trash. You're not saying that some of it may not be true."

His eyes and brain occupied with events outside the Lexus, Cormorant does not answer me. I turn and see running along beside us a black man who begins to pound on the roof. He is angry enough that if he had a pistol at this moment, he would shoot us. Seeing him, Raven hits the accelerator as she turns out of the parking lot, and we narrowly miss a cameraman who has positioned himself in front of the car. I have a sick feeling in my stomach and realize I am almost panting from fear.

"Just go on!" Cormorant screams from the backseat.

Raven runs a yellow light as she speeds down Roosevelt, and suddenly we are free of the mob. "I'll never go to a zoo again," Cormorant says, making us all laugh at the plaintiveness in his voice.

"It'll be over September 10th," I remind him. Cato has scheduled just two days of trial. I don't think he likes Minor Latting, but it may be just wishful thinking. Back in chambers he told us he didn't believe in gag orders. *I can't gag the media, and I'm not going to spend the next three months trying, either,* he told Latting, who had asked for one as a way to preemptively deal with the pretrial publicity. Later I will get a look at the prosecutor's file. Latting, who seems decent enough to work with, told me earlier that I won't have to jump through any hoops. Younger than I expected (he looks about forty), he seems fairly restrained for a prosecutor. He has to be worried about a change of venue with the way Ezekiel Merriweather is carrying on. If I had been in his position, I would have acted no differently. Judges often take their irritation out on the lawyers when they are mad at someone else.

Instead of driving Cormorant to his home, where presumably reporters will be waiting to try to follow him into his bedroom, Raven drives us circuitously to her house downtown to drop off Beth and allow Cormorant to get a quick shower before we head to her office for our first strategy session. Later, they will drive to Helena to talk to Mr. John. Since I don't have my own office here, she has graciously offered to allow me to convert a break-room in her suite in the Lafayette Building downtown. As we get out the car, Cormorant breathes a sigh of relief, and I know why: there is not a reporter in sight. In her yard are two majestic oaks and in front of the house are azaleas, honeysuckle, and roses. I look back across the street and see sitting on his porch a black man whom I assume is the same guy I saw last night, who right at this moment seems anything but a drug dealer. Even if it is illusory, for the moment life appears normal.

Inside I call Laurel to tell her how things went and afterwards she dutifully asks to speak to Beth. I stand in the hall listening to Beth rail against the events of the last twenty-four hours, and I realize that she must truly love Cormorant to have stayed with him all these years. Oddly, when she has had a couple of drinks, she says, playfully, she would have been more comfortable with a man like me. Her husband, she is fond of saying, takes his own opinions far too seriously. *You had enough sense to learn when to shut up and leave well enough alone. Cormorant never has and never will,* she said last year on her birthday when we were alone together at the table for a few moments.

I knew she was referring to events almost thirty years ago when, fresh out of law school, I returned to Lee County to farm and practice law and foolishly tried to play the role of the honest broker between whites and blacks during the year-long business boycott of merchants in Marianna in 1970. As I wait for her and Laurel to finish the call, my mind defaults to that year when I saw this much hatred in the faces of blacks. Even now, I wonder why we could not have avoided the boycott. Last year I read Taylor Branch's *Pillar of Fire*, about Martin Luther King in the years '63-'65, and there was not a single mention of Arkansas in the index. I still don't understand why the civil rights movement took so long to get to the Arkansas Delta. If it hadn't been for the federal government putting in the health clinic with those VISTA volunteers, who knows when it would have started? Despite almost three decades' distance, my face begins to burn as I think of how naive I was, remembering how in one memorable two-hour negotiating session I was called both a "nigger-lover" and a "honky planter." I should never have gotten involved. I learned then that politics, as Beth reminded me the night of her birthday, is not my game. Law is much easier.

Beth, crying again, looks at me, and I think, not for the first time, how miserable we both would have been had we for some reason married. She hates the Delta and has escaped. Poor Laurel never has. "Did you need to talk to her again?" she asks, rubbing the knuckle of her right forefinger under her nose like a child.

It is an endearing gesture, and after she hangs up the phone, I am moved to say that I can't imagine a jury will convict Cormorant. It is not a promise I should make, and I undercut it by saying, "Unfortunately, If they want to convict, sometimes the evidence doesn't seem to matter."

As Raven enters the den bringing her sister-in-law a cup of coffee, Beth says, trying to sound brave, "There's no motive. No jury can convict without a motive."

I explain that establishing a motive is not an element of the crime of murder and watch Beth's eyes fill with tears. I hug her briefly, thinking her life with Cormorant has never had an easy year. I look at her and try to smile.

When Cormorant, refreshed by a shower and shave, emerges twenty minutes later from the bathroom, he suggests we head immediately for his sister's office. Given that all we are going to do is to begin to map out a plan for defending him, we could stay here, but we all seem to sense that we need to get away from Beth if we are going to do anything except weep and complain about blacks. We leave her on the phone with their children after they briefly speak to their father. With their exams over in a week, they will be home for the summer from Maryland and Ole Miss. I don't envy their summer.

Ten minutes later we are seated in Raven's third-story office in the Lafayette Building, still on Louisiana but ten blocks north of her house. I almost have to pinch myself to realize that the petite woman across the desk from me is responsible for meeting the payroll of the ten people outside this room. Though I have known that Raven owned her own ad agency, I realize that until now I have never quite believed it. In the past my mind has gotten stuck on her messy divorces with their charges of adultery and kinky goings-on that none of the parties wanted to see the light of day. I've always admired her ability to turn a phrase and to think on her feet and stay cool under fire, but, in truth, I've never gotten beyond the image of a hard-drinking Chi O who ran through men like a star Razorback fullback. Yet, now that I think about it, the last divorce was five years ago, and on the other side of the door, there is the distinct smell of money being made.

"What I was talking about last night is that we've got to make this case boomerang on this Ezekiel character," Raven is saying as she removes her right gold earring and lays it on the desk in front of her. "He's trying to make a martyr out of his brother, yet maybe the best thing we can do is to let that happen at first."

Cormorant, who is staring out the window as if he expects Ezekiel Merriweather to show up on the Allright parking lot across the street, turns and frowns. "You mean with the media outside Arkansas?"

"Precisely." Seated behind her desk, which is the size of a small island, Raven rocks back in her chair, the only delicate thing in the room. On the walls are blown-up photographs of Little Rock's latest attempts to create a downtown: the river market, a downsized replica in some respects of Seattle's, a children's museum, and the new library, which boasts in granite around its parapet the names of diverse politically correct writers such as Aristotle and Lorraine Hansberry. Raven brings her perfectly manicured nails together. "The bigger the book gets outside the state, the more unconscious resentment it will begin to generate among some of the jurors even if they haven't read a word. They'll hear about it, and it will rub off."

Typically, Cormorant dismisses the notion out of hand. "It'll never be taken that seriously. As I've been trying to say for three weeks, as a history, the book's awfully thin. And it's nothing new. We're not talking about the discovery of the Dead Sea Scrolls," he adds snidely. "Some woman at the University got a Ph. D. out of the Slave Narratives a few years ago; the county historical quarterlies have referenced them; Bob Lancaster did a popular piece on them for the *Arkansas Times* a few years ago."

Raven rubs her temples with the tips of her fingers. "That's not the point, Cormorant. We all know Merriweather hasn't written another *Mind of the South*. It's more of the quality of Uncle Tom's Cabin Comes to Arkansas, hopefully complete with an appearance on Oprah by the grieving brother. With any luck, Don Imus will scarf it up and do a show in which he bashes the entire state. What we want to happen is that by the time Miller gets up to make his opening statement, the whites on the jury will be so hunkered down the only bullet left they'll have left to fire is an acquittal, and they won't even know why."

Directly behind Raven's head is a blow-up of a photograph of a model of the Clinton Library which is to be located a few blocks east of the river market and basically in a black area of town. "You're sure that if all this happens," I ask doubtfully, "a jury won't get on the bandwagon? What better way to demonstrate its moral purity than to offer up Cormorant as a sacrificial lamb?" I turn back to Cormorant for his reaction, but he is still studying the view. I wonder what he's feeling. Normally, he would have already taken over the conversation.

Raven hugs her bare arms. It must be sixty-five degrees in here. "Unless I'm way off, it'll be the Whitewater reaction in Arkansas all over again. We sit back and watch Ezekiel do Ken Starr in blackface."

I reach over to her desk and take a tissue from a box and blow my nose. "What you can't forget is that Kenneth Starr got a conviction of a sitting governor," I say when I'm through. "They may have held their noses, but they did their duty."

"They had a paper trail the length of the Natchez Trace!" Raven fires back. "All the prosecutor has is the fact that Cormorant was there that afternoon and his pistol that was stolen. Isn't that right?" she says, directing her question to her brother.

Cormorant turns away from the window and says evenly, "That's all they could have."

Quieter than I would like for him to be, Cormorant comes

and sits beside me. "My feeling," his sister continues, "is that there will come a time before the trial when we will spin the story our way and get our local media to turn on the Merriweathers big time. It would help if we can get some dirt on these guys. It's not going to be enough for Miller to stand in front of the jury and tick off the names of half a dozen racist groups who hate the book."

I have been thinking along the same lines, but Cormorant doesn't respond. I nudge his shoulder, hoping his mood is the result of a bad night's sleep. When attacked, his normal response is to defend himself. As if she were giving a pep talk to a wavering client, Raven continues, "If the O. J. Simpson trial was the book on how to play the race card, we can't afford to leave it unread on the shelf."

Cormorant seems nonplussed. "Whites have always played the race card," he observes, bobbing his head slightly as if to give emphasis to his words that his tone lacks. "It doesn't always work anymore."

I have the sense that we are having this conversation too soon for Cormorant. Normally, he will give a dissertation on any subject. "It's not the race card we want to play," I suggest, "but rather the 'Arkansas versus the world' theme."

Cormorant looks down at his hands and asks, "What about finding Merriweather's killer?" he asks quietly. "What are the odds of that happening?"

I feel immediately on the defensive, though I shouldn't. "I told you last night that's exactly what we are going to try to do. In just a few minutes I'll go look at the file and get an idea if there were other suspects, but you've got to realize from the beginning that Raven has a point. Jurors aren't blank slates. I'm serious about you writing out all you know about the Merriweather brothers. We need an investigator, too. The more we know the better off you'll be."

Ignoring me, Cormorant, his voice urgent, says to Raven, "Let's go see Daddy. He's probably beside himself."

Instantly, I understand that Cormorant and Raven should have driven to Helena as soon as he was released from jail. His father's reaction is what he has been worrying about since he has been charged. I try to put myself in his place, but know that it is Cynthia I would have worried about first. All his adult life, Cormorant has talked about his father as if he were an inconsequential figure in his life, and yet he spends much of his spare time back in the Delta, returning much more than Raven, who was their father's favorite. "That's probably a good idea," I agree, nodding at Raven. Until he has done that, he isn't going to even think about his defense. I tell them I will be going home tonight, and Raven graciously offers me a room in her house any time I need to stay over. Since Cormorant's children will be home this summer, I will take her up on it.

By the time I get over to the prosecutor's office across from the courthouse and get a copy of the file, the reporters and cameras are gone. Alerted to my presence, Minor Latting, the prosecutor for the 6th District, comes out of his office to shake hands. Outside of the courtroom and away from the media, he is even more unprepossessing and invites me back for a cup of coffee, perhaps to size me up. Delighted to have this opportunity to visit with him privately, I follow him to his personal suite and sink gratefully onto the leather couch across from his desk. He doesn't speak until he has personally served me a cup of black coffee in a mug that advertises the Blues Festival in Helena. "Miller, I know a lot more about you than you probably know about me," he begins amiably. "You have quite a reputation in the Delta. At our meetings, you have prosecutors moaning from Blytheville all the way to Lake Village. It's an honor to try a case against you."

Knowing I am easily flattered, I try not to smile, but this man is so down-to-earth outside of a courtroom that I find myself grinning. This morning before the judge he was a little stiff, and I suspect he lets his deputies try most of his important cases, which in a big district like Pulaski County he can easily afford to do and not hurt his reputation among the voters. His job is to take the credit as well as the heat and then remind his deputies who hired them. "Thanks," I say and kid him about the bond. "Next time you'll have to offer my client the hospitality suite if you want him to stick around."

He bursts out laughing, no small gesture since he had to endure the judge's sarcasm along with it. "And I thought we were good ole boys over here," he says amiably. "Damn, Henry did everything but break out the Jack Daniels for you."

I look around his office which is crowded with photographs of politicians, both Democratic and Republican. A Democrat all my life, I still am unnerved by the growing strength of the Republican Party in the state, but have accepted the truism that with Lyndon Johnson's support of civil rights, it was only a matter of time before the South became Republican. The wonder is that it has taken so long. "Henry's quite a bit younger," I reply, "like most people these days, so I didn't know him. I've heard of him, of course. He probably feels like he got out of the line of fire just in time."

Latting shakes his head as if the recent past is a mystery to him. "I must have been the only person in Little Rock not to get a subpoena. Speaking of stirring things up, nobody knows where Ezekiel Merriweather is going to show up next. I hate like hell for my office to look as if he's pushed us into charging your client. The perception it creates cheapens the criminal justice system, but I'll be damned if I know what to do about it. I don't want to try this case in the media any more than you do."

We both know that he can't admit how much pressure Ezekiel Merriweather has been able to apply on him, but apparently it has been considerable. Though he isn't going to admit it, I suspect he bypassed municipal court to give Ezekiel fewer opportunities to grandstand for the cameras. I sip my coffee, thinking I know the reason for his hospitality. He wants to know if I or my client is going to be another Ezekiel. I'm not under any obligation to tell this guy anything, but I like to play it straight with the other side. The practice of law is hard enough without all the games lawyers play. "Not having seen this," I say, patting the file on my lap, "I can't say for sure what we're going to do. If we have to try it in the media, so be it. I doubt though that Ezekiel is going to split the profits on the book."

Not a man who got elected on his looks, Latting shows a mouthful of dingy, gray teeth, his blue eyes twinkling. "Too bad for us. I read it this past weekend, and despite the bombast, it kind of got to me. I realize that some of you who still live in the Delta might take a different view."

"The little I've read so far is convincing," I admit. "My great-grandfather owned about forty slaves. All I ever heard was that they had their feelings hurt because they ran off when the Yankees came, meaning, I guess, they thought they treated them pretty good. Apparently, though, they voted with their feet."

Latting opens a drawer and pulls out the book and studies Merriweather's picture much as I did yesterday afternoon. "You'll see in the file that despite what you implied in your statement there are a number of people who won't present your client's relationship with Merriweather in quite so sanguine a light."

I feel my neck muscles tense, fearful that Cormorant's uncompromising bluntness has finally done him irreparable harm. I am burning to look at the file and get to my feet. "What

I'm already curious about is how you are going to convince a jury that a man would deliberately shoot another one," I say, having nothing to lose, "if he knew he was already dying with a painful disease."

The prosecutor pushes himself up and offers his hand to me again. "If I had to prove why people did things," he says easily, "we could keep everybody we convicted right here in my office."

Despite what he has said, Minor has to be concerned about proving first-degree murder. For whatever reason, he has not filed a capital murder charge against Cormorant, suggesting to me that at some point he may be amenable to knocking the case down to something like negligent homicide. I smile, knowing neither of us has revealed to the other a damn thing but not sorry I had this opportunity for a visit. There almost always comes a time before trial when the prosecution and defense sit down together and discuss a way to avoid going down to the wire. As I walk back the six blocks south through downtown Little Rock to the Lafayette Building, I admit to myself how unlikely a plea bargain seems in this case, but stranger things have happened. Even as honest as Cormorant is, he may not have yet told me the whole story. Accidents do happen. If he was angry enough, I can imagine my old friend threatening to do someone as outrageous as Merriweather bodily harm, and possibly he took the gun inside the house and fired it accidentally. At the corner of Capitol and Center by the Sterling variety store I almost am run over by a black prostitute, who on second glance is a transvestite, proving that life is seldom as straightforward as it seems. People change, and I don't know Cormorant as well as I once did. I am convinced that his basic integrity is unchanged, but I may be, as I often am, guilty of wishful thinking. I can't wait to get into the file, but I caution myself that I am nearly always too optimistic about what I will find. To my knowledge, we don't have these characters in Marianna, but maybe we do. Thirty years ago we didn't have crack cocaine either.

Twenty minutes later, I am back in my third-floor makeshift office in the Lafayette Building combing through the material in the file. I begin to see what Latting was talking about. A Detective Sizemore (presumably the black guy Cormorant mentioned) has taken a number of statements in which Cormorant reveals a long history of criticism of Damascus Merriweather. Not as concerned with a motive at the moment, I lay these statements aside to try to piece together how much time might have elapsed after Cormorant left Merriweather's house before his body was discovered. Though I have not said it aloud, my first thought was that Merriweather's murder may have been a robbery that turned into a homicide. Strengthening this possibility is that his murder occurred in his brother's home on Palisades Drive overlooking the Arkansas River, one of the most expensive sections in Little Rock. A pharmacist as well a businessman, Ezekiel may have kept a stash of drugs at his home. I suspect that occurs more than generally admitted.

Toward the bottom of the file is a statement by Rafe Kennedy, a work-study student who had been taking Damascus's mail and students' term papers from school to the Palisades address for the past couple of weeks. He says that, as instructed, he showed up at four that afternoon and rang the bell and knocked on Merriweather's door for five minutes. Since Dr. Merriweather, though known to be seriously ill, had always come to the door, he went back to his car and called him on the cell phone but couldn't reach him. He became worried and called the emergency number he had been given by Ezekiel and got a display pager. He remained in the car and within a minute Ezekiel Merriweather phoned him back and said he would try to reach his brother. About three minutes later, Ezekiel rang him back and told him there was a key under a flower pot by the door and to get inside the house and call him immediately once he found out about his brother. He did as he was told and found Dr. Merriweather slumped over in a wheelchair in his study. Thinking he was still alive, he dialed Ezekiel from a phone on the table, who told him he was on his way but to call 911. He did, but it became obvious that Damascus was already dead.

I put down the statement and look for the notes from my conversation with Cormorant. I find he says he got to the house about three and stayed approximately twenty minutes, which leaves about a forty-minute window. Continuing with Kennedy's statement, I find that Ezekiel had gotten to his home minutes before the ambulance.

Apparently suspicious of the student's story since he was admittedly at the house by himself, the cops took Kennedy into custody and did everything but x-ray the kid to see if he had swallowed the murder weapon. Even though every word checked out and there was no trace metal on his hands, he was obviously considered a suspect until Cormorant's pistol was found two days later. In the lab report section I learn, to my dismay, that the only fingerprints on the pistol were Cormorant's, who, as it turns out, didn't reveal to the police that he had been to Merriweather's house until three days after the shooting.

In the statement he gave four days after the murder, Cormorant says that immediately after he left Merriweather's that Friday afternoon, he and Beth had driven to Lake of the Ozarks in Missouri for the weekend. He knew nothing about the murder until he got back in town Sunday night, and then, on his own initiative, he had called the police the next day and told them he had been to the house on Palisades Drive that afternoon. He said he had visited with Damascus about three o'clock for close to half an hour, and that, as he told me, he had discussed his request to fill in for him on a panel at the law school. "Damascus was tired, but he bantered with me like he always did."

I put down the file and get myself a Coke from the refrigerator, thinking how bad it looks for Cormorant to have immediately disappeared for seventy-two hours but feel somewhat reassured when I come back and read that the murder weapon was found in the brush within yards of the Arkansas River behind the house. If Cormorant had wanted to get rid of the pistol, why didn't he take it with him and dump it in the Lake of the Ozarks? Obviously theorizing that the murderer had panicked and had tried to throw his weapon from an upstairs deck into the river but had fallen short, the cops have measured the distance to the shoreline, a distance of one hundred and sixty feet. As I expected I would, I read further on that a ballistics expert has determined Cormorant's pistol to be the murder weapon. I look out the window into the sun and think of Laurel's comments that Cormorant has been set up. Who would do it and how, I wonder. Obviously, somebody who knew he kept a gun in his car and had an appointment with Damascus. The kid? Maybe both of them had given him bad grades and he figured he would kill two birds with one stone. Cormorant, because of his mouth, could easily have pissed off a student or maybe even dozens and not even be aware of it.

As I continue through the file, it becomes apparent that, as we suspected, Damascus had his own enemies list. Ezekiel turned over two hate letters his brother had forwarded before the murder to the house on Palisades, where, in his poignant words, he had "…brought my brother to spend his final days." Others have been received since his death, which is not surprising, given Ezekiel's public pronouncements, and have been made a part of the file. The letters are naturally unsigned:

I have tried to read your book, but it is obvious why niggers were made slaves. You weren't good for anything else. We didn't beat your kind enough. As for your excuse that white men had sex with nigger women, so what? You weren't there and so you don't know if they wanted it or not. Given the fact that they were little more than farm animals they surely did just like you see dogs go into heat. Nigger, you are better off dead than being allowed to write such garbage.

Another letter is not as ignorant, and I am drawn to its contents:

I have begun to read your book, but it upsets me so much that I find I can't get through but a few pages at a time. How dare you call yourself a professor of history? Any person who would write a book so incendiary without more documentation surely has a death wish. How can you look at yourself in the mirror after naming the names of innocent people, black and white, who have nothing to do with any of the events you describe except carry the genetic reminders of their forebears? Truth is often another name for bitterness, and, Sir, you have written the last word on this topic. You will reap what you sow.

I wonder how hard the cops looked for these correspondents, and for every person who takes the trouble to write, surely dozens share the same feelings and don't. There are other letters along the same lines. I stand up and go to the window, knowing I could have written this last letter or at least its sentiments. It sounds as if the writer is some quivery, boozed-up old fart who bursts into tears every time he goes into his attic and gazes upon his great-grandfather's buttons from his Confederate cavalry uniform. Jesus, is that what I am becoming? For the first time since I talked to Cormorant, I am intensely curious about who did kill Merriweather, which is not the textbook way to defend a client. Though Cormorant obviously would like an immediate dismissal of the charges and a public apology, the most likely scenario will be one the most distasteful to him; that the jury must approach the evidence as he approaches history: if there is a reasonable doubt about what happened, the jury must not come to any conclusions. What is Cormorant guilty of? Hubris, arrogance, racism, but also the integrity and honesty people claim to want in racial conversations, but none of those, bad or good, make him a murderer. If Cormorant shot Merriweather in a blind rage, of all the people I know on this earth, he will be honest enough at some point before trial to admit it.

In the file are several pictures of Merriweather's body, but the most revealing is still the photograph on the book jacket taken by Ezekiel. I study it at length and realize how much the two brothers looked alike. They had the same busy eyebrows, broad nose and lips, but it is the intensity in their eyes that mark them as brothers. They radiate the gleam of zealots the world over from the deserts of Mongolia to the jungles of Colombia.

I find the autopsy report, much of which is about the cancer which had metastasized all over Merriweather's body. Whatever happened on the afternoon Damascus was killed, he had nothing to lose. He was a dead man already, and the only thing he had to live for was to see his book become a success.

I find the ballistics section again, thinking the police at first might have thought it was a suicide, but without a weapon that notion was quickly dispelled. I am not beyond arguing that it was a suicide made to look like a murder to gain publicity for the book, but too many facts stand in the way. The first and foremost is that the state crime lab has analyzed the blood spatter on the table from the wound and concluded that he was shot from a distance of approximately ten feet. Still, the suicide angle is worth some thought, and I get on the Internet on the computer Raven has provided at my request and type in the words, blood, spatter, and suicide. I'm delighted by how much material pops up. Suicide is an argument made regularly by attorneys who often have little else, but it occasionally works. I will need some expert guidance from a pathologist and an expert on blood spatter to determine if Damascus could have committed suicide through the injection of a drug and then been shot afterwards to make it seem like a murder, but the woods are full of hired guns on these subjects.

It does not help that the only fingerprints on the pistol were those of Cormorant. Statements taken from Ezekiel's employees and customers at his North Little Rock pharmacy indicate he was working in the store all afternoon, so my thought that he was involved in his brother's death is a stretch.

I work my way back to the statements of Cormorant's colleagues and realize that regardless of how Cormorant may have thought Damascus felt about him personally, his African-American colleague had more reasons to dislike him than simply his opposition to his hire and tenure. As I read and make notes from the statements of faculty members in the history department, it is apparent that Cormorant spared no one his thoughts and beliefs, no matter how politically incorrect. Cormorant made no secret of the fact that he felt white Arkansans (including himself), consciously or unconsciously, believed that blacks were genetically mentally inferior to whites and had not flinched from saying so about five years ago in front of a room filled with history professors including Damascus. According to a statement by a Dr. Carole Matso, Cormorant had said that whites, rightly or wrongly, would continue to believe that test scores measured intelligence until blacks quit using racism as an excuse and simply outperformed whites like they did in athletics. "Cormorant could be insufferably dogmatic when he thought he was right," her statement reads. "In that meeting of about five professors that included Damascus, Cormorant said that affirmative action was the single worst remedy ever imposed by the judicial system to overcome racial discrimination. It was very embarrassing for all of us, and I could tell that it humiliated Damascus, though he said he wasn't going to debate a subject as ephemeral as psychological testing. Cormorant was oblivious to the effect he had on people. Though his reputation as a historian is impeccable, on a personal level his insensitivity to the feelings of others can be overwhelming…"

There are two additional statements along the same lines, and I begin to wonder if one of Cormorant's colleagues could have set him up. There is no inkling of any animosity toward Damascus, who apparently was well liked and respected by his white colleagues. I rub my eyes, thinking that Cormorant's mouth has finally caught up with him. Yet, he said nothing in that meeting that wasn't true at least in the Delta. He and I both know that it is an unspoken article of faith in the white community in the Delta that whites are intellectually superior to African-Americans, and, I suspect much of the rest of Arkansas as well, though it is a subject that is publicly off-limits and for good reason.

I go through the file again and find that I have overlooked a statement from the dean of the Little Rock law school, who confirmed that he had talked with Professor Merriweather about participating on a panel to discuss the *Brown* decision, but disturbingly he does not recall giving him a date. For the first time, I have to wonder whether Cormorant is telling me the truth about the reason he went to see Merriweather that afternoon.

On my notepad, to see where it gets me, I begin to make a list of possible suspects other than Cormorant. Rafe Kennedy, who describes himself in his statement as a "student of history," seems the most likely candidate to begin with. Even if he turns out to be clean, he may know more than he thinks or than the police think. Certainly, he may have been familiar enough with Cormorant to know he had a pistol in his glove compartment.

He also could have been lying about Damascus failing to come to the door. Ezekiel, because of his relationship to his brother and his vigorous finger-pointing, I list too. The letter writers are also suspects. As far as I'm concerned, anybody who knew Cormorant could have stolen his pistol, kept his own fingerprints off of it, gained access to the house and shot Merriweather and then thrown the gun off the balcony. Though Cormorant could have been set up by a colleague, I will be starting from ground zero.

I get up and walk to the window and look out over the bus stop across Louisiana and notice a man preaching to a small group waiting for the bus. I assume he is preaching because he is holding a Bible and gesturing wildly at his listeners. For all I know he isn't saying a word. Is there something this obvious I am missing in this file? Is there an elaborate pantomime going on in front of me, and I can't see it? I crack the window and hear the street minister referring to God's final judgment. Not a good sign, I think and shut the window. White-collar criminal activity is not so distracting because it's usually all on paper. There is so much noise in Cormorant's case I realize I can't hear anything. I look out the window again and watch the preacher point his finger at the transvestite whom I saw earlier in front of Sterling's. He is standing on the corner of 6th and Louisiana with his hip cocked provocatively in the preacher's direction. If I turn down the sound in Cormorant's case, who do I see is directing the players? Ezekiel? Perhaps, but he seems as if he is one of the actors, playing the role of a devoted apostle. Damascus, it seems, is directing this show from the grave.

5

Back in Little Rock unexpectedly, on my way to a funeral near Conway only four days after Cormorant's arraignment, I take the opportunity to find the house Rafe Kennedy shares with two other students off Fair Park Boulevard within walking distance of UALR. According to Cormorant, this section of the city, called Oak Forest, was all white thirty years ago until the federal government required a big housing project to the east in Pine Forest to accept black applicants. It was a target of blockbusters as blacks who could moved west to find decent housing and a safer environment. Cormorant, who has an opinion for every subject, has quipped that the real estate industry would have had to invent blacks if they didn't already exist. According to him, Adam Smith's unseen hand in central Arkansas is moved east to west by the perception of the effect of blacks on the real estate market. I had hoped to begin my investigation at the crime scene, but Ezekiel Merriweather claims to be ill, and we cannot just walk into his house any time we want.

In the last forty-eight hours, we have decided how we will proceed with the investigation. Since he is basically free for the summer, Cormorant will participate as long as he keeps himself out of the limelight. This means, Raven has reinforced with him, no interviews with any source or potential witness. His primary job will be to find out all he can about the past of Damascus Merriweather; Raven will track the publicity the case generates and its impact on potential jurors, and I and the investigator we hire will do the legwork on anybody we think can be shown to have had a motive and an opportunity to have framed Cormorant. This means I have sat Cormorant down and made him promise to go through a list of his students, colleagues, tenants, and anybody else who may have known or heard about his relationship with Merriweather and knew or could have heard that he carried a pistol in his vehicle. Having thought about it, Cormorant now believes the last time he saw his pistol in the glove compartment was in the first week of April, two weeks before Merriweather was killed. Now that the shock of the arrest has begun to wear off, I have been able to convince him that he knows more than he thinks about who could have set him up.

More than I would, Cormorant continues to worry about his father's reaction to his arrest. According to Raven, Mr. John acted with predictable outrage but suffered nothing worse than the loss of a night's sleep. The old man has demanded to read a copy of Merriweather's book, and since there has been so much publicity about it on television and in the papers, Cormorant has had to promise to send him one. Raven quipped that if the book doesn't kill him, then he will outlive all of us. If he died tomorrow, she might (or might not) shed a tear, but I would hate to see the effect on Cormorant. I need him to stay focused until this is resolved, and his father's death would send him into mourning.

Kennedy, a stringbean who answers the door himself in jeans, bare feet, and a dirty white tee shirt, isn't what I was expecting. Though Cormorant says a good portion of UALR's students are older and work at full-time jobs, there is something almost redneck about this raw-boned kid, far from the stereotype of the beer-guzzling fraternity boy. The right paw covering mine is large, red, and rough as he grips down hard. His reddish hair is closely cropped, and he has the tight, pinched look of poverty, as if he has just arrived here off the farm from the Delta or from a chicken farm in the Ozarks. He is easily 6'5", and there is not a ounce of fat on him. He looks no more like a "student of history" than the maintenance man in the Lafayette Building, whom he resembles. Fearful he would hang up on me, I did not call him in advance, nor has Cormorant, who had him in class first semester (typically, he couldn't remember him), prepared me for him. I explain who I am, talking a mile a minute like a salesman trying to get his foot in the door and ask if I can confirm some of the things he has said in his statement.

"Sure," he says in a hillbilly voice, "come on in. I saw you on the tube and wondered if you would come by yourself or send an investigator." Because of his size, I wonder if he is a basketball player. UALR has tried for years to become a basketball power, but seems destined to play the role of an unwanted cousin to the Arkansas Razorbacks in Fayetteville.

Pleasantly surprised by his friendliness (he knows I am not a friend), I enter a sparse living room furnished with a Goodwill-green couch, a couple of folding chairs, a coffee table, and a lamp. He allows that he would offer me a cup of coffee, but he and his roommates are having a problem with the plumbing and the water is temporarily shut off. He says he has a paper due tomorrow or he will receive an incomplete, but he can take a break for a few minutes and invites me to sit on the couch.

"I've said everything I know a dozen times," he says, his voice cracking like dry brush. "They finally told me I wasn't a suspect any longer, and I guess Dr. Ashley's arrest proves it. I hope he isn't guilty. He's a great teacher. His lectures on Jefferson were awesome."

Over the years I suspect I have heard them all in one form or another. Thomas Jefferson fascinates Cormorant, who says the only President since who has rivaled him in intelligence and complexity is Bill Clinton. I sit down, delighted that this kid is favorably disposed to Cormorant, yet a little taken aback by his self-confidence. I tell myself that even if he didn't kill Merriweather, he may be able to help us. "You must have gone through a miserable experience, finding the body and then the cops treating you like you had killed him," I say, noticing a long, jagged crack in the ceiling and deciding he is too poor to be a college athlete.

His long face narrows further into a scowl. "I knew before this that you can't trust government at any level, and this just confirmed it. They figured they could browbeat me into a confession, I guess."

I feel a stab of guilt. He appears so sincere and trusting that it seems wrong for me not to say that if I can point a finger at him at Cormorant's trial, I will, but I don't want him to clam up. "Is that why you refused to take a polygraph?" I ask, pulling out his file from my briefcase. His unwillingness to give one has been a principal reason I think he has some more explaining to do.

"Damn straight," he drawls. "If the government wants you bad enough, it'll do what it takes. I wasn't gonna make it easier on 'em. They knew I didn't have any trace metal on my hands. I let 'em check for that. They knew then I hadn't shot him. When they got through questioning me, I checked with a professor in criminal justice. It would have shown on my hand so soon after shooting a gun."

If this is not an act, where does this kid's utter cynicism about government come from? I am guessing from his accent that he is straight from the hills, and his old man, if he knows who he is, is still making moonshine. "I guess you didn't have a lawyer."

He picks up a paper cup from the coffee table and spits what I assume is tobacco juice into it. "I can turn on the tube and see all the lawyers I want. Paying 'em is something else. I guess they would have given me a public defender if I had been charged, and I would have been on my way to the pen, come September."

I know some decent public defenders, but this isn't the time to sing their praises.

Instead, I spend almost an hour going over the details of his statement, but I don't learn anything that makes me think this kid killed Merriweather. As a work-study student, he did whatever he was told. Taking mail and papers to a sick professor seemed like a stretch of his job description but he wasn't in a position to complain. According to him, he didn't have anything against Merriweather, who was always cordial even though he could see he was in a good bit of pain, usually coming to the door in his wheelchair. He claims to have no special relationship with either professor, but apparently no axe to grind either. Knowing I can't eliminate anyone at this point, I ask repeatedly about Ezekiel's behavior when he arrived at the house and found his brother's body. "I keep thinking," I muse out loud, "that Ezekiel wanted you to be the first person to find his brother." I watch as the kid misses the inside of the cup and tobacco juice trickles down the side. I'm surprised he doesn't have a hole in his jaw already.

Kennedy wipes his mouth with the back of his hand and says, "You wouldn't think that if you had seen how upset he was. He kept saying his name and shaking him, but he was dead as a doornail as far as I could tell."

"What did he do while you were waiting for the ambulance?" I ask, not willing to give up on the idea that somehow Ezekiel was involved. If Ezekiel set this up, he knew his reaction would be the first thing the kid would be asked about once the cops figured out they had a homicide case.

Though he might have told his story repeatedly, Kennedy's voice suddenly becomes hoarse. "He cried at first. He didn't wail or anything, but his eyes were wet. If he was faking, I couldn't tell it. Then, he started acting kind of hyper, I think he was looking for a gun. Dr. Merriweather was slumped over, and I didn't know at first he was shot until I noticed the blood on the table. When he couldn't find a pistol or knife or anything, he started getting suspicious and asking me questions like if I had already been in the house before I called him. They didn't make a lot of sense, and finally he told me to go wait outside for the ambulance, and I did. It must have been then he called the cops. A few minutes later he came to the front and stood at the door watching me, I guess. Actually, he called me and apologized a couple of days ago for being so suspicious."

I think of Ezekiel's fiery visage. I suppose he is capable of emotions other than anger, but I haven't seen them. Over the weekend he was on television and in the pages of the *Democrat-Gazette* every day. We have been deluged with calls from neighbors, acquaintances, and reporters. Disturbed by the attention at first but quickly getting used to the excitement, Laurel cracked this morning that James Earl Jones, who seems more sanctimonious with each role, will play Ezekiel in the movie. Billy Bob Thornton, whose mother lives in Little Rock, will be cast as Cormorant, and she will be portrayed by Emma Thompson, whom she will coach personally to get the accent right. Shaving, I asked who would play me, and she said some unknown character actor.

"What did he actually say?"

"Just that he kind of lost it when he didn't see a gun," he says, spitting into the cup again. "He said that all he could think of was that I was at the house and that I must have gotten into an argument with his brother and shot him. He said he knew later that it didn't make any sense. Hell, I hardly knew him."

I lean back on the couch, making the springs squeak. For either to be a suspect, one of them would have had to have stolen Cormorant's gun and kept his fingerprints off of it. And how to explain the lack of trace metal on Kennedy's hands? I realize now more than ever that Ezekiel was never seriously considered a suspect. He was at the pharmacy in North Little Rock all afternoon. Still, I wish the cops had checked his hands, too. Of course, by the time they got to Cormorant it was too late, and Cormorant knew it or maybe hoped it was.

What I haven't considered, I realize, is that both of them could have been in this together. As I watch Kennedy wipe his mouth with his knuckles, my mind can't take this possibility seriously. Why would Ezekiel trust a student, especially one like Kennedy? No jury would buy that for thirty seconds. "Did you ever have Damascus as a professor or read his book?"

Kennedy, who must have been asked this question by the police, frowns before replying, "I didn't read it until a few days ago, but I can't prove it. Do I think it's garbage? Yep. If that makes me still a suspect, then I reckon most of the white population of this state ought to be trying to remember where they were that afternoon."

This boy has said this with an air of dignity that embarrasses me for still trying to come up with a motive for his involvement. All he did was take a dying man his mail. I hand him my card and tell him to call me if he remembers anything at all that he hasn't told the police. "It's natural to have your mind on automatic pilot when you're the subject of an investigation, but now you're not a suspect, you can step back and perhaps see a bigger picture," I encourage him. "When you saw Damascus and Ezekiel together, assuming you did, what was the emotional atmosphere? Did you pick up any tension between them?"

Kennedy shakes his head as he studies my card. "You see the guy on television and think he's some kind of agitator. In person with his brother he was as gentle and concerned as you'd ever want a person to be. They seemed to like each other. It wasn't anything Ezekiel did, but you could tell he cared about his brother even before he was shot."

So much for my hope that Kennedy is suspicious of Ezekiel, too. "It's crossed your mind," I say, "that for some reason Ezekiel was setting this up, hasn't it?"

"A lot of things have crossed my mind in the last three weeks," Kennedy says, his voice rueful. "That was one of them, but from what I saw and heard, it never made any sense."

"What do you think happened?" I ask, with nothing to lose. "Could it have been a student or a professor setting up Dr. Ashley? You probably hear a lot of gossip. Was there some bad blood between him and anybody that you knew of?"

Instead of laughing out loud as I feared, Kennedy seems to give my question some thought. "Dr. Ashley can piss you off," he says finally, "but you have the impression that he doesn't even know or care who the student is. I know some girls who've cried because he can be real sarcastic when somebody gives a dumb answer. But he's so oblivious that you can't take him personally. Merriweather was just the opposite. Though I never had him, his reputation was he learned his students' names even if it was a big class. Dr. Ashley wouldn't know your name unless you were really smart and then you'd have to be a senior. Merriweather had an okay reputation as a teacher, according to my friends who took him. As far as what professors thought, I don't know."

Before I leave, I ask what is his paper about.

"Thomas Paine," he says, standing up. "You remember him?"

"Vaguely," I say, as I get to my feet. He didn't trust government either.

Since the funeral isn't until eleven o'clock and Mayflower,

where the service is to be held, is only a twenty-minute drive west on I-40, instead of getting back on the interstate, I head north past the zoo and War Memorial Stadium into the Heights and pull in at the curb in front of Beth's Varsity Shoppe, an up-scale women's clothing store on Kavanaugh she owns with her best friend. I have not talked to Beth since the arraignment, and I want to visit with her alone to see how she is going to manage this summer. I have the sense she and Cormorant haven't been getting along for some time, and if she decides to move out before the trial, it will have a disastrous effect on not just Cormorant but the public's perception of his guilt or innocence.

"How are you doing, Beth?" I ask, finding her in the front unlocking the door for business. It is just now ten, and there are no customers. As usual, she is turned out beautifully in sandals, a lavender silk top and rose-colored skirt.

"Standing by my man," she says, giving me a brittle smile as she offers me her right cheek to peck, "just like I'm supposed to. You know, you find out who your friends are real fast when your husband is charged with murder. I've always tried to explain his nuttiness away to our friends, but this is just a little much, don't you think?"

Her make-up is perfect, so I can't tell how much she is sleeping. Probably not a lot.

I follow her around the store like a trainee as she goes from rack to rack straightening up clothes that don't seem a bit out of place to me. "Think of Hillary trapped in the White House for all that time," I say, trying to cajole her into a lighter mood. "This will be over before you know it."

Inspecting a cashmere sweater that must cost two hundred dollars, Beth says brightly, "I've never understood why you like Cormorant so much. If you hadn't rescued him every time he gets in trouble, maybe he would have learned something and not gotten us into such a goddamned mess."

"Maybe you're right," I say, not believing it. "But isn't he worth rescuing one more time?" I am cheered by the use of the word us. "You've been the best thing that ever happened to him. He needs both of us and Raven so he can be him. If we didn't have people like Cormorant who sniff out the bullshit, the world would be a much poorer place, don't you think?"

"Just because you grew up was no reason not to let him. His children and I are the ones who bear the consequences of all this wonderful truth telling. Do you remember reading *The Misanthrope* by Moliere? That's what being married to Cormorant has been like. For good reason, people eventually start hating back."

Beth and I were both in a world lit course in Fayetteville a hundred years ago, and I reach back and get a dim picture of a book about an idealist who made everybody around him miserable, himself included. "I think you told me once how much you admired that character."

With a tiny pair of scissors Beth snips a loose thread from a blouse. "I was twenty-one years old. Cormorant conned me into marrying him, Miller, and you know it."

I don't deny the truth of what she is saying. In those days, Beth, with her oval face, long black hair, and magnificent figure, could have had any boy she chose, and to prove he was a man to her and not just a big talker with an oversized brain, Cormorant gave up his student deferment and spent a year in Vietnam, though he hated the war and could give six good reasons why we shouldn't be there. Underneath the uniform, he was still the same ole Cormorant.

"No marriage is easy, Beth. Just ask your sister-in-law," I say, giving her an opportunity to feel superior if that is what she needs to get through the summer.

Beth, working her way toward the back of the store, scratches a long, red fingernail against a cotton fabric, removing an invisible mote of dust. "What woman wouldn't grow up and act crazy in that family? Raven is okay now. I wish I had her business sense."

"I wish I had it, too," I admit. Now that they are both entrepreneurs, Beth apparently is more charitable to her. In the early years of their marriage, while Raven was going through one man after another, Beth publicly supported her sister-in-law, but in private, in a memorable conversation one afternoon as they were sunbathing nude on our deck, she told Laurel she thought Raven was a nymphomaniac, a term more common a generation ago, but a quaint one in an era when it seems mandatory for everyone to enjoy sex. Laurel had laughed at her and passing along these comments to me that night, Laurel said she thought Beth was jealous of Cormorant's relationship with his sister because they had remained so close. I had come to that conclusion many years earlier.

"How do you and Laurel stand it in Marianna?" Beth turns to me and asks, her eyes suddenly red. "If Cormorant gets out of this, and tells me he wants to move back to the Delta, he can go by himself. If my mother weren't still alive, I wouldn't go at all."

I am tempted to tell her how close Laurel seems to be to leaving, but I am afraid it will harden her attitude. I answer with a question. "How are the kids taking this?" I ask, reminding her that she has responsibilities this summer beyond herself.

To hide her tears, she shows me her back and says, her voice brittle, "Miller, you're in your lawyer mode. You don't want to know; you just came by to make sure I'm not going to make this situation any harder than it already is. We'll survive. I promise I'll be a good little wife and won't cry any more on television. God, I've got enough role models in Little Rock after Whitewater. All those brave female faces. How come it's never the other way around? I'd like to see a brave little man, holding his wife's hand for a change. Wouldn't that be novel?"

I didn't make this world, I want to shout at her. I am tempted to turn around and walk out and find Cormorant and tell him I can't do this case. "Beth, it's not easy being Cormorant's friend and his lawyer at the same time. I told him to get somebody from Pulaski County, but neither he nor Raven will hear of it. Maybe he will listen to you."

From her wounded expression, I can tell that merely to suggest such an idea represents a betrayal, and I understand more fully than I ever have that Beth, whatever her faults and weaknesses and whatever happens, will stay the course. She just needed to complain. Now, she says quietly, "You know how he is. He would let you do open heart surgery on him."

Knowing I have nothing to fear from Beth now, I say bluntly, "There's a lot I don't understand. Why did you suddenly decide to go out of town? I can see you acting that spontaneously, but Cormorant has to read a book on the subject before he leaves the state."

For the first time, Beth genuinely smiles. "He's not as rigid as he used to be. You don't see him that much. Occasionally, he'll surprise me," she says. "I've thought about it a dozen times, and I know Cormorant didn't shoot that man. I just can't imagine the circumstances that would lead him to do something that stupid. He talked about Merriweather some, but not a lot. The day he was shot he didn't even mention him. When we got home and heard he was dead, he was genuinely shocked and called the police instantly to tell them he had been out there that afternoon. I would have been able to tell it if he were lying."

"How did he act on the trip?" I can't help but ask. A reason to get out of town for a few days would be to make less likely that the police would be able to determine that he had fired a pistol recently and to give him time to come up with a credible story. Most people I know aren't methodical enough to get away with crime. Cormorant is. That's what makes this scenario so unlikely. If somehow he was going to murder a man, it wouldn't be like this.

Beth leans back against the counter and says easily, "We had a good time. He's still capable of having fun when I can get his nose out of a book or a newspaper." She eyes me suspiciously, "You don't seriously think he could be guilty, do you?"

"No," I reassure her quickly. "I don't. But we have to anticipate what the police will make out of him leaving town on the spur of the moment without reservations. A good prosecutor can make the most innocent of actions seem suspicious. Did Cormorant say anything about taking Merriweather's place on that panel?"

"No," she says, looking up as her first customer of the day enters the store, "but he wouldn't automatically tell me something like that. He knows how bored I am by politics."

I know she wants to go speak to her customer, but I tell her, "I want you to start thinking about everything Cormorant has told you about the Merriweathers or who could have set Cormorant up. You probably know more than you realize. Did the police want to talk to you?"

A professional smile now on her face as she brushes by me, she says, "Cormorant said not to."

I want to ask her how she felt about that. Beth is the type of woman who will give you an earful when she thinks she or somebody she cares about is being abused. She already knows I am headed for a funeral, and I leave the store with a wave but without speaking to her again. We both know we will see each other often this summer.

Sitting on the fifth row of the Mayflower Baptist Church, I listen to a preacher who obviously didn't know my friend Otha Pape from a hole in the wall, and wonder if I got anything from Rafe Kennedy except what he wanted to give me, and that was the feeling that neither he nor Ezekiel is involved in the murder. Why should I doubt him? Somebody had to discover the victim's body, so why does it bother me that Ezekiel didn't tell the kid to leave the mail on the porch and go home? In his statement I think I remember he had told the cops that he wanted help in case he needed to carry his brother to his bed. That seems reasonable enough. Besides, in times of stress, people don't always act reasonably, I think, as I listen to Otha's minister puzzle over his suicide. Sustaining a friendship that developed in law school, Otha and I had traded visits over the years and met at Razorback tailgate parties occasionally, but Laurel and his wife Belle have had little to say to each other after their children were grown, and Otha and I kept in touch mainly over the phone. At the cemetery, I hug Belle and see in her ravaged face at once that she didn't have a clue. "He seemed fine!" she whispers, shocking me with the intensity of her words. "We still can't find a note."

Afterwards, I hurry back to the Delta for a meeting with a client at two in Forrest City and brood about my friend's death. He did seem "fine" the last time I talked with him a month ago. Speeding eastward on I-40, I force myself to slow down and console myself with the belief that we don't really know another person unless we live with them day in, day out, unless maybe it is our spouse, and right now I am not sure how well I know Laurel. You're so stubborn, she told me two nights ago. Is that why I won't leave and become an absentee landowner? As I whiz by the cotton, beans, and rice that seem to be doing better than my own, my thoughts become a blur. If Otha was "fine," then maybe he was murdered, too. But Kathy, his sister, told me he was found with his pistol beside him.

"Privately, Damascus could sometimes be as hard on blacks as he was on whites," Cormorant says as we pull up behind a Little Rock Police Department vehicle in front of Ezekiel Merriweather's house to view the crime scene on May 30th. "He just didn't write about it. I used to argue with him that blacks had no history of capitalism in Africa, and that's one of the principal reasons they've had such a hard time adjusting in this country, but he would say the answer to that was two words long: Ezekiel Merriweather. Look at this house!"

Though Cormorant does not live far from here as the crow flies, I have never been on Palisades Drive in Little Rock. Though nice and on a double lot, the brick home in front of me doesn't appear to merit his exclamation. Yet, I know what is being paid for is the view of the Arkansas River, which it overlooks, and the exclusivity of the address. "We need the names of people who personally took offense to him," I say, continuing to press Cormorant at every opportunity to find out as much about Damascus and Ezekiel as he can. I look up and down the street and guess the homes with a view of the river sell for half a million dollars. In Lee County, as depressed as real estate is there, the same house might be under a hundred thousand. "I doubt if Ezekiel has many black neighbors," I add, opening the door of Cormorant's Taurus.

I can't think of a single black person in Marianna who could afford this neighborhood, but I am not surprised that Ezekiel had the money to get in here. In the time since his arraignment, Cormorant has put his history degree to use and begun to find out about the Merriweather brothers. It is Ezekiel who actually fascinates me the most. Though a pharmacist by training, it is the free enterprise system in which he has his most advanced degree. Cormorant has discovered he owns five separate businesses, including pharmacies in both North Little Rock and Little Rock (not one, as the media reported), and has real estate investments in Cabot and Bryant, both white-flight areas in central Arkansas. Undoubtedly, his business shrewdness has made him successful. In addition, he also owns forty acres of land in St. Francis County outside of Forrest City in the Delta where two brothers still live. His wife was killed in a car wreck five years ago, and he never remarried. Damascus had been with him in the house one month. Older than his brother by a decade, Ezekiel has two grown children living outside the state. Confirming an earlier guess, Cormorant has learned for certain that it was Ezekiel who had paid for the book's initial one thousand copies and somehow arranged to have them distributed through Ingram's, a national book wholesaler. The book is already in its second printing, but we haven't been able to confirm a number. Cormorant has also found out the name of a black woman in Little Rock who served as an unpaid editor for the book.

Before Cormorant can respond, the cop is upon us. Squinting into the afternoon sun, he asks, "You're Ashley's lawyer, right?"

I shake his hand, and he introduces himself as Officer Tate, our tour guide this afternoon. In his thirties, he is squat as a fire plug, but if I were a dog, I would think twice about pissing on him. He looks fit. Cops generally make me nervous. I have cross-examined too many of them.

"Merriweather's not home?" Cormorant asks, though I have

assured him that he will not be here to monitor us.

Officer Tate pulls out a key as we follow him up the walk. He says, sneeringly, "It's just us and that nigger's ghost."

I make a mental note of his attitude, but I suppose it shouldn't surprise me that there is no love lost between a white cop in the Little Rock Police Department and the Merriweather brothers. Tate can't afford to live here and probably resents the fact that a black man, who has a mouth on him like Ezekiel, can. In the past week, Ezekiel has been in the news twice as he continues to hawk the book and complain about the bond. An article in the *Democrat-Gazette* yesterday again mentioned the growing outside interest in the case. The *Memphis Commercial Appeal* had a long story in its Sunday edition.

Inside the house, I see immediately I have underestimated its size. It is on two levels, and though I have been expecting it, the view of the river from the picture window in the main dining room is lovely. On the other side I can see North Little Rock, which is linked by six bridges to Little Rock.

"Gorgeous, isn't it?" Cormorant murmurs, coming to stand beside me.

"I guess I could live in Little Rock," I admit, thinking how much Laurel would like this house. Officer Tate seems in no hurry to move along, and I take my time, hoping to get a better feel for Ezekiel Merriweather, who seems determined to influence this case one way or another. Though I continue to resist the notion of some elaborate setup, I keep coming back to Ezekiel and the way he might have arranged to find the body. It is at least possible his employees and customers were mistaken that he had been at the pharmacy all afternoon until he was called by Kennedy.

On the walls and in the corners are a number of artifacts that suggest the man has traveled extensively. Particularly interesting are the masks, which to my untutored eye appear museum quality. Ezekiel was a collector and apparently didn't mind spending money to get what he wanted. The motive of robbery seems out since nothing was reported taken from the house. If Cormorant is spooked by being here, I can't tell it. He seems content to allow me to take my time and is as interested in the furnishings as I am. "Was this the only time you were in this house?" I whisper though Tate is leaning against the opposite wall and seems about to doze off.

Cormorant, who is dressed in jeans and sandals, answers, "Yeah. Damascus lived far more modestly. He had a house in Oak Forest near UALR. I'm surprised he didn't just stay in it, but I guess his brother could care for him better in his home even though he hadn't gotten to the point where he needed hospice."

I nod, thinking that stomach cancer sounds like a horrible death. Again, I wonder, why kill Merriweather if he was dying anyway? Unless he got angry, it doesn't make sense. Cormorant leads me a room off the living room and says, "This is where we talked that last time. He wheeled himself in here and faced me across this table."

According to the photographs and sketches in the file, where Cormorant is standing is where Merriweather was shot once in the chest in his wheelchair. It is unnerving to realize that Cormorant is standing in the exact spot. Knowing I won't find them, I look for the splatter of blood stains on the glass table, but they have been scrubbed away. I whisper softly, "You're standing exactly where he was killed."

I see the muscles of Cormorant's throat tighten, but he doesn't move. "It makes sense, doesn't it? He probably came in here to work every day."

I acknowledge that it does, but perhaps to get Cormorant away from the spot, I walk around the room examining the book shelves lining the walls and wonder if actually it was

Damascus Merriweather who was the more intellectual of the two brothers. I have never seen so many books outside a library in my life. I squint at the titles and am flabbergasted by the range of reading material. There are books on birds, alchemy, Catholicism, chemistry, and mathematics as well as foreign writers like Milos Kundera. "Do you think these are all his books, or were they his brother's?"

Cormorant casts a practiced eye on the shelves and says, "I never heard Damascus talk about anything but history and politics. If his mind was this eclectic, I never knew it. He used to brag occasionally about Ezekiel, but it was usually about his business sense. Over the years, he came by the department a few times, but we just nodded."

We have discussed who in the department knew that Cormorant had a gun, but, to hear him tell it, the entire campus at UALR kidded him about his .22. One thing we will have going for us for sure is that Cormorant will look like a young Arthur Schlesinger in his fussy little bow ties. I watch Officer Tate slide open a glass door and disappear onto the balcony. He is supposed to keep an eye on us at all times, but he has correctly pegged us as basically harmless. "Who was your worst enemy in the department?" I ask, not for the first time. It is not an easy subject for him. By his own admission, he has no close friends in Little Rock, nor does he want any. After reading all day, he comes home and reads some more. By the same token, he can't conceive that he has enemies either. People shouldn't take what he says personally, even if he is attacking their integrity and honor. I don't remember him being quite so abstract, but time rarely makes people less eccentric or rigid. If he has loosened up, as Beth has suggested, I can't tell it.

"You still don't get it," Cormorant replies as if I were a dumb student. "These people have their own fields of interest. They don't sit around carping at each other. They bitch about money occasionally, but basically they're reasonably content."

In perhaps another context, Cormorant's naivete would be charming—the absent-minded professor above the fray, too distracted to notice the petty but inevitable jockeying for prestige and power that accompanies all human endeavors. People keep score, and historians especially, surely have long memories for slights. I know I should be concentrating on the physical layout of the house, but I have an inescapable sense that the key to understanding Merriweather's death lies somewhere in the relationships Cormorant has or had with others, whether he admits it or not.

"Don't pretend you don't have a way of pissing off people," I say and remind him of his colleagues' statements. "Pinpointing what they felt about you may be the most important thing you do in the next three months. Our main hope may be giving the jury some reason to think somebody else wanted Merriweather dead. So you need to come off Mount Olympus, okay?"

Cormorant merely shrugs. "Anybody could have done it."

I tell him that isn't going to be enough, and then exasperated, follow Tate through the door onto the open deck and stare with him over the railing at the Arkansas River. "You think you could chunk a gun all the way to the water?" I ask him. In the middle of the river is a barge headed downstream, its cargo concealed.

Tate, who is about thirty, crushes the tip of a cigarette against the underside of the wooden railing, a gesture that seems to signal his disrespect for the owner. "When the adrenaline gets flowing, you'd be surprised what a man can do."

Or thinks he can do. I look down at the overgrown area that stretches to the shoreline. Cormorant, as a boy, had a habit of panicking under pressure. My most vivid memory is being in a boat with him on the St. Francis and floating under a tree that had a water moccasin climbing along its branches. I could have easily fended it off or killed it with my paddle, but Cormorant, about sixteen, began to scream like a small child and came perilously close to tipping us over, which could have been a problem. That and a half-dozen incidents over the years have made me aware how unequipped he is to deal with stress when a situation threatens to get out of hand. Though I have not said it to him, in the last week as I have reconstructed our childhood, I have concluded that he is certainly capable of wildly irrational behavior if enough pressure is exerted on him. What I can't understand is what, if anything, would lead to a pivotal moment in which he would fire a bullet into a man's chest and then totally spooked, race out to where I am standing and try to throw the murder weapon to the river and then run like hell. What the police surely know, though it wasn't mentioned in the file, is that the trip out of town was a spur of the moment thing, though he and Beth had discussed going up before.

With Tate leading the way, we tour the rest of the house, but I don't find anything inside that makes me think I understand this case any better than I did before I came. On the floor downstairs on the walls in the hallway are photographs of Ezekiel Merriweather's two grown children. If they aren't his, they have had plastic surgery to look like him. I wonder if they approve of their father's crusade.

There is a door at the rear of the house, and Officer Tate follows us outside. Theoretically, it is not impossible that whoever killed Merriweather went out the front door and ran around to the back, hid or planted the gun in the bushes, and got into a boat and crossed over to North Little Rock.

There is a cleared space of perhaps fifty feet behind the house. Merriweather's property is not marked by a fence or visible boundary but merely becomes brush where the lawn ends. It is a steeper climb down to the bank than I thought and I see no point in walking all the way down in my slick shoes. The humidity is oppressive. From the police sketch of the property, I noted there was no particular place for a boat to put in, but I suppose it wouldn't have been impossible. What makes it unlikely to me that the murderer came from the water is how easily he could be seen coming by Merriweather or his neighbors. Anybody who happened to be out on his deck that day could have easily seen an intruder and had a look at his face with a decent pair of binoculars. His neighbors, who have been interviewed, were not home that afternoon. For me, what makes it reasonably certain is that if the killer came from a boat and had an ounce of sense, he would have carried the pistol at least down to the water's edge and thrown it in from there. Unless he wanted it found.

Reading my thoughts, Cormorant comes over to me as I stand on the brick patio behind the house. "If it was somebody who came by boat," he says, looking over with me toward North Little Rock, "he went to a lot of trouble when he could have driven up and knocked on the front door."

"We can't eliminate the possibility that was what happened though," I say, not really believing it. I look at my watch, ready to get on the road to Jeffersonville. It is our anniversary tonight, and I promised Laurel I would be home by six. Cormorant was my best man, and I remind him where we were thirty years ago today. "Who could have predicted we would be standing here today?" I muse. "We had blacks serving the food and liquor at the reception. Not a one of them earned enough to pay the taxes on this house."

Cormorant gets a faraway look in his eyes. "Daddy was so proud of all of us back then. He still thought I was going to come back and farm even though I couldn't start up a tractor up without breaking something on it. Now, he thinks we are all crazy, with

Raven having had three husbands, me charged with murder. He says you hardly ever come by to see him."

I should care more but I don't. For some reason I have always been irritated by how much Mr. John still keeps up with my life. Since my own father died when I was nineteen, he has considered himself something of a father figure to me, though, in truth, I've never held him in awe the way his own children have. In all the time I've known him, he has never said a kind word about his son in my presence. "I'm sorry," I say automatically. "I never know how much he understands."

"More than you think," Cormorant replies. "You just have to be patient. He thinks the charges against me will be dropped when all this hoopla over the book dies down."

Cormorant and the nurses he hires for him are the only people who understand the old man, according to Beth. I guess I should feel a little guilty. Ashley Plantation (though their land is now rented out like mine) is only twenty minutes from me, and I could easily get by to see him more. "Surely he's not that out of it," I reply, remembering the old man's violent temper. I was scared of him, I realize. He was hard as nails, and if he had any redeeming features, I don't remember what they were. I look up at the house and see Officer Tate staring down at us from the deck. Cormorant is still operating in full denial. "Not that it appears so far he had anything to do with it," I say quietly, "but the man who owns this house doesn't seem inclined to let that happen."

Cormorant slides his sandal across the grass like a child who wants to play. "I bet he won't give you the time of day."

I pat my pocket for my keys. I have told Cormorant and Raven that sooner or later I am going to try to talk to Ezekiel Merriweather. Starting week after next, I have a few days in a row when I can concentrate totally on Cormorant's case.

Cormorant has picked up some gossip that Ezekiel has said he is not totally convinced the cops have charged his brother's killer. "All he can do is tell me to go to hell," I say, doubtful he will talk either. But six months from now, I don't want to be wondering why I didn't at least make the effort.

"What really irritates me about this book," Laurel says, looking up at me from the chaise lounge on our patio, "is that it has no balance whatever. We couldn't have been as horrible as he makes us sound. Do you remember this part? *Arkansas, like all other Southern states, even today in a period of prosperity, bristles with an inferiority complex because of its relative poverty. But unlike the Deep South, established earlier in time, it had no white aristocracy, however depraved and corrupt, from which someone might summon the courage to rebel. Its Delta has produced no important writers, no Faulkner to meditate on its great evil. Too insecure for meaningful introspection, its people have never been comfortable with any analysis that does not begin with the excuse that it is a poor, small state. Thus, the personality of Bill Clinton, its premier native son, is the perfect metaphor for the state's lack of depth and maturity. So badly wanting to be liked, so trapped by his need for acceptance, the President in Little Rock at the 40th Anniversary of Central High could not summon the courage to do the one thing for which his administration might have been remembered one hundred years from now: atone for the nation's shameful legacy of slavery. The President, blessed with a keen intelligence and a sensibility long attuned to the pain of others because of his own childhood, and educated outside Arkansas at the nation's finest schools, remained an Arkansan at heart, and as usual, consulted the polls and thus squandered his place in history.*

Laurel puts the book down on her lap and exclaims, "The nerve of that man! Who did he think he was! No wonder someone killed him!"

The smell of the beef as I turn it on the grill makes my mouth water. So far, it has been a perfect anniversary. We have made love only once since our trip three weeks ago. But from the moment I pulled in the driveway and was met by Laurel in lavender bikini underpants and a halter top, it has been more like the old days when we both were more content with our lives. I showered, and she joined me. Afterwards, we took the phone off the hook in the bedroom and for an hour we didn't talk about Cormorant or the Merriweather brothers, but now that Laurel has condescended to read the book, she can't stay away from it.

I look out toward the bean fields, thinking that when we returned home, we were worried about high water; today, after reading the long-range forecast in the *Democrat-Gazette*, I know my renters are fearful of a drought. This heat is unusual even for the Delta this time of year. Laurel's nose could be said to be a bit out of joint. I have never thought of myself as an aristocrat, but she has taken the past more seriously. Having read the book and had a chance to let its shrillness pass through me, I am stunned by a sudden but obvious insight. "Who does that passage sound like to you?"

"Cormorant!" Laurel snaps, her mind always running more quickly than my own. "He had the same anger this man does."

"Absolutely," I say, wondering why it has now just occurred to me. Cormorant has always been hard on everything Southern, regardless of its color. On this very deck he has contended that had it not been for the carpetbaggers who came to Arkansas with their interest in public education and economic development we would have remained even more feudal than we are now. I remember him saying once that the notion that Arkansas was raped by Reconstruction was one of the most preposterous ideas ever inflicted on the mentality of the state. It was his contention that if the carpetbaggers had stayed away, Arkansas would have developed on its own about as well as Mexico. On the Saturday before Easter, holding forth with a bottle of Jack Daniels in his hand, he told our twenty guests that when Bill Clinton dies, the pathologists will cut him open and discover the homunculus not of his hero Jack Kennedy, but of Lyndon Johnson. *If Bill had gone to Arkansas State instead of Yale, he would have been just like Johnson, openly seething with class resentment at east coast intellectuals. Clinton learned to hide his inferiority complex behind a good education, but he's got one just the same. Both of them wanted the country to give them the love they didn't get from their daddies.* Cormorant, I realize, could have easily written the paragraph Laurel just read me.

I put my spatula down and climb back up the steps of the deck to sit for a few moments and sip my glass of bourbon. Laurel has resumed reading to herself, and I wonder uneasily if I now understand what Cormorant's motive might have been to kill his colleague: Merriweather stole some of the ideas for a book of his own and never even mentioned Cormorant in a footnote. The longer I talk to Cormorant, the more I wonder if he is telling me the truth about his relationship with Damascus. Though Cormorant must have infuriated him, he probably respected him. I sit down in the chair opposite her. "Have you always found Cormorant to be truthful?" I ask Laurel, finally realizing that my assumption that we share pretty much the same view of him may not be correct.

My wife taps the book on her chest and scoffs, "Men like Cormorant don't know what the truth is because they don't know what they feel. Though he's driving me crazy, this man understands that the past is as much about feelings as it is about facts. Cormorant pats himself on the back every time he's pinned one down. Who cares? Somebody should have written a book like this a long time ago. Your family owned slaves. I wonder how they really did treat them? I can feel that 'buck'. It makes me want to get up and walk around. And sex! Merriweather says that no historian in Arkansas has honestly dealt with the way white men went into the slave quarters and produced all those mulatto children." She adds, her voice high, "Cormorant should have written this book, but he didn't have the guts."

Should or could, I think to myself. I look at Laurel and wonder if she believes what she is saying. I respond, "He'd say that he didn't have the facts."

"Don't you see how evasive that kind of response is?" Laurel says, picking up the book again and flipping through it. "Only a white Arkansas male would make it. Have you forgotten this?" She finds her place in the middle of the book and reads: *The hypocrisy of the white Arkansan on the subject of his sexual treatment of the slave is mind-boggling. Rape has always been rape no matter how much white male historians try to hide behind historical relativity and their pose of objectivity. What we, black or white, male or female, have all known is that the white Arkansas male's greatest fear was that black males would someday take revenge for what the slave owner was doing to their women. Even the thought of sex between a black man and a white woman made him crazy with fear, made him utter the most idiotic pronouncements ever to come out of a human mouth. In his book,* Negro Slavery in Arkansas, *the white historian Orville Taylor dutifully reports the words of the Arkansas Supreme Court that a white woman could not possibly be attracted to a black unless she were depraved. In a case in which the defense attorney had the temerity to suggest that a white woman had consented to sex instead of being raped, the chief justice of the Arkansas Supreme Court said in* Pleasant v. State: *"But surely, it may not be unsafe, or unjust to the prisoner, to say, that, in this state, where sexual intercourse between a white woman and negroes is regarded with the utmost abhorrence, the presumption that a white woman yielded herself to the embraces of a negro, without force, arising from a want of chastity in her, would not be great, unless she had sunk to the lowest level of prostitution."*

Laurel looks over the top of the book at me and laughs. "What utter horseshit! If the judge had said it was regarded with the utmost fear, he would have been closer to the truth. How did these men look their wives in the face the day after their little mulatto children were born? And if things were tense in the big house, imagine what was going through the mind of the black men on the plantation the instant they saw that light skin! I think if I had been the slave master that day, I would have said that this morning we were going to weed the cotton by hand and keep the hoes locked up."

Puzzled by Laurel's reaction, I stand up and go back down the steps to check the meat. She is hardly a feminist crusader, and has never expressed the slightest interest in slavery, but clearly this book has touched a chord. It has been the account of the beatings that moved me in Merriweather's book. The part of the book devoted to the "sexual predators of the South," as Merriweather called the section she is reading from, is more hysterical than anything. "Who knows for sure if the men thought anything?" I say, taking the steaks from the grill and putting them onto a platter. "I think these are ready."

Laurel ignores my question and does not look at the meat. She begins to read out loud again. *To pass over such lunacy from the state's highest judicial body without comment as Orville Taylor does in his book in the guise of objectivity is to dignify the Supreme Court's words, which are nonsensical cant, offered to rationalize the criminal behavior of the society which their white male counterparts controlled. No historian today excuses the Holocaust on the grounds of historical relativity, and any attempt to justify the absence of an examination of this subject on the theory that the state does not have adequate documentation about it is ludicrous. It is true that the Slave Narrative interviews do not contain accounts of Arkansas slave women speaking about how they were raped by their masters, nor should we expect them to be there. Perhaps if there had been female African-American interviewers, this painful subject would have been explored, but it was certainly too much to expect a former black slave to open up on this subject to a man or to a white woman whose male ancestors easily could have been involved. If we take seriously Orville Taylor's incredible suggestion that some black women may well have been willing for the master to come to their beds, we ignore the fact that it was the master, his family, and employees who were regularly whipping her, her children, and her men to compel their obedience. Only a white male steeped in the arrogance of his culture could suggest that slave women willingly consented to sex with their owners in light of their treatment. And only a white man drunk on power could perpetuate the legal fiction that a white woman could not conceivably be attracted to a black man (unless she were a whore) when all around him white men were trotting off to the slave quarters.*

I come back up the stairs with the platter of meat, suddenly feeling tired. "I've never read Taylor's book. Is that what he actually says?" I ask, hoping to tone down this conversation so that we can eat. We'll take a bottle of champagne into the bedroom with us. Laurel needs to get some food in her.

"Since I haven't read it either, I don't know, " Laurel admits. "You know how dramatic this Merriweather gets. But think about this. If somebody as high-minded as Thomas Jefferson was regularly bedding down with a slave girl like Sally Hemmings, then you know what the average Arkansas male was doing.

Imagine Bill Clinton owning slaves. He could have fielded his own pro basketball league by the time he was through."

I laugh, but make the point, "This is just what Cormorant was talking about. If you reduce history to the level of *The Jerry Springer Show*, it won't be worth very much."

Laurel stands. "And that's Merriweather's point! Arkansas history is not worth a damn thing now, because our historians are too worried about their reputations to try to write the truth."

I reach for my glass of bourbon on the railing. I have rarely seen her so animated over a subject before. I have mixed emotions about Merriweather's book. In many ways, it is outrageous, one unprovable salvo after another. "You've not exactly been on the barricades for blacks these last few years, yourself," I remind her.

Laurel looks toward the river. "I'm not saying I like the present. It's terrible! But I don't have to have burned my bra to know how powerless women have been historically. I've asked the library to get me Taylor's book through interlibrary loan. I want to see for myself if Merriweather is right about what this Orville Taylor said."

I balance the platter on the deck railing and reach over and take my wife's hand and pat it between my own. "I'd like to read it, too, " I say. "Why don't we eat now?"

Laurel jerks her hand away. "Don't pat me like I'm some hysterical female!" she yells. "This guy knew what he was talking about even if he was bitter as hell at whites."

I stare at Laurel, trying to assess where this anger is coming from. Having known her for so long, it is difficult to believe that she has been radicalized overnight. Merriweather's book doesn't say much that is new. It is how he says it that gets your attention. I think she is mad at me, because I won't sell our land. "Some stuff he does know about," I admit, backing away to give her some space. I don't want her picking up a knife right now. "Have you talked to the

Harkritters about being in the book? I'm surprised Claude hasn't called me about whether he can sue for libel."

"He can't sue!" Laurel says, jabbing her finger at me. "Because it's true! If you had checked the footnotes, you'd have seen his great-great-grandfather put his slave daughter in his will and the Arkansas Supreme Court upheld it. Daisy Hought, who is almost white, the one who works at the Thrift Store part-time, is Claude's cousin. People have gossiped about that for years, and you know it."

There are plenty of stories about liaisons between blacks and whites in Marianna and not necessarily from the days of slavery. "He must have cared about her," I respond, "or he wouldn't have put her in his will."

Laurel puts her hands to her face. "For God's sake, Miller! You sound like one of those fools on the Arkansas Supreme Court. It wasn't what he thought that was important. It was what she thought, and she, whoever she was, didn't have any choice but to submit if she wanted decent treatment for herself and her family."

I have the feeling that relationships between them were more complicated than men acting on the level of barnyard animals, but Laurel has become too emotional to discuss this subject rationally. "We'll sweat through our clothes if we try to eat out here," I say, picking up the platter. Let's take this inside. The potatoes should be about ready."

Hugging the book to her tee shirt as if it were a favorite child in need of protection, she says, "You don't get it, do you?"

Unless one of us backs off, the rest of the night is ruined and it had been so promising. "If we can't even understand why we act like we do in the present," I say, trying to smile, "how on earth can we be so certain of things that happened so long ago?"

Laurel, whose hair is now ratted with sweat at her temples, fixes me with a look that makes me feel as if we are complete strangers. "In case you've forgotten, this is the South, Miller. Some things never change." She brushes by me, and repeats, "Some things never change."

Though we get through dinner by changing the subject (Laurel has gotten back our pictures of France and we get a long phone call from Cynthia), we go to bed angry with each other. Still, Laurel is able to drift off to sleep at her usual time after the ten o'clock news (fights don't bother her sleep) but I am too restless to stay in bed and go upstairs to the guest bedroom that overlooks the deck. I go to the window seat where my great-grandfather's few remaining possessions are kept. For years I have accepted the story that a fire in 1900 burned almost everything they had from the days of slavery, and though I have nothing concrete to challenge this view, I have recently begun to wonder what happened to the contents of a commissary which was torn down when I was a boy. It could have contained records from the plantation, but now I have no idea where they would be.

In a scrapbook I find what I am looking for and carefully turn the pages to the journal fragments my grandmother copied by hand. As I remembered, my great-grandmother had recorded one of her slaves' deaths. *Sunday night. Sent for doctor. Davy very sick. Can't keep anything on his stomach according to Lula. She claims he has been dreaming of his death for weeks. I so wish Jay were here! Martha says Davy is sixty years old. Jay bought him in 1840, and he has been with our family ever since. A good and faithful Negro! If he dies, we will miss him! Monday morning— Poor Davy breathed his last. Doctor Lyle said he thought there was some kind of block, and Davy was in great pain at the end. His children look at me with such sad eyes. Jay won't believe it. Damn*

*this war! Tuesday. Davy buried this morning. I've felt sick all day.
He was a good man and Jay's favorite of our slaves. Poor Lula. She
has cried and cried. If I can get the preacher to come out, I want
her to talk to him. Lula said she doesn't believe in heaven! How
strange! I thought they all did. No wonder she cries and cries. If
this war kills Jay, I don't know what I will do. We will not have
enough food this year.* Here, water stains or something have
obliterated the next two pages, and then I find a familiar passage
with not even the day of the week to mark her anger and sense
of betrayal. *Gone. Every last one of them! Ran to the Yankees with
not even a word. As if I would or could have stopped them. Not one
shred of loyalty or gratitude for all we did for them. No one was
better treated and cared for! Let the Yankees feed them. God knows
what they will do free.* The last entry is marked *Tuesday. What
will become of me?*

I hear a sound downstairs and wonder if Laurel has gotten up
to go to the bathroom and is looking for me. I read the last entries
again and then walk down the steps, trying to imagine what kind
of person would feel so betrayed by their slaves running off. It
sounds absurd, but maybe anybody would, human nature being
what it is. God knows what they thought they would find. From
the hall I see the light on Laurel's side of the bed. I look at my
watch and am amazed it is just now midnight. It is as if I have
been up all night.

"You weren't too worried about me," I say lightly, hoping we
won't argue.

Laurel, who has taken to sleeping nude since our Paris trip, yawns.
"You were stomping around so loud up there," she says, her voice
good-natured, "I was afraid you were looking for his sword."

I strip off my underwear and get into bed. Laurel knows me
better than I do myself. I roll in toward her and put my arm
around her waist as she reaches for the light. "Maybe there's some

old papers mixed in with the files in the attic. I'll look tomorrow, and maybe I can find a confession that great-granddaddy raped them all and sired twenty children. That ought to satisfy you."

Laurel titters in the dark, and I know she is no longer mad. "My poor baby," she says, patting my thigh. "I'm never satisfied, am I?"

Though I know she is teasing me, I resist telling her that she used to be satisfied. Whites have been leaving the Delta for years. Four of our best friends moved to northwest Arkansas five years ago. But what do I think is going to happen—that one day I'll wake up and Lee County will be like it was when we were growing up in the '50s when I never thought for one minute that our lives would change? "Nostalgia is a powerful thing, isn't it?" I muse, glad that she snuggles in against me. For some reason, she has unilaterally declared a truce, and I am loathe to disturb it.

She brushes her knuckles against my penis. "Awfully," she agrees, pressing her face into my neck and opening her hand to cup me.

As we begin to make love for the second time tonight, I know that this hiatus will be brief and the tension that has been building between us will return and grow stronger. Like a dormant virus, it has been there perhaps for decades, and now that it has surfaced it is all we can think about. Maybe anything would have touched it off, but it seems to have started with Cormorant's arrest. Perhaps, if he is acquitted, we can get back to normal. Laurel presses hard against me as if the power of sex can overcome my stubborn refusal to leave this place.

"The Delta has always been a time bomb," Laurel says fifteen minutes later as we lie side by side, both of us spent.

For an agonizing moment, I think she is going to launch into another diatribe, but as if these words were a magic incantation to summon the god of sleep, in a moment I hear her gently snoring beside me.

6

Dr. Carole Matso's office, at least as much as I can glimpse of it without appearing too obvious, is about what I have come to expect of a history professor's office since I have begun contacting Cormorant's colleagues at UALR: it is small and crammed with books and journals. Square in the middle of the wall over her desk is a familiar art calendar—in fact, the same one that now hangs in our kitchen in Jeffersonville. The artist Gustav Klimt has recently become a favorite of Laurel's. If our calendar is any indication of his work, the orange-colored nudes who decorate our wall each month often seem lost in fantasies that have little to do with external reality. I wonder what her students think. She has not wanted to talk to me; understandably none of her fellow professors have opened up to a lawyer either. Cormorant, true to his word, has no friends on the history faculty, and his indictment has not endeared him. In fact, to say he is persona non grata on the campus does not put it too strongly. He has confirmed there is a tacit agreement that he won't come around the department this summer except to pick up his mail. I would have preferred he talk to as many colleagues and students as possible this summer, but that obviously is not going to happen. Cormorant has no talent for small talk or the common courtesies of academic life and is emotionally incapable of approaching others for help. As has been said about other men who live and die by their tongues, his opinions were his only friends. We have agreed with the university administration that he will take a sabbatical this fall, understanding it will end on September 10th if he is convicted.

A specialist in Latin American history, Dr. Matso, fortyish, is not unattractive, with her clear gray eyes and generous mouth. Cormorant says she is by far the best writer in the history department, but she has published little since becoming tenured, preferring to work with students and other university departments. "I don't think I can add much to the statement I gave the police," she says, spreading her palms outward in a gesture that tells me this conversation will be short. "I know I said more than I wanted to, but the detective kept pressing me."

Pleased and surprised she would concede this much, I take her written statement and place it on the desk between us. If she wants to recant, I'm not going to discourage her. "Sometimes, they can put words in your mouth. Cormorant says that actually he got along with Damascus Merriweather better than people think."

Dr. Matso frowns and sweeps back a lock of brown hair from her forehead with a hand so delicate it looks translucent. "It's possible, I guess," she says, carefully. "For years, I don't think they did more than nod at each other. Yet I do know that for *Coming To Terms*, which I read a draft of last year, Cormorant served as sort of a devil's advocate. I would ask them to shut the door because they could get so loud. Cormorant's office was next to mine. Frankly, what bothers me about Cormorant is that he never offers any constructive criticism. It's all negative. He can be absolutely scathing. I don't know how Damascus put up with it. To be quite blunt, Cormorant can reduce me to tears, so I avoid discussing my work with him. He's an excellent historian, though."

I try not to stare at June, the nude of the month, who

announced her presence at our house two weeks ago yesterday. The figure behind Dr. Matso has her left hand hidden between her bare thighs and appears to be in ecstasy. "Doesn't some of *Coming To Terms* sound like Cormorant?" I ask. I don't want to put any ideas in her head, but if this is something the police figured out earlier, I don't want to be the last person to know.

"Cormorant wouldn't dare write a book like this," Dr. Matso says firmly. "There're hardly any footnotes at all in some of the chapters. I'm sure he's told you that he thinks a book like this is destructive of our credibility as historians. I'm sure you must know that if you've been his friend besides being his lawyer. I've heard of him speak of you before. He calls you the only honest attorney he knows."

I'm not sure whether I am being insulted or complimented. Dr. Matso's manner is somewhat dry despite her apparent openness. I ask, "But wouldn't you agree that, for example, the section on Bill Clinton could have come out of Cormorant's mouth?"

Dr. Matso again brushes her hair back from her forehead. "But he wouldn't put it in a book like this. I'm not sure this helps you though."

I look down at the paper in front of me, hoping she can't read my mind. "I"'m just trying to understand the relationship between the two men. It seems rather complex to me. Will you admit to not liking Cormorant if the prosecutor calls you as a witness?"

"Obviously, I'd prefer not to be within a mile of the courtroom the day that trial begins," she says abruptly. "I think what he calls honesty is simply a form of narcissism. It took courage for Damascus to have that book published. It's not the kind of book that advances your academic career." Too polite to tell me to get out of her office, she looks at her watch. She has previously told me that she is teaching summer school.

"Do you know Ezekiel?" I ask, unwilling to take the hint. I like this woman. She doesn't pull her punches. "Judging by what I see on television and read in the paper, he was devoted to his brother."

"Absolutely," Dr. Matso says, a hint of a smile coming to her face. "He told me the one time I met him that he thought Damascus was the most persistent man he had ever known. But when Damascus finally admitted no publisher was interested, Ezekiel took over that end of it immediately. I don't know what the financial arrangements were, but I suspect he's going to end up making money off of it. As you probably know, the reviews so far have been very positive."

"What do you think of it?" I ask, wondering if I am going to get the feminist line.

"I think it was long overdue, and he said many things that needed saying," she says, her voice intense. "For your information, with the exception of Cormorant, Damascus was quite well respected by the history faculty. He did solid research over his career and published much more than I have."

I note that she hasn't told me what she thinks of it. "One of the things that seems a bit of a stretch in the book is the chapter about black ancestors," I say, hoping to fish out her opinion. "It seemed to me as if he was trying to make some kind of political statement. It seems hardly more than gossip."

"I totally disagree with you," Dr. Matso says flatly. She turns to the wall of shelves behind her and pulls a copy of the book from it, saying, "I can't vouch for how careful Damascus was in his research, but this section has great emotional impact. If the book will be remembered fifty years from now, it will be because of the way he introduces this part." She turns to the one of the last chapters and reads: *White Arkansans of a certain age pursue their family history as almost a spiritual quest. Even the smallest libraries in the poorest of Delta towns house a genealogy room. Their patrons, once the daily passions of life have begun to cool, intuitively sense*

*that the most important aspect of their beings are their personal
identities—who they were and who they are now. Out of shame
they fail to name and identify their black ancestors. By so doing,
they dishonor the nobility of their search for personal meaning,
and in the process rob their descendants of gifts far more precious
than the family silver.* Dr. Matso, reminding me of a look
Cormorant gives me, frowns ruefully, as if I were an inattentive
but promising student. "I find this part of the book enormously
compelling. One hundred years from now, hopefully, there will
be people from the Delta honoring Damascus for what he
preserved for them."

I stare at the calendar behind her, searching for clues as to
what gives this woman such hope that another century will make
a difference in race relations in the Delta when the last two
hundred have been so bleak. "Do you think that was his
motivation?" I ask, trying not to sound too skeptical.

"Unlike your client," Dr. Matso says, her voice becoming dry
again, "Damascus was not cynical. He just wanted the truth to
come out about slavery."

"I'm not sure anyone knows the truth," I mutter, knowing this
conversation is ending. She has begun to gather up her books
for class. "Why didn't he write an academic work? He could have."

Dr. Matso looks over my head as if it pains her to look at me.
"I think he felt that this state is still so racist that only a white
historian's work would be accepted as the truth. And, of course,
it turned out that he didn't have time. "

Emboldened by her candor, I ask, "I know you've probably
been asked this by the police. Do you know of anyone who might
have wanted Damascus dead? Perhaps a student?"

Dr. Matso stands up, forcing me to scramble to my feet. "I
really have to do some work," she says, coming around her desk,
"but to answer your question, I'm not aware of anybody, Mr.

Holly. Damascus encouraged his students, black and white; he didn't teach by intimidation. He was loved by many of them for the respectful, caring way he treated all of them. For those of us who knew him personally, some of the book is a surprise, because, outside of it, he was a gentle, kind man. Your client pushed his buttons, but he was one of the few in recent memory, and you have to remember, also, this was a man who was in pain the last few months of his life."

St. Damascus. Somehow, I can't fathom it. A man who would write a book as sharp-tongued as this one, even if he doesn't pick on students, has to have some enemies.

Professor Matso looks at her watch again, and I thank her for her time and leave the campus, which is far bigger than I realized. As I turn north onto Fair Park, no matter how much I try to dismiss it, I have the uneasy feeling that Cormorant was having a serious quarrel with Damascus and that it had more to do with ego than history. Instead of going straight at the light to get on the freeway to head back downtown, I turn east on 12th Street and realize that I will drive by Ezekiel's Little Rock pharmacy. As I pass through the light at Cedar, I see his Cadillac to the right of the building, and think that all he can do is tell me to get the hell off his property. It is almost six, closing time, but nothing ventured, nothing gained. I had thought to wait until later, but realize I have simply been putting it off for no good reason.

"Mr. Merriweather," I ask, my heart beginning to speed up, "would you give me a few minutes of your time?" I say quickly as I approach the front counter where he is standing by a cash register. "I'm Miller Holly, the attorney for Cormorant Ashley." I had not counted on being nervous, but now that I am face to face with the man, I feel intimidated. The television camera does not capture his presence. Even though on tv there is a steeliness in his visage, in person he seems to positively glower.

"I know who you are," he says, his voice loud and resonant. There is no one in the pharmacy except two clerks, both black men, and they now look at me as if the devil himself had entered the premises.

For a long moment, he stares at me and I think he is going to order me out, but he says gruffly, "R.T., start locking up. This won't take long."

Before I can respond, he disappears and then comes out a side door from the left and says brusquely, "Follow me."

He turns, and I trail him back through the door into an office whose green walls are decorated with those old-fashioned calendars you see in car garages of women in skimpy clothing, but the models are all black, I notice. Rows of filing cabinets line the wall behind a gun-metal color desk, and a computer sits atop it. He sits down in a swivel chair across from me and says, "Close the door and tell me what you want."

I figure I have about fifteen seconds to make some sense. According to an interview given by Merriweather to the black-owned weekly *Arkansas State Press* last week, he is no longer convinced that Cormorant is the only suspect. I take the paper from under my arm and slide it onto his desk. "I suspect you probably have a better idea than the police who murdered your brother, and I can't imagine you'd want to see the wrong man convicted."

Unlike the other times I have seen him, Merriweather today looks like a pharmacist. He is wearing a white jacket, khaki pants, and white shoes I've seen medical personnel wear in hospitals. He leans forward, resting his weight on his arms and replies, his voice sarcastic and strained, "Innocence is a relative term, don't you think, Mr. Holly? Your client is hardly innocent of racism, arrogance, and what my brother used to call the southern white male syndrome of believing, despite the demographics to the contrary, that the world will always be your oyster. Now, whether he is guilty of murdering my brother is, in the grand scheme of things, not that important. Whether he's convicted or not won't make up for all the discrimination, beatings, whippings, and rapes blacks have suffered at the hands of whites in Arkansas. Nothing can undo that. Nor can anyone bring my brother back."

He looks hard at me, and I can feel sweat dripping under my arms. He seems somehow detached, not the same person I saw being interviewed on tv or at the jail the day of Cormorant's arraignment. Perhaps the hate mail he has publicly complained of receiving has walled him off from the emotion he once felt. Or perhaps his public behavior is an act.

Though Cormorant has found out a good deal about this man, he has only scratched the surface. We now know that Ezekiel, unlike his brother, is a religious man, or at least that he regularly attends a black church downtown. His well-to-do white neighbors have nothing to do with him, nor he with them. And though it may have set off tremors five years ago when he bought the big house on Palisades, no one has had cause to complain nor, at this economic and social level, did they expect to. Ezekiel Merriweather is hardly the sort to sit out on his front lawn in his undershirt drinking beer and listening to rap music.

"As a historian, your brother would have wanted the truth about his murder to be known," I say, knowing I sound fatuous, but hoping to touch something in this man. As formidable as he seems, he wouldn't be putting himself through this if he didn't care deeply. "That much is obvious."

Ezekiel Merriweather's jaw tightens as if he were bracing for a shot of Novocain. "Your client didn't think my brother was much of a historian," he notes coldly. "I think he would have let him sweep out his office, but I'm not so sure about that. He was just a dumb nigger in way over his head who benefited by affirmative action."

I tell myself to keep my cool. If this guy runs out of steam, I think I can talk to him. "It was a lot more complex relationship than that," I say firmly, "and I think you know it. Your brother wouldn't have invited him over to your house to substitute for him on that panel, and Cormorant wouldn't have bothered to accept if there hadn't been respect on both sides. The man I represent is not an easy person to please. My wife is still furious that he wouldn't write a letter recommending our daughter for graduate school," I confide. "He said the world didn't need another mediocre graduate student."

As I hoped, this makes Merriweather laugh out loud before saying, "See, if it had been me, it would have been the other way around. If I'd had to listen to this kind of shit, I'd be the one charged with putting a bullet in your client's chest. I don't know where Damascus came from in our family," he adds dryly. "On a face-to-face basis, he could put up with white people's crap way past the time most of the rest of us would have tolerated your nonsense."

I can feel my face begin to flush, but I have expected to feel anger and try to ignore it. "That's why I don't think there was even an argument between them that day. Whether either admitted it or not, I think they respected each other for saying exactly what each thought. Why else would your brother have asked him to be on that panel talking about the '57 school desegregation crisis?"

Merriweather looks down at the copy of the *Arkansas State Press* and rubs his thumb over a crease in the paper. "So if your client didn't murder my brother, how do you explain his pistol with his fingerprints on it? From what I understand, his are the only prints on it and the cops say it was the murder weapon."

I feel extremely uncomfortable revealing our strategy to this man, but if he were to testify at the trial he still had doubts that Cormorant shot his brother, I might well get at least a hung jury. Given the make-up of the jury pool in Pulaski County, there will doubtless be a couple of blacks and maybe more hanging on Merriweather's every word. "Don't you suppose that it's at least possible that he was set up? It would have been easy to do for somebody who hated what was in your brother's book and knew them both. Cormorant made no secret of the fact he kept a gun in his glove compartment. I think that kid who brought him his mail knew way too much. If he didn't do it himself, he could have orchestrated your brother's murder easily."

Merriweather checks his watch but asks, "How do you figure?"

Despite appearing as if he isn't interested in this conversation, I notice Merriweather hasn't ended it. "Just since Cormorant was charged," I reply, "we've heard that the kid has a redneck uncle living in Pulaski County who was outraged by the section of the book that purports to identify present-day Arkansans whose ancestors raped their female slaves. He's a member of a survivalist group that meets from time to time. They aren't too fond of minorities." This information, obtained by Cormorant yesterday through a call to one of his former graduate students who was a friend of Rafe Kennedy, has not been verified, but sounds possible.

"Purports?" snaps Merriweather, scowling. "The book didn't prove a damn thing to you, did it?"

"Actually, it did," I answer, dumbfounded that Merriweather seems to be more interested in my reaction to his brother's book than in finding a possible suspect. Yet perhaps he knows more about the kid's uncle than we do. "What your brother put into the book from the Arkansas Slave Narratives didn't seem embellished to me. It was obviously a lot more brutal and degrading than whites care to acknowledge." As I say this, I find myself choking on the words. Though I have come to believe it, I feel blackmailed into this statement.

Merriweather folds his arms across his chest as if I were a son of whom more has been expected than has been delivered. "You people are amazing," he murmurs as if to himself. "Every single one of your families ought to be outed for the rapists they were. Did your family own slaves?" he demands.

Shades of Laurel! I don't owe this man an answer, but I refuse to let him bully me.

"My great-grandfather owned forty slaves in Phillips County. That's about all I know."

"That's all you want to know is what you mean," Merriweather says dismissing me as if I were a delivery boy. "It's like Damascus said in the book: You people claim to know every damn thing else about your ancestors, so it's strange you don't know about this part of their lives. I've got to lock up," he says.

I get up and walk toward the door, pissed that I thought I could reach this guy. However, as I put my hand on the doorknob, Merriweather asks quietly, "Do the cops know about Kennedy's background?"

I turn, wondering what really motivates Merriweather. He may just like to bait whites until he can get the response he wants. I know I don't like the son of a bitch. "I don't know. Once the prosecutor charges somebody, the police aren't interested in hearing about anybody else." I am hoping he will realize he may have responsibility here. Minor Latting may well have charged Cormorant sooner than he wanted to, just to take the heat off.

He lets that go, and as I head back out through the pharmacy where one employee is still left, I suspect Merriweather will follow up on Kennedy. He is too obsessed to ignore him.

"What did he say?" Cormorant demands as I sit down behind my desk in my temporary office in the Lafayette Building and tell him I just met with Ezekiel.

He knew I was meeting with Matso, too, but that conversation is easily forgotten. "Get Raven and I'll tell you."

He nods and obediently heads for the door. I am finding that I prefer to have Raven present when I have something worth telling Cormorant. Though he may trust me, it is his sister who can get him to be still and listen. If she is not there, he tends to rant and rave, and I have decided to try to include her in every important exchange of information. I am wondering too if I like having her here because I want to have a record of our conversations. When it is not focused, Cormorant's memory is as convenient as my own. If he is convicted, I'll want Raven to remember what was said and done. I don't want Cormorant writing his own history and having it come out with me as the villain.

Five minutes later he returns with Raven in tow. She looks tired, but it is the end of a workday. They sit down on opposite ends of the leather couch Raven has placed in the converted break room. We could meet in Raven's bigger office, but she seems to prefer to walk down the hall to the room she is letting me use. It is becoming difficult to remember that she ever seemed the less stable of the two. If Mr. John had turned loose some of the family money, Raven could have probably started her own business much sooner, and perhaps would have avoided her marital difficulties. Cormorant says she has never asked their father for a thing though he would have gladly given her, unlike him, whatever she wanted. "Sorry, I was on the phone," she apologizes unnecessarily, sitting down across from me.

"You've got to make a living," I say, and smile at her. Because I have seen Raven repeatedly at her worst and never flinched, she has treated me with a measure of deference in the last few years. When we were kids, it was much different. She was Cormorant's tomboy sister who was smeared with grease from working in the tractor shed and made fun of me because I was such a beanpole back then. She probably should have stayed on the farm, she has admitted to me. I have spent four nights at her apartment in the last couple of weeks. Doubtless, the drug dealer across the street thinks she is having an affair. From his porch he occasionally nods as if he approves of the new man in his neighbor's life. As long as I am not a cop, we won't have any problems.

"Tell us what he said, " she says, rubbing her eyes. During the day, Raven often dresses in red power suits and two-inch heels. When she comes home, sometimes not until nine, she changes into baggy shorts and a tee shirt. Some nights she is too tired or distracted with work to ask much about the case, and we watch the news at ten together in her den like an old married couple. In the morning, armed with a cup of coffee, she pads around in curlers, her nose buried in the *Arkansas Democrat-Gazette*. At work, however, Raven is all business. She has been the biggest proponent of a conversation with Ezekiel. She has studied every public utterance looking for clues to the case as though he were speaking in code. What we both noticed was that in his last two appearances he has quit talking about Cormorant and only mentions the book, and with the latest statement in the *Arkansas State Press*, we decided it might be worth a surprise visit with him. "A little," I say and reprise our brief conversation as literally as I can. "Unlike his brother," I conclude, "I think he now despises whites."

Raven draws her legs up on the couch and replies, "Why shouldn't he? We killed his idol. Whether he thinks it was Cormorant or some redneck, he's bound to believe the murderer was white."

I reach behind me for the file that we are compiling on the Merriweather brothers. Through my representation of white-collar criminals, I have learned the hard way that most people leave a longer paper trail than they think, and this case is no exception. However embittered Ezekiel is now, Cormorant has found out that Ezekiel has occasionally worked closely with whites, usually on some business deal or another. The most recent venture was a low-income apartment complex five years ago that had a number of white partners. When I commented on this apparent contradiction, Raven pointed out that a black businessman can't avoid whites in Little Rock if he wants to be successful, saying that almost everything he needs is still controlled by a white male power structure—money, expertise, access to the legislature and regulators. *He's still stuck with dealing with good ole boys, no matter how much their suits cost.* As a businesswoman, Raven has developed a healthy respect for Ezekiel which she says neither Cormorant nor I can appreciate. Going up regularly against the bigger firms, she appreciates how difficult it is to compete without the built-in social connections she compares to the infrastructure of a modern city.

I flip through the file and find that the number of reviews of the book is up to fifteen, and her secretary has just posted a copy of a glowing review from *The Washington Post* from a clipping service.

"Thirty years ago Ezekiel wouldn't have come after you the way he has," I opine to Cormorant. In the file we have a clipping of Ezekiel being named as the first black to the Little Rock Zoning Commission. Another article recounts he was the first black appointed to some obscure board by the County Judge. In addition to being one of the state's first black pharmacists, he owned a small hauling business.

Meanwhile, his brother was beginning to toil through a doctoral program in history at the University in Fayetteville. We have found out that Damacus has had two wives. From the divorce settlement in 1975, it appears his first wife may have supported him through graduate school, but she has been out of the picture so long any animosity on her part doesn't seem worth pursuing. He has no legal judgments against him, and a search of the title on his house shows no liens. We have waited to see if his estate will be probated, but so far nothing has been filed and may not be. I still want to know something about his children, but so far we have little but their names. I glance at the clock on the desk. A private investigator we have hired is coming by at seven to give us a report.

While he waits for his trial, Cormorant is growing a beard and now strokes it as if it were a hair shirt. I have insisted that he shave it off before the trial, but right now it is snow white. He looks twenty years older. "That's because thirty years ago Ezekiel probably still thought real integration was a meaningful possibility," he reminds me. "You had whites like Winthrop Rockefeller running around the state preaching that a new day was dawning. Blacks were going to get jobs, education, and respect, and we'd all live happily ever after together."

I cannot keep from shaking my head as I recall Winthrop Rockefeller, the first Republican governor since Reconstruction. This transplanted millionaire-many-times-over Yankee, shy and bumbling as he preached the gospel of racial progress and harmony in the '60s in Arkansas, was hard to take seriously as a politician until he won the governor's office once and then again. Arkansas blacks provided the difference in both elections. "What was Ezekiel like this afternoon?" Raven asks, bringing us back to the present.

"As asshole as usual," I respond, recalling his scowl when he realized who I was. I've begun to wonder if Ezekiel influenced Damascus more than we think. Until now, we have assumed that

Ezekiel has just picked up the torch; maybe he lit it for his brother.

"But he may feel some guilt now. I don't think he'll rest until he's satisfied he knows who killed his brother," I say, explaining how the conversation ended. "He got in his licks, but he was listening to me, too."

Raven, I am learning, is not comfortable unless she is making a list, and she walks over to the window where she keeps a flip chart and begins writing. In the past week we have expanded our possible suspects on the chart to include one of Cormorant's disgruntled tenants whom he evicted in February after an ugly confrontation in which Cormorant ran back to the Taurus and actually got his pistol. His tenant, a black, out-of-work carpenter with an obvious drinking problem, by the name of Waymon Duffy, had threatened to "get him" after Cormorant had served him with an eviction notice. Though Duffy later cleared his family out and didn't trash the place, he stole several items, including a microwave. Cormorant is convinced the man stalked him for a period which coincided with the disappearance of his gun. The day after Cormorant was charged, he got a crank call from someone who screamed into the phone that it was "payback time." Cormorant thinks now it might have been Duffy who stole his .22. If we could somehow show that, I might be able eventually to persuade Minor Latting to dismiss the case. The prosecutor has become increasingly annoyed with Ezekiel since his interview in the *Arkansas State Press*. Though he thinks Cormorant is guilty, Latting has all but said he was stampeded into charging Cormorant as soon as he did.

Raven writes Ezekiel's name on the sheet in front of her. "Would he talk to Cormorant?" she asks me. "If you could arrange a meeting between them, don't you think it would help?"

I turn and see Cormorant stiffening in his chair, remembering how the day we went to the crime scene the last person he wanted to see was Ezekiel Merriweather. Before Cormorant can dismiss this out of hand, I say quickly, "It's worth thinking about. Once Ezekiel gets through venting, he's probably not any more unreasonable than anybody else would be in this situation. I don't have the impression he's totally beyond the pale."

"I have to believe," Raven says, "Ezekiel has gotten some information that he's not telling the cops yet. The problem is that because we aren't black, we are never going to really know who were Damascus's enemies or even if he had any. If Cormorant talks to Ezekiel, maybe he will be convinced he didn't do it."

Cormorant asks me, "Is this really a good idea?"

I lean back in my chair. Every instinct tells me that it is always preferable to advise a criminal defendant to sew his mouth shut until the trial and usually then, but this case may be different. "Not in my experience," I say. "He'll repeat everything you say to the cops, and the prosecutor will put his own spin on it. If a defendant testifies, and I'm assuming right now that you want to, the fewer times he's told his story the better. But we can think about it."

Cormorant stands up and walks over to his sister and takes the magic marker from her. "I've been telling you both for a month," he says, his voice rising, "that I liked the man personally. Why would I kill him? It's ridiculous." He begins to draw the outline of a face, a facility of his that has always amazed me. Cormorant, Laurel says, could have been a commercial artist. To my brain, which only thinks in words, this ability to draw seems like magic. It implies another world, one which I have not been permitted to enter.

"Certain passages of the book sound like you," I say to him for the first time. "If the jury recognizes that, they will think you killed him out of jealousy or because he stole your ideas." I turn to his sister for confirmation. It is something we have not discussed. I realize I have been harboring this thought like a guilty secret.

Cormorant, who has already sketched the unmistakable nose and chin of the Merriweather brothers, also turns to Raven, who suddenly looks uncomfortable. If his sister and best friend are slow in arriving at this obvious insight, it must be because we lack perspective, which is why I should not have agreed to represent him in the first place. It occurs to me that one reason I have been successful as a lawyer is that I immediately assume my clients are guilty and work backwards. "Whether he stole some of your ideas or not," she says, bringing her hands to her face, "I can see them arguing that as a motive. Can't you?" she says to her brother.

Instead of denying what we have both implied, Cormorant returns to his drawing and with a flick of his wrist somehow makes Ezekiel emerge from the pen strokes rather than Damascus. It is something about the eyes that are immediately identifiable. Damascus had the sad, moist look of a dreamer, that far-off gaze that sees the past and future but not the present. Ezekiel, Cormorant's drawing tells us, has the look of a man who comes to life in the moment. He says easily, "There's nothing original in his book, so there was nothing to steal."

Raven does not challenge her brother but sends me a look that says he is in denial.

Until this moment I can tell that she has never doubted her brother. I have taken the precaution of having Raven sign a form I use for employees and I have actually paid her for her time at the rate of fifty dollars an hour so I will be able to claim her conversations with us are privileged. Since we both began with the utmost belief in Cormorant's innocence, it didn't seem particularly necessary; now it does.

Cormorant replaces the cap on the magic marker and adds stiffly, "On the other hand, one thing I haven't mentioned is that before he started writing the book, Damascus asked me more or less to collaborate on it with him."

The hair on the back of my neck begins to stand up. How could I have not figured this out? Trying not to make him defensive, I ask, "Why didn't you tell us?"

Before he can answer, his sister yelps, "Damn, Cormorant, what took you so long?"

Cormorant looks puzzled by our consternation. "It was a long time ago; I blew him off. It wasn't much of a conversation from my point of view. I haven't thought about it until now."

I don't believe him. "What exactly was said and was anybody else in on this conversation?"

Cormorant looks back at his drawing on the easel. "It wasn't a big deal. He just came to my office about three years ago and asked if I'd like to work with him on a history of race relations, focusing on slavery. He said he'd do most of the work, but my name would give the book the credibility it needed to be taken seriously. If I remember the conversation right, he actually said that if it was going to be accepted inside the state, it would need a white historian's name on it and somebody with my reputation. Nobody else was there."

I can see Raven holding her breath, thinking, I imagine, of what that conversation must have been like for Merriweather. It was more important to him that the work get done than who got the credit. She says, "So why didn't you do it? Miller's right. Some of this sounds like you. The part about Clinton and the mind set of the state really does remind me of you."

As if this conversation could not hold his entire attention, Cormorant flips back to a new page and begins to sketch the outline of the state with amazing rapidity. "How many times do I have to say this? Unless you turn the history of slavery into one long gossip column as he did, there's no more work to do on it in

Arkansas. Orville Taylor was as careful and meticulous as any historian could have been. I wasn't going to dignify the Slave Narratives, and I told Damascus that."

I can feel my pulse quickening as I race to what seems like the logical conclusion. "Don't you see? Whether you thought you were or not, you humiliated him, and he must have told Ezekiel, who would like nothing better than to see you convicted."

Raven shakes her head. "The problem with that scenario," she replies, "is that Ezekiel has begun to come off Cormorant as the murderer. What bothers me about this is Cormorant looks worse than ever." She turns to her brother. "It makes you seem more jealous, because your name isn't even mentioned in the acknowledgment section."

Cormorant rolls his eyes and scratches his ear with the opposite end of the magic marker. "I told him I didn't want to see my name within a hundred feet of that book."

I watch Cormorant as he begins to sketch in the St. Francis River which flows in front of their plantation near Helena. For all its alleged deficiencies, the book contains powerful sections of writing, which the reviewers have all noted. Factor in the undeniable truth that the author was writing at breakneck speed to complete it before his death, and any lack of documentation may well be overlooked by sympathetic critics. Though Cormorant is a purist when it comes to history, time has not diminished his ego.

"He must have talked to you a lot about the book, anyway. Dr. Matso said she could hear you arguing over it on more than one occasion."

Cormorant draws two stars surely indicating the locations of our families' respective plantations. "Sure, he did. He knew I was his harshest critic. If he could defend it against me, which he couldn't, he could defend it against anybody."

Across from me, Raven's bosom rises and falls in a sigh. "It just looks bad to me. The more information that comes out about your relationship, the more a jury will wonder if there wasn't some kind of fight."

Ignoring her, Cormorant says to me, "You know, the word 'plantation' is really politically charged, isn't it? The dictionary doesn't associate it with slavery, but that's the first thing that comes to mind. Guilt by association. The American way."

Before I can respond, there is a knock at the door, and Raven introduces our investigator, a man I have spoken to only over the phone. After one false start that cost us a couple of weeks, we are hoping we have the right person. Steve Crisp is a thin black man about six feet tall, who says he has no interest in history, black or otherwise, and has never worked for Ezekiel Merriweather though he has had a prescription filled by him at the Little Rock store. Forty years old, he has worked for a private investigator I used during Laurel's last divorce who vouched for his methods and results but said he was already free-lancing, which doesn't bother me. Cormorant and I shake hands with him, while Raven gets another chair.

"So, you're the professor, huh?" he says easily to Cormorant. "You look like one."

I'm not sure what Cormorant was expecting, but a sad smile spreads across his face as if he is wondering if he will be teaching in prison this fall instead of UALR. "Just call me Cormorant," he says, pumping Crisp's hand. There was a time in our history when Cormorant and I did not shake hands with black men. Nor did they call us by our first names without adding the word 'Mister' in front of it. If Cormorant senses any irony in the situation, I can't tell it.

We engage in some chitchat, mainly to get a feel for this guy since the one we thought we had hired took three hundred dollars and promptly disappeared. My experience, some good, some bad, is mainly with investigators out of Memphis, but as Raven guessed, they have all been white, and we need someone who knows the black community. He tells us he first got interested in his career when working for a nursing home as an aide in college. The white girl working with him for two weeks turned out to be an undercover investigator from the state attorney general's office. "One day she was emptying bedpans," he says, gesturing broadly with his big hands, "and the next she was on tv in heels and a suit with the AG telling reporters how all the patients were practically chained to their beds. I got the bug then."

What I like about Crisp is that he was born and raised in Little Rock and has connections in the black community that nobody white possibly could have. Two years of college in Pine Bluff was all he could stand, but we are not looking for an intellectual to debate Cormorant.

"What do you want out of me?" He asks, his voice betraying impatience though he has remained poised throughout the interview.

I explain to him we are interested in finding out who were Damascus Merriweather's enemies and whether he had any vices that nobody knew about, and I summarize for him what Cormorant has already found out. We give him Waymon Duffy's last known address in hopes he can track him down.

Crisp writes down his assignment on a small notebook he carries in his shirt pocket. "Do you know the names of any of Merriweather's friends?" he asks me.

I look at Cormorant and shrug. "We don't know that."

"Do you know where he likes to hang out?"

Cormorant shoves his hands in his pockets. "I doubt if he goes out that much."

"What makes you think that?" Crisp asks, a smile turning up

the corners of his mouth.

"You should see the library in his house," Cormorant says. "He's not all that young either."

Crisp laughs. "You guys might sit in the house all night and read books, but that doesn't mean everybody else does. You know if he belongs to any clubs?"

I don't know what clubs black men belong to in Little Rock. Irritated by how little we know, I answer, "This is why we're hiring you." I have made a copy of part of the file and hand it to him, reasonably satisfied that we have the right man. Actually, I have no idea whether I am wasting Cormorant's money, but, in truth, the segregated lives that blacks and whites lead in Little Rock leave us little option but to hope Crisp can track something down for us. In Lee County, if I know a man's name, I can make a maximum of five telephone calls and find out what I need, but the greater Little Rock area, depending on how you define it, is upwards of four hundred thousand, big enough to hide in. As I point out to Cormorant after his sister escorts Crisp out thirty minutes later, it is not surprising that we have so little idea of how black people live. For the most part, the races, except in downtown Little Rock, live in parallel universes. They intersect at work, and that is about all.

"I like this guy," Cormorant says as his sister comes back into the room. "He seems sharp. We don't seem to be getting anywhere. Maybe he can."

I glance at Raven, whose lips are pressed together as if she has swallowed something that does not agree with her. Turning back to Cormorant, I say bluntly, "You are beginning to remind me of somebody else I trusted once. Remember Clinton's expression when he said, 'I did not have sexual relations with that woman—Miss Lewinsky,' I was stupid enough to believe the son of a bitch because he looked and acted like he meant it.

Am I being stupid now?"

"No, you're not being stupid," Cormorant says to both of us, his expression serious but not angry as I had feared. "I wouldn't have wanted you to represent me if I were guilty. I couldn't have lied to you."

Despite a little warning bell that has begun to go off regularly these days, I still don't think he can either. Something is rotten in Denmark, but I'll be damned if I think it is Cormorant who's stinking up the place. Somehow, I still can't shake the feeling that it is Damascus who is manipulating us. Perhaps even Ezekiel. I again pick up the file containing the reviews, which, I suppose, are an author's dream. I look at his sister, wondering what she is thinking. After all, she knows him best.

Raven has begun to cry.

7

"Don't you think we're making some progress?"

I nod vigorously at Raven, who is standing in the doorway of my makeshift office with a newspaper under her arm, and then glance down at the calendar she has provided for my desk. June 28, a week into summer. In the last three weeks, thanks in part to Raven, we seem to have our defense efforts finally organized, and I have gotten through to Cormorant that his salvation may well lie in persuading a jury that the Little Rock police screwed up the investigation rather than us being able to actually hand over to the cops Merriweather's killer, though that is not as far-fetched as it once seemed.

For the past twelve days I have walked Palisades Drive from one end to the other in the sweltering heat with a notebook and interrogated residents about what they remember seeing the afternoon of April 21, and, just as importantly, found out if they have been interviewed by the Little Rock Police Department. If we can find just one person who remembers an unidentified vehicle coming through the neighborhood near the time of the murder, it could help enormously. The next best thing will be to find people in the neighborhood whom the police didn't get around to interviewing. Though several residents have been out of town and their stories remain to be checked, so far I have not found any discrepancies in the LRPD's investigation, but all it will take is one person who has a good memory. As quickly as Cormorant was charged, I am convinced we will find something or somebody that was overlooked if we are patient and methodical.

"Are you talking about Duffy or Kennedy's uncle?" I ask Raven. I have a meeting this afternoon with a man who claims to have some information about the boy's uncle. And just last week we turned up Waymon Duffy in the North Little Rock municipal jail on a charge of attempting to pawn stolen property, including Cormorant's missing microwave oven. Whether he has an ironclad alibi for his whereabouts the day of the murder we still don't know, but our spirits have been boosted by his refusal to talk to the cops, which indicates to me that he has a lot more to hide than a few household appliances. I have made a lot of noise over his silence to Minor, who knows he has a problem in Cormorant's case unless he can get Duffy to open up. I would be more than delighted to have Duffy take the 5th Amendment at Cormorant's trial. I have a secret hope that Duffy will confess to the murder in time for us to celebrate the dismissal of the charges against Cormorant at our annual 4th of July party in Jeffersonville next week.

"I was really thinking about the media coverage and the reaction to it," Raven says, handing me a copy of the weekly *North Little Rock Times* turned back to the editorial page. "If letters to the editor mean anything, at least people north of the river are getting sick of the Merriweather brothers. This is what I've wanted to happen all over Pulaski County."

I silently track the first part of a letter by a man named Kendall Arcineau, who professes to be mystified by the continuing outside interest in Merriweather's book and the trial. I read aloud the part I know Raven wanted me to see. *Merriweather's book and his subsequent murder are merely the latest excuses for east coast intellectuals to continue to bash Arkansans when, in fact, they have just as many Wal-Marts and bad politicians as we do. The hypocrisy is enough to make you gag.* I put down the paper and smile encouragingly at Raven, who earlier today made a presentation to do some work for the city of Little Rock and is still dressed for the occasion in a tailored blue business suit that makes her look professional and sexy at the same time. "Wouldn't he make a great jury foreman?"

Raven passes by me and stations herself by the window overlooking Louisiana and peers down into the street. "What this man is expressing is the pent-up frustration repeated criticism engenders," she says. "You eventually want to take it out on somebody."

Yet I wonder if it is her own frustration she is talking about. I watch her carefully. Raven admitted to me one night this week that she has begun to experience again the severe mood swings that used to plague her regularly until she got out of the serial marriage business. I tried to reassure her that as much as she cares about Cormorant, her reaction is normal. There have been times recently when she has seemed on the verge of telling me something, but has held back. Because we have known each other so long, I'm aware that Raven has had her own battles with issues of self-esteem, primarily, I think, because Miss Ella, her mother, was appalled by her daughter's aggressiveness and regularly told her she was growing up to be a lesbian, which, Raven laughingly says now would have saved her a lot of trouble. Her three marriages, in retrospect, seem like long battles in a war that may not yet be over. Despite her success, Cormorant's ordeal appears to have awakened her old insecurities. "You've been right on the money so far," I acknowledge.

"If Cormorant weren't such a lightning rod," Raven says unhappily, "this would be a lot easier. Aren't you afraid he's going to self-destruct on the witness stand?"

"He's learning fast," I say, thinking about the dozen or so interviews I've had with UALR professors and students from names he has given me. "I think at first he was in denial, which is understandable. If you're innocent, a murder charge is probably like being told by your doctor you have to quit smoking or you're going to die. At first you can't make yourself believe how serious it is. He knows now what he has to do. One way or another," I say, getting up, thinking I need to get on out to that bar on the strip that divides Pulaski and Saline Counties, "we're going to have the last laugh in this case. I can feel it in my bones."

"I think so, too," she says, turning to me with a hopeful look on her face. "Let me come with you. I've got some time now."

I shake my head. The man I am meeting wouldn't open his mouth around a woman like Raven, and I am doubtful that he is going to talk to me. For the past six weeks we have been unsuccessfully trying to find out something about the membership of "The Resurrection," a group reportedly devoted to establishing a white nation within the Ozark Mountains of Arkansas and Missouri. However, the information that Rafe Kennedy's uncle is supposedly an officer in this organization has been impossible so far to pin down. Doubtless the F.B.I. has a file a foot thick on it, but my requests for information from a variety of sources have come to nothing. Our best lead has come not from the Ozarks but from a contact in Lee County. An old bankruptcy client of mine (known by the unfortunate nickname of "Cuckoo" Watson) with views similar to this group has made some phone calls resulting in this interview. Though he has not said it in so many words, I suspect his son used to be a member and has arranged this meeting. I tell Raven I will see her at the house later this evening and head out into the heat.

As I drive west toward the small community of Alexander on

I-30, I take off my tie, thinking I don't want to come off looking like some yuppie Little Rock lawyer who has wandered off the main drag looking for trouble. I don't really know what is going on with Raven, but I am pleased with Cormorant's attitude. In Laurel's words, he has to get his hands dirty, too, and he has gone back through his recent classes for names of students whom he flunked or pissed off. And though none of my interviews at UALR have resulted in a particular suspect other than Kennedy, Carole Matso's characterization of Cormorant as inspiring fear mixed with awe has been reinforced repeatedly. As a historical gatekeeper, my old friend is a tough nut to crack and gives offense easily and often. As a result, I am convinced these meetings have been worth the time they took.

I find the Dark Room with little difficulty. Within sight of the interstate, it is a nondescript hole in the wall, but the big Confederate flag above the bar gets my attention. I have been mysteriously told by Cuckoo that I don't need to ask for anybody. Since it is only five in the afternoon, the long bar is deserted except for a couple of guys in the middle identically dressed in boots, jeans, tee-shirts, and baseball caps with Arkansas Razorback insignia. They are drinking draft beer, and I order the same from a man who squints at me as if I am not quite speaking English. The beer, Miller Lite, tastes good. I look around to get my bearings and spy a couple of pool tables off to the right by a juke box playing an eerily familiar song by the "Doors," and all I need is some marijuana and combat boots to drop off thirty-five years. Fifteen minutes later the bar begins to fill up. A couple of women in their thirties in shorts come in together as well as more men in jeans, and it is apparent I am the only stranger. I am about to decide to leave when one of the two men who have been there all along sidles over to me and says, "You're Miller Holly, aren't you?"

"Yes, sir." Automatically, I hold out my hand, but it is not taken, and feeling foolish, I rest my knuckles on the bar like an unwanted used car being sold at an auction of junkers.

"I understand you're looking for somebody," the man says, his voice not unfriendly, and I am tempted to hope that in the dim gloom of this almost windowless establishment he just didn't notice my hand.

"Well, I'm more interested in learning something about him," I say, wondering if I am looking into the eyes of Kennedy's uncle. Whoever this is, his face, now that I can see it better, is hard and unforgiving. "Are you any kin to the Watsons in Lee County?" I ask, hoping to turn this encounter into an exchange that doesn't resemble dialogue from a bad spy movie.

My contact is having none of it. "I'm not particularly a friend of the guy you're looking for," he says, his voice still neutral, "but I've got some news for you."

For an instant I am tempted to put down my beer and turn around and walk out. This all seems too silly, but the signs are that I've walked into another world out here, one that has nothing to do with what is going on in Little Rock just twenty minutes away. "What is it?"

The man leans against the bar and says from the side of his mouth, "Don't try to pin this on the Kennedy kid. His uncle is a rough customer, and so is the group he belongs to."

I am glad Cormorant is not here to make some sarcastic retort. If this man weren't so serious, it would be funny, but, in fact, it is not. On this guy's waist is a sheath with a knife in it. The Dark Room is not the sort of place that asks its customers to pass through a metal scan, and I wonder what other weapon he may be carrying. I have not been involved in a fight since high school, and not only do I feel out of place but effete as well in my white cotton shirt, black-wing tip shoes, and suit pants. "The problem," I say, trying not to sound ironical, "is that I have a client to represent, and Rafe Kennedy admits finding the body of the man my client is alleged to have shot."

As if he is talking to a child instead of someone twenty years older, the man says patiently, "Believe me, you don't want to mess with these people. I hear Rafe told his uncle he didn't do it. I'd accept that if I were you."

I feel the hair on my back of my neck begin to prickle. This is like talking to a wall. "Can you tell me just a little about the group?" I ask, keeping my voice low. For all I know, the annual stockholder meeting may be about to start. "How big is it? When did it get started? Have any of its members been convicted of anything?"

For the first time, the man almost smiles or perhaps it is a sneer. "My Dad said you would be like this. I'm trying to help you not get yourself killed, Mr. Holly. The less you know the better."

So his father *is* Cuckoo Watson. I feel relieved to know that much, though it isn't doing me much good. "That isn't generally the way lawyers work," I respond, no longer able to keep sarcasm from my voice.

"Let me walk you out to your car," he says firmly. "All these people know is that you're the lawyer defending that professor accused of killing the nigger who wrote that book. They're not interested in you stirring up trouble."

Cuckoo's son is not asking me now; he's telling. I take out a five and leave it on the bar and with him by my side head for the front door to the strains of Bruce Springsteen's "Born in the U.S.A." Though he does not try to take my arm, I cannot resist the feeling that I am being publicly humiliated and know my face is scalded red. Maybe there will come a day when I will be grateful to Cuckoo's son, but it won't be any time soon. Outside, he speaks to a man twice my size. The guy, all duded up in a biker's outfit, replies warmly but unintelligibly. "You could have saved me a trip," I complain when I get to the Olds.

The other man touches my shoulder for the first time. "You would have snooped around on your own," he says gruffly, "and somebody would have felt like he had to teach you a lesson. Now, that we're out here, I can tell you this much. If somebody from the Resurrection had wanted to take out that professor, they wouldn't go through a kid. When they finally do something, it won't be one person at a time."

For just a moment, I can hear in his voice the paranoia of a lieutenant in a paramilitary organization that is waiting for the signal to begin the Apocalypse. I can't tell whether he is merely pretending not to be a member, but, judging by the gleam in his eye, I would bet he is. Despite being certain it won't make it back to the Dark Room, I hand him a card as if he were a reluctant witness to a car accident. "I'd appreciate it if you'd call me if you get any information you're willing to share."

Cukoo's son shrugs and without another word heads back towards the bar. I drive back toward Little Rock on Highway 5 instead of the Interstate, wondering how long my investigator Steve Crisp would have lasted in the Dark Room. As I hit traffic streaming out of Little Rock, I have the feeling Watson was telling me the truth. I know I have gone as far as I can without assistance from law enforcement, and what would that be? It is not a crime to have an uncle who is preparing for Armageddon. Yet even if it will be something to raise at the trial, it is unsettling to encounter the hatred and potential violence that lies just beneath the surface of daily life. I have the uneasy feeling I am fooling myself that we are "making progress" in this case.

"Do you think Cormorant and Beth will come?" I ask Laurel as I sweep off the deck in preparation for our annual 4th of July party. "He swore yesterday they would, but I think he's a little worried about the reception they'll get."

It is almost six, and guests will begin to arrive at any moment. As usual, we will eat on the tables under the trees and have them serve their plates from here. It is pot luck as usual. We expect only around thirty this year. In the fifties, my parents planned for over a hundred and spent two days roasting pork over a fiery pit behind their house just west of here in a scene that was positively medieval. Family lore holds that these Holly 4th of July celebrations were interrupted only by the Civil War but promptly resumed when Arkansas passed the 14th Amendment and rejoined the country on June 22, 1868, in time to celebrate that year. Though I have trouble imagining what the earlier picnics must have really been like, my memories of my parents' parties, I realize now, are idealized. Before the civil rights movement, before drugs, before Vietnam, they were celebratory of life when it seemed more innocent. In the last quarter of a century, our parties have come to seem more like wakes. Now, it is easier to call ahead and order barbecue from the family of Walter Jones, a black man who has been famous in Marianna for decades for his sauce. To Laurel nothing illustrates better what is happening to our lives than our annual party. We've tried inviting the deserters, but they now have their own gatherings, and it is generally cooler in places like Mountain Home on the 4th of July than the Delta. Perhaps as a way of emphasizing our personal stake in the exodus, Laurel refuses to invite the few new people who move into Marianna, and so these parties have come to resemble "last man clubs."

"Sure, they will," she replies, wiping off a table beside me. "They know they'll be with friends."

"Mostly, I guess," I mutter. It is not so clear that every one will feel that way. "I hear Ted and Ann blame Cormorant for the book being so popular. I got an earful from Clay this morning."

Laurel, dressed patriotically in white sandals, blue shorts, and a red blouse, pats her right temple, which is moist from the heat and humidity. "I suspect there's more than one person," she says dryly, "who wishes Cormorant had never been born."

Ted's family has gotten a couple of pages in Merriweather's book, which quoted extensively from a letter by Ted's great-great-grandfather that turned up in a probate file in which he acknowledged he had fathered a daughter by a slave woman in 1850. Her descendants, who have lived in St. Francis County since the Civil War, are quoted in Merriweather's book as saying the story passed down in their family was that she had been forced regularly to have sex with him against her will. Ted has denied even the authenticity of the letter, though according to Merriweather it had been admitted into evidence in Phillips County probate court. "They're probably just frustrated by all the publicity," I say, having known and admired Ted's family, including his brothers and sisters, for the way they have persevered through hard times. "After all, despite the fact that he visits as often as he does, Cormorant hasn't lived here for over thirty years. I can see why they wouldn't be all that sympathetic."

Laurel looks up at the sound of the first car arriving, and I follow her gaze. It looks like Cissy and Chan Henderson's Pontiac. Since Laurel's outburst on the deck on our anniversary more than a month ago, she has read Orville Taylor's book and insisted that I read it, too. "Ted," she says, "would never admit Merriweather was right in a million years."

I bend over to pick up a dime that is wedged in the corner. "I don't think I would either," I reply. "That section of Merriweather's book is by far the least compelling. If everyone he wrote about had submitted to DNA testing, maybe he could have proved something, but right now it's just hand-me-down gossip."

Laurel hands me the rag she was using. "Not if you're Kendra Davis and her family," she says archly before heading into the house to open the door for Cissy and Chan. "It's part of your family history. And, of course, that was Merriweather's point, too. If a white wrote something down, it became trustworthy. If it came from the lips of a black person, it wasn't worth mentioning."

I bite my lip to keep from yelling after her that family histories are just as full of falsehood as anything else. Just a week ago we had a bitter argument over Taylor's book, which she said vindicated what Merriweather said in his. According to Laurel, Orville Taylor's book is what Merriweather claimed: history written by a white man for white men to feel better about themselves. I doubt whether she truly believes what she is saying, but she is sticking to it. I have argued repeatedly that Cormorant is right: we don't know what actually happened and will never know. She insists we know more than we will ever admit.

In the Hendersons' back seat are Nancy and Sam Cheek, and within ten minutes of their arrival, all four approach me separately and ask if I think Cormorant will be convicted. None of them has been particularly close to Cormorant, but Sam adds, "It's so obviously a setup that it's a joke he was charged."

I open a Rolling Rock for Sam and hand it to him. At the 1972 picnic and with Laurel's consent, I invited two black couples (I was still in my idealistic phase) and had to retract their invitations when Sam organized a boycott that would have left us with about sixteen guests. "Who do you think set him up?" I ask, curious about what he will say. Sam has a law degree, but he went straight to the bank as a trust officer and has never practiced a day.

"Hell, that damn brother of his," Sam says angrily after knocking back half of the bottle in one thirsty gulp. "That son of a bitch is a state-of-the-art demagogue. Can you imagine our fathers putting up with this kind of crap?"

I smile at Nancy, who was in my class all thirteen years in Marianna, including kindergarten. Awkward as a child, she is said now to have the best golf swing, man or woman, in the Arkansas Delta. I can still remember the day she whispered to me that Sam had wanted to kill me for inviting niggers. She said she personally wouldn't have cared. "They lived in a different time all right," I reply noncommittally, not wanting to argue with Sam who, like me, probably started drinking around noon. At least he has that reputation on holidays. Earlier in the morning I had been paired with Sam's thirty-year-old son in a golf tournament at the country club. It is too small a town to stay mad at your friends.

Cormorant and Beth drive up around seven as the party is getting in full swing and are immediately treated like celebrities. Laurel is right: they *are* among friends, and Cormorant is in his element, telling an attentive audience seated among the tables that Damascus Merriweather was an intellectual charlatan who wrote a modern-day *Uncle Tom's Cabin*. If anyone besides Laurel has any doubts, they do not voice them, for this is a celebration by those of us who feel a need to close ranks even more than usual. Cormorant, proclaims Dub Dilday, who farms three thousand acres in northern Lee County, his beard dripping barbecue sauce, is a victim of a conspiracy by the NAACP. I glance at Laurel, who in the past might well have agreed with this assessment, and notice she has been holding the same glass of wine since the party began. She knows what alcohol will do to her tongue.

Later, after we go inside to escape the mosquitoes and humidity, I caution Cormorant not for the first time that everything he says is grist for the prosecutor's mill, but tonight he is like a politician who has returned to his roots, greeting and hugging friends and acquaintances who haven't seen him since he was charged. If we could have the trial here, all of us could stop worrying.

At his side every step of the way is Beth, who has worn a colorful gypsy skirt and silk blouse, which makes her overdressed in this deliberately casual group who have the money to doll up when they wish, but as Laurel has said, it is Beth's way of saying she doesn't belong here any longer. Though carefully made-up, even Beth can't hold back the clock, but I can tell from their faces that at least the men in the room consider her the most attractive woman present or maybe they know she could have chosen any of them and are wondering what it would have been like.

It is impossible to keep the conversation away from the book, and not unexpectedly, Ted, who is still farming today because of the bankruptcy laws, asks me what kind of recourse someone would have against a book like Merriweather's.

Cormorant, sitting directly across from me, fixes me with a stare that says he is equally interested in my answer. Not the only lawyer in the room, I glance at Dave Potts and Lawrence Tabor, but they both nod deferentially as if it is my place to deal with this question. I suspect that Ted has talked to both of them, and neither of them thinks he has a case. Until relatively recently, libel was a much easier proposition in Arkansas because the defamed person didn't have to prove actual damages. Injury could be assumed, but in a recent opinion, the Arkansas Supreme Court caught us up with the rest of the country and prospectively announced the rule has changed.

Before I can reply, Ted says harshly, "They can't say somebody was raped when they don't know a damn thing about it, can they? We're talking about my family's honor here. We've been here as many generations as anybody in this county, and I'll be damned if I'm gonna let some nigger get away with an accusation like that."

Individual conversations have come to a halt all over the room.

If only by omission, Ted has publicly acknowledged for the first time that his great-great-grandfather had fathered a child by a slave, a concession I find rather amazing given Ted's feelings about blacks, which are as extreme as anyone's here. "As far as I know," I say cautiously, "we've never had a libel case like this that has made it to the appellate level in Arkansas. Though in theory you could bring suit, you have to be careful, because my recollection of the book is that Merriweather only says her family has repeated her family's story from generation to generation. He doesn't come right out and say she *was* raped."

Besides driving his tractors, Ted works on them, too, and from my seat on the couch beside Laurel, I can see the oil and grease under his fingernails, though he is wearing clean khakis and a red pullover shirt that doesn't have a wrinkle in it. "He might as well," he complains. "That's what he means. Hell, they were property; you couldn't rape them."

I glance at Laurel who gives me a knowing smile, and I say hastily to Ted, "We can talk about this next week if you want."

Ted, who now knows none of the lawyers present want to help him, nods brusquely and stomps off into the kitchen. For different reasons, Merriweather's book is troubling a number of us, and as the party starts to wind down around ten, I find myself listening closely to a conversation Cormorant is having with Midge Weaver, who teaches history at Lee Academy, our private school. Midge, whose physician husband Ned died last year from lung cancer, asks Cormorant if he agrees with Merriweather's prediction at the end of his book.

"Which one?" Cormorant asks carelessly, his tone relaxed and thick with Wild Turkey. "He makes several."

It has been, if not a triumphant night for Cormorant, an evening in which he has been consoled as a martyr. As if she has been waiting for this conversation, Laurel reaches behind us to the bookshelf and and hands our copy to Midge, who is rich enough to move anywhere but clings to the Delta because her sons Ed and Casey are two of the largest farmers in Lee County.

"This one," she says and begins to read in her best schoolteacher's voice: *Were it not for the federal government, African-Americans living in Arkansas would have no rights today in the Delta, and when, as inevitably it will be, federal protection is again withdrawn, as it was after Reconstruction ended in 1875, African-Americans will once more be subjected to the systematic discrimination and brutality they have always endured at the hands of white Arkansans. Because they will not come to terms with their behavior during slavery, white Arkansans cannot come to terms with the rest of the state's racial history: an unrelieved story of intimidation and lynchings (Arkansas was third in the nation in 1917), economic exploitation, and official and unofficial discrimination which resulted in the treatment of African-Americans as a caste distinct as the "Untouchables" in India. The shame and guilt white Arkansans bear has long been transmogrified into contempt for their victims' powerlessness and indifference to their humanity. Because they will not come to terms with their own historical guilt, white Arkansans have given themselves no choice but to consider black Arkansans inherently inferior. In their minds and hearts they must continue to insist that black Arkansans are not their intellectual and moral equals; to do otherwise would open wide the questions about their past treatment. Today, political correctness dictates that each race wear a mask. Some day, perhaps very soon, the masks will again drop from our faces.* Midge stops and looks up, and realizes that all of us are listening. She says to Cormorant, "What do you think he means?"

Cormorant, who has had his eyes closed as if he were listening to a student recite her lessons, now opens them and replies calmly, "Every group in society with an axe to grind sooner or later stoops to this form of psychologizing and then tries to dignify it by calling it historical analysis. Instead of analysis, Damascus allowed himself to indulge in the politics of *resentiment* that Nietzsche so brilliantly identified in *The Genealogy of Morals.* I told him when this book was still in manuscript form that every loser in the history of the world tries to make the winner feel guilt for having triumphed over them."

Midge, whose rough, sunburned face belies her status as a long-ago honors graduate from Southwestern and the closest thing we have to an intellectual in Marianna, presses the book against her chest as if she were a mother silencing an unruly child, and sighs before replying, "It sounds as if he is saying that unless white Southerners experience some form of primal collective guilt, we will never resolve the problems of race. Wasn't the last sentence a threat?"

Patting her knee paternalistically in a gesture reminiscent of her late husband, Cormorant replies, "Remember during the boycott when we thought there might be a race war? We've always overrated their capacity to act together. It's just basically a war of words."

I listen carefully, wondering if this part of the book was not a warning to Cormorant. Because of Cormorant's honesty, Damascus saw him with his mask removed. Did he in turn remove his own at some point in their relationship? It flashes in my mind that Cormorant never really took Damascus seriously and probably never believed the book would be published.

Martin Spain, a CPA who has testified for me as an expert more than once, asks Cormorant if he thinks that Merriweather's book doesn't wildly exaggerate the predicted effects of a withdrawal of the federal commitment to civil rights. "There's always been a bunch of liberals in Little Rock," he says, hissing the word *liberals* as if it were a synonym for communists, "who are just as bad as the North."

Cormorant shakes his head. "No, actually that's not true. There's a crowd in Little Rock who get together every few years and pat themselves on the backs for opposing Faubus during the Little Rock Central crisis, but hell, they weren't liberals, and they weren't even moderates as they like to make themselves out. They just wanted to get the schools open. Most of them didn't care about civil rights and would have been more than happy to delay desegregation for another century. There was a total of one liberal on that School Board, by the name of Ted Lamb, and he promptly got run off. But every time they tell the story, they become more saintlike. There're very few liberals in Little Rock or in the state who *have* or ever *had* any power. It doesn't really matter. You can't keep people from privatizing everything that matters to them, and that's what's happening."

Laurel, who has played the efficient hostess as usual, smiles at Midge as if this exchange were merely idle chitchat, and reaches for Merriweather's book. "Do you mind?"

Her hand shaking either from age or emotion, Midge gives it up, and Laurel opens the book from the back. "You don't think we need a South Africa type 'Arkansas Truth and Reconciliation Commission' as Merriweather proposes?" she challenges Cormorant and then begins to read from the last page before he can answer. *There can be no hope of understanding present-day race relations in our state until Arkansas whites accept that their version of the past is only part of the story and until they want to know the truth. Some of it can be found in the Slave Narratives; some of it resides in the untold or whispered stories in our communities both black and white; tragically, much of it lies beneath the ground, never to be known. Do Arkansans want reconciliation, or are we too weary of each other to care?"*

Not taking her seriously, Cormorant rolls his eyes and mutters sarcastically, "That's what we need all right. I'd be called as the first witness, and after I denied I shot Merriweather, they'd charge me with perjury and lock me up for good."

Yawning so hard that it makes my jaw ache to watch, Davis Yarborough, who set the Marianna shot put record when we were in school, says, "What I care about is some black buying across the street from me and chopping the house into apartments and renting to five families who are living on SSI checks."

I have always had a soft spot in my heart for Davis, whose career as an offensive lineman for the Chicago Bears was cut short by a knee injury in the sixties. Afterwards, he came back to Marianna and watched helplessly as one business venture after another failed including a car wash, restaurant, laundry, and hardware store. Now, he runs a gas station on the way out of town on Highway 79. Liked by both races, he served as mayor two years ago. As power shifts to the blacks, he probably has seen his last term.

"I heard the Parsonses only got twenty thousand dollars last week," Betty Rich chimes in from the couch. "That was a beautiful house once."

"At least it didn't go to one of *them*," Dotty Thompson sighs. "We were really worried, but T. J. went on and took it, though I heard Jessica wanted to keep it on the market and would have sold it to anybody."

As the conversation continues in this vein, the party begins to runs out of gas. As long as my friends vent about Merriweather's book, they stay energized, but as so often happens these days, the worry about property values and the future brings them back to reality and turns the mood gloomy. We have been beaten down too long to believe Merriweather's prediction that whites can gain control again in Marianna. As people begin to leave, I think about Sam's comment about our fathers. In fact, they *were* dinosaurs, but they didn't know it because they didn't recognize the end was coming for their way of life.

The party ends as suddenly as it began, and the prospect for a confrontation between Cormorant and Laurel disappears as quickly as it arose. Only twenty minutes from his father's house on the "low road" to Helena, Beth and Cormorant could stay, but they are out the door with the others. I promise to call him this week, and he waves perfunctorily as if it doesn't matter. Tonight, he doesn't want to think about who will have the last word.

While we are cleaning up, I ask Laurel what she thought of the party, and when she merely shrugs, I add, "Merriweather's book has made most of them more paranoid than usual," I say, rinsing the smell of bourbon from a glass. "Ted will find somebody who will sue for him, but I'm not fooling with it. He ought to just forget it."

"I guess I've been converted," she says ripping off a section of aluminum foil and covering a plate of meat with it. "I never used to believe in the idea of collective guilt, but if you can feel pride in the past, you can feel guilt, too. Just because we won't deal with it doesn't let us off the hook."

I should be more amazed at this transformation of my wife's beliefs, but it has been coming for weeks. Collective guilt! What good can it possibly do? I can't imagine that Ezekiel Merriweather wants reconciliation, and at this point I can't believe Damascus wanted it either. He wanted us to wallow in humiliation. I feel my face growing as hot as the dish water. Usually, a couple of Laurel's friends stay to help clean up, but tonight Carolyn Mayo went home early with a headache, and Daisy Tedford called to say she and Bob couldn't come. "Why didn't you say so?" I ask. "I'm surprised you didn't."

"You heard how Cormorant talked to Midge," Laurel says, handing back to me a spoon that doesn't meet her standards of cleanliness. "He's become so defensive that it's hard to tell him apart from mossbacks like Ted any more. He's scared to death."

The truth of this remark sinks home as I think of his bombastic performance tonight.

In his own way, Cormorant now seems to be no different from our fathers who both long past any reality repeated the mantra of states' rights. As Laurel has just intimated, Cormorant's denunciation of Merriweather's book sounds increasingly shrill. No longer does he sound like the academic who took the book apart on scholarly grounds. Tonight, he sounded for a moment like an old-fashioned Southern demagogue. Raven's strategy of converting this case into a public relations war will have to be implemented soon, for Cormorant, I realize, has begun to hide his fear beneath a grandiose bravado. It isn't an attitude that will impress a jury. "I wish Raven had come," I respond. "I wonder what she thinks. She knows him better than anybody."

Laurel asks, swiftly putting away the silverware, "Why didn't she?"

Our regular weekly meeting is in two days. Out of town on business, she has missed the last two. "She had a party in Little Rock."

"Is she afraid to show her face around me?" Laurel asks, her voice brittle. "You're not sleeping with her, are you?"

I turn from the sink to see her face, but she is behind me, putting leftovers in the refrigerator. "No, I'm not," I say evenly. "Would you like for me to start staying in a motel when I spend the night in Little Rock? I will."

She replies, her back still to me, "No, I'm just talking crazy, but I'll be so glad when this summer is over."

I can tell from her voice she is crying, but I know from experience that she does not want me to touch her right now. "I will, too," I assure her. "I will, too."

8

"Your Honor," I begin on July 20th at the omnibus hearing to move trial preparation along, "we have an expert witness available to inspect the crime scene, but the prosecutor seems to have some difficulty with that." Actually, it is not Minor Latting who is resisting but Ezekiel Merriweather. "We don't plan to do any testing; I just want him to be able to go through the house and the grounds."

Minor stands up and gestures at Ezekiel, who is sitting in the second row of the courtroom. "Your Honor, I feel obliged to point out to the court on behalf of Mr. Merriweather that he objects to another tour of the house. The defendant and his lawyer have already been through once."

Knowing he cannot win this argument—and he does not—Minor barely goes through the motions, but Ezekiel has continued to command attention in the case as the national media have begun to show the interest that Raven expected. Though he has not appeared on *Oprah*, a reporter from CNN interviewed Ezekiel last week and called Little Rock "a troubled community that appears to be haunted by its racial past." For his part, Ezekiel was somewhat muted, but continued to plug his brother's book as "the truth about slavery."

As expected, our motion is granted, and I continue, not having forewarned Minor this was coming. "Your Honor, the defense moves for a change of venue. Because of the pre-trial publicity this case is generating, my client cannot get a fair trial in Little Rock. Since the death of Damascus Merriweather, his brother, Ezekiel Merriweather, has appeared on Little Rock television stations, counting rebroadcasts, more than twenty times and this case has been covered nonstop by the local print media." I point to the mound of material in a box on the table Raven's secretary has prepared for introduction as an exhibit. "Even before charges were filed, Ezekiel Merriweather was appearing on television calling for the arrest of a professor at UALR, and though these interviews have slacked off, the book that Damascus Merriweather published shortly before his death and which has generated enormous publicity locally is inextricably linked to my client in the public's mind since he was a colleague of Dr. Merriweather's."

I continue in this vein for another ten minutes, deliberately omitting mention of the favorable reviews the book has received outside the state. My press conference afterwards will deal with that. As I sit down, I glance over my shoulder at Raven, who is on the third row by herself. Last night as we were preparing the exhibit for the hearing, we agreed that it is highly unlikely Cato will grant a change of venue and, in fact, we do not want him to do so, since it is the locals who feel the most beleaguered by the state's most recent negative publicity. My research shows that Cato has never granted a motion for a change of venue, so it is a safe bet he won't in this case. Though it feels cynical to file a motion we don't expect or want to be granted, I have come to agree with Raven that there is no other way of dealing with Ezekiel's ability to keep the media interested in the book and his brother's death.

As expected, Minor lets a deputy respond on his behalf, arguing that the state can show that Ezekiel Merriweather has recently questioned publicly whether the defendant is his brother's killer, and that in any event, the prosecutor should be given time to respond to our motion. Clearly irritated that I have waited until now to file this motion, Cato, of course, sets a new hearing date, and I turn over the materials to Minor himself, who is pissed I didn't tell him this was coming when we shook hands this morning. I would have preferred to have kept this case confined to the courtroom, but as Raven continues to remind me, the media's ability to be everywhere at once has changed forever the practice of law for the trial attorney. *Every lawyer who has a high-profile case should be required to take Public Relations 101 before he sets foot in a courtroom,* Raven told me last night for the third time since the trial began. When I protested to her that I had not really expected this case to become a battle of the press agents, she professed to be amused. *Then why was I the first person you called?*

I didn't have an answer, not a good one.

Once outside the court house, I say briskly to the assembled reporters, "I'd like to make an additional point that I didn't make in my argument to Judge Cato this morning."

Raven has tipped off the local stations that they should cover the hearing. Usually, omnibus hearings produce little in the way of news, but as if on cue, Dana Sanders from Channel 7 signals her camera person and shoves her microphone in my face. I try to seem casual, but the timing of this moment was a product of intense discussion between Raven and me. She argued that it may be too soon for this tactic and that we should send up a trial balloon to see if the local media is ready to bite. If we get no response, we should wait until closer to trial. I said that if we waited until the eve of trial to file a motion for a change of venue, my remarks at a later press conference would not be taken seriously, and would be seen as totally a public relations gesture. She conceded the point.

Looking directly into the camera, I say firmly, "The difficulty in this case is not so much yet the reaction inside the state but the inevitable pressure being brought to bear by those who see this case as another opportunity to bash Arkansans." I wave the stack of reviews in front of the camera as if it were a newly discovered piece of evidence. "Nearly every one of these is a glowing review of Dr. Merriweather's book, and as those of you in the media already know, nearly every one of them takes a shot at the state. Wittingly or unwittingly, we have become the nation's whipping boy once again, and it is my client who will pay the price if the jury in his case allows itself to provide a scapegoat."

Beside me, Cormorant, who has a new Razorback red bow tie for the occasion, stiffens, but as his sister and I have implored, he resists the urge to push me out of the way and commandeer the cameras. He has reservations about this strategy, but Raven and I have convinced him that the climate surrounding his trial will be just as important as the jurors themselves. As Raven pointed out to him yesterday in a dress rehearsal that lasted until ten last night, the public's emotions of love and hate grind exceedingly fine. As if I had planted this question in advance, Barry Clark of Channel 4 dutifully asks, "Do you have an example of what you're talking about?"

"Certainly," I say, and pull the review from the *Washington Post* off the top of the stack. "I won't read the entire piece, but listen to this paragraph. *Like a bad penny, the state of Arkansas keeps returning to the nation's attention. We have begun to suspect the state's problems are, as the author of this unflinching study suggests, all of a piece: first, slavery, lynchings, and segregation, followed by the 1957 integration crisis at Central High School in Little Rock, then the debacle of the Clinton Presidency, and now the murder of an African-American history professor who has written a book exposing longstanding character defects that seem embedded in the psyches of the insiders that control the state."*

I slap the paper against my hand and slide my voice into a higher register as Raven has coached me. "It is no secret to us that historically, Arkansans, like the rest of the South, have long been regarded with unrelenting contempt born of arrogance during the era Arkansas was a slave-holding state and which has continued unabated through the Clinton Presidency. Most unfortunately for my client, Dr. Merriweather's book, regardless of its intent, further inflames the nation's prejudice against us, instead of dampening it, as evidenced by these reviews. It is my fervent hope that if this case is tried in Little Rock, we can find a jury that will refuse to allow itself to be bullied by northern and east-coast intellectuals into blaming a local critic, which is precisely the extent of Dr. Ashley's involvement in this case."

Vickie Thomas from Channel 11 thrusts her square chin into the air and asks suspiciously, "In filing this motion today, aren't you blaming the media?"

Raven, who played Vickie Thomas in our dress rehearsal last night, anticipated this question as well, and I answer, "Not at all. All I am trying to do is see that when Dr. Ashley walks into a courtroom on September 9th, the jury isn't already looking for a victim to offer up to the nation to show that we are civilized down here. I simply want what every criminal defense attorney wants and is entitled to: a presumption of innocence."

Barry Clark tries to give our motion a racial spin by suggesting, "Are you saying the prosecutor charged your client because he was a convenient white male?"

Involuntarily, I glance at Raven and see a smile of satisfaction on her face, because this is the question she wanted them to ask most of all. I turn back to Clark and say, "Our motion to change venue isn't about race, but that is precisely what outsiders would like to see this case become, and this is exactly what we are determined to prevent. The people who are writing these reviews want nothing more than to reduce Arkansans to worn-out Southern stereotypes, in which we are still portrayed in the most elemental terms and which bear no relation to reality. We are determined not to try this case in the media, but I began Dr. Ashley's defense almost two months ago by suggesting that the relationship between him and Dr. Merriweather was collegial, nonadversarial. That does not mean they were friends or that they didn't have real disagreements over history. They did, and that will be freely admitted at trial.

"What I am suggesting is that Dr. Ashley's trial must not be influenced by how outsiders insist on portraying Arkansans. As anybody who has lived in Arkansas realizes, we are far too sensitive and concerned with our public image, but, in truth, we know from these reviews what the nation thinks. We are still Dogpatch and Daisy Mae, moonshiners and hillbillies, rednecks and welfare moms, good ole boys and trailer trash. Little Rock is portrayed as a place where tractor trailers are backed up to the State Capitol so legislators can more easily haul off the loot. We are at liberty to debate these characterizations to our hearts' content. Indeed, it is the job of historians to debate the truth about the past and come to their own conclusions. No one disputes this, but the truth today is that Arkansas is under attack, not a new situation to be sure. My job is not to defend the state, but to defend Dr. Ashley and make sure he gets a fair trial. Because of the ferocity of these attacks, and the publicity resulting from Dr. Merriweather's book, I do not think Dr. Ashley can get a fair trial in Little Rock."

I hold up my hand to signal I will not answer any further questions, and we move through the crowd of reporters to Raven's Lexus waiting across the street.

"Good job," Raven whispers as she speeds us away from the

court house. "You said just enough."

"Shades of Orval Faubus," Cormorant chuckles, having kept his own mouth shut, a remarkable feat.

I look back at the gaggle of reporters, and think sadly how easy it is to become a demagogue in this country. All you need is a microphone and a camera. In the fifties, nobody was better at stirring the passions of the public than the governor of Arkansas. I wonder if that is what I have become. Even as conservative as they were, my parents were appalled by Faubus's pandering to those elements who viewed race-baiting as an acceptable tactic. "It's not quite the same thing," I mutter, defensively.

Ever the historian, my oldest friend gives me a knowing smile. I know now that he did not want to travel down this road and had he been allowed by to take my place in front of the cameras, he would have intellectualized it. But even that would have amounted to a form of demagoguery. It so happens I am much better at it.

Taking her eyes off the road, Raven twists her head around to her brother in the back seat as she turns on Markham and drives by the Old State House, where Arkansas voted to secede from the country and asks, "You want to be acquitted, don't you?"

Cormorant fusses with his bow tie. "Yes," he says through clenched teeth. "I want to be acquitted."

In the next month Raven arranges for me to give a variation of the press conference in the form of a speech three more times and makes sure that there is media coverage for each event. In succession I speak at the Jacksonville Lions Club, a Kiwanis Club in west Little Rock, and then on August 20th, the downtown Little Rock Rotary Club, whose invitation, according to Raven, means I am striking a chord. These groups (which now let women have the pleasure of boring themselves silly) usually reflect rather than mold public opinion, but the downtown Rotary feeds at its noon meeting a collection of local heavyweights, ranging from bank presidents to real estate developers. As a member of the Marianna Rotary for a quarter of a century, I am at home with the chicken-and-green-peas crowd no matter where it meets and find there is little real difference in either place. Big or little, Southerners love boosterism and nostalgia, and between songs ("Sweet Adeline" and "Someone's in the Kitchen with Dinah") I talk to the man seated to my left at the head table about the 1969 Razorback game against Texas. A CPA and head of his own firm, he tells me he sat so close to Richard Nixon that he could have spit on him. I tell him I was at that game, too, and we agree that no politician could be elected President in this country unless he professed a love of sports.

In addition to being introduced as Cormorant's attorney, I am presented by the program chairman, a vice-president of TCBY, to the hundred or so members and their guests as "a prominent citizen of Lee County whose family has farmed for nine generations the rich soil of the Arkansas Delta." As I have at each club, I announce that I will not directly discuss nor answer questions about the specifics of the upcoming trial.

I then proceed with my now stock presentation, which has been refined to mention Cormorant's own infamous letter to the *Arkansas Democrat-Gazette* since it is likely I will get a question on it here as I did in Jacksonville. I scan my audience and see Raven schmoozing at a back table. Although not a member, she has managed an invitation for herself and seems to know everyone here. She undoubtedly regards this visit to the heart of central Arkansas capitalism as a business opportunity.

"The difference between a rebuke of Arkansans leveled by, for example, the *New York Times* and essentially the same criticism by a native Arkansan in the editorial pages of a local paper is that the Arkansan must live with the consequences of his or her actions, and the outsiders, who feel so superior to us, do not. Those of us who call this state our home take responsibility for what we say and are accountable for our remarks. A book critic who sneers at us from his lofty east-coast perch can get away with the worst form of character assassination and call it a book review. We saw it all through the Whitewater years, and now we are seeing it again in the guise of literary criticism."

As at Jacksonville and in west Little Rock, I get questions about both the book and Cormorant, and reply to one of the women in the audience, "I'm not speaking for Dr. Ashley, whom I have advised not to comment on this matter until after his trial, but I will tell you this: I found Dr. Merriweather's book to be stories about slavery rather than a factual account of slavery in this state. But it doesn't matter what I think: history and historians will ultimately judge the merits of his work. What we have to be on guard against is our tendency to accept the version of ourselves given to us by outsiders whose motives are often driven by such pomposity and self-righteousness as would be laughable if we weren't inclined to take them so seriously. Why do we do this? Though it has become commonplace to point it out, our state's historical inferiority complex remains just below the surface, and it is this festering insecurity that often leads us to substitute others' judgments and opinions for our own."

Though a few blacks are in the audience, the overwhelming presence is white, and it is this group as well as others like it that are most concerned with the image of the state, primarily for business reasons, but for reasons of state pride as well. According to both Raven and Cormorant, Little Rock hasn't truly experienced the growth it expected to since the 1957 school desegregation crisis, and, indeed, more than forty years later, litigation continues over the public schools, which are mostly black. From a table near Raven, a stooped old man (who I find out later is an old-time segregationist and a former Faubus lieutenant) stands and says in a wavering voice, "I appreciate your comments because I've been saying the same thing for years. We're always going to be on the bottom unless we learn to ignore the rest of the country and go our own way." His old man's mouth quivers as if he wants to add something else, but he sits down suddenly as if he has forgotten what else he wants to say.

This group is too sophisticated to rally around such a know-nothing sentiment, and I get a pointed comment from a man at the front table, who says, "The trouble with Arkansas is all we *have* done is go our own way. But it doesn't matter what people outside the state write about us. They don't vote down here to keep our schools underfunded and potholes in our highways. We do that to ourselves."

When he sits back down, I respond as if I agree with both men. "Whatever is said, inside and outside the state, and whether we believe it or not, the quality of justice we provide our citizens in the courtrooms of Arkansas is our responsibility and ours alone."

Afterwards, Raven gives me a dubious compliment. "Maybe when this is over, you can run for office," she says as we walk back to the Lafayette Building. "You were very diplomatic."

My undershirt is soaked with sweat, and it is not just from the ninety-degree heat. I feel increasingly ambivalent about what I am doing in this case, and yet I know it is necessary if we are going to go into the trial with a decent chance at winning. Now that he has seen the house and gone through the file, our forensic expert from Memphis will testify that Rafe Kennedy or someone else could have easily committed this murder and set up

Cormorant. The problem is that it is not going to be an easy sell. We have the real difficulty of explaining why there was no trace metal on Kennedy's hands. "I learned long ago," I say, giving her my arm as we cross the street, "that I have no business trying to get people to work together. Besides, I'm afraid I would like it and turn into the kind of backslapping good ole boy we usually elect to the legislature."

Raven squeezes my arm and laughs. "You're far too much the Southern gentleman to wear a hog hat. I'm surprised I've gotten you to do as much as you have. I was afraid you'd refuse to get down and dirty in this case."

I look across the street and see one of the two uniformed Little Rock policemen who patrol the downtown area on horses. A young woman is flirting with the officer, patting his horse. A robbery could be taking place ten feet away, and he would never know it.

To me the city's horse patrol seems a ridiculous waste of money, but I suppose it is part of influencing the public. I have surprised myself and wonder if I would have been so willing to try to manipulate the public's perception twenty years ago. It seemed natural to turn to Raven for help at the beginning, but now that I have, I feel I have never been in control of the case a single moment. Of course, I cannot blame Raven for a single thing. She has only done her job. As we walk south back along Louisiana, I raise my suspicion that the law was never meant to mix so thoroughly with the public relations business.

"I wish Cato had imposed a gag order in this case," I say gloomily. "This isn't how the law was meant to operate."

Though it is humid to the point of stickiness, she leans against me for a moment and says affectionately, "You are *so* dear, Miller. I know how uncomfortable you are in this role, but you know as well as I do that Ezekiel gave us no choice but to fight fire with fire. If he hadn't been in such a hurry to turn this into a crusade, the police would still be looking for his brother's killer, and you'd still be the country squire. The fact is, you're the reason we may pull this off. You're so dignified that you don't come across like a sleazebag lawyer. You sound honest and sincere, and that's why I've been able to get you invited to speak three different places. Cormorant has no idea what this is costing you, but I do, and I'll never forget it."

Regrettably, it has been easier than she knows. God, what would my father think?

9

"Mr. Holly," Steve Crisp says over his cell phone, "I've got some information for you. You want me to come by? I'm downtown."

He needs money, I think, having learned his modus operandi in the last month. I tell him this is as good a time as any, and in my makeshift office in the Lafayette Building, I continue to review Raven's file containing the most recent media coverage. I am encouraged. With four weeks to go to the trial, we are seeing further evidence that our media strategy is working and that the tenor of local reporting about the case has finally begun to soften toward Cormorant. Raven is convinced it was the language in Judge Cato's written opinion on August 5th denying our motion for a change of venue that began the turnaround. *The presumption of innocence of a criminal defendant must be real and not an idea to which the judge and jury give lip service,* he wrote in an order which was quoted in a lead editorial in the *Arkansas Democrat-Gazette* this last week. *If the search for Justice becomes a witch hunt in the community, in the long run the search for Truth in the courtroom doesn't matter.* The editorial applauded the court's decision not to transfer the case out of Little Rock but in a telling paragraph underscored the court's point. Raven has placed the editorial on our bulletin board, and I take it down and reread the part she has highlighted with a yellow Magic

Marker. *What Judge Cato didn't say but runs through every line of his ruling is that Arkansans are fiercely independent and stubbornly resist any thought of political correctness. We are confident Professor Ashley will receive a fair trial in Little Rock. The reputation of our community demands nothing less.* As Raven has pointed out, if we are so damned independent, why worry about our reputation? The clincher for me that the media has begun to blow in a different direction were the comments on *Arkansas Week* on Friday night in which Mona Davidson, a columnist for the *Arkansas Times*, said she thought the editorial was needed because Arkansans were no longer laughing anymore at jokes like the one about Ken Starr having to throw out the blood test in the Monica Lewinsky scandal because everybody in Arkansas has the same blood type. Dave Harris, a writer for the local AP desk, had responded, *We've taken one too many punches here in Little Rock to think jokes like that are very funny any longer.*

I remind myself that none of these responses will mean anything unless they have filtered down to the level of a jury pool, which in our meetings Cormorant, in his condescending way, calls "pond scum" because so many qualified jurors are excused. Horrified, I have reminded him that it will be pond scum who will decide his future and have warned him to quit being so cavalier. I flip through the stack of papers and find the first hint of editorial criticism toward the Merriweathers in a piece from the *North Little Rock Times*:

We agree that Professor Ashley can get a fair trial across the river, but justice will not be served by the media continuing to make a martyr out of a man who wrote a book as sparsely documented as Coming To Terms... *The tragedy of Dr. Merriweather's death and the trial of his alleged killer is a separate issue from the merits of the book for which he is apparently becoming posthumously famous. News coverage of these events thus far has often seemed like a promotional ad for the book, which, in our view, is seriously lacking in substance. A year from now, when the trial is over and all the hoopla is behind us, history, not the daily headlines, will be our judge once again.*

I put the papers away, wishing the editorial writer had mentioned Ezekiel by name and, still waiting for Crisp, pull out the brothers' file. It has begun to accumulate some details, but so far it is like looking at a road map, where you can tell distance but not elevation. A part of me still wants to believe that Ezekiel had something to do with his brother's death, but the evidence thus far is not there for it. Steve has interviewed the North Little Rock pharmacy employees personally and is satisfied their boss was present the afternoon of the murder.

The more we learn about Ezekiel, the less we understand him. According to Steve, and indirectly confirmed by Cormorant through some research of his own, he has been generous with his money, something I would not have associated with him. In fact, he has given away thousands to Philander Smith College, a small black school in Little Rock, and is responsible for sending dozens of black kids to college, and not only to Philander Smith but to black schools all over the South. He has employed teenagers, both girls and boys, in all of his businesses, and has health care programs for all his employees. With all his good works and philanthropy, if Ezekiel has employed or helped a white person in the last twenty years, Steve Crisp has not been able to find out about it. But so what? From his perspective, whites have all the help they need.

At the same time, Ezekiel does not tolerate much funny business in the black community either, having shot and killed a black drug addict who was robbing his North Little Rock store in 1980. At the time, the shooting caused a small stir only because, typically, Ezekiel gave it a racial twist, having been quoted in the old *Arkansas Gazette* after the prosecutor publicly declined to prosecute him that he was lucky that the victim wasn't white.

Cormorant and I have discussed the possibility that Ezekiel has been spoiling for a fight with the white community for most of his adult life, and finally his brother's book gave him the opportunity he had been looking for. Though Cormorant is lukewarm toward this idea, I have begun to wonder if the passion in the book might have been inspired by Ezekiel. As I come to know him better, it is Ezekiel whom Cormorant resembles, not Damascus.

I pull out my checkbook, hoping Steve has something worthwhile, because I have begun to wake up in the middle of the night and worry. Unlike what I expected by this time, we are running out of options. The Little Rock Police Department, I am now beginning to concede, has done a decent job. I have nothing to show for my more than one hundred hours in the Palisades area except confirmation that the cops nailed this part of the investigation shut. Waymon Duffy is still in jail and still a candidate for the murder, but I hate to think he is Cormorant's best shot at an acquittal. As Minor will doubtless point out to the jury, the jails are full of criminals who don't talk about what crimes they have committed.

I walk down the hall to see if Raven is back yet from a meeting, but Khala, her secretary, a girl who moonlights as a model, tells me she has gone to a meeting with a client. I am regarded with studied impassivity by Raven's staff. They have come to accept me, but nobody mentions my role, perhaps having been told by their boss the subject is none of their business. Raven, I am learning, is anything but laid back as a boss, laughing, cursing her way through the vicissitudes of the advertising business. I heard her scream at a commercial artist over the phone that if he was one more day late, she would personally see that he never worked again in Little Rock. Then she sent him flowers two days later. "Nick Never-On-Time," she calls him.

Steve Crisp arrives and, for the first time since I have known him, is smiling. He gets down to business without his usual patter. "I've got a bombshell. You ready for this? Merriweather was doing Dominique Marsden," he says, his voice low and raspy from an apparent cold, "and her old man found out about it."

"Ezekiel?" I ask, flabbergasted by this news. Though until now it has seemed irrelevant, the older Merriweather has since his wife's death, again according to Steve, been something of a ladies' man, even at the age of sixty-five. The thought of his involvement with his brother's editor is a stretch, though Dominique Marsden has been unwilling to talk since the beginning of the case. A thirty-five-year-old English teacher at Central High, she never gave more than a cursory written statement to the cops, presumably because she had no information to give them.

As usual, Steve heads for the window so he can keep an eye on his Cadillac, which he routinely leaves in the Allright parking lot without putting any money in the payment box. He could bill me for the expense, but for some reason he gets a kick out of risking a tow. "Damascus was the man, not Zeke. She's not really foxy, but she's not bad either." He pulls out a snapshot from his left front pocket and hands it to me.

I squint at the photgraph, a black-and-white. I don't know what qualifies a woman as a "fox," but this woman is attractive, her solemn but pleasant face reminding me of Clarence Thomas's accuser, the law professor, Anita Hill. "How could that be? Stomach cancer doesn't seem like much of a turn-on," I say, already allowing myself to be excited by the possibilities if it is true.

"The buzz," says Steve, "is that Damascus wasn't that bad off until a few weeks before he died. What I'm hearing is that her old man Bobby didn't find out until right before the book came out and then the shit hit the fan."

"Has he got an alibi?" I ask, wondering what Cormorant and Raven will make of this revelation.

"Not as far as I can tell," Steve hoots, apparently as pleased as I am. "Get this. He's a self-employed locksmith who works out of his house. The story I got is that he came back from out of town from a friend's funeral a day early, couldn't find his wife, and confronted her when she came home the next morning from Merriweather's. He beat her up and kicked her out of the house. Somebody called the cops that night—I've got an incident report on that—but she wouldn't prosecute. I figure Merriweather could have talked to her enough about your client so that Bobby knew about the pistol in the car, and he put on a pair of gloves, stole it, and let himself into Ezekiel's house and shot Damascus and then threw the pistol out in the backyard for the cops to find."

Crisp is making too many leaps for my mind to follow. "Still, if he was so sick, how could they have been having a torrid affair? He was dying."

Steve unwraps a stick of gum and pops it into his mouth. "Maybe he wasn't as sick as everybody thinks, and that's the last thing that goes," he says, shrugging his shoulders. "Maybe she just confessed they used to have sex. But whatever, he was pissed enough to throw her out of the house that night and she didn't complain when the cops showed up."

"How did you find this out?" I ask, knowing that without a black investigator we never would have heard about a relationship.

"He told a couple of guys he kicked her out and they've been talking. He's got a history. He served some time for terroristic threatening when he was in his twenties. The details are hazy, but that involved a woman, too. What I hear is that he's got a jealous streak a mile long and doesn't like to get shit on."

Steve's eyes widen as he continues to stare down across

Louisiana. "She's not gonna say shit. I figure she thinks she's lucky to be alive. Sometimes guys like Bobby will kill 'em both. I gotta go outside. I'll be back. Here's the report," he says and hands me a file folder.

I look at the police report and note that though the victim was reported to have a bruise over her left eye, her collar torn half-off her dress, and was reported to be visibly frightened, she refused to say that her husband had hit her. Mr. Marsden had told the police that "…she came home looking like that." As I read through his notes, Raven appears in the doorway shaking her head. "Isn't that our investigator across the street arguing with a parking attendant?"

I wave her on in and tell her about Steve's information and hand her the police report.

"What do you think?" I ask when Raven looks up at me.

"It's like reading the Starr report," she says, scowling unexpectedly and dropping the paper on the desk as if it were a soiled tissue. "Is this the best this guy can come up with?"

I am surprised by her lack of understanding of the significance of what Steve has found. "In a criminal trial," I remind her, "the defendant need only raise a reasonable doubt. He's a locksmith; he's served time for threats; he had reason to hate Damascus."

In a gesture of weariness that is foreign to her this time of day, Raven sits down heavily across from me and rubs her right eye. "When you first came over here this summer, I assumed sooner or later the hysteria would die down and the police would find some student druggie who stole Cormorant's pistol and then thought he could rip off a stash in a pharmacist's home and got surprised by Damascus and then panicked. Well, that hasn't happened. Now all we have are these wild theories that aren't going to persuade anyone who thinks about them for five minutes and who doesn't want to be convinced. A student who's got an uncle who's a Nazi, an angry ex-tenant, racist letter writers, and now an angry husband? If I were on his jury I'd laugh at you and ask, where's the beef, counselor? Miller, we're in la-la land, and you know it. Every time we talk to Cormorant, we find another indication there was a feud between him and Damascus."

She breaks off sharply, and stunned by her pessimism, I look over and see Steve striding confidently back in the room as if he were vice-president of the company. Raven has always liked him, but instead of being welcomed by her as a savior, he enters the room to stony silence. I write him a check for his time from Cormorant's trust account, and tell him I will be back in touch with him soon. Probably used to conflict involving his employers, he handles the changed mood in the room with far more tact than I would have, nodding at Raven and saying he will wait for me to call him. As he leaves, I realize that Raven has begun thinking like Cormorant's thoroughly disillusioned sister and no longer like a member of his defense team.

When Steve shuts the door, I ask, "What has happened? Something else is bothering you. You and I both know how unlikely it is that Cormorant shot Merriweather. He could have had fifty good reasons, but he still wouldn't have taken a gun and shot an unarmed man, especially not one in a wheelchair. You know that as well I do."

Raven runs her hands through her thick hair. "You don't know him as well as you think. Do you remember my last divorce, the one that was so messy?"

All three breakups have had their disastrous moments, but how could I forget her marriage to Ben Strickland? At one point, his lawyer was threatening to introduce pictures of Raven that still make her blush. "Sure," I say. She was drinking heavily back then, possibly doing drugs as well. If Strickland hadn't known we could have proved he was a crook, Raven would have walked away without a dime in order to keep from being humiliated.

Raven whispers furiously, "Cormorant took his gun and went to Ben's apartment and swore if it was the last thing he did he would blow Ben's brains out if he didn't give him the negatives and go away and let me take the divorce. He didn't do it for me. It was the Daddy thing all over again. He was convinced that if there had been a trial and all the crap I was doing at the time had been brought out, Daddy would have had a stroke years before he did."

I feel myself growing almost dizzy with this revelation. What has made me think I still knew either one of these people? "Why didn't you tell me this?" I yelp, feeling totally betrayed.

"I swore on Mother's grave that I wouldn't tell you what he had done," Raven says, beginning to breathe hard, "and the only reason I'm telling you now is that it isn't fair to you to have to represent Cormorant thinking he isn't capable of murder. He most certainly is. Do you remember that Ben moved to St. Louis?"

I laugh, but the sound coming from my mouth is like the self-conscious snicker of the rube who finds out too late he has been scammed by someone he thought he could trust with his life. "All this time I thought I had missed my calling as a domestic relations lawyer," I say ironically, and add, "If Mr. John knew what a tough guy his son has turned out to be, he would be delighted, wouldn't he?"

"This doesn't have to mean Cormorant is guilty," Raven insists, but she sounds as if she is trying to convince herself instead of me. "I just have begun to think that he may not be telling us the whole truth about what happened between him and Merriweather."

I have had that sense all along, but unraveling their relationship seems more like a job for a shrink than a lawyer. This case is beginning to seem like a bottomless pit. What else don't I know about my oldest friend? "I take it that you've asked him if he threatened Damascus?"

Raven, whose voice has become so low I can barely hear her even though she is leaning on her arms across the desk that separates us, replies, "He insists that he didn't, but I don't know. I know that to protect our sacred father, Cormorant is capable of anything."

I drop my eyes. The pain in Raven's face is difficult to bear. "If he did, and Damascus told his brother, I think we would know by now."

Raven shrugs as if we have no idea what is still to be learned about Cormorant, and she may be right, but from purely a defense perspective, information coming in at the eleventh hour can be made to smell awfully bad. If Ezekiel is holding something back, we might not be able to make it boomerang on him. "Could Strickland have done this?" I ask. "Is he back or what? He has a score to settle."

Raven studies the ceiling and then says, "I just can't see Ben involved in something like this. He was a greedy bully but not a murderer, I don't think. Besides, I haven't seen or heard from him in years."

It is something to check out, I think wearily. God, I want to kill them both. There is a knock on the door, and thinking it is Raven's secretary, I turn away, but it is Cormorant, who is thirty minutes late for our weekly strategy session. He explains he is tardy because he had a flat tire, and I ask, remembering his childhood incompetence, if he changed it himself. Seriously and without even a hint of irony, he replies that emergencies are why he has an AAA membership.

We arrange ourselves in our usual seats, me at the desk and the Ashley siblings across from me. Raven masks her earlier emotion by immediately telling Cormorant that Steve has given us some good news and I recap for him our conversation, saying none of the information has been confirmed. "It's something to argue, at least."

Cormorant bobs his head furiously. "Hell, what do you mean, *argue*? Steve's found Damascus's killer! Where's Steve? I want to talk to him."

I find myself listening hard to Cormorant's tone and realize I am not sure if I believe him. It is an unnerving sensation, and for the first time I understand that it is not Cormorant I trust but his sister's assessment of him. Now that she is doubting him, I have begun to as well. "We can call Steve back any time we want," I say firmly, "but we need to do some work first ourselves. Spouses have affairs all the time and nobody gets murdered as a result."

"But you said this guy was a self-employed locksmith!" Cormorant screeches. "You think that's just a coincidence?"

Raven interjects almost scornfully, "Do you think every time there's a burglary and there's no sign of forced entry that the police arrest a locksmith? It's something else to pursue, but let's not go off the deep end."

Cormorant shoots a hard look at his sister. "Why are you so pissed?"

"Because you're not telling the goddamned truth and you know it," Raven yells at him. "You don't give a shit whether people like you or not, and yet you've been obsessed by this man and his book. What the hell was going on?"

Cormorant looks at me as if Raven is crazy, but I tell him, "It doesn't add up. You've admitted he asked you to collaborate on the book, admitted that you talked with him about it. The damn thing even sounds like you in parts. Something else happened. What in the hell was it?"

Cormorant turns back to his sister and says coldly, "You told him that I threatened that asshole of a husband of yours, didn't you?"

"Thank God she did!" I reply. I push myself to the edge of my chair. "Get real, Cormorant, for once in your life," I plead with him. "You've got less than a month. If I don't know what went on between you and Merriweather, we don't have a chance of getting you off."

For a long moment Cormorant does not speak, and for all I know, he may never say another word to Raven. He goes to the window and then turns and faces us and says abruptly, "Before he was killed, Damascus tried to convince me that our great-grandfather fathered one of his slave's children. I told him that if he printed it, I would sue him for libel."

My skin gets clammy as I remember the intense expression on his face the night of the 4th of July party when Claude was asking me about a lawsuit. I look at Raven. He had told me that neither of our families was in the book. Raven demands, "Who was it?"

Cormorant shrugs as if this is not a subject worth pursuing, and perhaps it is not since Damascus omitted it. I say, "In the grand scheme of things, I don't think it matters."

Cormorant crosses back to the easel, and turning his back to both of us, he flips over the sheet. "It might," he mumbles.

Stunned that he has waited so long to tell us, I ask, "Does anyone else know this?"

For a long moment as he draws, he does not answer and then he steps back from the stand. He has sketched, in just a few strokes, a black infant with his own father's high forehead and cheekbones. "That's why it might be worth the risk of talking to Ezekiel again, to see what he knows."

I shake my head. "It's not in his statement, and so far there's nothing in the prosecutor's file. If we tip him off, it will give the prosecutor the motive he's been looking for."

Raven asks loudly, "Who was it, Cormorant? Was it the one they called Little Tina?"

I begin to feel sick to my stomach. Watching Raven interrogate her brother is like watching someone's face being hit. With each question, Cormorant turns a brighter shade of red. I want to run from the room but know I will not.

Cormorant swallows hard twice before he speaks. "It would have killed Daddy for someone to write this."

I marvel at the noose Mr. John has kept wrapped around his son's neck. I thought I knew the Ashleys, but obviously I do not know enough. Feeling weak with what I am about to ask, I whisper, "So you murdered Damascus to keep this a secret?"

Ripping the paper from the easel, Cormorant snaps, "Of course not! There's no proof anyway."

The weakness of his response is appalling. He must think we are idiots. Guessing what happened, I demand, "Did he tell you he would put it in the second edition?"

For the first time today, Cormorant loses his composure. His face crumples, and his long lashes begin to flutter. "Yeah. I got mad but I swear to God I didn't kill him, nor did I threaten him either."

Do I believe him? I don't know. Raven rises from her chair and walks up to Cormorant and, her face terrible, slaps him with her left hand, sending a clean, cracking sound through the room. "Goddamn you, when are you going to get over this Daddy shit!" she hurls at him. "What has he ever done for us except to remind us once a month that we have spent our lives disappointing him?"

Cormorant's face radiates hatred. It is the look of unadulterated contempt that family members reserve for each other, and I stand and put my hand on Raven's shoulder to restrain her. "Who was Little Tina?" I ask, determined to get everything out in the open so I can begin to understand it.

"Her granddaughter's still alive," Raven says, her voice suddenly cracked and spent. "I saw her last year in Helena at the nursing home. No wonder she's smiled at me all these years."

Sensing the fight has gone out of his sister, Cormorant crosses in front of us and slumps in my chair. "Don't act as if this story were any shock to either of you," he says. "It's surfaced before. Little Tina was supposedly James Ashley's favorite house slave. There are some references to her in a diary our great-grandmother kept."

"What's this woman's name who's still alive?" I ask, remembering I have heard this gossip before.

Raven gives me a tight smile. "Octavia Haskins. She's lived at Elaine all her life. She must be eighty."

God, it never ends, I think. There was an infamous black uprising or a slaughter of blacks, depending on what you believe, in 1919 in the southern part of Phillips County near Elaine. "What does she look like?" I can't resist asking, glancing at Cormorant, who is now staring past us, unseeing. The high Ashley forehead is prominent in both the two descendants present.

"She's obviously got a lot of white blood in her," Raven says. She has returned to her chair. Her voice now barely reaches me.

Cormorant strokes his beard. "That could have come from anywhere in the last hundred and fifty years," he says, the anger having gone out of him, too. "There's no proof. There's really nothing in the diary. Octavia has always been a little crazy, anyway."

Raven, whose red fingernails show the results of professional care, begins to gnaw at her thumb like a child. "What difference would it make if it were true, Cormorant?" she asks her brother. "You're just scared of Daddy being disappointed in you for the millionth time."

Taking Cormorant's seat, I ponder the truth of Raven's remark. Cormorant, who couldn't keep a tractor going straight for two seconds, couldn't keep a black man from printing gossip that would sully the Ashley name.

"Jesus Christ!" Cormorant snaps, coming back to life. "I don't care what he thinks."

Like a student making fun of her teacher's sanctimoniousness, Raven rolls her eyes at her brother. I study Cormorant's face, wondering if he can possibly be so out of touch with himself that he does not recognize the hollowness of his claim. Am I this out of touch, too? Damascus Merriweather's words about the consent of the slave women have haunted me and I am again forced to think about my own family's participation in slavery and the years that followed. If my own great-grandfather engaged in intercourse with a slave, it didn't necessarily mean it was rape. But, as Laurel has said, I don't get it.

Cormorant lectures us. "Daddy used to tell the story about how all the former slaves came back to his grandfather's funeral after the war. If they had hated him, they wouldn't have come. Besides, history is full of former slaves who decorated their family trees with gold balls that don't belong there. If you credit this gossip, you never find the truth."

I start to protest his logic, but it hits me that the stress that Cormorant is under must be overpowering. When it comes to his father, he is like a child.

Raven has put her hands to her face and says through them, "Let's ask Daddy. He knows the truth."

"No!" Cormorant shouts back at us. "It might cause another stroke."

Raven turns her head to me and says in a stage whisper, "My brother, the great truth seeker." She turns back to Cormorant. "You know he knows. You and I had this same discussion years ago, and we both chickened out."

How odd they haven't asked before, I think, and odder still that the three of us have not discussed this subject. Yet, I wouldn't ask Mr. John a question like that, and I'm not even related to him. His stare alone would have reduced me to jelly. God knows what he would have said. Now, nearly helpless, he doesn't seem so intimidating.

"What if he says 'no'?" Cormorant asks her, his voice mocking. "Would you believe it then?"

Raven cocks her chin as if she were about to take a punch, and we all three know the answer, although she is silent. Cormorant, now in full professor mode, spreads his hands in a gesture of helplessness that signals his frustration. "That's what makes oral history so suspect: It depends on the era you're living in whether it seems credible. The Slave Narratives seem more credible the further we get away from them. They become very tempting to believe according to the politics of the era. As white males, especially southern white males, fall increasingly out of fashion, the Narratives seem like a godsend in their ability to teach us what slavery was really like. But to the honest historian, they are as suspect as ever. And so is an old man's memory of what he was told about the past."

My old friend's didacticism makes me want to argue that he is begging the question. Is there such a thing as an honest historian? I am beginning to have my doubts. "What if you ask him and he says, 'yes'?" I ask, trying to keep my own growing resentment out of my voice. "Will you believe him then?"

Cormorant drums his fingers on the desk. "It would depend," he says, his tone limp. "It would still be hearsay."

Raven buries her face in her hands. It is apparent that she thinks Cormorant is hopelessly compromised by his relationship with their father. And, yet, if I am honest, I must admit that I am beginning to see his point. The truth would surely be easier to determine if this were rocket science. As a phone begins to ring on the desk beside Cormorant, I remind myself that what I should be listening for is how any of this impacts on Cormorant's defense. I have only one job here. If I lose sight of that even for a moment, I risk failing my obligation as a lawyer. Yet, even as I think this, I know my mind for the last month has run on parallel tracks as I have wondered about my own past. While Raven answers the phone, I again propose hiring a second lawyer to help me at trial.

"No," he says flatly. "I'm paranoid enough as it is."

I hope that is all it is. Raven says abruptly that it is her best client calling with an emergency, and she leaves to take the call in her office.

There is an awkwardness between us. We are both embarrassed by his fight with Raven. He returns to the easel and begins to draw, asking over his shoulder, the words barely reaching me, "Do you think I have a Daddy problem?"

As I consider this question, he brings into being with just a few lines a suggestion of an old man—his father, of course. There is no question that my own father's death when I was twenty liberated me. Though a kinder and far less intimidating man than Mr. John, his views on everything from politics to race shaped my consciousness far more than I knew at the time. Outwardly, he encouraged independence, but while he was alive, I realize now I was little more than a clone. "Most of us over a certain age have had Daddy problems in the Delta," I say, ruefully. "Until the sixties, they were as good as their word, and everybody knew it. The kind of power they wielded creates a myth about the world that some of us never seem to get over. As a child, it makes you feel they are omnipotent. What's remarkable is you've been as ornery and independent in your own way as your father has been in his."

Cormorant sketches in his father's wide mouth. "I suppose I had to show him."

While we wait for Raven to return, I tell Cormorant a story I heard from a federal bankruptcy judge while we were waiting for a black lawyer to talk to his client. He and a friend from Birmingham were in downtown Denver having a drink outside a brewery when three gorgeous people, dressed to the teeth, sauntered by. The man was black and handsome, the woman white and stunningly beautiful, and the child, who could have been a Gap model, a lovely chocolate shade in between. "He said he looked at his friend and wondered aloud if that was what we had been worried about for the last hundred and fifty years."

Cormorant smiles, but it is the smile of someone who has not given up the fight. "You don't believe I'm telling the truth even now, do you?"

I feel my face heating up. I don't know what to believe. "I don't think you are lying to me. It is so far from my experience of you that you would even threaten to kill a man that *none* of this makes sense to me."

Cormorant's voice goes high. "You just don't have the same sense of family and place or you would understand."

I've always thought I did and thought that was what bound us both to the Delta, even though he left it. "Don't you see how twisted your logic is? Merriweather's book only hurts you if you let it. You said a hundred times that it's nothing but gossip. What if he did put the Ashley name in there? Next year at this time, do you think anybody will remember or care?"

"That's bullshit, Miller," he says soberly. "If it were *your* family, you'd care, too."

The hypocrisy of what I am saying hits me full force. Of course, I'd care. But though I don't say it, I'm starting to believe Cormorant needs a therapist as much as he needs a lawyer.

10

"Turn on Channel 7's early morning show!" Raven calls down to me from the top of the stairs the next morning. "Ezekiel's at it again!"

I put down the *Democrat-Gazette*, hurry into the den and click on the Sony. There is Ezekiel holding up a copy of a paperback book with a nightmarish picture of a hooded Ku Klux Klan figure standing over a black male's body. The interviewer, a serious blonde in her twenties with the willowy figure of a fashion model, asks, "what is this second book about and will it be as controversial as the first?"

In a dark pin-striped business suit that gives him the look of a successful banker, Ezekiel, who had been quiet recently, solemnly intones, "*Salted With Fire* is what my brother called the rest of our story in Arkansas. It picks up with our persecution during Reconstruction and follows our history all the way to the modern civil rights era, which my brother saw ending with the year-long boycott in Marianna in 1971. And yes, it will be as controversial as *Coming to Terms*."

I put down the cup of coffee I am holding, feeling my chest tighten. I will definitely be in this book. When was it actually written?" the woman asks. "It was the public's understanding that Dr. Merriweather was suffering from cancer when he was killed."

Ezekiel looks older, his beard whiter than when the summer

began, but then I probably do, too. He says, "My brother wrote much of the material in the last decade. In the last weeks of his life, he was feverishly working on this book and knew I would publish it after he died. It has recently been edited by Dominique Marsden, who also worked on *Coming to Terms* with my brother, and I owe Mrs. Marsden an enormous debt for pulling together this book from his writings. An English teacher at Central, she has made the publication of this book possible."

Raven comes into the room, her hair in curlers. Nodding at the screen, she exclaims, "I can't believe Sissy didn't call and warn me about this. I gave her the first real job she ever had."

Thinking of what Steve Crisp told us yesterday, I say under my breath, "When did Dominique Marsden have time to work?"

"What do you consider is the principal difference between the two books?" Raven's former employee asks. "Or is it a continuation?"

Ezekiel tugs at his beard as if this were a harder question than it sounds. "What is similar about both books is that my brother felt that though present white historians writing about race relations in Arkansas since slavery have been much more candid about the subjugation of blacks until the modern civil rights era, the average adult in Arkansas has little awareness of the violence that has been perpetrated against blacks because there has been no inexpensive paperback book exclusively on the subject until now. My brother wanted in this collection of essays to begin the process of forcing whites to confront exactly what it has been like for blacks to be dominated by them since the slave era, and to begin coming to terms psychologically with their actions. My brother's thesis in *Salted With Fire* is that Arkansas's historians until the modern civil rights era had no sense of objectivity about the subject of race, either ignoring or distorting the truth when they did mention it. In the process, much has been lost because so many of the participants are now dead.

Damascus especially wanted to challenge present-day whites in *Salted With Fire* because of the tendency to view slavery as an era for which nobody has to take responsibility because it was so long ago. After slavery and up until the modern civil rights movement, African-Americans have been lynched, exploited and cheated in Arkansas, but, as with slavery, my brother believed the white population has never admitted its responsibility. Even in Germany, there has recently begun to be a public discussion of responsibility for the treatment of the Jews."

Even this young interviewer is old enough to know the button Ezekiel has pushed, and she exclaims as if on cue, "You're not comparing what happened in Germany to the treatment of African-Americans in Arkansas, are you?"

I feel my mouth go dry, and I lean forward to hear his next words.

"My brother felt there were more similarities than the typical Arkansan, black or white, might think. May I read a brief paragraph from the introduction to give you a flavor?"

"Please do," Sissy says, nervously, and looks away from the camera, presumably in the direction of her producer. This may be her last day on camera, or it may be the first day of a memorable career.

Ezekiel opens the book and reads: *The Holocaust, it has been documented, did not occur in a historical vacuum. Just as Jews were demonized by the Germans long before any official action began against them, after Reconstruction ended, the white establishment in Arkansas, for political reasons (as in the rest of the South), from governors on down, became race-baiters of the first order, and thus prepared the way pyschologically for the violence that was to follow. Thus, for example, when confronted with accounts of an atrocity, such as the Elaine Massacre in 1919 in Phillips County, the reaction of the white power structure was to deny that a wholesale slaughter of African-Americans had occurred in the Delta and to maintain blacks were about to murder whites, when, in fact, black sharecroppers were simply trying to organize a labor union. Hundreds of blacks may have been killed in Elaine. The official record is that only a few blacks were shot and those in self-defense.*

"In *Salted With Fire*, my brother documents this tragic phenomenon over and over in post-slavery Arkansas: any sign of labor unrest among the black population has been met with immediate force. Yet, in Orwellian fashion, throughout the systematic oppression of blacks in this state, it was the official view of white community leaders until the modern civil rights era that, in general, race relations have been good. As my brother documented in chapter three, white Arkansans have so deluded themselves with this myth that when the civil rights movement finally began to gather real force in the Delta in the late 1960s, incredibly, they seemed to be genuinely shocked by the firestorms of protest that engulfed them. As is acknowledged by all historians now, until mechanization began to transform farming in the 1940s, blacks were seen as an absolute necessity to the survival of the Delta because of the need for their labor, and it was for this purpose only that their presence was tolerated in Arkansas. White Arkansans can no more admit today that the history of race relations in this state until relatively recently, has been one of systematic oppression, intimidation, exploitation and violence than the ordinary German who lived through that era can openly talk about the horrors of the death camps. But until that day comes, there will be no honest dialogue on race as the President—an Arkansan—had hoped would be one of his principal legacies to the nation."

Sissy, now visibly nervous—she can't be older than twenty-five—cannot keep her right hand from her hair. She frowns. "But to compare the Holocaust in the same breath as race relations is bound to bring charges that all your brother was trying to do was to make matters worse instead of better."

"That was never his intention," Ezekiel says flatly, holding up the book again. "At the very end of the book, which was concluded in the last days of his life, you will see that he wanted all of us to realize the enormous complexity and even the emotional richness of individual relationships between blacks and whites—but in order to get to that point, whites have to truly understand and acknowledge the history of your conduct toward the black population of this state. You frankly have no idea how horrific so much of it was. Even though historians in Arkansas have begun to acknowledge and write about these events in a truthful way, there has been little public interest shown in them."

Whether it is the producer's intention or time is up, Sissy concludes the interview by saying the book will be distributed locally beginning today, and I click off the program dumbfounded by what I have just watched. "If Cormorant had a clue about this second book," I tell her, "he never shared it with me."

Instead of replying, Raven picks up the phone and calls her brother, waking him up.

He professes to be as mystified as we are. "Ezekiel and this woman must have cobbled together some of his old research," he guesses when Raven hands me the phone, "and put it together as quickly as possible so he would get the most mileage out of it."

Raven absently picks up my coffee cup and nods in agreement as I say, "After the trial, he wouldn't be able to give the book away. Do you know Dominique Marsden? You've never mentioned her."

"I met her once when she came to Damascus's office and had to wait for him," he says vaguely.

After I get him off the phone (Cormorant says he knows where he can probably get his hands on copies of the book for us before the bookstores open), Raven and I agree it is more crucial than ever to talk to Dominque Marsden as quickly as possible. Undoubtedly, the media will be after her, too.

"The timing on this may be perfect for us," Raven says, already in her professional mode. "If the media outside the state jump on this, what you have been saying will have more credibility than ever."

I stand up to go shave, still fearful of how I will be portrayed in this new book. "You should hire Ezekiel," I tell her, chagrined by his ability to dominate the news. "You have to admit he's able to swing the momentum back to Damascus whenever he's ready."

Raven nods and predicts Ezekiel will be everywhere today promoting his brother's book, and just an hour later, we see him on Channel 11 pitching *Salted With Fire* with the fervor of an evangelist preaching about the end of the world. I would love to be inside his head for one minute and figure out how he managed to pull this off. For an instant I wonder again if I am now part of a giant public relations plot to sell books. If there is life after death, Damascus Merriweather, wherever he is, must be relishing this moment.

"Mrs. Marsden," I say quietly, hoping not to attract attention as she comes out of the convenience store toward her Escort. She has a quart of milk in her hand. "It's crucial that we talk a few minutes. I'm Miller Holly, and I represent Cormorant Ashley. It's not about the books."

She stops abruptly in front of the door and stares at me. I have startled her, and she gasps. "Have you been following me?"

Mrs. Marsden, who was interviewed fifteen minutes ago in the studio of Channel 4, glowers at me as she waits for an answer, but she shows no signs of bolting back inside the store. She is taller than she appeared on television and even more attractive in person, with a lovely mouth, I think, remembering her picture. Her large brown eyes dart from me to the street as if she is considering her options. For her television appearance, she was wearing a blue jacket over a gray skirt, but she has taken it off in the afternoon August heat. Underneath is a starched white blouse that shows not a wrinkle. Not wanting to admit that I raced from the Lafayette Building to the Channel 4 parking lot where I saw her getting in her car, I say simply, "I know this is awkward for you, but I feel obligated to verify some information before we go any further with it. Will you sit in your car for a moment while I go over some things with you? It won't take but a few moments."

She shrugs, as if today will never end for her. In her interview, she confirmed that she was hired by Ezekiel to work through a collection of unpublished essays as well as some recent material written by Damascus before his death, and to edit and organize the material into a book. Though she refused to say how much she was paid, she admitted that she wanted to spend much more time shaping the material, but her contract called for her to finish the work by the end of July. Having now spent much of the day reading the book, I have to admit it holds together rather well. Since my name is mentioned only once and not in a disparaging way, I have been able to read it somewhat dispassionately. Even Cormorant has admitted that Damascus had done some decent work in parts of the book.

"I have nothing to say to you, Mr. Holly."

"It's about your husband, ma'am," I say, trying to keep my voice down. The place is swarming with customers stopping off from work.

She sighs and barely nods. I follow her to her car, but instead of getting in, she turns and leans back against the front door. "What do you want?"

This is not the place for this conversation, but she is leaving me no choice. I look across Markham at the oasis of green which is the campus of the state schools for the Deaf and the Blind. If we are on a wild goose chase, now is the time to find out. "I want to know if it's true that you were having an affair with Damascus Merriweather and your husband found out."

Her eyes narrow into slits, and through clenched teeth, she demands, "Who told you that? That's the most ridiculous thing I've ever heard!"

I can't tell whether she is genuinely outraged or putting on a show. "I have a police report in my car," I reply, "that shows your husband beat you on the night of April 16th, but you wouldn't prosecute him. And we know that you had come from Dr. Merriweather's house."

Mrs. Marsden stands ramrod straight. "You are out of your mind!" she says loudly, her chin thrust forward. "I demand to know who told you this!"

I begin to feel increasingly uncomfortable in the fierce heat, standing here in front of passers-by. A Little Rock patrol car sits on the grass across the street on the campus of the School for the Deaf. I may be waiting for the first hard freeze before she says another word. I pull out the card from my wallet and scribble the number for Raven's firm.

"Please let me talk about this with you in private. I'm not trying to embarrass you."

Mrs. Marsden suddenly begins to cry, but instead of lashing out further, she says abruptly, "Follow me."

Without another word, I get back into the Oldsmobile and trail her Escort into the neighborhood which Raven has identified for me as Capitol View, an integrated area which contains some lovely old homes that remind me of houses on Pearl Street in Marianna.

Raven has said that this middle-class area has in the past

received publicity for having two neighborhood associations, one black and one white, a sign of the continuing racial mistrust which dogs the city of Little Rock even in areas which seem successfully integrated. True to its name, Capitol View is only blocks from the State Capitol, and I can imagine it was a pleasant walk to work at one time for state employees. Despite appearances, some streets are not safe in Capitol View because of drugs, according to Raven.

"My daughter is at a friend's," Mrs. Marsden says as I enter her brick two-story dwelling behind her. "But if she comes in, I want you to leave immediately. She wasn't home that night, but she gets very upset when it is brought up. If you don't, I'll call the police."

"Of course," I say, wishing I had suggested Raven's office to talk, but I know I am lucky to be having this conversation at all. Steve's report had not mentioned a child, nor had there been any mention of one in the police report. The first piece of furniture I notice is an upright piano against the far wall, and above it a picture, presumably of her daughter, a pretty teenager in a Central High cheerleader's outfit. I feel my sense of awkwardness growing by the second, but after she puts the quart of milk in the refrigerator, she finally invites me to sit down across from her at a dining room table covered by a lace tablecloth.

Steve's report says the husband threw her out of the house, but they must have later agreed on a separation. We don't know where he is living at the moment. "All I want to do is to confirm this information. If it's not true, I need to know it."

"I don't understand," she says, sounding genuinely uncertain, "how my marital problems are any of your business."

She seems intelligent, and I can't believe she could have edited Merriweather's books and not have an understanding of what her role might be in this case. "If your husband believed you were having an affair," I say, spelling it out for her, "he might have been jealous enough to have murdered the person he thought you were involved with."

"But I wasn't! Damascus and I had been friends for years, but our relationship wasn't like that."

Why couldn't she be telling the truth? After all, I, a married man, have routinely spent the night this summer in the home of a woman I consider one of my closest friends and have not slept with her. Why should Dominique Marsden be any different? "But your husband thought it was," I say, pushing her to admit his state of mind. If she will, it won't matter whether it was true or not.

"Bobby is not a murderer," she argues. "He wouldn't kill a man. That isn't how he would react. He would take it out on me."

He did take it out on her. Unsaid is that he might have killed *her*, but he didn't. "So you will admit he was jealous."

"Damascus was feeling really bad that night," she explains, "and my husband was out of town. My daughter was spending the night out, and when Damascus got sick, I thought I should stay and be with him. He was depressed more than anything. Can't you understand this, or do you not want to?"

She is looking at me so intently that I understand this woman realizes the risk she is taking in talking to me. "Of course I can understand, but you know that my job is to represent Professor Ashley, and if there is a possibility your husband murdered Dr. Merriweather, I'm under an obligation to show that."

Her face turns to stone. "Then I'm not going to talk to you," she says firmly. "You don't care about the truth. You just want to protect your client."

I have heard this more than once this summer. I realize I was hoping she would be able to tell me that Damascus, in spite of Cormorant's racism and his feelings about his competence, had somehow liked Cormorant anyway. Cormorant had implied that, and this woman would certainly have been in a position to hear about it. "Cormorant said he's met you," I say, trying to establish some kind of personal connection between them.

Dominique Marsden swallows hard as if the mere mention of Cormorant's name leaves a bad taste in her mouth. "Yes, I've met him."

Cormorant was probably rude or condescending without even being aware of it.

"Do you think he's guilty?" I ask.

For the first time Dominique Marsden smiles as if it is I who is naive. "You really don't understand, do you?" she says softly. "I've heard enough about your client to think he was envious of anyone who dared to say anything new about the past. Damascus used to say that he was simply too worried about his professional reputation to risk telling the truth about race relations in this state. All he ever wanted to do was to hide behind a footnote."

I have to keep from nodding in agreement, for this woman has confirmed my worst fears. I reply, knowing I sound absurdly stiff, "Dr. Ashley has quite a reputation in his field."

Dominique Marsden, who has been sitting with her hands folded in front of her, now spreads them and exclaims, "But don't you see? This is one of Damascus's main points in *Salted With Fire*. On the issue of race, none of the so-called experts in the field in this state have been willing to come out and say publicly to what degree their profession failed until recently to document the state's treatment of blacks. So much of our history is now lost because of it. They're like you lawyers, protecting your own behind a wall of secrecy.

"Damascus was convinced Dr. Ashley knows exactly what racist nonsense the teaching of Arkansas history about blacks has been in the schools. I know you haven't had an opportunity to read the book, but let me read you one passage."

She takes a copy of the book from the shelf behind her. I nod, pleased she is at least talking to me. In fact, I have spent almost the entire day reading *Salted With Fire* and have felt strangely conflicted. As in *Coming to Terms*, Merriweather offered little in the way of what Cormorant calls acceptable documentation, but his conclusions have begun to nag at me. As someone who thought he knew the history of the Arkansas Delta, my ignorance is disturbing.

Glancing from my face to the page in front of her, Dominique Marsden begins to read: *The story of whites' treatment of blacks in the Natural State from slavery until the modern civil rights era is like the story of the man in great pain who finally goes to the doctor with his wife. The doctor takes the wife aside after the examination and says her husband has an inoperable cancer. On the way home, the wife tells him that he merely has a case of indigestion. When he stumbles into his living room, he tells his teenaged daughter that he has a little stomachache, and when he dies in agony the next week, his obituary says he passed away peacefully in his sleep of natural causes.*

All blacks over a certain age have the shameful memory of segregation in this state burned into our brains along with all the reasons for obeying its unconscionably degrading restrictions. We knew the brutal stories our parents and grandparents had told us about what whites had done and still could do to us. For example, we knew that the events in Elaine in 1919 and St. Charles in 1904 had not been blacks rioting, but massacres; we knew from our experience in desegregating Central High in 1957 and other schools that at any instant whites would fire us and our parents and make us destitute. Every black person of a certain age can tell you stories of someone who has been harassed, beaten by whites, and then arrested for trying to defend himself, and then of having the official story—that is, the story told by whites—reported in the press be that the black person had been the violent aggressor and had earned his own punishment.

Mrs. Marsden puts down the book and stares mildly at me. "You're from Arkansas. You know this is so."

Though I have already gotten an earful this afternoon from Cormorant, who insists that no historian knows exactly what happened at Elaine (the most widely publicized of these incidents—I had not known of the killings in St. Charles) or how many blacks were killed, after reading *Salted With Fire,* I can no longer say I have no idea what Merriweather is talking about. As I was growing up, a black person dared not fail to call my father or me "Mister" and would have been shocked to have been shown the same respect. And had a black man ever reacted familiarly with my mother, I do not like to think what my father's reaction would have been. Segregation in Arkansas, I have admitted to myself after reading Merriweather's second book, was not rooted in custom and preference as my parents claimed, but in the implicit force exercised by white society to keep our blacks in place. As Merriweather says in the first chapter, white children raised in the South began to absorb even in our cradles the knowledge that the deference to be shown us and our parents by blacks was a matter of our very birthright, and the disrespect we showed blacks in almost every aspect of their lives was appropriate and contributed to the social order.

I tell her that I did read the book today and admit he made some good points. I concede, "Some of the chapters hit home, but it would be more convincing if it contained other eyewitness accounts to the incidents he describes."

Mrs. Marsden's voice, surprisingly rich and decorous on television, now sounds weary. "You wouldn't believe them anyway if they were black," she says. "You know you wouldn't. And now it's too late in most cases because so many of the eyewitnesses are dead. As Damascus said, our history was destroyed along with our dignity."

The phone begins to ring, but she does not answer it. A click signals that her answering machine is full. Undoubtedly, her friends are calling her from all over. I am surprised that someone has not come over to the house in the last twenty minutes. She stares at me as if daring me to disagree. Earlier in the day, I read a passage in *Salted With Fire* that made me understand what she is saying. In the final chapter, almost an afterword, really, Merriweather was writing about the difficulty whites have in believing any version of history but our own. He had said that our sense of superiority and arrogance was so deeply imbedded in us that it is next to impossible for a white to believe a black person's story if it conflicts with the "official" version. When I had finished the book this afternoon, I called Laurel to tell her about it. She had laughed and said that now I know what it is like to be a woman in the South.

"I know you want me out of here, but if I subpoena you to testify at my client's trial," I ask, "will you tell the truth and at least admit your husband thought you were having an affair with Merriweather?"

Dominique Marsden folds her arms across her breasts and scowls. "Before you publicly try to ruin my reputation and my husband's, don't you have to verify if he was somewhere else first?"

"Of course," I say automatically, but I know I will be obligated to try to discredit any alibi he offers. This woman seems so fundamentally decent I feel a wave of nausea churn my stomach. I find I am intensely curious about her relationship with Damascus but ask dutifully, "Do you know where your husband says he was that day?"

"It's never occurred to me to wonder until this moment," she says, putting her right hand to her face. "Have you asked him?"

I have to restrain myself from replying sarcastically. Can she be so innocent? I have trouble believing her first thought when she heard Merriweather had been killed was not that her husband had done it. "Our investigator is looking for him. Do you know where he is?"

She wets her lips with her tongue, and for an instant, I think she is going to tell me, but she says, "Forgive me, Mr. Holly, but I don't trust you. I'm sure you understand."

More than ready for me to leave, she has moved to the edge of her seat, but I nod and ask, "Why didn't you tell all of this to the police?"

She stands, and I scramble to my feet. "I really had nothing to tell them. I was Damascus's editor and friend, but not his confessor. And I don't know who killed him."

Her expression is one of strange calm. My lawyer's mind wonders if she could have been involved in her friend's death in some way or at least knows more than she is telling.

"You don't think Cormorant Ashley killed him out of jealousy?" I ask, trying not to sound mocking.

She begins to walk me to the door, and I feel I have no choice but to follow. "Unless there's a confession," she says, turning to me when we get to the hallway, "I don't know that we'll ever be certain what happened. Damascus said once that Dr. Ashley wasn't really any different from other white males. If that's true, anybody could have done it."

I put my hand on the door and open it. "Even Ezekiel?"

Her eyes widen in surprise at such a heretical notion, but she goes through the motions of pretending to contemplate this possibility. "I've never seen brothers who cared about each other so much. No, not Ezekiel, Mr. Holly."

"Could he have helped him commit suicide somehow," I ask quickly, "and then shot him to make it look like murder?"

Before she can answer, we both see her daughter walking up

the steps. Not bothering to dignify this question with an answer, Dominique Marsden opens the screen quickly and lights up the room with the warmth of the smile I saw earlier on television.

The girl, who is a copy of her mother but darker in color, is wearing jeans and a tee shirt that advertises the "Race for the Cure," making me wonder if Mrs. Marsden is, on top of everything else, a survivor of breast cancer. The girl looks questioningly at me and then her mother and says to her, "I've been trying to call you! You did so good!"

Mrs. Marsden introduces me, by saying, "This is Mr. Holly." To me, she says, unable to keep the pride out of her voice, "This is my daughter, Margaret."

Margaret, who has her mother's voice, must assume that I am from the press and gives me a brief smile. "Hi," she says and, undoubtedly anxious for details, looks back at her mother.

Dominique Marsden does not explain further, and I pass her my card, asking that she call me if she would like to talk again. She gives me the noncommittal nod one would give to a vacuum cleaner salesman, and I walk to my car with the sound of her daughter's excitement in her ears.

Back in Jeffersonville by nine (I have several routine hearings in bankruptcy court in Helena tomorrow), I hand over to Laurel my copy of *Salted With Fire*. It is too humid to sit on the deck, and while she skims through the book seated at the kitchen table across from me, I down a well-deserved bourbon and Coke and munch on the plate of ham sandwiches and potato salad she has taken from the refrigerator. "Merriweather tries to make the case," I say, "that we, meaning our generation of Arkansas whites, have repressed our consciences so completely that many of us, even after reading his book, won't be able to admit that we know what he is talking about. There's a lot in there I didn't know, and if you can look at the past hundred and fifty years from his point of view, it's sobering, to say the least."

"What does Cormorant say about it?" Laurel asks, turning the pages slowly. When she met me at the door she hugged me so tightly that I thought she was about to tell me that she was leaving.

The bourbon tastes exquisite, and I try not to gulp it, but I know I will soon be at the liquor cabinet for another one. It has been a long day. "That as propaganda the book will be an instant classic. As history, it's merely a retelling of what academics have already said in the quarterlies in the last thirty years. He relies heavily on a book called *Arkansas Odyssey*, a new history by a professor at Arkansas State that has come out in the last decade. He says it makes it possible for whites, who are willing, to wallow in guilt."

"Does it?" Laurel inquires, knowing I have spent the day reading it. She puts the book down between us. Her understanding and appreciation of the sexism that permeated Orville Taylor's book on Arkansas slavery has made her, though not sympathetic to the present state of affairs, more sensitive to the past, and I must take her question seriously or risk an argument. I wipe my mouth with one of the red cloth napkins that Laurel insists on putting out for everyday use.

On the drive home I realized that perhaps I had never allowed myself to worry about the treatment of blacks because I, too, based on my experience of them, have believed that we had no choice. According to Merriweather's preface, Delta whites believe that blacks are so fundamentally inferior to whites that they, like good-natured dogs, patiently accepted their lot without uttering an intelligible complaint until outside agitators stirred them up. In the last chapter, Merriweather summed up his position that holding this belief system together also demanded that we whites blind ourselves to the reality by which we have held power—by physical force and intimidation. I asked myself if Merriweather's analysis rings true in my own case, and I have been turning the answers over in my mind ever since.

In answer to Laurel, I pick up *Salted With Fire* and turn to Chapter 5 and read aloud the first paragraph to her: *Upper and middle-class Arkansas whites from inside and outside the Delta have long defended themselves when confronted publicly by the state's appalling image broadcast around the world from Little Rock in 1957 with the argument that the overwhelming majority of them have not taken part in acts of oppression of blacks and did not even come into contact with blacks on a daily basis. If blacks were poor, it was because they were lazy and ignorant and content to remain so. Why else live like they did? Like those Germans who still claim they didn't know what was happening to the Jews, their protests of innocence reek of the most transparent hypocrisy. Who do they think has been in power in Arkansas? In the small Delta towns like Marianna and Helena, these claims are especially outrageous. Each time whites picked up their maids or laundry from the squalid shacks in "Niggertown," they knew blacks had no paved streets, no street lights, and often not even sewer connections. The dwellings, often owned by whites, were in deplorable condition and little more than firetraps. Separate never even came close to meaning equal in Arkansas. And the rest of the country knew it. For example, to the embarrassment of white Arkansans,* Life Magazine *ran pictures in 1949 showing the "separate but equal" school systems in West Memphis on the banks of the Mississippi. A new school had just been built for the whites, giving them two schools for 900 students; photographs and the accompanying text revealed that 310 black students and their five teachers were crammed into five rooms of their fire-gutted school, and 370 additional children were packed in a single one-room black church.*

Maya Angelou, a native of the town of Stamps in southern Arkansas, who was chosen by President Clinton to read her poetry at his first inaugural, recalled the degradation of segregation in her best-selling autobiography of her childhood, I Know Why the Caged Bird Sings. *Taken to a white dentist in an emergency by her grandmother, who had at one time loaned the man money, the response was, "Annie, my policy is I'd rather stick my hand in a dog's mouth than in a nigger's." The moral deadness that lay at the center of the white power structure in Arkansas throughout the period of segregation was profound and total.*

I put down the book and tell Laurel, "Yet even if every word of this book is true, you know just as well as I do that given the situation, there was no alternative to segregation in Lee County. There's not a white here who would have stayed."

Laurel, who was already thin at the beginning of the summer, has become almost gaunt, her skin stretching tight against her skull like that of a cancer patient. For the first time I see a glimpse of what she will look like when she is old. "That's not what I'm asking: Is he *right*? Has it all been based on force?"

I sip the bourbon, wishing I hadn't been so hungry and could have relaxed before I ate. From the expression on Laurel's face, I can tell her question is not rhetorical. Maybe the difference between men and women in the South comes down to the fact that a woman would have to ask this question. Even someone as clear-eyed as Laurel has to have some hiding place from reality. "Would you rather that they had been in control?" I respond harshly. "Would you trust an all-black sheriff's department or police force around here? Equality wouldn't have worked. The whole system would have collapsed within a week. They would have stolen whites blind. Now they'll do the same thing through taxes when they take over completely."

Laurel has the stricken look of a woman who, before becoming angry, has just been slapped. "Do you really believe it had to be like it was?"

"Would they have been better off in Africa during that time?" I answer, angry that she is trying to distance herself. She was a part of this, too. "Would they have been better off starving and murdering each other in tribal warfare like they are still doing now?"

Laurel snatches the book from me and gets up from the table and goes into the den.

I know immediately that she will not sleep until she has read it. I call after her but she does not answer. I pour myself another bourbon and sit alone in the kitchen, thinking not about the book's substance but about how it will affect Cormorant's trial. A racial backlash against the Merriweathers, Raven predicted again this afternoon, will crest (if we exploit this new book correctly) right at the trial. As Dominique Marsden was coming on television this evening at five, Raven began to crack her knuckles, a habit from her tomboy years, and said that the Merriweathers have declared a holy war against the state of Arkansas and wondered aloud if she really wanted to fight them any longer. When I asked her months ago what she thought about the merits of *Coming to Terms*, she had said blithely that the only thing that interested her about the book was the size of the author's ego. And yet reading *Salted With Fire* today has unnerved her as well. Neither of us is so young that we don't remember what segregation was like. Mr. John's birthday celebration is tomorrow, and we are to talk again afterwards.

"Miller?" Laurel calls me from the den as I am brushing my teeth for bed. I go in and she arches her back against the leather couch. "Do you think your father cheated blacks?" she asks, her voice innocent as a child's.

I am standing in my underwear and can hardly wait to get into bed. She is acting as if she were not born in Marianna, and if her father had not run a grocery store and made blacks wait until everyone else, including white children, were waited on first. "Maybe you should ask yourself the same question. Actually, I thought about that on the way home," I say wearily, unable to imagine my father or hers deliberately cheating anybody, but I do know whites who would have. "Did my father make a profit off the items he sold to blacks in the commissary when they didn't have any other place to buy them? Undoubtedly. Should he have sold everything at cost because he was only paying them three dollars a day to chop his cotton? I'm sure Merriweather could make a case that he should have. He wasn't charged with peonage, if that's what you're getting at." Merriweather has reported instances where Arkansas planters received national publicity because of exploitation of blacks in the cotton fields. His point, I note, made relentlessly throughout *Salted With Fire*, is that white Arkansans, left to our own devices, would still be treating blacks little better than serfs if we could get away with it.

Laurel shrugs as if I haven't answered her question. "He says fifteen blacks were killed in 1891 in Lee County after they tried to organize cotton pickers on the plantations. I didn't know that. Is that true?"

I explain to her what Cormorant told me. "Apparently, it's not the facts that are new in this book, but the interpretation he gives them. The federal government is the hero, and the state is the whipping boy. It's nothing new, but it's how he puts our treatment of blacks in an ethical and moral context. We are made to seem like absolute monsters."

Laurel nods and lowers her head to continue reading. She has not thought much of our efforts in the last month to portray the state as a victim of lingering prejudice against Arkansans, saying the average juror doesn't care enough about the state's honor to make the connection to the case. For Cormorant's sake, I hope she is wrong. Privately, I think her negative attitude is because it was Raven's idea, and there is nothing she can do right while I use her house and business this summer. Though Laurel has recently insisted that she is not jealous, it is clear that she is. Though it is she who claims to want to leave the Delta, she has resolutely failed to travel from it this summer since our return from Paris, which seems a lifetime ago. "Are you going to be as sympathetic to this book as you were to his first one?" I ask.

"I might," she responds, not looking up again at me. "So far he makes sense."

I suppress a sigh. "We're no different than any other Southern state," I say, but know it is a sorry response. Yes, I feel attacked. It is as if Cormorant and I are suddenly to blame for the patriarchal arrangement in the state. I want her to come to bed, but she will not. I pad over to her in my slippers and bend down to peck her on the cheek.

"As Merriweather points out," she responds dryly, not even turning her head, "that kind of response is an evasion of collective responsibility. This is what we did."

I stand up straight and hear bones pop in both knees. "Don't you think you ought to read the rest of the book before you come to any conclusions?"

Laurel replies haughtily, "I haven't come to any."

Frustrated, I get into bed but cannot sleep. My mind has begun to race in earnest. White Arkansas women don't escape Merriweather's judgment, but because they have rarely held positions of leadership in the state, Merriweather has less to say about them. The brunt of this book is reserved for the white male power structure, whether in the Delta or the rest of the state. In instance after instance, he portrays us collectively as willing to go to any lengths to preserve our control over the black population for the purpose of economic greed and points as a prime example to what he terms the Massacre at Elaine.

I toss in the bed, knowing that when Laurel gets to that section of the book she will wag her finger at me. And if I am honest, I will admit that it was our darkest hour because of the way the legal system in Phillips County and the state Supreme Court failed to operate in any way but a sham. A "mask," the U. S. Supreme Court called the proceedings in which six blacks were tried and convicted of murder in a single day. How many blacks were killed at Elaine? Merriweather asks repeatedly, knowing that it was the last fact that anyone in authority in Arkansas has ever been interested in finding out. Typically, not a single white person was arrested, with the exception of the son of the white attorney who had helped black sharecroppers to deal with planters who were alleged to be cheating them.

Laurel's question about my father cheating blacks nags at me. Though for forty years my father farmed and had sharecroppers on our place, I don't believe he cheated them. The "not my family" theory of history, Merriweather calls it. *Every white person over a certain age is implicated in this story.* His treatment of the boycott in Marianna in 1971 is somewhat muted, perhaps because of the intimidation and violence which he concedes was perpetrated by blacks whom he claims had stayed nonviolent in the state until the death of Martin Luther King. His sentence about me has left me nonplussed as I mull over that period. *Miller Holly, a young white lawyer just out of law school whose planter family has farmed for generations in Lee County, haplessly tried to negotiate a settlement.* Hapless, all right, I think, hearing Laurel in the kitchen. There was so much bitterness and mistrust on both sides that I may as well have been trying to bring together the walls of the Grand Canyon. I get out of bed and find her running water from the kitchen tap into a glass. She takes a long drink.

"I'm coming to bed," she says. "It'll keep until tomorrow."

I look at the clock on the microwave. It is midnight. For some reason I am comforted by this neutral statement and nod. She puts her arm around my waist and says, her voice full of affection, "You look like a child waiting to get a spanking."

Minutes later as she lies down beside me naked in the dark, I know she is right. This book does trouble me, and I admit to myself finally how much Merriweather's first one does, too. "He overstates so much," I complain as she nestles against me. "He makes it sound as if it were all a giant conspiracy from the beginning. I have to think that it was pretty rare after slavery that people sat around thinking about how to keep blacks down. Sometimes disastrously, we just reacted to events. Like I did."

"That's too easy," Laurel says, turning on her left side, her favorite position to sleep.

I slide behind her spoon-like and put my arm across her chest. Though the air-conditioner is going full blast, she feels almost hot against me. "Every generation of white Arkansans has been in denial since we bought the first slave and brought him or her here," she says, her voice soft. "Since you've had the power, you can't admit it."

White males, I think wearily. She has not even gotten to the parts about the Ku Klux Klan that operated in Arkansas after the Civil War, and its more civilized revival in the 1920s when nationally it became a respectable and potent political force which baited foreigners, radicals, Jews, and Catholics, as well as blacks. If Merriweather is quoting correctly, Little Rock and Pulaski County boasted 7,800 members and its organization swept county elections in 1922. I wonder how much of that hatred of outsiders still exists.

I start to reply, but like someone exhausted, she falls immediately asleep, and I am left to brood alone. Is that why I have been willing to represent Cormorant? Is this a way to stay in control? I feel now like we are now trying to ride the back of a tiger.

11

The Ashley plantation in Phillips County lies along the "low road" to Helena and like our place must be disappointing to visitors who are expecting Tara, but the fact is that the Arkansas Delta, younger than the "Old South" just across the Mississippi, contained relatively few ante-bellum mansions, and fewer still have survived. According to Cormorant, the home built by his slave-owning great-grandfather was relatively modest, a two-story affair containing containing less than three thousand square feet and no columns. After a fire destroyed it in 1925, his grandfather had it rebuilt it along similar lines on the same spot, and though it has undergone extensive repair and the installation of a central heat and air system, Cormorant says it is not too different from the original dwelling built in 1850.

Since Mr. John's stroke five years ago, this annual celebration of his birthday has been confined to his immediate family and Laurel and me. Before his impairment, other guests were invited; but always vain, Mr. John, now seventy-five, is appalled by his own appearance, which actually seems remarkable given his lack of exercise and the paralysis that affects the left side of his body. Laurel and I arrive at the appointed hour of six, our gift a Land's End long-sleeved shirt he will rarely wear since he only leaves the house occasionally in cold weather to sit in a wheelchair out front where, if the leaves are off the trees, he can barely see the Mississippi across the gravel road and cotton fields a quarter of a mile to the east, raging past. Though the house was built on one of the slopes along Crowley's Ridge, the floods of '27 and '37 got inside the first floor each time, but these disasters have always been regarded as the price to be paid for such fertile land, and the house, again according to Cormorant, was cleaned and refurbished to await the next flood.

"What would he do if we didn't come?" Laurel wonders as we walk up the driveway.

We have parked behind Raven's Lexus. Ahead of it is Cormorant's Taurus. Though his sister could ride over with him and his family, she never does, declining to spend the night in the family home or with us though we have offered a number of times. Whatever voodoo Mr. John worked on his son, it didn't take on his daughter. She wouldn't be here tonight if it weren't his birthday. "He'd send Cormorant to fetch us," I reply, knocking on the door. "He likes you best. You act like the daughter Raven won't."

"It's no trouble," she says, more to herself than to me. Despite her desire to flee the Delta, Laurel insists on preserving its rituals, and one is paying respect to its old, a good custom. She has dropped by to see Mr. John several times this summer, an act which pleases Cormorant as much as it does the old man.

Cormorant greets us at the door and, as usual on his father's birthday, plays the gracious host, but this year, inevitably, the atmosphere is strained as we go through the motions of celebrating Mr. John's birthday in the big dining room before we eat steaks Cormorant will grill on the patio behind the house.

Cormorant's children are present but seem flustered, uncertain about what can be said and what is off-limits this year. Though I have been by Cormorant's home in Little Rock often this summer, this is the first time I have been with the whole family together. Miller Ray, my namesake, and always quiet, is even more silent than usual, the flickering smile on his face unable to conceal that he'd rather be anywhere but in Arkansas this summer. I wonder how often he will come back if his father goes to jail as a murderer. He and Cormorant have always gotten along well, his father accepting his homosexuality better than his mother, who has yearned for an upper-class Leave It to Beaver family life and has not experienced one moment of it since Miller came out to them when he was fifteen. After a year of wringing their hands, Cormorant and Beth found a gay therapist in Little Rock who conducts group sessions with gay teenagers, and Miller survived his teenaged years in the South—no easy feat, he has said. A pre-architecture major at the University of Maryland, he has his father's brains but understandably not his penchant for controversy.

In the family, only Catherine, who physically resembles her father rather than having inherited Beth's lovely features, has lived her life the way her mother would have preferred. A Chi O at Ole Miss without an ounce of ambition except to marry well and begin a family, Catherine, Beth confides, would do better to not come back to Little Rock either, whether she graduates or not. She can put her to work selling dresses part-time, but there is too much competition to bring her into the business. Reading between the lines, I gather that even if he is acquitted, her father has become too notorious, and she is too plain to achieve her goals in-state. While the presents are being opened for Mr. John, I stand by Catherine and Miller and whisper anecdotes from their father's youth. "Your grandfather couldn't trust your dad to go to the hardware store without your Aunt Raven," I murmur. "He couldn't tell a nail from a screw." Having heard these stories all their lives, they laugh dutifully, but both are plainly miserable. Their father is not an easy man to console.

Having not seen me since his son was charged, Mr. John reproaches me in his increasingly strangled voice, which I have rarely understood since the stroke. Interpreting, Cormorant excuses me by saying how busy I have been on his behalf and keeping up with my own practice. Cormorant has given Doris the night off, but I am curious what she would make of our conversation tonight, which in part centers around the reaction to Merriweather's latest book. Mr. John had seen Ezekiel touting it on television yesterday, and pointing to a picture of him in his lap from today's *Democrat-Gazette*, asks if I think Ezekiel is crazy—or at least I think that's what he has asked.

"Crazy like a fox," I respond loudly as if he were deaf instead of partially paralyzed. "He's trying to sell books and doing a good job, I bet."

He says something that I do not catch, but Cormorant translates. "He wants to know what you think about it."

I look at the circle around Mr. John, and realize everyone is waiting for me to respond, including Laurel. I know Cormorant trusts me not to put him on the spot or upset his father. "There's a lot of sound and fury in it," I say neutrally, "but I'm not sure what it signifies."

Raven, who has been helping to open her father's presents, says boldly, "He makes it clear how difficult it was being black in Arkansas."

Cormorant shoots her a warning glance, but her father nods his head as if he agrees and says something with the word "farming" in it. Cormorant explains, "He says that they didn't have anything to do when farming was mechanized."

Without warning, Laurel says, "Merriweather says that after Reconstruction ended and the federal troops were withdrawn, we kept blacks in their place basically at the point of a gun. Is that true, Mr. John?"

Even with half his face frozen, the old man is able to convey his frustration through his tone, but again his words are unintelligible. This time it is Raven who translates, "Daddy says nobody is controlling them now. Besides, they could have left and a lot did."

Cormorant alone is watching his father carefully for signs this conversation is too much for him, and I know he is annoyed. Yet implicit in Mr. John's words is some kind of admission, and to soften the impact, I blurt, "You mean if they stayed, they were going to have to accept doing things our way."

Out of his line of sight, Laurel rolls her eyes at me and asks, "What happened at Elaine, Mr. John? What did you hear about it?"

Cormorant pats his father's shoulder and whispers something in his ear that none of us can pick up. The old man shrugs and takes a deep breath, and the word "revolt" is plainly heard, but I can't quite get the rest. Cormorant is about to speak, but Raven says quickly, "He said blacks staged a revolt and started killing whites. The governor called out the troops and put it down."

Knowing where this is about to lead, Cormorant again puts a hand on his father's arm and pleads loudly, "Are you tired of this? You want to eat dinner?"

Mr. John shakes his head. He hasn't had the one cocktail he is allowed and motions with his good arm that he wants his drink. As if she and Laurel had planned this together, Raven produces his bourbon and water from the tray on the dining room table, and hands it to me. Greedy for one of his few pleasures, Mr. John knocks half of it back and puts it down on the plastic board that straddles his chair.

Laurel, absently kneading with her hands the soft fabric of the sweater Beth has painstakingly knit for her father-in-law, says, "Merriweather says that hundreds of blacks may have been killed. Do you think that's possible?"

The old man belches gently and then grunts out a long sentence that says, according to Cormorant, Governor Brough had no choice but to use whatever force it took to put down a rebellion. Probably not many blacks died since it was over so fast.

Looking straight at her brother, Raven says, "Daddy, in the first book this Merriweather wrote, he says that some whites in the Delta had children by the slaves. We all know that's true."

"Raven!" Cormorant yells, interrupting her, "we're not getting into this!"

For an instant it is as if we are children again, and Raven is spraying the .22 dangerously close to the house. Though she was an an excellent shot and knew exactly what she was doing, anything could happen if the bullet ricocheted off a piece of metal. She continues, "Cormorant and I heard that a slave called Little Tina had at least one child by your grandfather. Is that true?"

The room is suddenly quiet and every eye is on Mr. John. I do not know what Cormorant has told Beth and his children, but each has a frightened look, as if this moment could actually end Mr. John's life. He fixes his watery eyes on his daughter. The longer he speaks, the easier it is to understand him, and I can make out the words, "Who told you that?"

Cormorant's face has gone hard, and I do not doubt at all that he once threatened to kill a man. He certainly seems capable of murdering another person. Raven moves closer to her father and says, "Cormorant and I heard it for years, and this man who wrote these books interviewed Octavia Haskins."

Mr. John, whose mind is sharper than it has appeared, gasps intelligibly, "Is it in the books?"

"No, Daddy," Cormorant says quickly, having waited a lifetime to be able to defend his father. "I told him I would sue him if he wrote that."

Mr. John raises the rest of the bourbon to his mouth and sips at it and looks around as if he is just waking up from a bad dream. Breathing rapidly, he says, or so I think, "That's what my father told me."

I look across at Laurel who nods at me to confirm what we both have heard. There is an unmistakable gleam in her eyes as if the chickens are finally coming home to roost and she is bothered not one bit by it. I am furious that Raven has forced this moment. None of this helps Cormorant, but she has insisted on it, and she seems determined to drive a wedge between them. Why? It scares me to think that she may, in fact, believe he is guilty and thinks she is forcing him to be honest with us. If Cormorant does admit to us he murdered Merriweather, I can't let him take the witness stand and commit perjury.

"Cool!" Catherine responds, incredibly, her voice sounding as sweet and clear as the peal of a church bell. "We have relatives I didn't know about. Who was she?"

Cormorant grimaces with obvious distaste, but I am reminded of Dr. Matso's reaction that someday people will thank Damascus Merriweather for rescuing their family history for them. Raven fills the growing silence by saying, "She was a house slave."

Whether she knows it or not, Catherine has struck the right note to end this discussion for the moment. Sexually active since she was sixteen, according to Cormorant, Catherine is not naive about either sex or race, and I would not be at all surprised if this is her own way of defusing a topic which resonates, for different reasons, more harshly for the rest of us.

"I hope he treated her well," Catherine says lightly and reaches over and pats her grandfather's good arm. His fragile state is obvious to all, and his pained expression makes clear that he does not want any further questions tonight.

If Damascus Merriweather were alive, doubtless he would argue she couldn't have been treated at all well, and my increasingly militant wife could surely make the argument for him, but she is smugly silent, as if this is victory enough. I feel as vulnerable and exposed by Mr. John's admission as if it were my own. Sitting here, I recall Cormorant's saying his father's statement would not be conclusive, and yet now I have no doubt Mr. John knows the truth. His eyes blink rapidly, and he reaches for his drink and finishes it.

Though the topic is studiously avoided during dinner, it resurfaces as soon as Mr. John, who does seem exhausted, is put to bed by Cormorant barely an hour later. Catherine peppers her aunt for information about Octavia Haskins and Little Tina, and the battle lines are drawn as Laurel and I fight each other through Catherine about issues of consent and the question of whether there could have been genuine affection between a slave woman and her master. I find it irritating that Raven has become her ally. Our unwitting mediators are Catherine and Miller Ray, whose comments prove to me what little stake they feel in the outcome. Born well after official segregation ended, they both express surprise that no one has asked Octavia Haskins for the stories *she* knows about her great-grandmother.

"Shame," Laurel pronounces. "Miller probably has a dozen black relatives, but he's afraid to find out."

I wonder if that is the reason. Beth, sitting to my right directly across from Laurel, puts down her wine glass, and says defensively, "How would you know whether she's telling the truth?"

Pushing away from the table, Catherine professes amazement at her mother's question. "Why would she lie?"

"I doubt if she would, but blacks have reason to hate us as a group," Raven says, "for what we've done to them. Read Merriweather's books. They'll send chills up your spine."

Catherine, who blithely claims she hasn't read a book outside of class in over a decade, puts her arms behind her head and stretches. "Maybe they'll make a movie."

Miller, who only recently has begun to like his sister, laughs but adds seriously, "Blacks my age don't seem to care that much about the past. They don't talk about it."

Raven begins to clear the table, and everyone but me joins her. "They didn't go through what their parents did. Who could blame them for not rubbing their childrens' noses in it?" she says. "It's bound to be painful to admit you were humiliated for much of your life. We're ashamed and afraid is why we don't ask. Daddy isn't going to tell us anything about how Little Tina and her child were really treated. He's not going to blame his ancestors at this stage of his life anyway. So we don't know anything except for a few references to her in a journal and some letters."

"But *they* know," Catherine says excitedly. "Surely those stories about what happened have been passed down."

Laurel, who has always dismissed Catherine as a frivolous sorority girl, smiles at her as she picks up my plate. "You should be the one to talk to Octavia Haskins. Since you're from a different generation, she won't be bitter toward you."

As the discussion moves into the kitchen, I feel my resentment toward Laurel growing. In the last two months she has become the patron saint of blacks, when, at home, her attitude is that they are responsible for the poverty in the Delta.

When Cormorant comes into the kitchen moments later, he says melodramatically to Raven, "If he dies tonight, we'll know why."

Raven, her expression unapologetic, hands him her dish towel and goes to stand by her nephew, who is observing us from a chair propped against the refrigerator. "For God's sake, it didn't hurt him to admit that."

"It did, too," Cormorant challenges her. "He wouldn't say a word when I got him into bed. He knows you hate him."

Raven's voice tightens as she responds, "I don't hate him. I hate how he's treated you all these years. You're like some anxious little dog around him hoping for a few table scraps. It's pathetic."

I have never mentioned to Laurel that Raven slapped her brother in front of me, and until now, I had assumed it had been forgotten, but perhaps because his children and wife are present, Cormorant can't allow her comment to pass. "I'm sick and tired of you turning the past into some psychodrama in which blacks and I are simply Daddy's victims," he says, his voice again rock-hard. "He was a product of his time just like everybody else. I owe him respect whether you do or not."

Raven whirls around to Miller Ray and says to him, "I hope to God you've escaped this blind loyalty fixation that infects the southern white male. It's warped the ones I know."

For the first time since we were children, I feel Raven's wrath, and it is not a comfortable sensation. "I take it that was meant for me," I say lightly, trying to contain my irritation. "I thought loyalty was a pretty good thing. You've certainly been its beneficiary over the years."

"I have," she admits, "but you and Cormorant are just so stubborn about the past."

"You mean we won't roll over just because an embittered black man writes a couple of books?" I say, glaring at her and getting up to leave. "No, I won't do that!"

On the way home, I feel more estranged from Laurel than I ever have. She drives, but we do not talk and are accompanied only by the night sounds of the Delta that murmur over the crunching gravel beneath Laurel's Voyager. Nearing the house, she says, finally, "I'm going to visit my sister for a few weeks and try to decide what I want to do the rest of my life. "

I cut my eyes to see if she is serious or is being sarcastic, but it is too dark to read her face. I am reminded of Cormorant's mother, Ms. Ella, whose disease-ridden mind at the end of her life thought it necessary to apologize for her great-grandfather's sermons. "So you want to spend the rest of your life," I cannot resist saying, "doing penance for our sins, huh?"

She turns in our driveway, and says, her voice a million miles away. "I don't like my life here. I've told you that."

We get out of the car. Now that I know it is serious, Laurel's threat to leave sears me as if she has poured a bucket of boiling tar over my head. "What is wrong with you? Aren't you forgetting you made a vow?"

Laurel acts as if she has not heard me and goes into the house.

After a moment to let her get away from me, I follow and fix a bourbon and Coke in the kitchen and then take it out to the deck, wondering if this would have happened anyway without Cormorant's trial to bring it to a head. Maybe it's me all along she has wanted to flee. I can't believe she will leave. This is our home.

12

"Mr. Holly," Kit Pierce asks, his Yankee accent grating against my ears, "what's your reaction to this most recent book by Damascus Merriweather from beyond the grave, so to speak? Your home state of Arkansas is compared to Nazi Germany. Do you think that's accurate?"

This is the third out-of-state telephone interview I've done this week, and the fifth since *Salted With Fire* was published three weeks ago. I am becoming accustomed to the hyperbolic mischaracterization of the book by radio talk-show hosts. "Nothing could be further from the truth," I reply, suspecting the guy has not read more than a few pages of Merriweather's book. "From the standpoint of most white Southerners who lived through it, a period of segregation was an inevitable transition, and no one denies it was often a difficult one for the African-American community." I add, having practiced this soundbite with Cormorant just last night, "But to compare it with the Holocaust is an insult to your Jewish listeners and contributes nothing to one's understanding of the period."

Though he may not have read the book, Kit Pierce, who is calling from a Chicago station, can't resist gigging us. "According to Dr. Merriweather, the word *difficult* doesn't describe the conditions endured by blacks in Arkansas, which I don't ordinarily think of as a Deep South state. Violence and intimidation were commonplace acts."

I glance at Cormorant who is sitting across from me. He is listening in. He mouths the words, *race riots*, and I say, hoping the guy doesn't cut me off, "I'm sure you know your history well enough to realize there were major race riots not only in rural Arkansas but in several cities in the north, including Detroit, Chicago, and Omaha during this same period. Eventually, what white Southerners came to realize was how militantly segregated the rest of the country was, too. If you are old enough to remember the television pictures from South Boston in the 1970s, you realize the former states of the Confederacy didn't have a monopoly on resistance to the federal government and the forced busing of children."

It is more or less a typical interview, and I have parried the usual barbs from the host and listeners alike. Moments later, the interview ends, and Cormorant concedes that I have become reasonably adroit in dealing with the media. I lean back in my chair and wonder if our strategy is working. By the time the trial begins next week, we are hoping Cormorant's jury, which will be overwhelmingly white, will tacitly identify me as having been Cormorant's surrogate as the state's defender against Merriweather's books. We have worked hard to keep the media informed of my appearances, and have been rewarded by a couple of articles in local papers. My interviewers, of course, would rather have Cormorant, but since I have continued to insist that it wouldn't be wise for him to respond publicly before the trial, the media have continued to accept me as the next best thing. Inside the state, the general reaction to Merriweather's second book has been strongly negative as a result of his Holocaust comparison even as it continues to leap off the shelves.

Raven appears in the door and shakes her head as Cormorant tells her about the latest interview. "This may work, but we'll regret this some day, Miller," she says to me, her tone sorrowful. "What Merriweather has written is basically true. There is no defense. We *are* like those Germans who shrug and say they didn't know what was going on in the death camps."

Cormorant, who has been encouraged by these interviews, wags his finger at his sister and says, "That's totally ridiculous!"

"The people in this state won't always be in denial," she predicts, ignoring her brother's reaction. "Because of these books, sooner or later, we'll realize what we've done and quit making excuses for it."

Though Cormorant professes to be dumbfounded by his sister's capitulation to Merriweather's books, I suppose I am not. Raven was always different. The surprising thing is that it has taken this long. Cormorant places his hands behind his head and says, "You know who you're beginning to sound like?"

"Our mother," Raven admit and laughs. "We used to think she was crazy. She just felt guilt."

The telephone rings on my desk, and I pick it up but nearly drop it in surprise.

It is Ezekiel Merriweather who says gruffly, "I want to meet with your client this afternoon after six at the pharmacy. Can you and he come?"

Elated that he wants this meeting, I accept on the spot and tell him we will be there a few minutes after he closes up. I put the phone down. "Ezekiel wants to meet with us this afternoon," I tell Cormorant, unable to keep the excitement out of my voice. "This is what we've hoped would happen."

Raven's eyes grow big. "Are you crazy? You and he are like two boys daring each other to jump off a bridge. You don't need this meeting. You wouldn't let another client do this!"

Raven means, I suppose, that because his brother's second book is taking a pounding locally for the Holocaust comparison, we don't need him to say at the trial that he doesn't think Cormorant killed his brother—but I know better. The trick will be to get Ezekiel to say this on the witness stand and get it into evidence. "I at least want a hung jury. If he indicates during his testimony that he thinks Cormorant is innocent, any blacks on the jury will follow his lead."

Cormorant nods. "I want to see the son of a bitch up close and personal," he says to his sister. "He's caused me enough misery."

Raven laughs. "Do you think he's going to apologize? You must be out of your minds."

The truth is that I don't know what he wants, but it will be better to find out, and I have no doubt he won't meet with me alone again. Raven, who started this, has lost her nerve, and I tell her as much while Cormorant does an errand for Beth at her shop. "We've got Ezekiel on the run," I gloat. "Arkansans resent this last book especially, and we've got to make sure it carries over to the trial."

Now seated in Cormorant's chair, Raven runs her hands through her hair. "You've become obsessed with the racial angle of this case," she accuses me. "It's going to backfire on you if you're not careful."

This was her idea, I want to remind her, but I know it will do no good. Guilt is generally a woman's disease, and the Merriweather brothers have pushed all the right buttons. I pull the file on the Merriweathers and marvel at how thick it has grown. When have we not been obsessed by blacks? Raven can't even go out at night because of them. "It must be nice to be so superior," I respond sarcastically. "Your brother doesn't have that luxury, I'm afraid. Neither does Beth."

Raven stands and goes to the easel and writes my wife's name. "I know you feel abandoned by Laurel and me, but it's really not like that."

"It's not?" I say, astounded she would deny it. In the last week, Laurel has called Raven from England at least once to talk about how benighted the rest of us are. "You know she's jealous of you. She was afraid you would try to seduce me this summer."

Instead of feeling embarrassed as I thought she would, Raven says gravely, "We talked about that. I should have been more sensitive to Laurel. She's felt a lot more insecure than I ever realized. I didn't know how unhappy she was. I always thought she was content to live out her life in the Delta."

It pisses the hell out of me that Laurel has confided in Raven. They have never been friends before. Now they talk about me behind my back. The phone rings again, and I pick it up, afraid it is Ezekiel calling to cancel, but it is Steve Crisp phoning from his Cadillac downtown. He says he has finally tracked down Bobby Marsden. I know Steve wants his money, and I tell him to come by now. I hang up the phone and ask Raven, "How're you going to feel when Cormorant is getting raped weekly down in Cummins by a gang of blacks? Do you think you and Laurel will be so sympathetic to them then?"

She throws down the pen and stalks from the room, and for the first time in three weeks I feel as if I have gotten her attention. I wait for Steve and think that the smartest decision Cormorant could have made three months ago when all this began would have been to hire a black attorney. I can't help but think he would know the full story on this case by now. Trust. It is a fragile commodity these days. I am reminded of the conversation Laurel and I had before she boarded the flight to England two weeks ago in Memphis. Even at the airport, I begged her to stay until Cormorant's trial was over, thinking if we could just get it behind us, the stress would be lifted, and she would settle down again. The last night I even offered to go to therapy, and she laughed, saying that neither of us was crazy and that we understand each other perfectly.

And if I am honest, I know I want her to come back for another reason as well. Earlier this morning in my office in Marianna, Peggy, my secretary, and I looked for a file for an hour that Laurel would have been able to put her hands on immediately. I have talked to her five times since she left, sometimes just to find a document Peggy can't locate. My law practice is quickly becoming a disorganized mess. Peggy, I remind myself, is doing the best she can and would be able to limp along if Laurel had helped her before she left, but all Laurel's energy was spent getting ready for her trip. I am realizing how much I have depended on Laurel all these years. I pretend that all is well at the office, but Peggy knows better and doubtless is talking.

What Laurel told our friends I can only begin to guess. I have been invited for dinner just a couple of times since everyone thinks I am spending all my time in Little Rock getting ready for the trial. No one seems to realize how much I have been in my office in Marianna out of necessity these last weeks because of Laurel's absence.

I go over to the window to look for Steve, who just at this point is pulling into the parking lot. Yesterday in the barber shop in Marianna, Dacus Terrell asked why people kept taking pot shots at Lee County. Before I could answer, Will Peyton, who has cut my hair for twenty years, cracked that just as the rest of the country loves to hate Arkansas, the Delta has replaced hillibillies as its favorite local prejudice. There is a lot of truth to that, I think.

I watch to see if Steve will put any money in the slotted board, wondering if *he* thinks Cormorant is guilty. As usual, he tempts fate and does not pay. The more fingers we try to point at people, the more money he makes. For all we really know, he is on Merriweather's payroll, too. Taken together, I realize the

Merriweather brothers have made us all paranoid.

When Steve saunters in, he is disappointed that we are not more pleased with his information. I'm no longer much interested in Marsden as a suspect because the prosecutor's file now contains statements by both Marsdens. It is as if the recent spate of publicity given to Dominique Marsden made Minor decide he better cover all his bases. The prosecutor has now been given an alibi, which seems solid enough. Yet when I went out to interview Marsden, he had moved again, and I have a nagging hope that he could turn out to know more than either he or his wife has reported.

"He's living in an apartment near McClellan High," Steve says, handing me an address on the back of his card and, as usual, forgetting I am not from Little Rock. "When I was a kid, it was wall-to-wall whites, a lot of them rednecks. Now, blacks live all around there."

I nod, but I have only a vague idea of where he is talking about. Steve lives in North Little Rock, which I know how to get around in even less than southwest Little Rock. Despite my suspicions about Steve, without him we have come up with next to nothing. Ezekiel has kept us off balance from the beginning, and I haven't had a handle on this case since day one. If I had insisted that Cormorant hire an attorney from Little Rock, he would have had no choice. What is it about me that likes to be the rescuer? I have tried to play that role all my life. Now, with Laurel in England and the dynamics of this case so confusing, it is I who need rescuing. I give him his check and tell him I will call him if we need him again. As he puts it in his wallet, I ask, "What did you think of *Salted With Fire?*"

"I'm glad I wasn't living a hundred years ago," he says, succinctly. "I don't think I would've made it a day. It's hard enough now."

I smile and shake his hand, thinking I know what he's talking about. In Marianna, an argument over the payment for a hamburger at a drive-in led eventually to the boycott. From the window I watch him walk across to his car, wanting to see if it has been hauled off. It has not, and I watch him drive off, wondering as Raven has suggested on more than one occasion, if he is heading straight to tell Ezekiel.

The meeting spot for our visit with Ezekiel is again his pharmacy, where I met him almost two months ago. From the beginning of this case until only recently, he has been in the driver's seat, but as I have realized time and again, his focus except at the beginning of the case has not been his brother's murderer but the content of his books. Why? The most obvious answer is that he can't bring his brother back, and that Damascus lives on every time he sells another book.

As he should be, Cormorant is nervous on the drive over to 12th Street. I have warned Cormorant that Ezekiel might be concealing a tape recorder. Cormorant, who has started smoking again and has begun to lose weight, drums his fingers on his knee. This summer he has taken to wearing jeans and sneakers, clothes he wouldn't have been caught dead in three months ago. For some reason, he has changed to slacks and a white shirt, as if Damascus's response to us depends on how much respect we show him. "I'm not going to say anything he can use against me," he says. "I just want to see him."

I shake my head but know the feeling. The old saying that a man who defends himself has a fool for a client could be expanded to include his best friend.

At five after six, Ezekiel unlocks the door and lets us in. No one offers to shake hands, and he leads us to the back room with a grunt. It is the first time I have seen him in person in months, and he looks smaller, less bearlike, as if the events of the summer have whittled him down to size. He motions for us to sit down. We do, and I notice that the calendars that were here are gone. He has been interviewed so many times that I wonder if they seemed appropriate, though they were hardly salacious. Yet I have learned that this man leaves little to chance.

"You know I now have some questions about whether you killed my brother," he says to Cormorant, "but before I talk about that, I want to know your reaction to my brother's second book."

I watch as Cormorant draws his hands together under his chin, a familiar sign that he has been taken by surprise. I want to warn him that this is apparently some kind of test, but it does not matter, because Cormorant will not answer this question diplomatically, regardless of what is at stake. In order to get some information, I would soften my answer. Cormorant will not. Predictably, he says, "Any time a man writes history with an axe to grind, he's always suspect. The book isn't even good journalism because we aren't sure if we really *know* any more than when he started. And that's all right, but he should have told his readers that at the beginning and repeated it in every chapter, so they don't come away fooled. Now Damascus has people thinking we know the truth about slavery, the truth about the South's oppression of blacks, the truth about the moral cowardice of white Southerners, when all we have is more questions, not answers."

I wonder if that's true. Despite Cormorant's cautionary statements about the Slave Narratives, I realize that for me they have conveyed the *truth*, whatever details might have been misremembered. Instead of going off on Cormorant as he did me, Ezekiel folds his arms tightly across his chest. "So, you're willing to concede my brother raised some good questions," he says, his tone ironical.

"But the questions have always been there," Cormorant says passionately. "Raising them the way Damascus did doesn't help answer them. It makes people think he was on to something, but, in reality, the latest history by Michael Dougan acknowledges many points your brother makes and in a less inflammatory way." We all know Dougan, a professor at Arkansas State, is white.

For the first time since we got here, Ezekiel shows signs of frustration. "But his main point—and you knew this according to my brother as well as any white historian—" he says, his voice rising, "is that we've never been accepted as *sources* of history. Until that happens, no historian's version will be accurate, and our story will be lost."

I am not part of this conversation, but Merriweather's eyes bore in on both of us. Despite his intensity, he seems to want to have a genuine dialogue. Cormorant pulls on his beard and says finally, "This is a problem for historians in many areas. For example, we don't know what women did or thought for most of human civilization, because they weren't considered, as you call them, sources either."

I cannot believe my ears. Cormorant, to my mind, has made a huge concession. I did not expect him to be capable of making any, and I am not sure of his motive. He is speaking as if Merriweather were, if not a colleague, at least a promising student. Yet even Cormorant knows he needs this man on his side, if at all possible. Merriweather responds, "So you agree that what my brother did in gathering oral histories from families about the rape of their ancestors in the Delta was worthwhile?"

Merriweather's voice has become tinged with condescension, but Cormorant treats this as a serious question and gives him a lecture that reminds me of his explanation of why historians have problems accepting the Slave Narratives. Merriweather seems to be listening, but I don't know if he truly is any longer. It is obvious he has nothing but contempt for Cormorant, who is pontificating on the difficulty of knowing the truth when it is clear even to me now that it is whites alone whose versions have been accepted and reported as truth. "It's not enough to know the stories," Cormorant is saying. "They have to be evaluated from many different angles."

Merriweather slowly shakes his head as if he is talking to an imbecile. It is hard to know which man is more arrogant. Abruptly, he says, jabbing his finger at Cormorant, "Damascus told me that one of the stories is that your great-grandfather bore a daughter by one of his slaves. You ever heard that?"

Cormorant drops his professorial manner and, scowling, replies, "I'll tell you the same thing that I told your brother— that if you ever print that, I'll sue you for libel."

Feeling as if I am in the courtroom being observed by a jury, I don't even swallow.

Merriweather laughs and says sneeringly, "Good. I'll ask the judge for a blood test. Her great-grandchild is ready and willing. How about your daddy?"

I do not expect Cormorant to admit anything on this, and I cannot imagine Mr. John, even under oath, testifying publicly to what he admitted to us. Given his physical condition, I can't imagine that a judge would force him to testify.

"Is this why you wanted to talk to me?" Cormorant asks, as if the thought has never crossed his mind. "Thanks to you, I'm charged with murder. I didn't do a thing to your brother except to deal with him as honestly as I knew how. You people say that you want a dialogue, and when you get one, you can't stand it."

Instead of making him angrier, this statement seems to intrigue Merriweather. He puts his right forefinger beside his lips. "So if you tell my brother to his face that his race is inferior to yours, that he's a joke as a professional, that nothing can be done to tell the truth about how your ancestors brutalized and raped ours, I'm supposed to thank you for talking to him? My brother figured you for a coward and racist to the core, but he didn't say you were stupid."

Cormorant blinks several times, a sign that I know from past experience tells me he is trying to control himself. "He said I was a coward," he asks softly, "because I told him what I thought?"

Ezekiel stares at Cormorant, his expression one of disbelief. "Because you didn't have the guts to risk your reputation," he answers, "when you knew what blacks had done to whites."

Cormorant opens his mouth to respond, but checks himself, giving me the chance to ask, "What is the point in going over this now? You knew what your brother thought when you called me."

Ezekiel shrugs. "I wanted to see what your client had to say for himself," he says to me. "I don't expect him to testify at the trial."

At this point, without other suspects, Cormorant doesn't have any choice. "You might be surprised then," I say.

Cormorant leans forward, his voice not quite trembling but hoarse. "Mr. Merriweather, I didn't kill your brother. I didn't have any reason to want him dead. And even if I had, why would I do it? We all knew he was dying."

"Why should I believe you," he says slowly drawing out his words, "when you admit that you don't believe us?"

The words are out of Cormorant's mouth before he can even think. "Because it's the truth."

Ezekiel smiles now, and as his silence fills the room, I am struck by how he has reduced this conversation to its fundamental meaning. It is as if all along he has been trying to teach Cormorant a lesson, and now he has. "What do you want?" I ask, hoping to get something out of this.

"To find out if your client," he says, "had the courage to pull the trigger. As far as I am concerned, you're both basically rabbits."

I feel my face flush and try to hold my temper, but Cormorant stands up, not willing to take any more abuse. "Fuck you!" he shouts at Ezekiel, who rises hastily to his feet.

For an instant, I think Ezekiel is going to reach into his drawer for a gun and shoot us, but all he does is gaze upon us with a bemused smile. Cormorant is shaking with rage. I follow him out of the room, but we have to wait while Ezekiel unlocks the door for us. Cormorant won't even look at him any more, but I do, and he gives me a cold stare as if I am beneath his contempt.

Once we are back in my car, Cormorant yells at me, "Why in the hell did we come here? He just wanted to provoke us."

Or try to make us understand something, I think but don't say as I turn left onto 12th Street and then right on Fair Park. I want to go to Cormorant's house and have a drink and try to calm down. My heart is beating fast. I don't know if Cormorant felt fear in Ezekiel's office, but I did, and I am ashamed and angry at the same time. "Well, we let him," I respond.

In the kitchen at Cormorant's house, I fix myself a bourbon and Coke and move into the dining room to rehash what just occurred. I sit down at the long table, a family heirloom from the 19th century. Cormorant sits down across from me with a beer. I am still angry but feel myself breathing more easily. I'm not sure we haven't somehow just witnessed a carefully staged performance. Naively, I had gone there hoping he might tell us who he thought did kill his brother. "I think he wanted to see," I say, "if he could make you lose your temper and find out what you would do. In his own mind, he may honestly be still trying to figure out if you shot Damascus."

Cormorant fingers his glass so hard that I am afraid it is going to slip and fly across the room. "He just wanted to humiliate us!"

I start to add that we should have been more conciliatory, and then feel disgusted. *Rabbits.* That son of a bitch! We talk for half an hour but succeed only in getting angry again. In order to get myself back under control, I know I have to get away from Cormorant and decide it is as good a time as any to try to find Bobby Marsden. Cormorant explains the easiest way to get to southwest Little Rock, and I get on I-30 toward Hot Springs. He offers to go with me, but I don't want him around for awhile. As I look for the Geyer Springs exit, I replay in my mind once again the conversation with Ezekiel and realize something rang false. Ezekiel had said that his brother basically hated Cormorant, but if that is true, why had he wanted him to substitute on the law school panel? Maybe, though, he had said that just to piss off Cormorant. Why had he asked him to collaborate on the first book? It has been impossible for me to understand what their relationship truly was. In his own way, Ezekiel seems just as curious as I am.

Within minutes I am threading my way through an area of Little Rock I didn't know existed and am struck by its size. An older and grittier area, the streets are jammed with traffic, and though it is not an attractive part of the city, it has a vitality that I thought was the exclusive characteristic of west Little Rock. As promised, I find Marsden's apartment complex near McClellan High School. On the second floor of an eight-unit apartment building, a black man in his forties comes to the door. I introduce myself and get a cold stare reminscent of our encounter with Ezekiel. "I know you've talked to the police," I tell him quickly, "but I need to check out some things myself."

About six feet three, Marsden, who is wearing threadbare jeans and a UALR Trojan tee shirt, doesn't invite me in, but he doesn't tell me to leave either. We stand facing each other on his balcony in the fading light, and his expression tells me that I am not going to have a lot of time to make my point. Though he probably already knows, I explain that I have talked to his wife and have read the police report about him. Instead of telling him I think he is a suspect (which seems extremely doubtful since the report says he has two unbiased witnesses, including a homeowner who will say he was in Conway that afternoon unlocking a chest containing the family silver), I ask him if he thinks it is possible that his wife could have been involved in some way in a plot to make it appear that Cormorant had killed Merriweather. "Even if she wasn't sleeping with him," I speculate, "I suspect she was as close to Damascus Merriweather as anybody but his brother."

As I had hoped, Bobby Marsden does not blow me off. "She thought he was God," he blurts, but adds, "She wouldn't have the stomach for that, though."

There is no breeze even up here on the second floor, and I wipe my face. Across the street from us, six kids, all black, are throwing a football in a vacant lot. The Razorbacks are supposed to be loaded this year. "She says she wasn't sleeping with him," I say.

Marsden bends down and places his hands on the balcony railing and watches the kids play. There are two other apartments up here, but fortunately no one else is out with us. "All he had to do was crook his finger," he says, "and she'd drop whatever she was doing. I couldn't even get her to go my uncle's funeral. I know why now."

Marsden, who looks as if he could have played wide receiver for the Razorbacks at one time, is not a bad-looking man. I suspect he would not have a problem finding female company if he wants it. "Did she ever mention that Damascus was worried," I ask, wondering how closely he is listening to me, "about whether anybody would publish his first book?"

"All the time," he says, nodding. "He had written this great masterpiece, and nobody was going to read it."

This guy is so angry that I am afraid he will say anything. "Was she thinking that he might commit suicide?" I ask, trying to keep my voice neutral. I am not the only one on this balcony who thinks Dominique Marsden, whether she will admit it or not, was in love with Damascus at the time he died. Even if she has convinced her husband that she wasn't having sex with him, that night was proof to him that he had lost her.

"She said she hoped he would," he says, surprising me. "She claimed he was in a lot of pain."

"Did she ever mention Cormorant Ashley's name that you can remember?" I ask, guessing that his daughter, too, might suspect that her mother had fallen for Damascus, and that was why she didn't want me to talk to her. Yet Dominique Marsden seems too respectable to be involved in a plot to frame Cormorant.

"I don't remember hearing his name," Marsden replies, turning to me, "until he got arrested."

I try to remember the sequence of events. Marsden probably wasn't around during this time, and I say, "You might have been gone."

Marsden looks back at the kids and says, "We talked about getting back together, but she spent every minute working on that damn second book. The brother wanted to make sure it came out before the trial."

He has told me something I already know, but this helps account for his rage. Even after Merriweather's death, his wife spent her time with him. For an instant, I want to tell him that my marriage has also been affected by Damascus Merriweather, but I doubt if he will be terribly sympathetic. I ask about Ezekiel, but he doesn't know him well.

"He stayed after Dominique," he says, his voice tight with emotion, "night and day until this book came out."

I wonder if they have talked since its publication. Marsden is clearly still in love with his wife, but perhaps she has moved beyond him. One of the kids, the smallest one out there, catches an impossible pass and immediately spikes the ball in the imaginary end zone. It is hard not to be reminded of my own situation. Has Laurel decided she has moved beyond me? I have never thought we would end up divorced after all this time, but now it seems a real possibility. It is not something I want to think about.

Marsden yells down at the child who caught the ball. "Good catch, Junior!"

I peer down at the kid who turns and grins at us. I hadn't known about the boy.

This guy's not a killer any more than I am. I can't resist asking, "Have you read the books?"

Marsden lifts his chin and ends our conversation by muttering, "I'm not going to read that shit." He stalks back inside after calling his son to come in.

I drive back to the Heights, knowing I have not found any evidence that will impress a jury, and that night in Cormorant's study after a dinner of corn, tomatoes, and veal prepared by Beth, who seems quietly to be preparing for the worst, I tell him that though I will do my best to implicate others, it will come down to whether the jury believes him. "As much as I'd like to believe that Ezekiel has shot the prosecutor in the foot by bringing out *Salted With Fire* before your trial, we can't take anything for granted. As comforting as it would be to believe that the jury's mind is already made up before we even step foot in the courtroom, we can't do it. We don't know what's going to happen."

Cormorant, still seething over his treatment by Damascus, has found little comfort in the fact that Bobby Marsden is also a victim of the Merriweather brothers.

"How can a jury not believe me?" he thunders from his recliner. His mood is bellicose. He has switched to bourbon, not a good sign.

Easy, I think. I'm not sure I believe him either. I look up at the wall of books in Cormorant's study. History, a ton of it. How odd that it takes a man's death to make him so fully alive.

13

"Judge, my position is that I agree with Mr. Holly," Minor Latting, sitting beside his top deputy, Slade Martin, argues in the judge's chambers moments before the trial is to begin, "that Merriweather's first book is central to the case, but the second one is totally irrelevant, and he shouldn't be allowed during *voir dire* to read portions of either one aloud to influence any prospective jury members who haven't read them."

Last night I'd dreamed the judge would not let me even mention the title of either books. Now, I'm fearful my dream is about to come true. "Your Honor," I respond, "it's crucial to both sides that we find out who's been biased by *Salted With Fire*. There are some extremely inflammatory passages in that book. We should have the opportunity to hear how a prospective jury member reacts to it."

Cato looks down his nose at me over his dollar-store reading glasses. "I'm not going to let you grandstand in the courtroom like you've been doing in public for the last month. These books are not on trial. Do you understand me?"

I feel shame radiating through me as if someone is running a hot iron up and down my back. No judge has ever accused me of playing to the public, but I can't deny that's what I've been doing. "Your Honor, this is the only way to find out," I say, just now realizing how much I've alienated this judge. It may be the worst mistake I've made. "I don't believe you, Mr. Holly," Cato says, his voice cold and distant. "You want everybody on this panel to hear Damascus Merriweather compare Arkansans to Germans *vis-a-vis* the Holocaust, and I'm not going to permit it."

I don't easily blush, but I feel my face turn red. I've never had my credibility questioned by a judge or another lawyer. I realize now this case is destroying a reputation I've spent a lifetime building. I'm no different at this point than certain lawyers I've always detested. "The court should have imposed a gag order," I say, not denying he is correct. "As long as Ezekiel Merriweather paraded in front of the media on a daily basis, I had no choice."

Now, it is time for the judge's face to turn red. He takes off his glasses as if he can't stand to see me. "You always have a choice. For you to complain now is sophistry, Mr. Holly. It's clear to me by your actions this last month that your motion to move the trial was not made in good faith, and I want you to know that when this trial is over, I'm seriously going to consider filing sanctions against you with the Committee on Professional Conduct."

This is not the time for me to lose my temper. "I'd like to move that the court ask the panel if there is anything in either book that would keep anyone from rendering a fair and impartial verdict."

"That's exactly what I've intended to do all along, Mr. Holly," he says, his voice clipped as if I have insulted him. "But let me be real clear: don't you go over the line when you talk to this jury. Do you understand?"

"I know how to conduct myself in the courtroom," I reply, glad his court reporter isn't describing my face or the tone of my voice. My voice has begun to quiver with rage, but I can't control it. He is treating me like a child.

Cato sets his glasses back on his nose, and his blue eyes bulge out behind the lenses. "You will not turn my courtroom into an exercise in demagoguery, regardless of how you characterize it. If you try it, you'll be sorry."

I swallow hard but do not trust myself to speak again. With his threat ringing in my ears, I stalk out of his office like a chastened schoolboy behind Slade and Minor to select the jury. All my life I have heard other attorneys complain about how judges treated them, and on many occasions I silently agreed their behavior had gotten them exactly what they deserved. Behind Cato's sharp words was the look of a judge who has had to deal with a run-of-the-mill jackleg.

"We're going to finish this trial in two days," Judge Cato promises the prospective jury in a strong voice that suggests he will tolerate no grandstanding from anybody. "We don't drag cases out in Arkansas like they do in the rest of the country. You can be assured that the defendant's rights will be fully protected, but I also fully expect the prosecutor and defense counsel to move things along."

He looks directly at Cormorant and me. If Cato is going to be this hostile throughout the trial, whatever jury is seated will be suspicious of me. I smile at the members of the panel as if I couldn't agree with him more. I usually do not let the pressure of a trial get to me, but at the moment my throat feels so tight I wonder how I'm going to speak. All I can do is hope Cormorant is not the one to suffer. There is no time to second-guess myself, but I knew from the beginning that I should have said I wasn't qualified to do this kind of trial.

I turn and see in the second row behind us Miller Ray, Raven, and Catherine, who gives me a little wave. Incredibly, Laurel has not returned from England. Beth and Cormorant will never forgive her for not being here. I have admitted we are having problems that don't have anything to do with them, but if the South is about anything, it is about preserving appearances, and they have a right to feel betrayed by her absence. I have begun to wonder if I will ever see her again.

Beside me, Cormorant is putting on a good show of pretending to be confident, but I know he is about to burst. As we were driving down this morning, he predicted that if he was sent to prison, the trial would insure he would be murdered by blacks within a week.

As Cormorant and I mull over the list of potential jury members, the witnesses are brought in for the panel to determine if they are familiar with them. Nothing, I fear, will be more important than the composition of this jury. The clerk's office has told me that a new term has just begun and this panel has not enough of a track record for anyone to make predictions. But, as a columnist in the *Democrat-Gazette* said in yesterday's paper, all bets are off in this case because of the publicity surrounding the case. Only the trials and grand jury deliberations during the Whitewater era have topped it.

Of course, it is Ezekiel who attracts the most attention, and the prospective jurors study him as if he were a visiting head of state. Though just days ago in his office he appeared worn out from the summer's ordeal, today, resplendent in a three-piece blue suit, he looks strong and confident. How can this not be an act? Since the publication of *Salted With Fire*, he has been bombarded with criticism, but now he faces the crowded courtroom with a proud and serene expression. It is as if he is actually relishing this moment, which I can't imagine he is. For the last three days, Cormorant and I have spent hours debating how hard I should go after him and what I should say in my opening statement. We both agree he is such a loose cannon that we don't know what he is going to say.

When Beth's name is called, every eye in the courtroom focuses on her. Today, she has dressed down as I instructed her. Though she could have chosen anything in her store, she is wearing a simple tan suit and flats. A professor's wife, not a killer's. Still, she has pulled herself together for this trial in a way that makes me proud of her. In fact, she looks astonishingly lovely, her hazel eyes clear and her skin healthy. If she does not break down, she could help Cormorant, who must surely be wondering how his life has come to this.

Good as his word, Cato begins jury selection by asking the entire panel if anyone has read *Coming to Terms* or *Salted With Fire* and fifteen people, eleven whites and four blacks, raise their hands. Not a single one says he or she can't be fair and impartial. Whatever their motivation, these panel members want to hear this case. Hoping to employ our original strategy of circling the wagons, when it is my turn to ask questions, I inquire if any one has read or heard about anything about the books in the papers or on television, and a number raise their hands. When I ask the first person, a retired postal employee, what she recalls, Cato interrupts and calls me and Slade and Minor to the Bench. "I'm not going to let you back-door me, Mr. Holly. You just want the others to hear and be tainted by some outrageous comment."

"Your Honor," I say, totally exasperated by this judge, "I ought to be allowed to find out what that person has read or heard. If you're worried, let's take them back in your chambers one at a time."

Cato shakes his head. He looks up and says to the hushed panel members, "Has anyone read or heard something about this case in the media that would make it impossible for you to be fair to the defendant or prosecution?"

Naturally, no one raises a hand, and Cato knew nobody would. Loud enough for the court reporter to hear, I object to the court's refusal to let me question the jurors more closely, but I know the judge hasn't committed reversible error. If Raven's strategy works, we'll never know it. I use my peremptory challenges by striking blacks and a woman who admits to having moved to Little Rock in the last six months from Boston, where she had worked as an editor for the *Boston Globe*. By the time Minor and I finish selecting the jury, we wind up with ten whites and two blacks and, because of the court's ruling, I know far less about how they feel than I would like.

"Ladies and gentlemen," Slade Martin begins from his chair an hour before lunch, "the State will prove beyond a reasonable doubt that on April 21st of this year, between the hours of three and four-thirty p.m., the defendant, Cormorant Ashley, shot a .22 caliber bullet into the chest of Damascus Merriweather as he sat helplessly in his wheelchair, causing his death instantly." He stands and strides briskly to the jury rail. "Before I go over with you each bit of evidence the State will introduce to prove the defendant's guilt, let me summarize this case by saying that the physical evidence in this case is extensive. The State will present undisputed evidence that the defendant was the owner of a .22 caliber handgun, and that by his own admission in a statement to the police he went alone to the residence of the victim at three in the afternoon the day of the murder. We will present evidence from the State Crime Lab that the defendant's fingerprints, and his alone, were on the murder weapon found in the grass behind the defendant's residence. And there will be further uncontroverted evidence from the State Crime Lab that it was a bullet from the defendant's weapon that caused Dr. Merriweather's death. And, equally important, there will be testimony that a full and thorough investigation by the Little Rock Police Department revealed that no one else had been present at the victim's residence after the defendant until a work-study student by the name of Rafe Kennedy arrived at four as he had done every day for the last two weeks to bring Professor Merriweather, who was suffering from stomach cancer, his mail." Slade, who has a nice easy manner, lowers his voice and stands dead still. "Before I go any further however, I want to tell you briefly about the victim and the man who we will prove shot and killed him in cold blood. The victim, Damascus Merriweather, was the first African-American to be hired and to receive academic tenure in the history department at the University of Arkansas at Little Rock. A full professor with his Ph. D. from the University of Arkansas in Fayetteville, who you will learn was respected and liked by his colleagues and students as well, Dr. Merriweather had published his first book, *Coming to Terms,* two weeks prior to his death. The defendant is a fellow teacher in the history department, and though the State is under no obligation to prove motive as part of its case, you will learn in the course of this trial that there was a long history of bad blood between him and the defendant. You will learn that the defendant is quite openly a racial bigot who had opposed Dr. Merriweather from the very beginning of his career, arguing against his bid for tenure, and even at one point in a departmental meeting causing a furor by announcing that most Arkansans, including himself, believe that African-Americans are genetically inferior to Caucasians."

I am not surprised that Minor has chosen to characterize Cormorant's views in racial terms, but I assume he is trying to beat me to the punch. Beside me, Cormorant bristles at these words, but I am not unhappy that the prosecution has chosen to go down this path. It will make my opening statement much easier for the jury to swallow. Cormorant starts to say something to me, but trying to hear Slade, I put my hand on his arm.

"You will hear evidence that on more than one recent occasion the defendant was overheard to argue loudly with Dr. Merriweather, and it will be established that the defendant left suddenly right after the victim's death to go out of state for the weekend—literally within a couple of hours of the time Dr. Merriweather's body was found— and didn't return until Sunday night. And the evidence will be that the defendant admitted to the police that in his words, he `bantered' with the victim, during the few minutes before he was fatally wounded." Slade lets a sardonic smile play at his lips before saying, "Ladies and gentlemen, I submit to you that by the time this case is done, the evidence will be that the defendant did much more than *banter* with the victim. The evidence will show that he shot an unarmed man…"

I breath a sigh of relief that nowhere in Slade's opening statement has there been a reference to a confrontation over the inclusion in the book of the story of Cormorant's great-grandfather having fathered a child by a slave. Though it would hardly seem a motive for murder to the average juror, if he got to know Cormorant well, he might think otherwise. Still, by the time Slade sits down twenty minutes later, Cormorant is about to come out of his chair. Slade has effectively painted a picture of him as a hot-tempered racist who lost control of himself. As I stand and smile at the men and women who will decide Cormorant's fate, it occurs to me they appear so uncomfortable because they expect a college professor to behave differently than a peckerwood shooting off his mouth in his neighborhood beer hall. If Minor's strategy of painting Cormorant as an out-and-out racist turns out to be successful, our plans may indeed backfire. College professors, of all people, the jury may think, should be above that sort of thing, and by design, Cormorant looks the part. Though I have told him not to react to any part of the prosecutor's opening statement, he has already begun to fidget and is ignoring my suggestion to take notes. Somehow the jury is going to have accept Cormorant as he is, not as I want him to be.

"Ladies and gentlemen," I begin, focusing on Calvin Jarvis, a CPA and the most educated man on the jury, "since the prosecutor brought up the question of motive, let us begin there and see what the evidence will show about who was really angry at Dr. Merriweather at the time of his death. Indeed, within the prosecutor's own files are unsigned letters from individuals who were furious with him for just having published an extremely controversial book on slavery in the state. Mr. Martin has already mentioned the ninety minutes or so between the time my client left 4616 Palisades and the time when Rafe Kennedy, the work-study student mentioned by the prosecution, called Ezekiel Merriweather to say he couldn't get in the house. Contrary to what Mr. Martin told you, the evidence will be that the Little Rock police don't know whether someone else was at 4616 Palisades during those ninety minutes or not. All the evidence will show is that the police say they investigated and didn't find any sign of another individual at the house. The evidence will show that Rafe Kennedy gave a statement to the police that he never went inside the house and that the police believed him. However, I submit to you that the evidence will show that Kennedy most certainly could have killed Damascus Merriweather. You will learn that Kennedy once had Dr. Ashley as a professor and, being on the campus day after day, had easy access to his automobile, and for two weeks prior to his death had routinely entered the victim's residence. Why would a student shoot his professor? Well, the evidence will show this student has an uncle in a local group known as 'The Resurrection' that is known for, among other things, its desire to establish a white nation…" As I speak, I watch the jurors' faces and decide that I will not mention Ezekiel as a suspect and wait to see what he says. If I name him as a suspect, despite the fact that all the witnesses are sequestered and instructed not to discuss their testimony with each other, I am certain he will learn what I have said in my opening statement.

I walk back over to the table and put my hand on Cormorant's shoulder. "Further, the evidence will be that contrary to the portrait of a racist painted by the prosecution, the relationship between my client and Damascus Merriweather was a professional one, admittedly contentious in the way of academics to whom the truth about history matters, but not one based on anger." I walk to the other end of the jury rail and fix my gaze on Deborah Hunt, a black home health RN who seemed to frown the entire time Slade was on his feet. "The first and foremost thing you will learn from the witnesses that the State of Arkansas calls is that Dr. Ashley is an accomplished historian who is known for his meticulous and scrupulous methodology. You will learn from the evidence that he did not single out an African-American man for censure, but, in fact, on occasion, has delivered stinging criticism to a number of his colleagues. The evidence will be that Dr. Ashley is a man of uncommon integrity, one who insists on telling the truth as he knows it. What he says may make you uncomfortable, but there will be no evidence that he is a murderer…"

I conclude by saying that I will present evidence that in fact Dr. Merriweather's death could well have been a suicide, staged to look like a murder to promote his book. I describe our expert witnesses' theory that Merriweather could have injected himself with a drug that escaped the notice of the Medical Examiner's office, and that another person could have collected his blood before his death and then splattered it to make it look as if he died from a gunshot wound to his chest, though again I do not mention Ezekiel's name. I have subpoenaed both Dominique and Bobby Marsden, and will argue to the jury that Dominique was in love with Damascus and that, as his editor, she had a vested interested in the success of his books.

By the time I am finished and the judge breaks for lunch,

Cormorant whispers to me that no matter if he is acquitted, people will never look at him the same again. "I'll always be the man," he says morosely, "who got away with the murder of the black history professor who wrote the books."

As Cato disappears into his chambers, I think that, although I knew Cormorant was afraid of what would happen to him in prison, this is the first time I have ever heard him express concern about what people will think of him even if he is acquitted.

Standing between her niece and nephew behind the railing, Raven catches my eye and we go over to her. "You and I and Cormorant can go to the Lafayette Building, and I'll send out for sandwiches," she tells us as we fight our way through the media, which is all over us. Not willing to risk the further ire of Cato, I refuse all comment. Cormorant, in a gesture that I have not seen for years, holds his sister's hand.

On the drive to the Lafayette Building, I explain that Cato wouldn't let me ask any questions about the books. "It might not be reversible error," I admit. "The trial judge has wide discretion over the jury selection process."

Stopped at the light at Louisiana and Markham, Raven turns toward me and asks, "How come you didn't mention Ezekiel as a suspect in your opening statement?"

I explain that we are waiting to see how he will testify. "I'm afraid to go after him because if he hears I have named him as a suspect," I say, watching to see if the media is following us, "there's no way in the world he'll testify that he thinks Cormorant is not the person who killed his brother."

"I thought the witnesses were instructed not to talk to each other about their testimony," she says, speeding toward the Lafayette Building. "And besides, how important is it if the judge lets him give his opinion?"

The first question is easier to answer than the second. "If you don't think he won't find out everything that happened today, I've got some swamp land I'll sell you. The truth is, I don't know how important his attitude will be to the jury."

Cormorant asks, "You can't come out and ask him who he thinks killed his brother?"

We pull into the lot I have used all summer. Outside, the black man who has been preaching to the bus stop crowd all summer is at it again. The necessity for belief is his theme. "It's not relevant, but perhaps I can ask it on cross-examination," I say, hoping Cato will let me. At the rate I'm going, the judge isn't going to let me do more than get people to spell their names.

As we ride up to the second floor, Raven says, "I don't think Cato likes you very much." Cormorant nods in agreement. Neither of them knows the half of it. Raven sends out a secretary for Chinese, and we troop into my office and spend most of the lunch hour trying to make Cormorant understand that the jury is watching him at all times. Seated next to him as she has been so many times this summer, she exclaims, "You have to start acting like you couldn't have possibly killed Merriweather! You look guilty, and you have to stop it!"

Cormorant bites his lip. "I can't help it, damn it. I get so mad listening to this shit, and then I think how easy it will be for the jury to believe the prosecutor. I can see that fat woman on the far end nodding every time Slade opens his mouth. She didn't move a muscle," he tells me, "when you were up there."

I know who he is talking about. I should have cut her. Marilyn Dowd, a rich housewife in her fifties who lives out in west Little Rock, looked all right earlier this morning, but for the last thirty minutes she wouldn't even look at me. I shrug, knowing I need to reinforce what Raven has told him. "We don't know what she's thinking," I tell him. "I've told you ten times you can't tell about jurors from their body language. She may be thinking about whether she left the oven on."

Raven reaches over and pats him on the cheek as if he were a child. "You can do this!" she says urgently. "I know you didn't kill Merriweather."

I wonder if she believes that about not being able to read jurors any more than I do. Our food is brought in, and Cormorant begins to calm down. Raven's presence is crucial to him, and by the time we head back for the afternoon session, I am feeling better about his mental state. If she thinks he is guilty, she is concealing it well. Someday, I'll ask her.

14

Minor begins the afternoon by presenting the physical evidence, and Slade, who handles most of his witnesses, does a good job with the forensic experts from the State Crime Lab. It is uncomfortable watching the evidence dealing with Cormorant's pistol being locked in before this jury. Our forensics expert from Memphis has found no fault with any of the tests of the weapon. All I can do is ask the ballistics expert if there was any evidence that Cormorant had fired the gun the day of Merriweather's death. Since it has already been brought out by the detective who questioned Cormorant that he went out of town Friday afternoon and thus was not available for tests to determine if he had fired the pistol, it has little impact and begs the question of why Cormorant decided on the spur of the moment to take off for Lake of the Ozarks that weekend. Suddenly I have a fear of Beth breaking down and confessing that Cormorant had told her that he shot Merriweather. Of course, I do not have to call her. On the positive side, Raven's lecture has calmed Cormorant, and he sits more quietly and calmly than I could have hoped.

On cross-examination of the state medical examiner, I have little luck in getting him to admit that Merriweather's death could have been a suicide. "There was just nothing I found," he says, "in my autopsy to suggest he took his own life."

Dr. Grimm, a man in his fifties whose hands rest comfortably in his lap, has the demeanor of a kindly grandfather. "Wasn't his body riddled with cancer?"

"Quite," Dr. Grimm agrees, and launches again into a vivid description of the tumors in the Merriweather's bowel and liver, adding that the cancer had spread to his chest.

"Your main duty, if you can," I ask, "is to determine cause of death?"

Modestly, Dr. Grimm allows, wheezing slightly, "It's not always apparent, but yes, that's what I'm paid for."

I notice the fingertips of Dr. Grimm's left hand are stained with tobacco, or perhaps a chemical. It's not a job I could do. "In fact, in Dr. Merriweather's case, it was relatively easy, since he had a chest wound apparently secondary to a metal slug in his chest. That often will result in death, won't it, Doctor?"

Dr. Grimm smiles at me without a hint of condescension. "It's my opinion it did in this case."

"When you've got a chest with a metal slug in it, blood spatter that matches the deceased's blood, and a stomach and chest full of malignant tumors, wouldn't that keep you pretty busy?"

"If you are suggesting, Mr. Holly, I overlooked evidence of a toxic substance In the victim's body," Dr. Grimm says with sudden passion, "I can only say my examination revealed no evidence of such."

I am tempted to conclude that Dr. Grimm is suddenly second-guessing himself, but that would be clearly wishful thinking. "Have you ever made a mistake," I ask, dropping my voice to a whisper, "in your ten years as medical examiner?"

Dr. Grimm has recovered his equanimity and answers politely, "I'm sure I have, and I can think of a case, one right here in this courtroom where a physician hired by the defense disagreed with me."

I smile along with the jury. "But that's how scientists often get at the truth, by disagreement?"

He replies blandly, "But usually it's done better in the lab."

Though I shouldn't do it, I let him think he has the last word, hoping I will figure out how to work his quip into my closing argument.

Slade's expert on blood spatter looks like he played football for a Big Ten School. In fact, with his shaved head and dapper three-piece suit, he reminds me of Telly Savalas, a dim favorite of mine, as he discusses the pattern of blood on the table, using photographs of the crime scene. "Would you concede the blood spatter could have been staged?" I ask, glancing at the jury to see if they are paying attention. It is four, and I have begun to notice a few yawns. According to the literature and my expert, the analysis of "blood spatter" is hardly an exact science, though it has its adherents.

Charles Shuttlesworth dutifully acknowledges the possibility. "You'd have to be awfully good to duplicate this pattern."

Delighted with this admission, I ask, "But it could be done?"

Shuttlesworth, who seems to be enjoying the attention, allows, "Theoretically, yes, it's possible to make it appear that blood has spattered in a particular pattern so that it looks like someone has been shot from a greater distance than he was, but in my ten years of analyzing blood spatter, I've never been to a crime scene where I thought it had been done successfully. Besides, we know it couldn't have been in this case since we know it wasn't a suicide."

I correct him, "You mean that you assume it wasn't a suicide because Dr. Grimm determined from the autopsy there was no evidence of it."

"Right," he says, making my point for me. "If Dr. Merriweather had committed suicide, obviously his heart would have stopped beating, and if somebody had shot his corpse afterwards, obviously there would be no resulting blood spatter, and it would have to be staged."

"The information you have about blood spatter," I ask next, "comes from your experience, but it is also a subject that has been written about, isn't that correct?"

"Definitely," Shuttlesworth says, doubtless prepared to name a handful of books to bolster the dubious reputation of blood spatter analysis as a science.

"So the information is out there for anyone to learn about?" I ask.

"Probably not on the best-seller list," he says, getting a couple of smiles from the jury, "but there are a few books on the subject. Not many."

As Detective Sizemore takes the stand, Cormorant stiffens beside me. "I hate this guy," he says of the black man who first questioned him and who made the arrest. "He had this smirk on his face the entire time he talked to me."

A tall, graying man in his fifties who appears comfortable on the witness stand, Sizemore draws back his lips from his teeth when he is listening to a question. Whether he is smiling or snarling, he is an effective witness, laying out the investigation in a clear tenor voice that keeps the jury focused on him. When asked if someone could have come in the house on Palisades after the time Cormorant admitted he was there but before Kennedy arrived, Sizemore explains that he has personally talked to every resident within four blocks on either side of the house. Two women who were in their yards gardening within the line of sight of Merriweather's home that afternoon remember seeing Cormorant going into the house. One remembers Kennedy pulling in the same spot as he had been doing for the last two weeks about four o'clock and then seeing Ezekiel's Cadillac fly by about thirty minutes later, presumably after Kennedy had called him on his cell phone.

Neither saw another car outside the house, and they were in and out of their houses all afternoon. No one had seen Ezekiel's Cadillac or him since he had left his house at seven in the morning. Cormorant sighs audibly beside me. He knows better than anyone that we have nothing to rebut Sizemore.

On cross-examination, I get him to concede that someone could have put in across the river and crossed by boat and not been seen since the neighbors on either side of the house were not at home that afternoon. Afterwards, Sizemore retracts his lips, and I share Cormorant's irritation because his expression somehow conveys to the jury how unlikely this scenario was. Though he has to admit that the identity of the individuals who wrote the hate mail to Ezekiel is still not known, on redirect, Minor brings out through Sizemore that the letters were sent to Damascus's house near the University, not to Ezekiel's residence on Palisades, leaving the inference that if the murderer had been one of the letter writers, he would have had to have found out that Damascus was staying with his brother. If the jury wants to acquit Cormorant, they will find a way, but it won't be because I have planted a reasonable doubt in their minds through Detective Sizemore.

Before we quit for the day, Slade puts on his first witness from the faculty, and perhaps because it is an attractive woman, nobody checks his watch. I'd have thought that Minor would have wanted to get Rafe Kennedy's testimony out of the way or even Ezekiel's, but instead he calls Dr. Carole Matso, who, as she told me the day I interviewed her, states clearly she does not want to be here, though that does not stop her from blasting Cormorant and making him sound like a schoolyard bully, daring anyone to challenge him. "Though he was visibly humiliated by Cormorant," she says, looking straight at the jury, "I saw no sign Damascus was afraid of him. They used to argue so loudly I'd shut my door."

As I have feared, she is an unnervingly convincing witness that there was a good deal of continuing friction between the two men, and I can do very little with her though I remind her she said it was "possible" that they got along better than she realized.

"I never saw anything," she says firmly, "except what I would term confrontation and tension between them."

Treating her with kid gloves since the jury seems to find her sympathetic, I suggest that perhaps it was a matter of perception. "Do you recall telling me that Dr. Ashley made you cry?"

Dr. Matso flushes with embarrassment. "Let me put it like this: In all the years I have been around the two men together, I rarely saw or heard them exchange anything but barbs or sarcastic retorts. Damascus obviously had a tougher skin than I did. Yes, I told you I cried once."

While Dr. Matso is speaking, I turn my back to her to distract the jury from her words and am thrilled to see that Laurel has come into the back of the courtroom. I had convinced myself it would be another two weeks before I would see her, if then. I am overjoyed she is home, and I have to force myself to attend to Dr. Matso, whom I ask, "You also recall, do you not, telling me that it was possible the two men had a better relationship than it appeared on the surface?"

"To get you out of my office, I conceded it was possible," she says, her voice indignant, "but my impression is that despite their continued interaction, these two men disliked each other intensely."

I should have cut her off, but I am distracted now. "And you'll admit you dislike my client," I ask, hoping I'll get an honest response. I turn again to try to catch Laurel's eye, but there are too many spectators between us. I hope she isn't too exhausted by the flight home.

"He's arrogant," she responds, "self-centered, and condescending, and, in my opinion, a bigot. No, I don't like him."

"But you also said to me that Dr. Ashley is a good historian, did you not?"

"Yes," she answers between clenched teeth.

I let her go then, and while Slade puts on two more witnesses from the history department who add little but generally corroborate Dr. Matso's version of the relationship between Cormorant and Damascus, my mind wanders to the back of the courtroom. Laurel wouldn't have come now if she hadn't resolved the relationship. Of course, I am guilty on most days of wishful thinking.

"Who do you keep looking at?" Cormorant asks, irritably. During the afternoon he has become a model client, which I owe to Raven.

I tell him, and he smiles wearily as Cato ends the afternoon's session. "That's good news," he says, probably interpreting her return as a favorable sign to his chances.

I agree and make my way to Laurel who, as I feared, is visibly worn out from the trip. Under her eyes are circles she cannot hide, but I am delighted to see her and tell her so in the crush of gawking spectators. "How's it going?" she whispers against my ear.

I hug her against me, and for the crowd around us, I add, "Not bad at all." In fact, this was a terrible day, but I remind myself that the first day of a trial for the defense is always rough. Though tomorrow's witnesses will be more spectacular, it may be the damage has already been done. The evidence is already in that can convict Cormorant if the jury chooses to believe nobody else came into the house after him. It is that belief I have to attack tomorrow.

Raven, who genuinely seems glad to see Laurel, insists that we spend the night with her. Laurel greets Cormorant a bit standoffishly, which I attribute to her embarrassment. We find Beth, who has been released for the day as a potential witness, in the hall two doors down from the courtroom, and Cormorant hugs her before telling her to go home with Miller Ray and Catherine since we want to get to work immediately. Beth, possibly still angry, speaks, but the two women do not embrace.

Outside the Pulaski courthouse, we battle through the media to Raven's Lexus with Laurel tightly clutching my hand. Though Cormorant and Raven are now used to the madhouse outside the courthouse, it is Laurel's first exposure, and she is wide-eyed as we push forward to the parking lot across Markham. Reporters yell questions (the most persistent is whether Cormorant will take the stand), but I am not going to risk pissing off Cato any further by speaking to the media, and we bull our way into the car with smiles pasted on our faces. While Raven drives us to Laurel's car three blocks away on Center Street, Laurel asks me, "How do you stand this?"

As Raven inches her way through the mob of reporters and spectators, Cormorant answers morosely, "It's not an acquired taste."

I put my arm around my wife and tell Cormorant to smile. At Raven's we make some sandwiches and fifteen minutes later leave Laurel to take a nap and return to the Lafayette Building for our final session.

Seated in my office, we turn on the six o'clock news and watch as Channel 7's Ramona Saunders describes the physical evidence introduced by the prosecution. She quotes a local trial attorney as saying it was a good day for the prosecution. "The question that will be answered tomorrow is whether Dr. Cormorant Ashley will testify on his own behalf. The attorneys familiar with this case I have talked to say he has no choice if he wants to be acquitted. The physical evidence is just too strong, unless there are some surprises tomorrow from defense lawyer Miller Holly."

Cormorant, now that he is away from the defense table,

displays none of the stoicism that he managed after lunch. "It's like having a noose tightening around my neck," he complains. "Of course I'll testify."

For the entire summer, I've been waiting for Cormorant to tell me exactly what happened that afternoon. Raven goes out of the room for a moment, and I press him hard. "If you have anything to hide, you have to tell me now, Cormorant," I demand. "You owe me that much. You've dribbled out bits and pieces of your relationship with Merriweather long enough. Whatever else happened, I need to know it tonight."

Cormorant, who cannot get through a conversation with me in this room without drawing something, goes to the butcher paper and picks up a pen. Instantly, he does an unmistakable caricature of me before the jury. In this rendering, I am a wispy figure, my torso far more insubstantial than my head. It is my jaw and forehead that make me an easy target for him. To say they are prominent is to understate the case. Laurel has teased me from the day we met, asking if I had ever fought as a welterweight in a Golden Gloves tournament in Memphis, meaning I suppose, I look like I can take a punch. The way Ezekiel has battered us all summer, I feel as though I have. For a moment, I think Cormorant is finally going to tell me the truth, but instead he tells me that I know as much about that afternoon as he does. He signs the paper at the bottom as if he were a famous artist, rips it off, and gives it to me. "This will be worth something some day," he quips. "The day you began your career getting off murderers."

For the briefest of moments, I think he has confessed to me, but as Raven enters the room, he reaffirms his innocence. "I didn't kill him, Miller."

Do I believe him? I don't know. We stay until eleven, rehearsing his testimony and working on answers for cross-examination. Exhausted myself, I need a good night's sleep, and, of course, I want to spend a few moments alone with Laurel if she is awake. After we drop Cormorant off, Raven asks, "Were you afraid that she wasn't coming back?"

Raven, who has confided so much to me of her own fears, deserves an honest answer, and I tell her that I was. "Do you remember how when we were kids we talked about how wonderful our lives would be? I've always thought the last thing I would see before I died as an old, old man would be Laurel's face smiling at me. I haven't thought that this summer until I saw her in the courtroom today."

As we turn into the drive, she reaches over and pats my arm. "I love you to death, Miller, but when it comes to women, I don't think you've ever had a clue."

She gets out of the car before I can ask her what she means. I want to tell her that I know that I have been selfish all these years, but stupidly, until recently, I thought Laurel was happy, or at least, happy enough.

Upstairs, when I go into the bedroom, she is asleep, and I slip naked into bed beside her. I am delighted to find that she is naked, too, and though I do not anticipate making love, this is what happens, and I find it delightful, despite our mutual weariness. She says little, but hungrily presses into me until I release myself. As a sexual experience, it won't be remembered, but for the first time in months, she seems truly needy and not merely dissatisfied. Her face is wet, and I ask in the darkness, "What's wrong?"

She turns away from me, fitting her hips snugly against my groin and takes my hand and cups her breast. She does not speak, and all kinds of thoughts race in my mind. She has filed for divorce; she had an affair with some rugged Scot. Finally, she says, "Miller, did you never suspect that Cormorant and I slept together two summers ago?"

I lie perfectly still, knowing my life has changed forever. I can't breathe. "What are you saying? Are you saying that you did," I ask, praying it isn't true, "or that you think I thought you had an affair with Cormorant?"

"It's true," she moans and begins to sob.

I can't bear to touch her any longer. I might begin to choke her. I get out of the bed and pull on my pants and sit in the chair across from her in the dark. Two summers ago I spent much of the time in Memphis, having been hired to help try a complicated bankruptcy case in which a wealthy Tennessee farmer had defrauded the federal government of a quarter of a million dollars. We had all the help we needed, and Laurel stayed in Marianna to run the office. I drove home some nights and was home weekends, and sometimes when I would drive in, Cormorant would be there on the deck with Laurel sipping bourbon, saying he had been over visiting his father and had dropped by. I remember now that I was happy to see him because I was gone so much. "No," I say slowly, "it never occurred to me that summer or since. I guess I've been pretty naive." As I say this, now I realize why she has been so jealous of Raven this summer, thinking it was payback time.

Laurel pushes herself up against the headboard. "It just went on that summer; I stopped it when that trial was over. I'm so sorry!"

I sit in the dark, trying to remember when that case was finished. The middle of August, I think. I wonder who ended the affair. Cormorant's classes started up again the last of the month. "Are you sure *you* stopped it?" I ask quietly. "And why? I guess it wasn't convenient with me being around."

"I didn't love him!" Laurel cries. "It was just stupid. I was bored and lonely. He can always make me laugh. He was always so damn human and alive, and sometimes you aren't."

I reflect on this comment for a moment and then ask, "Because

I didn't cheat on you, I'm not human or alive?"

"No! It's just he's always made himself vulnerable; you haven't in a long time."

My eyes are accustomed to the dark, and I can see the outline of her breasts. I can't believe we just made love, and now she's told me this. I am beginning to think that it hasn't been the Delta she's grown to hate but me. "I thought Cormorant was more interested in his brain than his dick," I say, thinking of the night of his arrest when despite all that must have been going through his mind, he smelled her perfume, and she let him. "Why did you want me to represent him?" As if she can not stand me staring at her, she pulls the sheet up to her chest. I wonder if we have awakened Raven two doors down, but I can't hear anything but my own breathing, which sounds labored. I take a deep breath.

"I think it was like I said—I wanted you to get your hands dirty," she says, reaching for a tissue on the nightstand beside the bed. "He's been your best friend your entire life."

I turn on the lamp on the nightstand. Laurel can't quite extend her hand far enough without exposing her breasts, and I hand her the box of tissue. I wonder if she thinks I would become aroused again at the sight of her. If she does, she must have me confused with someone else. "I thought he was my best friend," I allow. "Why are you telling me this now?"

"Because it's so horrible what this case has done to you," she cries. "To try to save Cormorant, you've become what you've always hated. You've become one of those lawyers who go on television and say whatever they can to manipulate the public. You used to say that to become a lawyer was a chance to become something noble. Now, I can't tell the difference between you and those demagogues you used to ridicule."

"Well, you got what you wanted. I seem, to myself at least, very human these days. I wish you had told me after it happened."

Laurel blows her nose, destroying the tissue completely, and I hand her another one. I wish I could cry, but all I feel is a numbness spreading through me. If it were not just my arms, I would think I was having a heart attack. She says, "I was afraid you'd kick me out. You have such a sense of loyalty about everything and I breached it."

I begin to rub my forehead which has begun to ache. "What good has it done me?" I wonder aloud. "Everything and everyone I've been loyal to seems to have been a figment of my imagination. Nothing's what I thought. You, Cormorant, this case. All summer I've wondered what my father and his ancestors were really like, but I'm afraid to find out."

Laurel sniffs. "Probably just like everybody else," she says, her eyes downcast. "How could they have been otherwise? I know you want to believe your family was better than everybody else, but they probably were just like the rest of us."

What an odd conversation this has become. I am finally beginning to feel angry. How dare she talk about my family! "What was Cormorant like in bed?" I say, "And did y'all do it in our bed?"

"Don't do this!" Laurel pleads. "No, not in our bed, and he was just like you'd think—short and not particularly sweet, and I hate myself for doing it. Do you want a divorce?"

"Maybe I need more than fifteen minutes to digest this," I suggest to her. What is amazing is that Laurel, who knows better than anybody what concentration is required to do a jury trial, would tell me now. "Is this your way of punishing Cormorant? How can I stand up in court tomorrow and defend him now? He probably killed Merriweather for all I know."

Laurel reaches over and turns off the light. "Please come back and get in bed. You know he doesn't have the guts to kill anybody."

She hasn't answered my question, and the surge of anger that I am feeling begins to melts into a great sense of weariness. I know I won't be able to sleep, but I am suddenly too tired to go anywhere else. Yawning, I slip off my pants and get back into bed as Laurel moves back toward her side. I doubt if she understands why she told me. How interesting that Cormorant never told her that he threatened to kill Raven's husband. It convinces me that he really meant it. "Who else knows? Beth? Raven?"

Laurel takes my hand. "Raven's guessed. She asked me last week on the telephone if that was why I went to see my sister. Beth doesn't know."

"What did you tell her?" I ask, beginning to now feel the horns of a cuckold sprouting from my head. How does a man who fucks your wife have the nerve to then ask him to represent him on a murder charge? Maybe, like Bill Clinton, he never thought of it as sex. No matter what, it implies a total lack of disrepect for me.

"Nothing," my wife says, turning on her side in the dark. "Instead, I asked her what she would have done if you had tried to seduce her this summer. She said it would have served me right, so I think she figured it out, but she said she would have given you a glass of warm milk and sent you back to bed. She thinks you're a saint."

I wonder if saints feel murderous. Cormorant is the ultimate user and betrayer. The hypocrisy of what he has done overwhelms me. All his so-called honesty has been a pose. "I just don't understand why you or he didn't have the integrity to tell me."

There is a long silence, and the possibility occurs to me that Laurel has been planning this since Cormorant was charged. "I can't speak for him," Laurel answers finally, "but I wasn't ready to get divorced."

I suppose this means she is ready now. "I can't even really

conceive of it," I admit.

Laurel squeezes my hand. "See, that's part of our problem. All these years I've helped you in the office, taken care of you at home, and every year that passes, you become more and more detached. What I've been trying to say all summer is, what good is loyalty if all it means is going through the motions and growing bitter because you can't control the future? I don't want to grow old with you if that's all our lives are going to be. I feel terrible about that summer two years ago. I'm weak; so is Cormorant, by the way. Compared to you, we all are, but your strength, if that is what it is, comes at too high a price."

I can't get the image of Laurel with Cormorant out of my mind. It sickens me, and I close my eyes, but it is still there. How many times? Did she enjoy it? I don't feel strong now. "What do I do when I see Cormorant tomorrow?"

My wife says quietly, "You'll do what you've always done your entire life. You'll do your best to represent him. You believe all that stuff."

I move to the edge of the bed so I don't have to touch her. What happened? I more or less believed everything would work out, but nothing has. Maybe the amazing thing is that my delusions were allowed to stay in place for as long as they have. I have sat by and watched it all unravel and pretended nothing too disastrous was happening. How foolish I seem to myself now. I want to scream out that I deserve better than this, but perhaps I don't.

15

The morning's testimony gets off to a troubling start as Minor calls the Dean of the UALR law school, who conveys a genuine air of puzzlement that Damascus would ask Cormorant to substitute for him. "If Dr. Ashley wasn't going to be able to appear," he testifies, "before he got someone else, I'm sure he would have consulted me. I didn't know he was so ill, though."

The implication is definitely in the air that Cormorant is lying about the reason that he went to see Merriweather, and I can't disprove it. Beside me, Cormorant has been worrying at a place on his chin where he cut himself shaving this morning. If he doesn't leave it alone, it will start bleeding again, and I will have to ask Cato for a recess he will be loathe to give. Part of me would like to sit back and watch him bleed. This morning when he came to Raven's at seven for a final strategy session, I could hardly keep myself from asking if he wanted to go up and get in bed with Laurel, who didn't come down until we were about to leave and is not in the courtroom now. Oblivious as usual to everything outside himself, Cormorant has surely assumed I have been cold to him because I am thinking about his case. I am, as best I can, but I notice that Laurel still has not come.

I whisper to Cormorant, "Did he say he was supposed to get his own substitute?"

Cormorant writes on the legal pad I have provided him, "I assumed he could."

Awkward on his feet (the jury seems to make him self-conscious), Minor hunches over the podium and puts his hand to his face as if to avert his gaze. "Why are you sure, sir?"

Dean Castleman is smaller than Cormorant and reminds me of Robert Reich, Clinton's first Labor Secretary. "I had told him I wanted his perspective, an African-American historian who would articulate the view of the plaintiffs with a certain, shall we say, sympathy."

By the time I get to my feet to cross-examine Castleman, I can do nothing except to reinforce his testimony, and I ask a single question: "Dean, you don't know what Dr. Ashley said to Dr. Merriweather, or vice versa, do you?"

All he can do is say that he does not, and I sit down, knowing how badly Cormorant has been hurt by his testimony.

The next witness is Rafe Kennedy, and I feel a certain amount of discomfort as he takes the oath. Assuming he is innocent, he can only hate the judicial system and lawyers, and though I did not mislead him, I was not candid with him either. Today, he looks even more raw-boned than when I first met him. Instead of clothes from the Gap or wherever kids buy their clothes these days, Kennedy is wearing a faded pair of jeans, and his long legs are jammed into a pair of cowboy boots. As before, he looks like a hick but not a murderer. Slade takes him through his statement, and I hear nothing new in his testimony. Slade, anticipating correctly that I will come after Kennedy, asks him if he had ever heard that Cormorant carried a pistol in his glove compartment. He claims he had not.

I can feel the tension gathering in me as I listen to the boy's testimony. If the jury is to believe that anyone other than Cormorant saw Merriweather that afternoon, now is the time.

With my cross-examination, I must make it happen. His story is effective, and Slade elicts his personal observations of Ezekiel, much as I had done when I visited him three months ago. When Slade is finished on direct, I am convinced that he never saw Damascus alive that day.

As I get to my feet, I realize my heart is not in trying to make this boy a suspect, nor do I think I can. As I walk to the podium, I wonder if my lack of enthusiasm is actually because of what I learned last night about Cormorant's infidelity with Laurel. Since I entered the courtroom this morning, I have consciously tried to block it out, but it is no use. I want to turn to Cormorant and say to him that he is a liar and a fraud and probably a murderer. Instead, I ask Kennedy if he does not have an uncle who is in a separatist organization that is known to him for its animosity toward blacks. Kennedy pokes his angular chin out at me and replies, "Sir, my family is my family. And as I told you, I read Dr. Merriweather's book and thought it was full of nonsense, and if that makes me a suspect in his death, so be it."

Elated that he has referred to *Coming to Terms*, I get him to acknowledge the title and then ask him, "You admit then that this book made you angry?"

"Not angry enough to kill Dr. Merriweather," he says sarcastically, "but it did piss me off because I think a lot of the stuff in there couldn't be verified."

Over Minor's objection on grounds of relevancy, I am allowed to ask him specifically which passages made him mad and why, and he recites the slave narratives and some of the reasons given by Cormorant the day he was arrested. I glance at the jury and notice they have become unusually attentive. If I can keep the focus on the books instead of Cormorant, some of the jury will be bound to resent Damascus before the trial is over. Unknown is the outcome, if any, of our initial strategy to start the trial with some of the jury panel hostile to Damascus; still, I am encouraged by my exchanges with Kennedy. I would like to be able to ask him about his reaction to *Salted With Fire*, but since it was published posthumously, it is so clearly outside the bounds of relevancy that I don't dare mention it. Cato would be sure to reprimand me for trying to incite the jury. As Kennedy answers my question about his reaction to Merriweather's naming of specific white families in the Delta whom blacks claim to be their ancestors, he cannot keep the contempt he must feel out of his voice. I think of Laurel's comment that I have become like those attorneys I despise. She wanted me to get my hands dirty, and I guess I am. At least I have an argument that the book had an impact on him, perhaps more than he was willing to admit. "What you can't deny is that you were there for a full thirty minutes before Ezekiel Merriweather got there. Isn't that a fact?" I ask.

"I've never tried to deny it," he says, his voice tight with anger.

"Are you sure you didn't steal Dr. Ashley's pistol, gain entrance to the house and shoot Dr. Merriweather or help your uncle do it?"

"No!" the boy shouts, rightfully furious with me. "And my uncle was a hundred miles away!"

I stop there, and Minor does not redirect nor does he need to. There was no trace metal on Kennedy's hands, nothing to indicate he had fired the gun. Yet, if some of the jury wants to believe he did, they have that option despite the testimony of the state's expert that trace metal would have remained on his hand and would have been detected since he was taken into custody immediately. Whether Damascus was already dead when Ezekiel arrived, the medical examiner can't say, but he can't say he wasn't, either. I do not like myself for what I did to Kennedy, but I had no choice.

After a short break, Minor calls Ezekiel, and the entire

courtroom hushes as he walks to the witness box. If he wants to indicate to the jury that he believes his brother's killer is still at large, the jury will be listening, for they have come forward to the edge of their seats. Though I never saw his brother alive, I cannot imagine he had the presence that Ezekiel communicates by merely tapping his fingers together as he waits for the court reporter to change a tape. Cormorant locks his own hands together, and I can only imagine what he must be feeling. While Minor asks some routine background questions, I study the jury and realize the man they are watching could have been an outstanding trial lawyer. I don't know whether they resent him or feel sympathy at this moment. Though his expression is grave, he does not appear sorrowful. Yet, as I know now, everything is theater with Ezekiel. He even gets attention when he clears his throat. As Minor continues, it is apparent he is not an easy witness to control, because he, of course, wants to talk about his brother's books, and several times, no matter what the question, he works them in to his answer.

"*Coming to Terms,*" he boasts, "would have found a commercial publisher, but my brother was too sick too wait any longer, and so I published it for him," he responds to a question Minor asks about why his brother came to stay with him.

I could object to the nonresponsiveness of his answers, but of course I am delighted. *Coming to Terms,* he informs the jury, is already in its fourth printing and has received forty reviews from all over the country. As we have expected, Ezekiel is determined to use the trial to get maximum publicity for the books and his brother's ideas, and on cross-examination I will be delighted to help him. During his initial testimony, he glances at Cormorant and at me, but I do not detect any overt hostility today. There is no love lost between the judge and Ezekiel, and Cato reprimands Ezekiel, but it is as if he does not hear him. He will say what he wants. "Tell the jury what you did the afternoon of your brother's death," Minor instructs him finally.

Ezekiel becomes less animated, but he gives a detailed account of his afternoon, informing the jury he had stayed at his North Little Rock pharmacy during lunch because an employee needed to take off to run some personal errands. Afterwards, he ate a sandwich in his office and worked back there, relieving his employees during breaks until he received the call from the student.

As he speaks, it occurs to me that though two employees have said he was there all afternoon, if his North Little Rock pharmacy is arranged like his Little Rock store, he could have left from a back entrance, driven to the north shore and crossed the river and been at the back of his house in fifteen minutes. "As soon as the boy called and said Damascus hadn't come to the door," Ezekiel says, his voice dropping, "I knew he was dead. Of course, I didn't know he had been shot, but I had a feeling I wasn't going to see him alive again."

Everything I know about this man makes me certain that he did not shoot his brother, at least not while he was alive. Minor asks what he did next, and Ezekiel says it took him about twenty-five minutes to drive to his house, and from there his testimony tracks Rafe Kennedy's statement. In a sheepish voice, he testifies that when he saw that his brother had been shot he immediately thought Kennedy had done it, began to question him, and finally ordered him out of the house while he called the police. He adds quickly, "I don't know who killed my brother. I thought I did, but I don't."

Cormorant grips my arm. I nod to show him I was listening. A host of conflicting emotions wash over me as I study the black jurors' faces. By their expressions, I am certain they took in exactly what he said. Even now, I don't know if he is sincere or trying to keep me from coming after him on cross-examination. To lessen the impact, Minor follows up by trying to lead him. "That's the job of law enforcement, isn't it, Mr. Merriweather?"

Ezekiel looks directly at the juror closest to him and says, "My people don't have a history of trusting law enforcement."

Minor has no choice but to hurry along with other questions as if this were an acceptable response, but the damage may be done. I whisper to Cormorant, "What do you think?"

He draws on his pad a simple question mark. Minor can not ask Merriweather questions about how his brother felt about Cormorant without an objection from me, and quite properly does not try. In a few moments, he is done, and we have the biggest decision of the trial. I get to my feet, knowing in my bones I have no choice but to try to offer the jury another choice. If I alienate the blacks and maybe even some whites by going after Ezekiel, so be it. The case against Cormorant is too strong to ignore the possibility that somehow Ezekiel may have set him up.

As I introduce myself to him, he gives me an ironic smile since there is no need for this courtesy. "I know who you are, Mr. Holly. We've met on two occasions."

If he is afraid of me, I can't tell it. "Mr. Merriweather, you've been a pharmacist for twenty years, haven't you, sir."

He smiles. "Yes, I have."

"And as a pharmacist, you would know that a drug such as potassium chloride, if injected into the human body in sufficient quantity, would cause death instantaneously, would it not?"

Merriweather, I am convinced, knows exactly what I am doing and answers smoothly, "It certainly would."

As I ask about whether he knows how to operate a boat and whether his office in North Little Rock has a rear entrance, he remains completely unperturbed, and I find myself doubting that I have made the correct decision, but having made it, I have no choice except to put the other pieces in place. "In the days and weeks before his death," I ask, coming around to the side of the podium, knowing Cato won't let me get any closer, "was your brother in pain?"

Merriweather folds his arms and answers softly, "On occasion he was."

He has nothing to gain by lying to any of these questions, and I ask, "If you know, would you tell the jury how much longer he thought he had to live?"

Minor shouts out a hearsay objection, but this question has already been answered by the medical examiner.

"Had he ever talked with you about ending his life?"

Again, Minor objects, but I argue successfully that I am not offering this evidence to prove that he did end it, only that he mentioned it.

Even after Minor's objection is overruled, Merriweather hesitates. "He may have mentioned it," he says as if he has to think about it. "I suspect most people in his situation would at least have that option cross their mind."

He knows what question is coming, and I ask, "Do you know if your brother committed suicide?"

"Of course not!" he thunders, his expression now the familiar scowl of his television appearances. "If you are are going to suggest to this jury that my brother injected potassium chloride into his body, and then I shot him and sprinkled his blood on the table, may God have mercy on your soul!"

I have no idea if he is acting. "Did you?"

Ezekiel sets his jaw and stares at the jury. "Absolutely not."

"But you'll admit that you told me once your brother disliked my client, won't you?"

"I suspect many people dislike your client, Mr. Holly," Ezekiel roars, "including my brother, so the answer is yes, but if he was going to commit suicide, the last thing he would have worried about is trying to make it appear that someone murdered him."

I look at the jury while I ask, "You'll agree that a charge of murder has insured maximum publicity for the book."

Merriweather is not going to concede anything. "The book didn't need publicity," he contends. "It was recognized on its merits."

"But you'll admit that you carried it around with you every time you held a demonstration or press conference?"

Merriweather responds quickly, "Yes, and I'll say this too. My brother's book angered many whites who don't want to hear the truth about the history of slavery in this state."

"And you've been quoted more than once that you don't know who killed your brother."

"I don't deny that," he says flatly.

This is what I want the jury to remember, and I choose this moment to sit down. Cormorant asks hopefully, "What do you think?"

I hold my breath until Minor decides not to redirect. "We have to remember that though he's milking it for all it's worth," I tell him then, "Ezekiel is not on trial. The jury doesn't know any more than it did before I got up there. It doesn't change a thing as far as your testimony." I confess that I do not mind seeing Cormorant sweat. I scan the faces of the people who will judge Cormorant and wonder if my cross-examination has had any impact at all. The problem is that we do not have any physical evidence of potassium chloride in Merriweather's body. All I can do is suggest that the medical examiner overlooked it. What is puzzling is that Ezekiel did not try to mention that Damascus had confronted Cormorant about his grandfather, and that Cormorant had threatened to sue him for libel. Nor apparently did he tell the police or anyone from the prosecutor's office.

Before noon Minor stands and says the state rests, and out of the presence of the jury I go through the motions of asking for a directed verdict to preserve our appeal rights. Cato barely listens and summarily denies it. The atmosphere in his chambers is frigid. I will get no breaks from him. He won't even look at me. As we stand to go out, Minor surprises me by whispering, "Will you come with me into the courtroom for a moment? I have an offer to make."

"Sure," I say, and follow him and Slade to a spot right outside the judge's chambers. With the trial in recess, the courtroom is mostly empty. All summer long, I have waited for this moment to come, but I had given up on it. Does Minor think Ezekiel has fatally wounded him? Except for Ezekiel's testimony, the case went in about as smoothly as it could have. I look at Slade Martin, but his expression tells me no more than Minor's. Perhaps Minor has been worried about the jury all along, and wanted to wait until he was in the strongest position psychologically before making an offer. If so, our strategy has worked. If we are going to deal this down, it had better be quick, and Minor wastes no time. He says, "I think Cato will accept negligent homicide. Your client will do a year, and because it's a misdemeanor he won't have to do his time in Cummins."

I look over at Cormorant who is waiting for me at the defense table. I feel like shouting for joy, but I know there are two problems. Cormorant will have to admit shooting Damascus, and he will have to keep his mouth shut for a year. I tell him that if I don't get back to him with an answer in thirty minutes that we can't accept his offer. He nods and with Slade at his heels, walks past Cormorant out of the courtroom.

I walk over to the table and sit down. "Minor is willing to knock this down to negligent homicide. You'll do a year in the county jail."

Though we have not discussed a plea bargain, Cormorant

remembers what it means. "I'd have to say that I shot him, wouldn't I?"

My pulse quickens. I realize I no longer trust Cormorant to tell me the truth about anything. It is a sad moment, but I don't have time to dwell on it. "Yeah, but you don't have," I say looking at my watch, "but thirty minutes to think about this."

Cormorant nods vacantly, and I can see that his mind is already at work. I want to say that if he didn't shoot Damascus, ethically I can't allow him to plead guilty to a crime that he didn't commit, but at this moment my old friend faces a situation no different from the plight of the average criminal who gets a break from the criminal justice system for one reason or another. He begins to draw on the pad in front of him. "What do you think will happen if I don't take it?"

Gone is the indignant, self-righteous Cormorant who has denied he murdered Damascus. He wants to know if he will be convicted, but I can't tell him. "If I had to handicap it," I say honestly, "I'd say fifty-fifty. Minor wouldn't be offering this if he was totally confident about this jury. I think he's worried about the impact of Ezekiel's testimony. The problem we have is that we don't really have any evidence someone else did it, only that it was theoretically possible. Minor knows that. I think, as we have said all along, it will come down to your credibility."

Cormorant draws back, and I look down see that he has sketched an unmistakable outline of the jury box. Inside it however there is only one figure—Damascus or Ezekiel, I can't tell which. He folds his arms against his chest and says, "What do you think I should do?"

I say carefully, "I won't answer that question no matter who asks it. You have to decide this one alone."

"You don't believe me, do you?" Cormorant whispers, his face incredulous.

I can't look him in the eye, and I stare back down at the sketch, realizing that for the last three months this has been the point made over and over again in one form or another by the Merriweather brothers: what most of us call history is simply what we are comfortable believing. "How could you," I say, choking out the words, "have slept with Laurel?"

The expression on Cormorant's face changes to one of utter shock. "She told you last night?" he gasps.

I had not intended to say this now, thinking I would be able to come to a decision after the trial, but now that I have, I feel a great sense of relief. "How dare you ask me to represent you after you betrayed our friendship that way! You son of a bitch!"

Incredibly, tears come to Cormorant's eyes. "It didn't have anything to do with our friendship," he says. "I'm sorry."

I look to my right at the bailiff, who is looking at his watch. I feel sick to my stomach. "You know that is such a lie!"

Cormorant looks at his own watch. "Miller, help me, Goddamn it!" he pleads. "This is my life at stake!"

Over fifty years of friendship lie like ashes in my mouth. Again, as I did last night I have the feeling that I have wasted my own life. Duty. Loyalty. It seems now as if all that has been at stake is my own ego. Though I have begun to sweat underneath my suit jacket, I give him a wintry smile. "I'll do my job, Cormorant. What will it be?"

Knowing perhaps another denial is so much hot air, Cormorant says stiffly, "I'm not taking a plea bargain. I can't go to jail."

I nod, knowing he is both dishonest and a coward. "Go to lunch, and you better hurry," I tell him. "Raven should be outside waiting."

He stands and asks, "You don't want anything?"

I shake my head and point with my chin to the double doors to the side. My stomach is churning too much to eat. I watch him go out the door, wondering if he realizes this may be his last decent meal for the rest of his life. For the rest of the hour, I sit and try to think about the trial, but I cannot concentrate. Usually, at this moment in a trial, I can focus beautifully, but now my mind is a jumble of random thoughts. As I try to review the evidence, my mind defaults to thoughts of Laurel and Cormorant together. I have never thought of myself as a failure as a husband, but no woman cheats on a man if she is satisfied emotionally with him. All I want is for this ordeal to end, but I wonder what I will do after it is over. Right now, I can't imagine going back to Marianna and pretending that everything is normal. Given my last conversation with Laurel, I may not have that option. Where is she? I never saw her all morning. God help me. Right now I can't even think.

16

I begin Cormorant's defense by calling Beth. As she walks gracefully into the courtroom, I cannot help but reflect that she, too, has been betrayed just as badly. Her life for the last thirty years has been lived at the whim of what I think now has been Cormorant's monstrous ego. While I feel strangely buffoonish standing at the podium, there is something valiant about Beth as she smiles stiffly at Cormorant, trying to overcome her natural fear of speaking in public and answer confidently the questions I put to her.

To her credit, she does rather well on direct in explaining how they decided on the spur of the moment to go to Lake of the Ozarks the afternoon of Damascus Merriweather's death. "One thing about living with a man like Cormorant is that outside of his classroom, he doesn't live according to a schedule." She had planned to take that weekend off from her shop, and he had known she was free. Somehow, she is able to convey a more carefree portrait of Cormorant than I suspect is true, yet she doesn't go too far. Nothing in his behavior seemed out of the ordinary that weekend. Since he knew it bored her, he rarely discussed his work with her and had not mentioned Merriweather's name that weekend. When his book had come out, Cormorant had dismissed it but had not seemed particularly concerned by it.

By the time Slade gets up to cross-examine her, it is obvious she has helped Cormorant, because she so plainly does not think he is capable of murder. Though their marriage is not on trial, Slade, given wide latitude by Cato, dissects it, and quickly manages to suggest through his questioning that these are two people who, despite thirty years of marriage, seem to know or care very little about each other's professional lives. Beth becomes defensive, which unravels her earlier testimony, and I decide not to try to rehabilitate her for fear she would sound even worse. Whether Cormorant confided to Raven at his abbreviated lunch that I knew he had slept with Laurel I don't know, but he genuinely seems moved by Beth's efforts to help him. God only knows what their marriage has really been like, or what it will be like in the future. So far as I know, Beth has kept her end of the bargain. I wonder if she would have agreed to testify had her husband confessed last night that he had spent an entire summer sleeping with my wife.

Hewlett Dutton, my expert witness from Memphis, is good for nothing more than a indiscreet sound bite, as he irreverently testifies that "…blood spatter is about as easily staged as a woman faking an orgasm." This ridiculous simile from such a dour man elicits laughter from some of the spectators, who are threatened with expulsion by Cato. Not a single member of the jury smiles.

On cross-examination, Slade, barely rising from his chair, asks, "Isn't it a fact that you've found no evidence to suggest that Dr. Merriweather committed suicide?"

After he replies that he has not, Slade keeps him on the stand for another five minutes, but he is already effectively destroyed. For the last fifteen minutes I have begun to feel a headache coming on from not eating, and it settles in with a vengeance. Despite everything, I know I desperately want Cormorant to be acquitted. Regardless of what he has done to me, I can't avoid the feeling he is being railroaded in this case. "Your Honor, I call Dominique Marsden."

I have been surprised that she has not been called by the prosecution, but I suspect Minor is saving her as a rebuttal witness. It is a risky proposition, but I want her to make a point. While she sits down primly in the witness chair, her Anita Hill air of wounded dignity already manifest in her expression, I am thinking she hasn't admitted the depth of her feelings for Damascus, and I suspect she has tried to protect her daughter. Wearing a blue dress that is less stylish than in her television appearance, she seems to be trying to avoid the impression of being a sexual person. I start off by getting her to tell the jury about her role as as editor for the books, and as I expected, she tries to make the relationship sound as professional as possible. "Mrs. Marsden," I ask finally, "were you in love with Damascus Merriweather?"

Dominique Marsden raises her chin slightly and her left hand flies to her face. She says, "He was my friend and in my opinion, a great man."

"Were you in love with him, Mrs. Marsden?"

Blinking rapidly, she looks down at her lap and in a quiet voice, admits, "Yes, I suppose I was."

"Did you have a sexual relationship with him?" I ask, feeling that this question is tawdry but that the jury expects it.

"He was very ill the last three months of his life," she says delicately, "and that's when I began to work with him."

"I understand, ma'am," I say quickly. "Do you recall our conversation the evening after you appeared on television on the day Dr. Merriweather's second book came out a few weeks ago?"

"Yes, I recall it," she says, her face somber.

"And I asked you the about the relationship between Dr. Merriweather and my client," I say, looking over at Minor. "Do you remember telling me that Damascus Merriweather once told you that he didn't think my client was any different from other white men in his racial attitudes?"

Minor is on his feet objecting to this question as hearsay, but I argue to Cato, "Your Honor, the prosecution has argued that my client was a bigot and that was a motive for the murder, so I'm entitled to show the victim's state of mind on this point."

Cato, like any trial judge, does not want to risk a reversal, and instructs her to answer. "He did say that," she says, "and he also thought your client was a coward for not risking his reputation to tell the truth about how terribly blacks had been treated in this state."

"How's that?" I ask, certain she knows the answer I want.

She turns her body to the jury and says, "Damascus had wanted him to help him write it or at least put his name on the book, but he wouldn't do it."

I let this sink in, and turn to Minor. "Your witness."

Obviously thinking that I have hurt Cormorant more than I have helped him, Minor lets her step down as Cormorant whispers furiously, "Why did you ask her that?"

I don't have time to explain, and instruct him, "Remember to talk to the jury, don't lecture them or condescend to them, because they will resent it. They give the grades, not you."

My heart is thudding as I say loudly to Cato that I call Cormorant Ashley. I look back to see if Laurel has come into the courtroom, but I don't see her. I force my mind to the front of the room where Cormorant takes his seat. He is clearly nervous, and as with any witness, I try to calm him with preliminary questions that let him get comfortable. Until last night, all I thought I had to do was to get the jury to understand Cormorant's complex personality. Now, with last night's revelations, I doubt if his salvation lies in explaining himself so thoroughly, but he has no choice.

After barely five minutes of hearing about Cormorant's career and credentials as a historian, Cato sustains an objection from Minor that I am taking too much time establishing my client's background, and I plunge in and instruct Cormorant to tell the jury about his relationship with Damascus Merriweather. "In your mind, did you get along with him?"

Cormorant pauses for such a long time that I'm about to repeat the question when he answers, "I thought I did. I never just agreed with him in the way so many whites patronize blacks. I don't think he liked me, but I think he knew I would be honest with him, and I think that's why he asked me to read a draft of his book. I thought it was badly lacking in documentation and told him so."

"You have heard what his brother said. Did you think he considered you a racist?" I ask, worried about an objection, but Cormorant should be allowed to explain his motivation.

Cormorant looks straight at the jury box and says, "If being a racist means being willing to acknowledge publicly that persons of European descent generally perform better on I. Q. tests and have higher test scores, and that some of this difference is probably attributable to innate ability, then, yes, I was a racist in his eyes, and in the eyes of the rest of my colleagues. In this era of political correctness, my views are taboo."

Out of the corner of my eye, I see the judge's jaw tighten and would dearly love to know what is going through his mind. If I were Minor, I would argue that the issue of race is a red herring; this case is about Cormorant's character. He is a liar, a deceiver, and willing to threaten libel and murder to keep the the truth from coming out about members of his family. "Did those views or any other lead you to fire a metal slug into your colleague's chest?"

It is time for Cormorant's own jaw to harden, and he replies angrily, "Of course not!"

"Did you argue with Damascus Merriweather on occasion?" I ask, knowing that the national media will tar and feather Cormorant for his answers. Yet if Raven's initial strategy turns out to be correct, it will be the only revenge they get.

Cormorant nods. "I did. As I've said many times, in my view, his methods were suspect. In his book *Coming to Terms*, he relied on historically dubious sources, and I told him so on more than one occasion. I remember telling him once that he should have been a gossip columnist. That was how we bantered. And it's obvious he never quit talking to me, since I was one of the last persons to see him."

"Were you jealous of Damascus Merriweather for publishing this book?" I ask, knowing if I don't ask him this question, Minor or Slade will.

Cormorant manages to avoid sounding sanctimonious as he answers, "Because of the lack of documentation, I don't consider it a historical work, and in fact, I think it is misleading, so, no, I was hardly jealous when it was published. I don't think it passes critical muster."

As he talks, I know that the jury is getting a dose of the Cormorant I've always known, but I can't tell how they are reacting. At this moment I know my own reactions are mixed. I don't want Cormorant convicted, but I wouldn't mind it if someone took him out and beat the shit out of him. When I ask him to describe his visit to see Damascus the day he was shot, his voice becomes surprisingly emotional. "We could have talked over the phone, but he said he had some papers he wanted me to see, so I said I would come by. When I got there, I tried to kid with him like I used to, but he seemed distracted to me."

The courtroom is quiet, and I ask, "How do you mean?"

Cormorant looks oddly distressed, and for just an instant I think he is going to cry.

He sighs and as if I am the only person in the room with him says, "I don't think he was listening, but for all I know, he may have been in pain. He never complained around me."

"Did you carry a pistol in the glove compartment of your car?" I ask, knowing it is crucial that he not sound overly concerned about his colleague's health. This jury would never buy it now.

Cormorant explains about the gun and manages to convey the impression that he is not a slumlord. "I was scared of some of my tenants," he admits candidly. "I never used it, but I felt better knowing I had it."

"Did you ever carry it with you to a tenant's door?"

"A couple of times," he admits. "But I felt pretty stupid since nothing happened."

"Did you have it in your car," I ask, slowing my words down, "when you went to see Damascus Merriweather the afternoon of his death?"

"It had been stolen," Cormorant explains, "but I didn't realize that until after Damascus had been shot. I hadn't looked in the glove compartment for several weeks and didn't check it until after I called the police when we returned from Lake of the Ozarks."

I take Cormorant back to the day of his visit and he testifies at length to what he talked about with Damascus. He sounds believable, but cross-examination will not be as easy for him. I end by asking one more time, "Did you kill Damascus Merriweather?"

He looks straight at the jury and says fervently, "No, I did not!"

As I return to my chair, I see Laurel has come into the courtroom and wonder how much of Cormorant's testimony she heard and what she thought. She is sitting at the back, apart from the rest of the Ashleys, but she may not have wanted to disturb me. Seeing her, I know that I will forgive her some day, but that may be the last thing she wants from me.

It is Slade who conducts Cormorant's cross-examination, and he begins immediately to discredit the reason for his visit to Merriweather's house. "Isn't it a fact that in all the years you had known Dr. Ashley," Slade begins, "you had never once been invited to his residence before that afternoon?"

I have warned Cormorant not to try to outwit the prosecution on cross-examination but to answer only the question asked, and, glancing at me, he does so now. A witness like Cormorant usually can't make himself wait for his lawyer to rehabilitate him on redirect.

"That's correct," he says, having previously admitted to me that he had never socialized or done anything with Damascus except at gatherings of the department at the University.

Slade is presumably laying the ground for a closing argument that Cormorant's story that he was asked to come out to see Damascus to discuss filling in for him on the panel at the law school was a fabrication. There is nothing I can do about it except hope Cormorant keeps his tongue in check. "And you admit that there was no immediate date set for the panel discussion at the law school?"

Cormorant cannot resist answering, "I don't know that."

Slade pastes on his face an incredulous expression. "You heard the Dean of the law school testify," he says loudly. "Do you know of any reason he would have for lying about that?"

For a moment I think Cormorant is going to make some sarcastic retort, but he says, "I can't imagine that he would."

I breathe a sigh of relief. If Cormorant becomes testy, it will look as if he has something to hide. Slade, who is twice Cormorant's size, drapes himself on the podium and hammers away at Cormorant's story that he went out to discuss substituting for Damascus. "You've admitted that you could have easily talked to him on the telephone and he could have sent you any papers by the student who was going out there every afternoon?"

"It didn't make any sense to me either," Cormorant replies.

"But that's your story!" Slade points out.

And it is in this tone that Slade exposes the weaknesses of Cormorant's testimony. There was no reason for him to drive out there, no reason to discuss the panel, no reason to suddenly take a three-day vacation. As Cormorant's answers become increasingly hollow, it becomes apparent to me that for a defense to make sense to the jury, I will have to concentrate my argument on the possibility that Cormorant was set up, which is the least likely scenario since we have no proof that he was.

It is Minor who gets to his feet to make the closing argument instead of Slade. I think this is a mistake since Minor is a poorer speaker, but perhaps Minor's ego is just as large as Cormorant's. He walks to the jury rail and begins to tick off the reasons why this is an open and shut case. I watch the jury, and am dismayed to see that they seem riveted by him, but, in truth, it is an easy summation. He has delivered what he promised in his opening statement. "Don't let the defense fool you. This wasn't a suicide, and there is not an iota of evidence to suggest that it was, and the evidence is what you have to decide this case on. Not a theory, not a possibility, but the basically undisputed facts in this case. All you have is the defendant's bare assertion that he didn't fire the bullet that killed Professor Merriweather, and what would you expect him to say? He even admitted he didn't tell the police his gun was stolen until after the police asked him if he owned one. He admits he was in the presence of the victim during the time fixed by the medical examiner for his death, and he admits he bantered with the victim, and he admits he unexpectedly went out of town immediately afterwards for three days. Why did he go to Merriweather's? He told you a story that even he admitted didn't make sense…"

As he continues, I fight down a sense of panic that when I begin my summation, the jury will no longer be listening, and when I do get to my feet ten minutes later, in fact, one of the African-American jurors does not even try to suppress her weariness and stretches. Though I am about to come out of my skin with nervous anticipation, I pretend agreement, and walk over to the rail, saying, "It has been a long two days, but now we lawyers are almost done, and you will be asked to make the biggest decision you have ever made in your life. What is this case about?"

I go back to the lectern and say, "Imagine you were in a classroom, and this was a history lesson you had just been taught. Would you believe it?" I turn and look at Cormorant. "You can find all the inferences that something occurred a certain way, but at some level in your heart you have to *believe* it, and that is what this case is about. When you strip away all the logic and rhetoric, it's about what you fundamentally believe Cormorant Ashley was capable of *doing* on that afternoon."

I walk over to Cormorant and put my hand on his shoulder. "When all is said and done, you have to make a decision about what you believe about this man, because there were no eyewitnesses to this murder. It was all circumstantial. No doubt the prosecution proved it was his gun, the bullet came from his pistol, the only fingerprints on the gun were his, and he was there alone with Dr. Merriweather an hour or so before he died. But you still have to believe he pulled the trigger and fired a bullet into his chest."

As I talk, I move back to the lectern and point at Cormorant. "Dr. Ashley says he didn't take his gun into the house. Why should you believe *him*?" Cormorant blinks and for a moment appears to think I am going to turn on him and denounce him as the liar and cheat I know him to be.

I turn back to the jury and say, "Whether or not you believe Dr. Ashley is complicated by a subject that we have all danced around throughout the trial, and that is the subject of race and the role it plays in this trial." I pause and take a sip of water and then go back to the rail. "Each one of us in Arkansas, whether we studied much history or not, knows that at one time in our past this trial would never have occurred, because no white person would ever be tried for the murder of a black person in the South except under the most obvious of circumstances and then, if he was, he would be routinely acquitted. Well, fortunately those terrible days are over. That wasn't justice. But the point I'm making is that trials don't occur in a vacuum; they occur in a tiny place and moment of time which we later call history. What I'm asking you to do is to realize as you apply the presumption of innocence to the facts of this case that you have already been influenced just as surely as white Southerners were influenced by their time and place in the distant past. Today, for complex reasons, blacks and whites live together in a time of such political correctness that it would be almost laughable if it weren't so tragic. In our heart of hearts, we all know that most of us harbor *beliefs* about each other that we can't possibly say out loud without unleashing anger, pain, and very possibly violence. So these beliefs about each other, right or wrong, true or false, we say only to our own people and then usually in code."

I go back over to Cormorant and stand beside him. "Fortunately, not every one of us acts as I have just described, and one of those people who doesn't is the defendant in this case. This is a man who has been willing to say what he thinks on the subject of race, regardless of what is acceptable in society. Now, what makes most of us even more uncomfortable is that while we would expect some redneck cracker to say what he thinks about the intellectual capacity of blacks, when a white professor says it, we all cringe just a little bit more, because we are not used to hearing that from an educated person. So, the truth is, my client sticks out like a sore thumb in this day and age when the easiest and most prudent course of action to take is to say nothing." I turn and look Minor in the face and say, "I can hear the prosecutor in my head telling you that this case isn't about this at all. It's about facts--fingerprints, ballistics, scientific evidence."

I begin to move toward the jury rail and say, "Well, I disagree. This case is about your gut feeling about Cormorant Ashley. Is he a man of fundamental intellectual honesty and integrity who insists on speaking his mind, or is he some hot-headed peckerwood who would shoot and kill another man because of jealousy or racism or whatever motive the prosecutor offers you? I think Cormorant Ashley is guilty of being an arrogant, intellectual elitist who insists on embarrassing his colleagues and others with his politically incorrect notions, but most of all he is guilty of being honest. That, of course, is not a crime, but it is dangerous. Because the past has not been fair to African-Americans, and because many people in this country are watching this trial, some of you, consciously or unconsciously, may think you have to show that the South has changed, and that we can convict a white man accused of murdering a black person. This is one of the influences that we in our time have to contend with—our guilty feelings over our past treatment of African-Americans."

I walk back to the lectern and say, "I think we have to consider another scenario of what happened April 21, and it all grows out of the extraordinary relationship between Ezekiel and Damascus Merriweather. What I think happened in this case was that several things came together in the last few months of Damascus Merriweather's life. He knew he had written an important book, but one that would be hard for white Arkansans to accept because it dealt with our deepest levels of guilt—the way our ancestors, whom we traditionally revere so much in this state, treated blacks. The most important thing left for him to do was to get this manuscript in book form and before the public, but he couldn't find a commercial publisher. Because it was so important to him, Dr. Merriweather had swallowed his pride and asked Dr. Ashley to appear as a co-author, something my client, in his typically arrogant manner, wouldn't do primarily because of his insistence that the book had to be documented in a historically acceptable way. In other words, it wasn't enough for African-Americans to tell us what happened, and for us to believe them. So, his brother had to pay to publish the book for him.

"I think at that moment Dr. Merriweather, who knew he was dying from cancer, wanted to accomplish two things. First, he wanted his book to become famous and be read by as many people as possible. At the same time he wanted to teach his white colleague how important it is to be believed, and so he conspired with his brother Ezekiel to make it appear that Cormorant Ashley murdered him.

"And the way this was accomplished was for Ezekiel or someone else to steal his pistol from the glove compartment of his automobile. When that was done, Dr. Merriweather arranged for Cormorant to come see him on a pretext, knowing it wouldn't make sense to the police. After my client left, Ezekiel went out the back door of his pharmacy and crossed from North Little Rock by boat, entered his own house, said goodbye to his brother and watched him end his life by injecting a drug such as potassium chloride into his veins, then shot him in the chest after he was dead. Then, using an atomizer or some other device he spattered blood that he had already taken from his brother on the table in front of his body. On his way out, probably still wearing gloves to keep his fingerprints off the pistol, he threw my client's gun into the bushes before taking a boat back to the pharmacy, knowing it would be just a matter of minutes before Rafe Kennedy would bring the mail by."

I stop and spread my hands, a gesture of appeal. "Could this have happened? I think we have to use our common sense. As arrogant as it sounds, there simply was no reason for my client to shoot Damascus Merriweather. He thought he had written a bad book, not a good one, regardless of how much attention he got. If he really had disliked Damascus Merriweather, he wouldn't have come near him after he became sick. The quite understandable anger and resentment came from the Merriweather brothers, who saw my client as the ultimate in white male superiority. But despite their hatred of him, I don't think they intended for him to be convicted, but to go through the humiliation of an arrest and trial and in the process help sell a ton of books." I go back to the jury rail. "Why do I think this? Ezekiel Merriweather went almost immediately from campaigning for my client's arrest to stating publicly that he thought that perhaps the police had the wrong man. He told you that today." Though I can't say it aloud, I know that if either Damascus or Ezekiel had really wanted to give the police a motive, all they had to do was to tell the police about Cormorant's anger at being told the apparently true story of his great-grandfather.

I finish my closing back at the lectern. "The Merriweathers got what they wanted. The books are selling well and have been reviewed quite favorably, especially outside Arkansas. Sometimes history cries out to be believed, and I think my client has been taught a lesson. The African-American community in Arkansas has waited a long time for common sense to prevail so that it can be believed about what the past was like. After this ordeal, I think my client and I can sympathize with this position. I hope you will exercise your common sense and find that there is reasonable doubt to believe my client is a murderer…" I end by mentioning Rafe Kennedy as a suspect and say that anyone could have come in afterwards, but I know I have lost the jury's attention and end too quietly, asking for an acquittal.

As I sit down, I have immediate misgivings about not focusing more on other suspects, but I have the feeling I would have been wasting my breath. It is Minor who delivers the rebuttal, and it is a stinging one. "Blame the victim!" he thunders from his chair. "Talk about arrogance!" He begins to pace as if he is furious. I had expected Slade would make the final argument, but for the first time I see the passion beneath Minor's typically calm demeanor. "Isn't that what we whites historically have done to black people in this state? And now the defendant's lawyer has the nerve to tell you to do it one more time. Based on what? There's no evidence of any frame-up. *Belief?* He is asking you to believe in a fairy tale, not an alibi. Do you honestly think that in the final weeks of Dr. Merriweather's life, this was what he was thinking about? Is there any proof of this at all? If it all it takes to acquit someone of murder is a wild fantasy, then we can do away with the criminal justice system, because that's all this is. Basically, this is nothing more than wishful thinking from a defendant who hasn't contested a single fact that has gone into evidence against him in two days of trial." Cormorant sits grimly beside me, and I wonder what he is thinking. I look down at his pad, but it is bare. What the members of the jury do not know is that Cormorant really is capable of murder. As the last one files out fifteen minutes later, I ask him how he is feeling.

"Numb," he says, sighing and letting the mask on his face crack for the first time today. "I remember seeing the police lights the night I was arrested and feeling the same way. It's as if I'm being sacrificed. I don't trust them not to carry it out."

"That may happen," I say bluntly, wondering if any members of the jury bought my closing argument. Now that it is finally over, I feel my anger giving way to a profound sense of weariness. I just want to get away from him, but there is no other place to avoid the media, and so we wait in the courtroom, and for the first time all day, I talk to Laurel.

"Did you believe what you were saying about this being a history lesson?" she whispers as we sit side by side at the back of the courtroom.

Her expression is one of frank curiosity, and I answer truthfully, "Most definitely. The Merriweathers were too smart for us from the very beginning. Could they have come up with a better way to get these books before the public? I can't imagine how they would have done it, and they got to kill two birds with one stone. I'm convinced if the medical examiner did another autopsy, he would find Damascus committed suicide, but because Ezekiel raised such hell, the State Crime Lab was forced to rush through an autopsy that seemed totally obvious. They set up Cormorant perfectly."

Laurel nods at Beth and Cormorant sitting in the corner five rows ahead of us. "Unless Cormorant is actually guilty," she says, her voice low and grave. A tiny smile comes to her lips as she takes my hand. "I'm not blaming him. I'd lie, too, if I thought it would save me. I don't think you would."

Exhausted by the last forty-eight hours, I feel limp as a rag doll. One thing is for certain: I had no business representing Cormorant and have begun to wonder if the Merriweathers had even taken that into account. I wouldn't be surprised. Blacks have studied us for years and know how we will react. "I don't know what I'd do," I say and squeeze her hand.

"Of course you do," Laurel says simply. "By the way, you know Raven's been in love with you for years."

I close my eyes, wishing I had a drink. At least I don't have *that* on my head. "You told me last night," I remind her, "that she would have sent me to bed with a glass of warm milk."

Laurel is wearing the same perfume she had on the night Cormorant was arrested. I can't think of the name of it, but it reminds me of lilac. How brazen that he leaned over and smelled her fragance that night! "The first time that you approached her, maybe. But if you had wanted her... The rest of the human race is a lot messier than you are, dear."

Dear. It is not a word that Laurel uses, and it makes me afraid that she has already decided to regard me as an affectionate memory instead of a living human being. "I didn't want her," I protest. "I've just wanted you."

"No doubt," she says. "I've always been so dependable and taken care of you and until recently, haven't complained. Raven would have driven you crazy. Most men don't really want somebody like her. She's too strong. She knows that."

My headache, which I had forgotten about, returns with a vengeance, and I ask for some aspirin. Laurel takes the tin from her purse and hands me two, which I take without water. She's right, of course. I have taken her for granted forever. I wonder if I could stop. The next three hours seem surreal, but as if by some prearranged agreement, Cormorant and I do not talk. I can't eat and spend part of the time talking to Miller Ray and Catherine about school, travel, politics, anything but the trial, because it makes us all too nervous. Catherine asks about Cynthia, who has kept her distance from both her mother and me this summer, guessing, I'm sure, that we were passing through a crisis that wouldn't be resolved if she put in her two cents' worth. Besides, her solution is well-known. Get the hell out of Dodge. Maybe she and her mother have been talking and haven't told me. I'm not sure her mother will even come back to clean out the house. "Do you think that when all this is over," Catherine asks, her blue eyes wide and disingenuous, "you'll track down your ancestors?"

She means my black ones. I treat the question as a serious one. "Maybe you can help me," I tell her, realizing that Catherine is the type of young woman who could perhaps make the "New South" work in the small towns of the Delta. She doesn't carry the baggage that the rest of us do. Maybe it will be whites like her who will come back to the Delta and contend with it more successfully than we have. I wonder if she knows about her father's affair and what she thinks.

"Miller?"

I look around and see Cormorant standing beside me.

I try to smile, but he looks so depressed I can't quite pull it off. "I don't think it will be too much longer," I say for Catherine's sake more than his.

"I need to talk to you. Can you give us a few minutes, Catherine?" he asks politely.

"Sure, Daddy," she says gently and pats his shoulder as she passes by him to go sit with her brother.

Cormorant sits down beside me and says under his breath, "I didn't tell you everything."

"What?" I ask, bracing myself for the worst. I have been waiting for this moment for months. The son of a bitch.

"That afternoon when I went to see Damascus, he accused me of hitting on Dominique."

I can't even grasp what he is saying. "What are you talking about?" I ask, trying to keep my voice low.

"That time I told you I met her--she was waiting for Damascus, and I invited her to wait in my office."

"Why in the hell did you do that?" I ask. In the last four

months I have imagined many possibilities, but nothing involving a black woman.

Cormorant blushes. "I don't know," he mutters. "I just got a wild hair up my ass all of a sudden. She's pretty attractive."

"Jesus Christ!" I say, "what did you do?" Horrified, I close my eyes and suddenly can see his father in his wheelchair admitting the story about Little Tina was true.

Cormorant clears his throat and then blurts, "I didn't really *do* anything. I guess I may have leered at her. I can't remember my exact words, but I said something like she could come visit me any time. I didn't know who she was then."

"What did she do?"

"She kind of shuddered and wandered down the hall away from my office."

Though I want to remain calm, I feel a tremendous urge to stand up and walk around. My mind begins to race. What difference did it make if he knew who she was? Was this about power or sex? I can't believe Cormorant let me call the woman as a witness. I feel my own face burning.

"Tell me what happened the last time you saw Damascus?"

Cormorant brings his hands to his face. "As I've always said, he had called me out there to talk about the panel at the law school, but it was as if he wanted to confront me about the incident with Dominique. Believe it or not, he said he forgave me. He said it was in our blood."

"Whose blood?"

"I took it to mean the males in the Ashleys, but I guess he could have meant all of us."

I whisper, "So you got mad and shot him?"

Cormorant shakes his head. "No, I swear to God I didn't. I admit it enraged me. He sounded so damn pompous. I *wanted* to kill him."

"Why didn't you tell me this?" I ask.

Cormorant straightens up and looks around the courtroom. "I knew you'd think I'd lost it and had shot him."

It begins to sink in that this latest information was never used by Minor. Why? If he had known, he would have eaten Cormorant alive with it. I can't imagine that Damascus didn't tell Ezekiel about it. "What did you say to him?"

"I called him a son of a bitch," he says. "The nerve of him saying he was forgiving me. It wasn't that big a deal."

"What did he say?"

"Nothing. He just smiled."

Out of the corner of my eye, I see Raven coming toward us. "They're coming back!" she says, as Cato's bailiff opens the door. Suddenly, the room is full as scores of spectators crowd in to hear the verdict. I can't seem to catch my breath as I walk to the counsel table with Cormorant beside me. When we reach it, I sit down and look at Cormorant's latest drawing. He has sketched a pair of hands around iron bars, not a good omen. He pants gently beside me.

At the very moment the foreman hands Cato the verdict, I turn and lock eyes with Ezekiel, who is staring straight at me. As Cato reads it, I have the unmistakable sensation that Ezekiel has winked at me. Cormorant has been found not guilty.

At Raven's, we hold a family celebration in the den and watch the news clips of the aftermath of the trial. I sit by Laurel on Raven's couch and watch Ezekiel display in front of him copies of both books and essentially give the same speech he has given on several occasions now. Nothing will bring his brother back, so this verdict doesn't change anything. Nothing the police will do will change the history of the state and make up for the treatment of African-Americans by white Arkansans.

The elation and euphoria that we felt immediately after the acquittal has already begun to wear off as Cormorant flips through the channels watching all the principals being interviewed. "The asshole," he marvels. "He isn't missing a beat."

For his part, Cormorant comes across on television relatively subdued, like a man who has just missed a plane which took off and crashed moments later and killed everyone on board. After all these months of silence, he has little to say. Repeatedly, he is asked how he feels, and candidly, he replies to one newscaster from Memphis that he has so little response because he has been preparing himself for a conviction. In an interview on Channel 11, now being shown on the ten o'clock news, he does manage to say that he feels enormous gratitude towards his attorney and oldest friend, Miller Holly. Beth raises her glass of champagne, which her sister-in-law has provided, and cries, "A toast to Miller! The world's greatest lawyer!"

Miller Ray has picked me up a pizza, and I manage to choke down a few bites as I listen to the tributes of the family. Though my sense of relief is overwhelming, in truth, I cannot avoid the feeling that I am the world's greatest chump. A few minutes ago I asked Cormorant as we were standing in the kitchen by ourselves for a moment if he had seen Ezekiel wink at me at the moment of the verdict, and he had said he didn't doubt it but that his eyes were closed. Why did the jury acquit? We don't know for sure, but one white juror who has already been interviewed by Channel 4 has been reported as saying that the victim's brother had seemed as if he knew who the murderer was.

At midnight, Laurel and I are too drunk to leave, and go upstairs to spend the night.

Brushing my teeth while she washes her face, I tell her about

Ezekiel's wink and ask her if she saw it.

Laurel pats her skin with one of Raven's expensive bath towels and tosses it in the hamper. "Surely you imagined it," she says and yawns, opening her mouth so wide that I can see a gold crown she had done five years ago. "I notice you didn't say anything to the media."

Following her down the hall to our room to bed, I think to myself that it is not a story I intend to tell publicly for a long time. Yet, in the way we have in the South, I know I will someday. It is too good a story not to. Will I tell the truth about Cormorant's final moments with Damascus? I don't know. In the grand scheme of things, what Cormorant said and did to Dominique Marsden was hardly of any consequence, simply another display of boorish male behavior. But if I think about it too long, I have to think about his betrayal of me with Laurel. If I hadn't idolized what I took to be his honesty, perhaps I would have figured more of this out. In Damascus's mind, Cormorant's behavior (assuming Cormorant is telling the truth) was all of a piece, connecting past to present. If it is all of a piece, then it must be about power and arrogance, not about sex. Or perhaps the absence of power. In our great-grandfathers' time, an encounter between master and female slave would have resulted perhaps in a rape. Today, it is reduced to an insult. Lying side by side in the dark room, I ask Laurel, "What will become of us?"

She yawns again. Outside, I can hear cars passing in the night and wonder if the man across the street is selling drugs. Laurel answers, "We'll go on with our lives until we decide it's time to do something else."

I think about her answer for a moment, not knowing whether to be encouraged or sad. I start to reply but hear her snoring gently beside me.

ABOUT THE AUTHOR

GRIF STOCKLEY grew up in Marianna, Arkansas, and graduated from Rhodes College in Memphis. For the past 28 years he has been an attorney for the Center for Legal Services in Little Rock, which provides representation for indigents in non-criminal cases. He is the author of a series of five mysteries based on Gideon Page, a fictitious Arkansas lawyer. Stockley was awarded the Porter Prize for literary excellence, and was inducted into the Arkansas Writers' Hall of Fame in 2000.